Born

To

Run

To Hannah

Best Wishes

Other titles by Graham Sclater

Ticket to Ride
Hatred is the Key
We're Gonna be Famous
Too Big to Cry
More Than a Woman
Love Shack
Cowboys and Angels
I Will Survive

Non-Fiction
WRITE ON!

For more information on Graham Sclater and all of his books,
see his website at **www.grahamsclater.com**

Born To Run

Graham Sclater

Tabitha Books

Tabitha Books
Exeter EX2 9DJ England
Tabitha books is a division of Tabitha Publishing Limited

©®

Tabitha Books
First Published in 2022 by Tabitha Books

Copyright © 2022 Graham Sclater

Typeset in Sabon 12 by Tabitha Books

Printed and bound in Great Britain by
Imprint**Digital**.com EX5 5HY

Cover design Denise Sclater

Front cover photo Graham Sclater

Rear cover photo Andy Dean

Acknowledgements

Karel at the Koopermoolen Amsterdam, the Amsterdam politie department, Barrie at Gomango Creative, Canal & River Trust, Domburg Tourist Centre, John Peters & Tracy at Venture Radio, Lug Gee, Gina Awad BEM, EDAA, and the wonderful music of Yola, Barbra Streisand, Andrea Bocelli, and many others, while I worked on this novel. And to Denise, my wonderful wife, for her ideas, proof reading and unwavering support.

Lastly, I would also like to thank the numerous radio presenters and media around the world who continue to support me, and all the readers who have bought my previous work.

The author in Hamburg

Graham Sclater lives in Exeter with his wife, Denise, two daughters and three grandchildren and is a successful music publisher. Prior to returning to Devon, in the late sixties, he was a professional musician playing across Europe and working as a session musician with many name artists. His first novel *Ticket to Ride,* based on his time living and playing in Germany during the sixties, was originally published in 2006.

Graham can regularly be seen talking in libraries, at book signings and literary events, as well as delivering creative writing sessions and enrichment talks to passengers on cruise ships. He is currently working on several television series and film scripts.

Born to Run is his ninth novel.

Graham can be heard on the BBC, regional and national radio, talking about various subjects close to his heart, as well as his monthly book review which is aired on stations around the world.

Check out his website for all the news, interviews and videos: www.grahamsclater.com

CONTENTS

Details of all titles written by Graham Sclater can be found on his website: www.grahamsclater.com

Zita whispered in Liam's ear. 'We have had fun... haven't we?'

ॐॐॐ

Dedicated to music journalist, Antje Voit, my long-term friend from Hamburg, without whose help my life could have been so very different. You will be sadly missed.

NEW

PROLOGUE

I Will Survive

Liam leaned back in his favourite chair and watched Zita as she carefully picked her way between the hand-painted pots overflowing with vibrant late summer flowers that still filled much of the houseboat deck. She finished deadheading her geraniums, penstemon, rudbeckia and the last of her roses then watered the huge sunflowers before leaning against the wooden handrail and looking contentedly down the canal.

She closed her eyes and faced towards the last of the cooling afternoon sun and spoke without turning around. 'Liam, do you know that next Thursday is your birthday?'

'Is it?'

'Would you like a special birthday present – to go back to Madeira for some time?'

'Madeira?'

She turned her head and looked directly at him. 'This time it is *our* exit route,' she said.

He smiled at her. 'Yeah. I know. Where we went to that café … in the garden …?' He reflected. 'I liked it there.' He nodded. 'Yeah – why not?'

She looked at his pale face. 'It is perfect for you. Not too hot. They say it is like eternal spring.' She paused. 'And I will take you somewhere special …' She smiled. 'To Reid's Hotel, for afternoon tea.'

Liam grinned mindlessly. He had no idea where or what it was, so he innocently reached out, grabbed her hand and kissed her on the cheek. 'Nice,' he said, considerately.

When they heard the motorbike, they both turned towards it. They watched the telegram boy as he rode slowly along the cobbled street at the side of the canal on a yellow and black livered machine. He stopped alongside their houseboat and checked the name on the envelope before turning off the engine. He walked onto the deck and spoke to Zita. 'Sigrid Obermeyer?' he asked.

She forced an exaggerated smile and nodded.

He handed her an envelope.

'Thank you,' she said.

She held it in her hand and watched as he climbed onto his motorbike and accelerated away.

Liam was in shock and mouthed her name. 'Sigrid–?'

'Fuck! So, now you know …' she said, exhaling heavily.'

He was totally confused and looked nervously at the envelope in her hand. 'Is that what I think it is – a telegram?'

She nodded.

'The last time I saw one of those – I was only a kid,' he said, recalling that afternoon. 'They told my mother that my father was being released.'

Zita lifted her head from the envelope and offered him an absent-minded gaze.

'Prison,' mouthed Liam.

She didn't respond and fiddled nervously with the envelope. After expelling a series of huge sighs and with heightened apprehension she took her time to open it. As she read the one-word message all colour drained from her face.

'What is it?' asked Liam.

'They know …' She exhaled. *'They know …'* She squeezed her bottom lip and repeatedly tugged at it. 'They know … I've broken *their* rules–'

'Who?'

She whispered her reply with trembling breath. 'Who do you think? Mossad. My bosses … and my handler–'

'Bosses?' He swallowed hard. 'But … but you don't have anyone like that.'

'Don't I?'

'Well …' He stared at her with his mouth wide open. 'Do you?' He shook his head in disbelief and shock. 'Is that why *they* used your *real* name?'

She replied in little more than a whisper. 'Yes, of course it is.' She swallowed nervously. 'It is their signal–'

'Signal?' He tried to stand but the shock was too great and he slumped back into his seat and looked at her bowed head. 'Fuck! What the hell is happening now?'

She looked up at him, her face dejected and bewildered. 'I have a handler. And … I can *never* leave them.' She paused and lowered her voice. 'Alive.'

'What?'

She shook her head. *'Dey* don't like it.' She held up the telegram and spoke as she exhaled, her voice fading to little more than a whisper. 'I broke their protocol. That is why they used my true name. My real name – who I really am. They know I used their … their special …' She paused and

17

gasped for breath. 'Their *secret* codes to hide our locations when ...' Once more she struggled to catch her breath before she continued. 'When ...' She paused and looked directly into Liam's eyes. 'Do you remember when I called Amsterdam and told Ribeker and Ackerman we were still in Berlin – when we weren't?' She swallowed hard. '*You know* ... that each time we weren't. We were with De Groot on the island and ... and *then* in Lisboa.'

'Oh, that,' said Liam, dismissively.

For the first time since Liam had known her, Zita openly displayed true fear. Still holding the telegram, she dropped the envelope. It was blown along the deck by the light breeze and settled between the flower pots. She slumped into her wooden seat, grabbed at the arms and squeezed them until her knuckles, starved of blood, turned white. Her body tensed as she stared blindly ahead. She took several ragged breaths and continued. 'They will punish me and ...' *She looked at the once wild Englishman now contaminated and tainted forever by the skilled ruthlessness that was second nature to her.* She sighed with forced regret. 'And maybe ...' She lowered her voice to a whisper. 'Maybe ...' She sniffed as her sad eyes burnt into him. 'You too,' she said, weakly.

Zita's fear now gripped him and quickly swept throughout his body. The ensuing tension caused the scar tissue in his brutally damaged throat to tighten. He coughed hard then retched painfully and vomited onto the deck. He turned his head and looked up at her. 'Do we deserve it?' he asked, although he already knew what her answer would be.

A beat.

Zita's head twitched uncontrollably and trembled as she looked furtively around. Once more, she released her mixed emotions with a deep shuddering sigh. She reached across and flicked the button on the portable CD player and after choosing the Bryan Adams 1985 song, *The Summer of '69*, she cranked up the volume.

As the music filled the deck she stood, walked unsteadily towards him and tugged gently at his hands. 'Liam … will you dance with me?'

He didn't move.

She tugged harder and reluctantly he stood.

She pulled him close to her and they hugged and moved gently, the opposite reaction of dancing enthusiastically to the pulsing rock track. The assassin's first bullet blasted the head of the huge sunflower, shredding it and spewing black and white seeds into the air and onto their heads.

Zita closed her eyes and pulled Liam tighter into her and as Bryan Adams sang "The best days of my life," she whispered in his ear. 'We have had fun … *haven't we, Li–?*'

CHAPTER ONE

Rescue me

Within a split second Liam found himself fighting to breathe in the cold, murky canal water. He felt a hand grab at his shoulder and pull him towards the opposite bank where he was finally able to grab at a chain. He spluttered as he expelled the water that had partially filled his lungs, while at the same time he tried to catch his breath.

Zita grinned at him mischievously while he wiped at his eyes. 'We made it …' She shook her head. 'We beat dem.' She took a deep breath and exhaled. 'Well, for a short while … anyway.'

Liam tightened his grip on the chain and struggled to stay afloat. 'What the fuck happened?' he asked.

'They wanted to kill us …' she said, as she dived and then reappeared. She exhaled as she shook her head and took her time to drag her fingers through her hair. 'Both of us,' she said, breathlessly as her face revealed a rare expression of deep concern.

Liam tried to ask another question.

She ignored him and looked up and down the canal.

She pointed to the nearest bridge, with its railings already illuminated with coloured lights. 'Do you think you can make it to dere?'

He took his time and mentally measured the distance. 'Yeah …' He paused to breathe and spluttered. 'Slowly … though,' he said.

'Of course. We can take as long as we want.' Zita turned and noticed a group of tourists and their guide walking along the canalside towards them. She pushed him tight against the wall, covered his mouth with her open hand and waited until they'd passed. 'Come on. Quietly – not too much splashing.'

They shivered as they waited under the bridge until the last of the autumn sun had set and the canal was clear of the daytime tourist boats. Zita hoisted Liam out of the canal and they made their way to the only place they could, what had been De Groot's best kept secret, his safe house, in Huidenstraat, the house, that held so many bad memories.

Zita ripped off the police tape, screwed it up, pushed it into her pocket and fiddled with the newly fitted combination lock until she heard it click. She opened the door, smiled to herself as they entered, and closed the door behind them. As she locked the door, she noticed the broken letter box, shook her head and slid the top and bottom bolts across.

With predictable and well-placed apprehension, they slowly climbed the stairs. When they reached the living room they stood in silence and shivered as the water dripped from their soaked clothes. They each replayed in their minds the violent debauchery and torturous events that had affected them, in very different ways, many months earlier. Zita finally moved and exhaled her anger at being naïve enough to have been held captive by an animal. She shook her head in disgust as she looked around the room where Erag, the Albanian butcher, had inflicted his vile acts on her and the girls from the Love Shack, as well as Bernie's lesbian lover, Detective Andrea Ribeker.

Nothing had changed.

It was still a mess. The smell of fear still hung in the air and their blood had now dried in dark patterns on the wall, floorboards, rugs, table and chairs, settee and armchairs.

Liam was the first to speak. 'I never expected to come back to this fucking place–'

'Who did?' gagged Zita. 'Who would want to?' She forced a grin and took a huge breath. 'But … no one will expect us to be here and it will give us time to plan what we need to do next.'

He nodded. 'Do what?'

Zita was gone. She spent the next few minutes checking every inch of the building.

Liam sat at the table, exhausted and shivering, his dripping clothes forming pools of water on the floor.

When she returned, she had already removed her wet clothes and wore a blood-stained dressing gown. She passed Liam two huge towels. 'Get your wet clothes off …. dry yourself and …' She handed him a thick overcoat. 'Put that on, or you will catch a cold.'

His teeth chattered as he pulled off his drenched clothes, threw them across the room where they landed with a splat. He continued to shiver as he dried himself and then pulled on the overcoat and dragged it around him.

Zita smiled. 'You will soon be much warmer. I have turned on the boiler so we will have hot water and heating.'

Liam looked concerned. 'Won't *they* notice the flue?'

'No. It is at the back – so "they" won't see the smoke.'

She walked across the room and checked one of the radiators. 'It is already getting warm but it will take some time for us to feel it. This place has been empty for months and has got very cold.'

He stood and pulled the overcoat even tighter around him.

'Do you want something to eat?' asked Zita.

'Eat?' he replied. He looked at her, opened his outstretched hands and shrugged his shoulders. 'Whatever.'

She was disappointed at his response and shook her head. 'Alright,' she said, half-heartedly. 'Leave it to me.' She shook off her apprehension with a shrug. 'But now we need to get cleaned up … Come and find yourself some dry clothes while I have a shower and then you can have yours.'

Liam grunted.

She walked towards the stairs and sighed loudly. She turned and glared back at him. 'Can you make us tea when you have your clothes? No milk in mine.'

He sloped across to the fridge, knelt down and opened the door. He pulled his head back as the stench hit him. 'Milk?' He picked up a bottle that had curdled and showed it to her. 'Fuck.'

When she reached the stairs, she turned and her face broke into a wide silent grin. She called back to him. 'Put it all in a plastic bag and I will get rid of it when I come back.' *Her mind was elsewhere. She knew they had outsmarted their invisible assassin but she had no idea for how long. She needed to have some sort of security or early warning system in place before she could relax?* She turned and rushed back into the room and leaned on the table. 'Liam …' She continued in a stern voice. 'We must *not* use the lights.'

'What the fuck?'

'Liam.' She pointed at the bare windows. 'It will give us away … They will know we are here.'

'Fuck.'

She continued. 'Please … *No lights.*' She paused and took her time to force a smile. 'I'm sure we can manage for a while. Okay?'

He sighed and shivered. 'Sure – no problem.' He cursed as he searched the drawers and cupboards until he found a ripped plastic bag. He knotted the torn corner and urged as he emptied the fridge of the rotten food and drinks that had been in there for more than seven months.

Zita showered and soon reappeared in an ill-fitting tracksuit.

Liam looked up and muttered to himself. 'Mmm … She would look good in a sack …'

She smiled at him. 'Liam, I have left some towels in the bathroom, you can go now and have a long shower.' She paused. 'You will feel so much better after dat.'

He nodded.

She leaned into him and kissed him on the cheek. '*Now* … I *will get* something for us to eat.'

He nodded and tugged the belt and pulled the overcoat even tighter around his body. He stood and watched her as she threw her head back, flicked her fingers though her wet hair and shook her head. She walked towards the window and, with seemingly no effort, dragged the blood splattered settee to one side, opened the window grabbed the foul-smelling bag from the floor and swung it over her shoulder. She crouched in the open window and turned back. She waited until Liam looked up before she spoke. 'Liam?'

'Yeas?'

She fired him a firm look. 'Liam … I am sorry to repeat something … but … *please* do not put on the lights.'

He looked confused.

She repeated herself. 'Liam … remember this place is empty, yeas?'

'Wha …?'

'There is no one here? So, we must not switch on the lights …'

His reaction was a knowing nod. 'Yeah. I *know that.*'

Zita climbed onto the fire escape and down the rough metal stairs. She stood in the cramped courtyard between the huge rusting freezers, a pile of empty vegetable boxes, empty rusty catering tins and a lean-to covered with corroded metal corrugated sheets. She leaned against the door frame, took aim and threw the stinking bag into the huge waste bin. She tapped on the open rear door of the Lost Tulip Café and waited until the owner and chef saw her.

He was visibly shocked. 'You? You've come back to this place.' He stepped into the yard and looked up towards the open first floor window. He stuttered as he continued. 'How could you ever think of coming back … a … a … after what happened?'

'We do *anything* we need to do,' she retorted.

He threw back his head and grunted. 'So?'

'We are hungry–'

'We?'

'Yes. "*We.*"'

He didn't know how to react.

Zita grinned back at him. 'Yes. *We* need something to eat.'

He screwed up his face and nodded.

'Can you let me have two pizzas?'

'Any preferences?'

She shook her head. 'Whatever you want to make.' She paused. 'Oh. And … I need a few other things.' She passed him a handwritten list.

He read it, nodded and slipped in his pocket. 'Okay. Give me ten minutes.'

She didn't move.

He looked at her and his eyes silently questioned why she was still there.

'I'll wait.' She paused a beat and smiled at him. 'Oh … Can I use your phone?'

He nodded his reply and pointed towards the phone on the wall.

Zita pushed past him, picked it up and dialled.

'Detective Ribeker.'

'Hello, Andrea, how are you?'

'Is that … Zita?' she asked, apprehensively.

There was a smile in Zita's voice. 'Yes, it's me.' She waited as the detective exhaled her relief. 'How are you?'

'I was going to ask you the same,' said Ribeker. She paused and grimaced while her face became instantly contorted and took on a look of confusion. 'Piet is out …' She couldn't hide her shock and continued to blurt out her words. 'He's got divers searching the Prinsengracht–'

'What?'

'Yeah, a tour guide on one of the boats said she heard shots and saw two people fall into the canal … from a houseboat – the Madonna.' She paused and took a deep breath and spoke as she exhaled. 'She said they were DEAD!'

'"Dead?"'

'That's what she said – *dead.*'

'Fuck.' Zita paused and took a few seconds to decide how to respond. She sighed heavily. 'Someone did try to kill us, Andrea … but … we mana–'

'Kill?!' she shrieked. '*You … and Liam?*'

Zita nodded to the invisible caller as her face broke into a mischievous grin. 'Yeah, scary, eh?'

Ribeker's voice waivered. 'I'd better get on to Piet and tell him to call off the search.'

Zita sucked hard on her bottom lip but didn't comment.

Ribeker picked up her walkie talkie and continued. 'So where are the two of you now?'

'We're safe,' said Zita. She paused and took a huge breath. 'Sorry, Andrea that's all I can say.' She took an even deeper breath. 'But … can you do me a huge favour?'

'Course, I will.'

Zita sighed heavily and took her time to continue. 'Will you ask Piet to have his men keep an eye on my home – my boat – Madonna.' She looked into the bustling café filled with customers enjoying innocent conversation and sighed. 'I don't think we'll be back for a while.' She paused. 'Well.' She turned and looked towards the flames inside the pizza oven and continued with a defiant tone in her voice. 'That is until I've sorted out this mess.'

Detective Ribeker and her lover, Bernie, had been caught up in the violent and torturous events above the Black Tulip Café months earlier and the memories of those days had affected everyone that was there. She remembered

27

everything so vividly. Her whole body shook and her voice cracked as the faked, sympathetic tone of her voice confirmed it. 'After what we've all been through Piet will be more than happy to have someone drive past and keep an eye out for you.'

Zita sighed with relief. 'Thanks, Andrea.' She looked into the restaurant and noticed the coloured flickering table lights. Her eyes glanced along the open shelves until she saw the tea-lights. She reached up, grabbed a handful of them, held them up to the chef, who nodded his agreement, and slipped them into her pocket.

He waved at her as he slipped the pizza boxes into an already bulging plastic bag. She acknowledged him with a twist of her head and finished her conversation. 'Look, Andrea, I have to go now.'

'Take care, Zita.'

'Bye,' she said as she replaced the receiver, leaving Andrea Ribeker staring vacantly at the handset in one hand and the walkie talkie in the other.

The chef handed Zita the bag.

She dug into the pocket of her tracksuit bottoms and paid him with a handful of wet notes. She sensed his initial resentment in wanting to accept them so motioned to him to dry them on the side of his pizza oven. She watched him as he carefully peeled the soggy mass open and laid each of the notes out on the warm front edge of the oven. When he'd finished, she whispered in his left ear. 'Tell no one you've seen me.' She leaned into him and stared directly into his eyes and waited for his response.

He squinted at her and, after rubbing at his tired bloodshot eyes, he shot her a puzzled look.

Her whole body stiffened menacingly and her nose touched his. 'You, tell … NO one. Okay?!'

He trembled nervously as he replied with a stutter. 'C ... c ... course not ...'

She knew he wanted to ask how long she would be around. She read his mind. 'Don't ask that either,' she said, as she turned and pushed past him.

He opened her note and read down the list. When he reached the last two items, he stopped and looked up at her. 'These will not be so easy to get for you.'

She nodded. 'I know.' She lowered her head and then raised it and fired him a look of desperation. 'But we do need them.' She tilted her head. 'Please.'

He folded the note and slipped it into his pocket. 'I will have everything by tomorrow.'

She reached towards him and kissed his cheek. 'Thank you ... very much,' she said softly. She turned and smiled to herself as she walked out into the yard.

CHAPTER TWO

One Day We'll Fly Away

Zita climbed the fire escape and in through the window. Liam, having showered, was now dressed in a pair of baggy check trousers, grey shirt and thick dark blue pullover. He sat waiting expectantly at the table in the semi-darkness, for something … anything … to eat. He watched as she took out the two pizza boxes and placed them on the table along with several cans of coke, a packet of cigarettes and a lighter.

He reached across the table and grabbed one of the pizza boxes and ripped it open. He tore into the pizza and ate like a ravenous animal.

Zita, surprised at the degree of Liam's hunger, shook her head and murmured to herself as she walked across to the fridge and took the remaining items from the bag. She placed the milk, ham, cheese and butter inside the buzzing fridge and, after brushing off the dust from the worktop, she placed the bag of croissants, bread rolls, tea and coffee on it. She lit two of the tea-lights and placed one of them on the table and the second well away from the windows.

They finished the pizzas in silence and as Liam wiped at his lips, he shuddered as he spoke. 'There sure are a lot of bad fucking memories here, Zita.'

She trembled and dropped her head. 'Too many,' she murmured, regrettably. She turned away and tried to hide her tears as she remembered the horrendous torture she had endured. She sniffed hard and continued. 'But, Liam,' She wiped at her eyes with her sleeve. 'There is nowhere else for us to go.' She sniffed again and paused. 'So ... we need to stay here for a while.' She paused and remembered the weak link – the front door. 'I need to make us safe and secure.'

Liam nodded.

He had been eyeing the cigarettes while he ate the pizza and now reached across the table and picked up the packet. He opened it and lit his one and only permitted cigarette of the day, something that was reluctantly agreed by the consultant after the lengthy and challenging operation to repair his damaged throat. He took a huge drag, sat back in the chair and gazed at Zita through the smoke. 'How did you know?'

'Know what?' He pretended to clear his throat with a cough. 'When to shove me into that vile ... bastard water.'

She regained her composure, sat upright, smiled at him and extended her head proudly. She took a huge noisy breath through her nose, pushed out her perfect pert breasts and spoke as she exhaled. 'I knew ...' She tapped the table rhythmically. 'I knew that after the first bullet missed us ... we would have two seconds to *live* ...' She fired him a solemn look. 'Or ... *die*.' Her voice faded as she ran out of breath.

'Fuck.'

'Liam.' She openly laughed at him and he recoiled. 'It's not like you see in de films.' She pushed herself back in the chair and waited for his reaction.

There wasn't one.

'*That* was for *real*,' she said.

She paused a beat.

'Don't forget, I was trained to do dat.'

He grunted. 'Um.' *Liam knew that for her it was a contradiction of her training – to save life and not kill.*

She continued. 'Whoever it was … they made a *mistake.*' She screwed up her face in disgust and sniggered. 'There is no excuse for dat,' she said, shaking her head and tutting. '*He* … or *she* … should have got one of us with the *first shot.*' She paused. '*But they failed,*' she said, with a low growl. 'That's a serious fehler.'

'What?'

She giggled. 'Mistake … Um. *They* made a big mistake … and it won't go down so well with their handler.'

Liam sat back and chuckled to himself as he realised what Zita had said. It took him a few minutes before he was able to speak. 'They did, didn't they,' he said. He nodded enthusiastically and finally realised how lucky they had been. He fidgeted nervously with the edge of the pizza box until he asked the question he had been waiting to ask since he'd walked up the stairs and into *that* building. 'So *where are* we going?' He paused and looked directly at her.

She lowered her eyes and as she slowly raised them, she fired him an extended blank look. 'I don't know yet,' she said.

He sighed and continued. 'But we can't stay here …' He leaned forward, rested his elbows on the table and leaned on his clenched hands. He sighed again and continued in a defeated tone. 'For the rest of our lives–'

'Course we can't,' yelled Zita. 'I am trying to think where we can go …' She clicked her tongue. 'And gain some time before dey find us again–'

'Find us?!' He took his time to take in what she'd said and looked around at what was their temporary home, tainted by their hellish memories, before he continued. 'So how long do you reckon we have to stay in this fucking place?'

Zita took a huge breath and swallowed hard before rubbing her chin with the palm of her greasy hand. In disgust, she wiped it in her tracksuit. She closed her eyes and spoke. 'Three ...' She took her time to partially open them and squinted at him as she continued. 'Maybe four days.'

He covered his mouth and repeated that to himself. While he took that in, he reached down and subconsciously picked at a piece of gaffa tape beneath the arm of the chair with his left hand. His whole body shook as he realised that he was sitting in the chair that Erag, the Albanian, had tied Zita to and then tortured her. He remembered when he broke into the flat and cut her free from the chair. He looked down at the blood-stained floor boards and recollected how she had used every last ounce of strength to crawl across the floor and rip out her torturer's throat. He shuddered and gasped for breath. He coughed and grabbed at his painful throat as he tried to relieve the excruciating pain.

'Liam, what happened?' screamed Zita. She took a slow breath and oozed concern as she realised why he was in so much pain. 'Of *course*, you don't have any more painkillers, do you?'

He shook his head and took huge gulps of air as he tried to regain his composure. 'I'm alright.' He took another gasp of air. 'I ... I ... I just need a minute ...'

She jumped up from the table, sending her chair crashing across the room. 'I'll get some for you.' Before Liam could answer she had climbed out of the window and disappeared down the fire escape.

She returned a few minutes later with a handful of painkillers. 'They are not what you normally have …' She looked him up and down. 'So be careful … They are so much stronger.'

While Liam swallowed them with the last of his coke, Zita reached across the table screwed up the empty pizza boxes and pushed them into the plastic bag. 'Let's go to bed.'

The houses in central Amsterdam were very narrow following the high taxes in the medieval times based on the length of the frontage. So, they were designed and built narrow and tall. Many of them having five and, sometimes six storeys.

Zita chose the top floor – the fifth. She sighed. 'Tomorrow, I will plan our next move … and …' She took her time to take in his pained, exhausted face. 'You need to rest.' She reached out for him and helped him off his chair. 'Come on.'

CHAPTER THREE

One More Try

The low mid-morning sun finally entered the bedroom and slowly crept across the room until it reached their exhausted faces. They both woke up at the same time and after opening their eyes looked up at the patterns created by sunlight on the cracked and peeling ceiling. Zita nudged him. 'It's too late for breakfast, Liam. I'll go and get us brunch while you make the tea, and then … we will have work to do.'

He rolled over.

Zita persisted and tugged the covers from him. 'Please, Liam, we do need to do this *today*.'

Half an hour later she appeared at the window with a box containing their brunch, and a bulging tool bag.

Liam looked at her from his seat at the table. 'You weren't joking were ya?'

'No, Liam. We must do this today.'

They finished brunch and Zita cleared the table and emptied the tool bag checking that everything she had asked the café owner to get for her was in there. She lined everything up in order. There was a claw-hammer, two boxes of screws, a box of cable clips, two screwdrivers, a reel of grey electric cable, two torches and a pack of batteries, a pack of latex gloves and two unmarked white boxes.

'How did you get all of this?'

She giggled. 'I placed an order with the owner downstairs–'

'Wha …?'

'I knew what I needed.' She ran her fingers over everything on the table and stopped at the boxes. 'Some of it was not easy.' She sniffed. 'But … he did it for me …' She looked up at Liam and continued. 'For us.'

Liam reached out for one of the boxes.

Zita smacked his hand. 'Please, don't touch.'

He lowered his head, slid his hand across the table and dropped it onto his leg. 'What the fuck is all this?'

She didn't answer. She stood up, grabbed the nearest dining chair and smashed it to pieces.

Liam watched in amazement. 'What the hell are you doing?'

She ignored him and broke up the larger pieces with the hammer. She picked up the biggest piece and checked it. 'I want you to screw that on the inside of the letterbox.' She took a deep breath and tried to hide her concern. 'So, they can't push anything through it.'

'What?'

'Liam, if they can't come inside … what do you think they would. do?'

He scratched his head. 'Fuck–'

'Yes, "Fuck!" Is right.' She breathed heavily through her nose and took her time to exhale. 'They … would try and kill us – maybe burn us alive,' she said, with heartfelt conviction. 'You remember what happened before?'

Liam shuddered and grunted. 'I get it.' He took the wood from her, grabbed a box of screws and screwdriver and left.

Zita picked up the hammer, walked part-way up the stairs, lifted the sixth and seventh tread and created a small gap beneath each of them. She opened the smaller box and took out two sensors and slid one into each slit. She bit off the end of the electric cable and connected it to each of the sensors and partially screwed down the treads. She tacked the cable to the stair stringer and up the side of the nearest door architrave and walked it up the stairs, tacking it to the wall every few metres and finally taking into their bedroom on the fifth floor. She opened the second box and connected the contents to the cable and placed it under her pillow.

Liam had finished sealing the letterbox and sat at the table sipping at his mug of tea. He grinned at her as she walked down the stairs. 'All done. They won't put anything through there now.'

Zita pushed a torch towards him. 'Always point it to the floor. Okay?' She picked up her mug and sat opposite him. 'Okay. Now I want you to screw all the doors closed except the bathroom, toilet and our bedroom ... and the front bedroom on the fourth floor.'

'Why?'

'It is so simple. Think about it.'

He shook his head.

'Well, if anyone does try to break in–'

'But the front door is bolted–'

'It is now ... but once we finish this ... we must ... *unbolt* it.'

'Why?'

'Because, if they realise the door is bolted from the inside ...'

Liam finished the sentence for her with a slow nod. 'They will know someone is in here – right?'

Zita slammed her hand on the table. 'That is exactly correct, Liam.' She stood up. 'So please screw the doors for me now. Remember to leave the bathroom and toilet, our bedroom and the front bedroom on the fourth floor.'

'Okay,' he replied. He couldn't hide his confusion and fired her a vacant look.

Zita continued. 'If … and I mean if, they are able to get inside … they will try each door and, as they are screwed closed, they will have no idea which room we are in … or, if there are more people in the building.'

Liam grinned.

'It will frustrate them and we will hear them before they reach our room on the fifth floor.'

Zita lay on the bed beside Liam and, having screwed so many doors closed, he rubbed at the sore palms of his hands.

Zita jumped up. 'Liam can you come to my side … please?'

'What?'

'I need to test something. Please move over.'

He slid across the bed and rested his head on her pillow.

Zita walked down to the lounge and then back up the stairs. When she reached the bedroom Liam was roaring with laughter. 'What the fuck was that?' He pointed at the pillow. 'This thing was vibrating … is that some new sex toy?' He shook his head. 'What the fuck next.'

Zita's face beamed. 'That is fantastic.'

'Really? What sort of a buzz can *anybody* get from a sodding vibrating pillow?'

'That is our early warning if anyone does break in.'

'Okay, but what the fuck is it?'

Zita sat on the edge of the bed and took the circular pad from beneath the pillow and held it in her hand. 'This, Liam, is used for deaf people.' She faltered. 'I mean people who cannot hear … anything … at all.'

'Right.'

'They connect it to a sensor in their doorbell so … if they are in bed, when it vibrates, they know someone is at the door.'

'Fuck me.'

'I have connected it to two sensors on the stairs so, we will get a warning before they reach us and …' She pointed towards the window. 'If they do reach us, we can use the fire escape.' She paused. 'If we need it.'

Liam shook his head wildly. 'What will the bastards think of next?' he said, as he closed his eyes.

'I know. Things are moving very fast these days, Liam.' She jumped off the bed and stood at the door. 'Can you help me please?' She turned. 'Bring a screwdriver.'

They walked down to the bedroom on the floor below and Zita squeezed behind the large dressing table. 'Can you help me move this.'

'Sure.'

'We need to remove the mirror–'

'Mirror?'

'Yes, Liam. I will explain.' She held the mirror while he unscrewed it.

'Now what?'

'We put it on the landing–'

'On the landing?'

'Yes. Come on.'

They lifted it onto the landing and rested it against the wall facing the stairs.

'Now what?'

She giggled at him. 'You don't know, do you?'

'Know what?'

'Every night we must move it across the stairs.'

'Really.'

'If… and I mean … if. If anyone does come in, they will use their torch to come up the stairs.' She paused. 'Have you understood?'

He shook his head.

'Think about it. When they shine their torch on this floor their light will reflect back to them – it will confuse them *and* maybe they will think there is someone else on the stairs.' She grabbed Liam. 'Who knows what will happen.' She couldn't stop laughing. *'They may even fall down the stairs.'*

Liam was speechless.

Zita continued. 'I did the same in Bergen … Norway … seven years ago.' She grinned proudly. 'He died and I didn't have to do anything.'

'Bloody hell. What a great idea … and … and so fucking simple.'

'It is … but it only works in certain places.'

CHAPTER FOUR

Something In the Air

Zita pushed herself up onto one elbow, looked down at Liam and shook his arm. 'I need to go back and get our passports, credit cards, cash and a few other things,' she said, with a yawn. 'Before …' She took a huge breath and continued as she exhaled. 'We can even think about going anywhere.'

He rubbed at his tired eyes and looked up at her. 'How do you plan to do that?'

She dug him in the ribs with her other elbow. 'Fuck you, Liam.' She forced a grin. 'How can you even ask me dat?'

Liam blushed and pushed his head deep into the pillow. 'I'll leave that to you then–'

'Sure.'

On the third day, and when she was sure it was safe, Zita was up before dawn Not wanting to disturb the snoring Liam, she crawled out of bed, and walked to the window. She grinned and whispered to herself. 'Perfect,' she said softly as she looked out at the dense fog that had consumed the buildings, streets and canals of the city and created an eerie atmosphere.

The café was closed, and she was left with no option but to leave by the front door. She stepped outside and shivered briefly while she decided on her route. She shook herself into action, left Huidenstraat and walked into Keizersgracht before crossing the bridge at Berenstraat. She turned left and walked until she was a hundred metres from Madonna, her houseboat, and her home for the past three years. She stopped and waited. When she was confident that she wasn't being followed and, keeping tight to the buildings, she walked the last few metres. The fog that enveloped everything was a perfect cover for her. She stopped in a boarded-up shop entrance and listened, double-checking that she wasn't being followed.

Nothing.

She crossed the cobbled street and climbed onto the houseboat. She unlocked the door, pushed it open a few inches and listened. She waited a beat before she opened it fully and stepped inside. She pulled a head torch from the drawer nearest to the door, flicked it on and positioned it before she slowly picked her way from room to room. The bed was unmade, the coffee in the percolator had dried out and the dirty spoons and open biscuit and cake tins still lay untidily on the worktop. She wanted to clean up and put everything away but after giving it a second thought shook her head, walked back into the bedroom and grabbed the most battered and worn backpack. She quickly filled it with basic toiletries and her underwear, and pants and socks for Liam. She flicked open the side pockets and filled then with their fake passports, credit cards and cash in various currencies. She filled a crumpled holdall with one set of clothes for each of them, a pair of her worn boots and Liam's shoes. She grabbed two worn jackets, pulled one on and forced the other one into the already bulging backpack. She took one last look around at what had been her home since arriving in Amsterdam before sliding the head torch

42

back into the drawer. She gave a final look around, sighed heavily and wiped at her tearful eyes as she closed the door and locked it behind her.

As she walked across the deck she glanced briefly at the fading potted flowers, shook her head and sighed. She noticed the blurred lights of a car driving towards her. It slowed down alongside the houseboat and she saw it was a police car.

It stopped.

She pulled back, hid behind the raised deck and waited.

The driver wound down his window and shone his torch into the fog towards the locked door. He found it hard to see clearly and squinted. He climbed out of his car and walked towards the boat.

Zita crawled back along the deck and crouched as low as she could behind the taller pots and held her breath to prevent it being spotted if she exhaled.

The policeman shone his torch across the deck and locked door before the beam moved and briefly hovered across the pots. He took a step back and flashed the light along the windows on the roadside. He gave one final flourish of his torch before he radioed in, wound up his window and drove away.

Zita waited for the rear lights of the car to vanish, almost immediately into the fog that still hung menacingly over everything, before leaving the houseboat. She took a different route and continued along Prinsengracht, over the second bridge and into Huidenstraat.

Two hours after leaving Liam she walked into the Lost Tulip Café. Although it was open, it was empty except for one waitress who swept the floor and a second waitress who was wiping down the tables and laying them up for breakfast. She acknowledged them with a smile and a nod and made her way into the kitchen. 'Ochtend.'

'Hallo.'

'Twee hartige pannenkoeken alstublieft.'

'Sure. It will only take a minute.'

The owner grabbed two large frying pans from the wall, placed them on the gas hobs, poured a few drops of cooking oil in each and waited. He turned to her and eyed the backpack and holdall.

Zita answered his silent question. 'Yes, we will soon be gone.'

He nodded, turned and checked the oil. As soon as it bubbled, he poured the pancake mix into them. He opened the huge fridge and took out a plastic container, removed several rashers of spek – smoked prosciutto and, after cutting it into smaller pieces, dropped it into the pancakes. He flicked them over to cook the spek and then back again. He added slices of cheese, black pepper and salt and rolled each of them into a box and handed them to her. 'Geneieten van.'

'Thanks, we will.'

Liam was sat at the table drumming his fingers but when he heard Zita's footsteps on the fire escape he rushed towards the open window.

She climbed through the window and he hugged her tight. 'Wow. I was worried.' He took his time to scrutinise the backpack and bulging holdall. 'So … that's all we have now, is it?'

She ignored him and placed the boxes on the table. 'Can you get the knives and forks.'

'Sure.'

She threw the backpack and holdall onto the settee.

He sighed heavily. 'Just *two* bags?'

She raised her voice, pointed her finger and pushed it gently into his chest. 'Can you remember what *you had* when you arrived here?'

He nodded slowly. 'Yeah,' he said, as he forced an embarrassed smile. 'Point taken.'

'Come on eat your breakfast.'

He opened one of the boxes and grinned as he cut into it.

While Liam ate, Zita emptied the backpack and placed everything neatly on the other side of the table. She grinned. 'This is *all* we need ... At this moment.' She grinned at him. 'We can go anywhere now ...'

'Yeah ... Where then?' He grinned brazenly. 'What surprises do you have for me *this* time?'

She licked her lips, tilted her head and shot him a nervous calculated smile. 'We're going to London–'

'Fuck!'

She raised her outstretched fingers in front of him and tried to calm him.

It had no effect.

Liam stomped around the room like a wild animal. He stopped suddenly and turned to her, his raised arms flaying in mid-air. 'You expect me to go back and ... and ...' He stuttered with a combination of disbelief and anger. 'And walk back into all that shit again?!'

Zita pulled down his thrashing arms and clamped them to his side. 'Listen. Liam. We can't stay on mainland Europe ... and ... and we can't go anywhere else for quite a while.'

'Fuck!'

'Listen to me, Liam. We need to go somewhere no one would expect.' She lowered her voice. 'Then … hopefully I can put a stop to it.'

'Really?'

She closed her eyes and nodded as she answered. 'I hope I can …' She sniffed. 'If not, we will never be able to come back here … to *our* city.' She opened her eyes and looked at him with a pitiful stare. 'Is that what you *really* want?'

He gulped for air.

'Well … you have to do this for me … and … if I can make this happen … both of us will be able to come back.'

She waited a beat.

Liam fidgeted nervously, picked up his passport and exhaled a long slow breath. 'Okay?' He lowered his head and flicked the pages. 'You are asking a lot of me … you know.'

She cuddled him and kissed his forehead. 'I know, liebling.'

CHAPTER FIVE

Don't Turn Around

They were up before dawn and while Liam was in the shower, Zita spent her time collecting and bagging up everything and anything that would give any indication that they had ever been there. She climbed through the window and dropped several bags in the large waste bins in the Lost Tulip Café yard.

When they were almost ready to leave, she spent an hour wiping down any finger prints on all the surfaces, chairs and door handles. As the sun finally appeared through the rear window, she checked her watch, walked across the room and stood a metre away from the second-floor front window. She anxiously watched the street below until she saw a mud-splattered twenty-year-old pale green Volvo estate car drive past, slow down and pull up a few metres from the café. She turned to Liam. 'Okay. Let's go.'

They each grabbed one of the bags and walked slowly down the stairs. They both felt unusually nervous to be exposing themselves to their potential assassin. Zita partially opened the front door and looked out onto the deserted street. She took a huge breath and spoke as she exhaled. 'Liam, go to the car … sit on the right side. Don't rush – walk slowly and don't look around.' She let out a sharp sigh. 'Go now … and sit in the back seat – remember

– the right side.' She tapped him on the shoulder. 'And …
put the bag on the floor beside you.'

After Zita briefly acknowledged the driver she
refixed the torn and fading police tape across the front door
then jumped into the car. As it pulled away, she threw the
backpack over the seat.

They all sat in silence as they drove through the
empty streets. Zita continued to glance over her shoulder
and the young female driver repeatedly checked her mirrors
to see if they were being followed. Twenty minutes later
they reached the outskirts of the city and they both sighed
with relief.

Zita reached between the seats and tapped Liam's
leg. 'This is my friend, Palina, from Iceland.'

The fair-haired, blue-eyed young woman looked in
the mirror, raised her hand and smiled at him. 'Hello, Liam.
I am pleased to meet you.'

Liam nodded and pushed himself back into his seat.
He suddenly lurched forward as he felt something jab into
his back. 'Fuck!' He reached behind him and pulled out a
keyring with two tiny, beautifully painted clogs.

Palina twisted her head to look at him. 'I am so
sorry, Liam.' She pointed at the keyring. 'We use this car for
the markets.' She smiled. 'You can keep it if you wish.'

He grunted as he pushed himself back into the seat,
closed the hand holding the keyring and fell asleep.

The two women talked excitedly throughout the
journey and Palina's excitement grew as Zita told her what
had happened to De Groot and his vile empire.

The car slowed as it drove through the picturesque seaside
smalstad and pulled into the car park near the sand dunes
which, except for a few avid wind surfers, was deserted. Zita

opened the door on the opposite side to Liam, reached down, grabbed the backpack and slipped it over one shoulder. She dropped the holdall heavily into his lap and he woke with a jolt. 'Come on, we are having some lunch.'

He shook his head and rubbed at his eyes. 'Okay.' He pushed himself up and after clearing the window of condensation, he peered out. 'Where the fuck are we?' He sat erect and watched the surfers shivering as they dried themselves before changing into their jeans, tee-shirts and bubble jackets.

Palina answered him. 'We're in Domburg, Liam.' She smiled proudly. 'A very famous townlet here in Zealand.' She beckoned him with flapping arms of excitement. 'Come. You will love it.' She opened the boot, pushed her bulging cardboard boxes of stock around and handed Liam a jacket that was much too big for him. This time he didn't care. After falling asleep he was freezing and was thankful for anything.

Palina handed Zita a dark blue logoed fleece then pulled on a red fleece with the same logo. She tapped Liam's arm and proudly pointed at the logo on his jacket and their fleeces. 'This is our business, *The Clog and Cheese Company.*'

Liam faked interest with a nod.

Palina locked the car and they walked along the pavements laid with dark brown brick paviours until they reached the centre of the town. It was so different to Amsterdam. Another world, resembling a model village with brightly coloured houses, neat gardens and, even at this time of year, flowers and shrubs. They turned into Ouuststraat and Palina guided them into the covered external seating area of the Restaurant De Visbar, a seafood restaurant, where two huge ugly copper illuminated fish hung from the ceiling. 'Here we have the best sea food from the North Sea,' she said.

The waitress knew Palina and welcomed her with a warm smile. She showed her and her guests to an inside table.

While Zita and Palina scanned the menu Liam sat at the table and fiddled with the tiny clogs on the keyring.

Palina leaned across to him and tapped them. 'Me and Jan make these and we sell them to the tourists at markets here in Domburg ... and other places.' She looked at Liam and then out of the window at the trees, their branches rocked by the wind as they shed the last of their leaves across the empty road and pavements. She laughed and pointed towards the lake. 'It is beautiful in the summer.' She briefly closed her eyes and remembered. 'Blue skies and warm sun ... almost every day.' She exhaled. 'And packed with tourists.' She nudged Liam. 'We love tourists.' She giggled. 'They always buy *something* from us.'

Palina ordered for them and while she and Zita ate brioche, smoked salmon and fried egg, Liam had a large piece of cod with chips and an excess of ketchup.

She paid the bill and they took their time to walk back through the village between the unique chocolate box houses and bungalows before they climbed up onto the dunes that towered high above them. The bitter northerly wind blew the sea fog onshore and hit them full on, taking their breath away and causing Liam to shiver.

Palina drew up beside him. 'That is the North Sea Liam and this time of year it always brings cold winds from as far as my home in Iceland ...' She took a huge breath of the cold but invigorating sea air and exhaled. 'And the waves for the surfers.' She faked a shiver. 'They love it.' She turned and pointed at the fanatics racing along the huge waves. 'Look.'

Liam turned to Zita and was stunned when he saw how far the village he had just visited was below them. 'Does the sea ... the North Sea ever come over the dunes?'

'Sometimes,' said Palina. 'After the last war Domburg was a mess and many of the buildings were little more than rubble and those undamaged were soon flooded and damaged by the sea water.'

Liam shrugged his shoulders.

She ignored him and continued. 'In 1948 people came back to swim and lay in the sun on the beaches and these dunes.' Palina reached out to Zita and spoke. 'There was another catastrophe five years later. At the beginning of February 1953–'

'What happened?' asked Zita.

'Jan was a little boy at that time. He told me the storm killed more than a thousand people and many animals died too. The cost was more than four hundred million guilders.'

Zita tugged at the sleeve of Liam's jacket. 'But as you can see, Domburg is beautiful once more. The Dutch have been dealing with this for hundreds of years. They are engineers ... very clever engineers.'

CHAPTER SIX

Turn Back Time

After driving for little more than half an hour Palina slowed down in front of a huge sign advertising the farm shop. She turned into the large car park filled with coaches and cars. Tourists were thronging excitedly between the racks of brightly painted clogs that filled both sides of the entrance to the shop. Some had already bought their gifts and souvenirs and were making their way back to their coaches with brightly coloured bags displaying the name of the *Clog and Cheese Company*.

In a pen near the front glazed doors were two brown and white calves which attracted a lot of attention from the younger children who had come with their parents. Liam tried to guess how many different nationalities were there by looking over the number plates. He gave up when he got to six and couldn't recognise any more.

Zita looked around at the mass of customers. 'Wow, you have worked wonders, Palina,' she said.

'Thanks,' said Palina. She exuded a huge grin. 'It has been such hard work … but we love it here.' She drove through the car park and between a pair of high ornate metal gates and stopped in front of a large house. She reached over the seat and nudged Liam. 'This is my home now.'

She leaned across and kissed Zita on the cheek. 'Remember?'

Zita grinned. 'Yes, of course I do.'

Palina turned. 'Liam, welcome to my home.' She flung open her car door. 'Come on you must meet Jan.' She opened the rear door which creaked loudly and leaned into the car. 'Come.'

Liam picked up the holdall and Zita grabbed the backpack. They stepped into the yard and avoided the chicken that clucked excitedly whilst they scavenged for food in the gravel.

Liam and Zita followed Palina towards the noisy machines housed in a large timber building covered with a corrugated iron roof, at the far end of the yard, and the recently delivered poplar and willow trunks neatly stacked along the length of it. Palina, Zita and Liam stood at the entrance and waited until Jan saw them and signalled to the machinists to turn off their woodworking machines and the overhead sawdust extractors.

They slowly ground to a whining, juddering halt.

Jan removed his goggles and ear protectors and as he walked towards them he exuded a huge welcoming smile. Jan was a giant of a man, in his early fifties, and much older than Palina, with flecks of wood shavings and sawdust in his wild dark brown hair and bushy beard. He shook his head and drew his fingers through his beard to release some of the unwanted debris before he reached out and kissed the diminutive Palina and then hugged Zita. He kissed her on both cheeks then reached out his hard dry hands and shook Liam's hand. 'Good to meet you?'

'Liam,' said Palina.

Jan's ruddy face beamed. 'Liam, welcome to our farm. I will see you later and we can talk some more.' While he replaced his ear protectors and goggles, he signalled to the two men who turned on their machines and returned to work.

They walked back to the car. Palina turned to Liam. 'If you wait here, we will be back,' she said. She pointed across the yard. 'We sometimes have tourists who like to stay here.'

He handed Zita his bag and Palina walked her across the yard and into the self-contained annexe.

Palina opened the door and Zita looked around. She remembered how she had stayed there several years earlier when she first deserted the Mossad and needed somewhere safe to hide before she finally moved on to Amsterdam, to disappear into the underbelly of the city and work for De Groot.

She shuddered.

Zita opened the backpack, took out their passports, debit cards and money and pushed everything into her jacket pockets, slid their bags under the bed with her foot, and pulled down the valance. She double-checked by looking back towards the bed, locked the door then joined Liam who was still standing at the car.

Zita and Liam walked across the yard to the house and into the kitchen.

Palina had already made a pot of tea and a large cafetiere of coffee and laid up the table with four mugs and tea plates and a huge apple cake.

Jan was already sitting at the table eating a huge piece of the cake. He stood with the rest of it still in his hand. 'Come sit down, you two. Enjoy this wonderful cake and have a drink.'

Liam had finished his second mug of tea and was eating his second piece of cake when Jan stood, pushed his handmade carver chair under the table and turned to Zita. 'I think you two have something to do … Don't you?'

Zita fired Liam a reassuring look. 'Yes, we do. Catch up on everything.'

Liam looked puzzled.

Zita and Palina grinned back at him.

Jan continued. 'Come, Liam, I will show you around.' He led Liam across the yard and into his now silent workshop. He pointed at a large tree trunk 'You can get about seventy-five pairs of clogs from one large tree but it takes about twenty to twenty-five years for a tree to be ready for harvesting so we need a lot of them every year.'

Liam feigned interest and asked the only question he could think of. 'What sort of trees do you need?'

Jan grinned. 'Good question … Liam. We usually make the clogs from willow or poplar wood.' He stooped and picked up a chunk of wood and showed Liam the grain. 'Because they split easily.'

'Right.'

Jan continued. 'In the Netherlands we make about six million souvenir clogs each year, so everyone is sure to find just the right pair to take home.' He paused. 'And we make the small samples – keyrings with the pieces of wood we have left.'

Liam slid his hand inside his pocket, fingered the keyring and pulled it out.

'Yes, that is what we make.'

Liam blushed 'Oh, no. Palina *gave it to me*.'

Jan grinned at him. 'Don't worry.' He laughed loudly. 'I expect you found that in her car. She has so much jammed in there to sell at the markets.'

'Yeah, she told us.'

'Come.' Jan reached out and guided Liam across the yard. 'My father, and his father too, made clogs but since then I have expanded and now … we make cheese …' He pushed out his chest. 'How-da, the most delicious cheese in the world.'

Liam nodded blindly.

'So, you see I make them - the clogs in the winter and … cheese in the summer.' Jan grinned proudly. 'I will show you now.'

They walked towards the sound of the cows mooing and into a much larger wooden barn. On each side of the building were beautiful cows that all had their names on metal plates on the beam above them. Jan proudly introduced each of them to Liam. 'When the cows have their calves, we milk them twice every day and then use it to make the cheese.' He paused. 'But this time of year, we don't make cheese … so we sell the milk.'

'I see,' said Liam.

At the end of one row in a separate pen were four calves. Jan realised that Liam was nervous. 'You can stroke them. They won't bite.' He took Liam's hand and moved it towards the nearest calf. 'The tourists and children love to stroke these. We change them at midday so they don't get tired from the children.'

Liam extended his arm and reached out tentatively. For the first time in his life, he stroked an animal other than a cat or dog.

He liked it.

Jan waited patiently while Liam reached out and stroked a second calf. 'Come. I will explain why we do these things and how we make our famous cheese.'

They left the barn and crossed the yard to what looked like a relatively new brick building. Jan unbolted the sliding door and slid it across. It led into a small reception area which had shelves lined with white rubber boots and hooks with white coats. 'We need to take off our shoes and put those on,' he said. He pointed at the boots. 'What size?'

Liam was caught by surprise and stuttered. 'N ... n ... n ... nine?'

Jan grabbed a pair of boots from the top shelf, checked the size and passed them to Liam. 'And now we need to put on one of these.' He unhooked two of the white coats from the pegs and passed one to Liam.

Liam slid his feet into the boots and pulled on the coat.

Jan looked Liam up and down and as he laughed loudly his whole-body shook. 'Like a doctor, eh?' He nodded. 'Yes. It suits you.'

Liam felt ridiculous and smiled back at Jan sheepishly. 'Yeah.' He sniggered. 'Not That I've ever wanted to be one ... or to look like this.'

'Let me show you the cheese we make from those wonderful creatures.'

Jan opened another locked door and they walked into a large room where the walls were fully tiled with white glazed tiles and filled on one side with stainless steel pipework linked to what resembled a huge stainless-steel bath with paddles suspended from an overhead gantry. 'We use that to make the cheese,' he said proudly. 'It has to be spotless ... and ... that's why we always wear these.' He said, as he pointed at the white coats and rubber boots.

Liam nodded.

Jan continued. 'We can't leave the cows outside in the winter. We keep them inside and that is when I make the clogs. In the summer, I make the cheese.' He couldn't hide how proud he was. 'It is a tradition, here in this part of the Netherlands. Other places grow many bulbs, millions of them ... tulips and other flowers,' he said flippantly, as though they didn't have the same value as his cheese. He turned. 'Come. He guided Liam into a large cool storeroom where there was shelf upon shelf of bright orange waxed wheels of cheese. 'So, you see we can be busy through the year on very different things.' Jan picked up a wheel of cheese and passed it to Liam.

He was surprised at the weight and nearly dropped it.

Jan took it from him and effortlessly placed it back on the shelf. 'That wheel weighs forty kilograms and they must all be the same weight.' His demeanour changed. 'There are now only two hundred farms that make ... *Howda* in this country.'

Liam nodded but tried to hide his bewilderment.

He failed.

Jan laughed. 'I think you know this cheese as Gouda, yes?'

Liam was none the wiser.

Jan pointed at the shelves of cheese. 'Each wheel has to be the same size – as I said ... forty kilograms.' Jan continued. 'We make it in the summer with the milk from the cows. We keep them inside in the winter because the ground is too wet but, in the summer, they can go outside and they are milked twice every day ... we use raw milk ... *not* pasteurised.' He pointed at the rows of cheese. 'The wheels are left in a salty bath in the vats for five days and then allowed to dry for twenty-four hours. When they are dry, we apply a wax coating, three times, all over them. When they are ready, they are taken by traders and kept in a warehouse, or store, for at least two years.' He pulled a trier from his overall pocket, pushed it into one of the wheels. He ran his fingers across the cheese and gently touched the crystals and holes. 'This is perfect.' He slid one piece into his mouth and wallowed in the sheer ecstasy of perfection. He finally handed a piece to Liam. 'Try it,' he said.

Liam took a deep breath and finally pushed the cheese into his mouth and forced a smile. He was surprised how soft it was. 'Um … Nice. I like it.'

Jan beamed. 'Wonderful, isn't it?' he said, proudly. He spoke while he readjusted the cheese wheel. 'Liam, where did you meet, Zita?'

'In Amsterdam. I was the manager of a bar … the Love Shack … in De Wallen–'

'Oh, really.' He paused to think. 'In De Wallen – the naughty district?' he said, with a hint of disgust in his voice. He continued. 'The Love Shack? That is a strange name.'

'Yeah, well it was a brothel and a bar …'

Jan showed his disapproval with a shake of the head.

Liam continued. 'I lost everything.' He paused. 'We were firebombed on New Year's Eve.'

Jan could see that Liam was upset. 'Wow. So now you decide to go back to London–?'

'For a while. My father is ill.'

Jan waited to hear more.

'Cancer–'

'I'm sorry to hear that, Liam.'

'Yeah.'

They walked back to the house in silence.

Jan opened the door and waved to Liam to enter while he took off his work boots. 'Please ...'

Liam stopped and froze, shocked at what he saw.

Zita was sitting in a chair and Palina was standing behind her. Zita looked up at him and smiled. 'Do you like it?' She giggled. 'It's the *new me*.'

Liam couldn't speak. He stood at the kitchen door stunned.

Zita's tousled blonde hair was gone and what was left was a shapely, dyed crewcut of dark chestnut hair that followed the contours of her perfectly shaped skull.

Palina removed the towel from around Zita's neck, ran her tiny fingers back through her short hair and tried to ruffle it.

Liam watched Zita check herself in the mirror and smile to herself. She turned to Liam and waited.

After a lot of thought and a heavy sigh he grinned back at her. 'I love it. I really do.'

She walked towards him and kissed him on the cheek. 'I am so pleased.' She took his hand and guided him towards the chair. 'You are next–'

'Me? Now?'

Palina motioned to him to sit down. 'Don't worry, I won't bite.'

Liam stuttered. 'Please don't make it as short as Zita.'

She chuckled. 'Relax. You can trust me.'

Liam sat down and fifteen minutes later he looked in the mirror. Gone was his straggly unkempt hair that had been hiding his ears. He now looked modern and much younger than his thirty-three years.

Zita was the first to complement him. 'You look really good ... very smart and ready for London.'

He checked himself in the mirror and briefly ran his hands though his hair and stood. 'Thank you Palina. You did that like an expert.'

She reached out and gave him a playful nudge. 'Liam, you are so cheeky. I was a hairdresser in Akureyri, the second largest city in Iceland.' She laughed. 'We call it a city …' Her laugh grew louder. 'But there are only twenty thousand people living there.' Her happy face suddenly turned morose as she remembered her attack. 'Before I arrived to Holland,' she said, dejectedly.

He didn't notice that Zita had reached over and squeezed Palina's tiny hand and a smile slowly returned as her demeanour changed and the smile returned. 'Okay.'

He glanced at himself in the mirror again. 'Thanks.'

Liam found it hard to keep his eyes off Zita. She looked so different.

'Tell, me the truth. Do you like it, Liam?'

'Yes, I do. I really do.'

CHAPTER SEVEN

I Don't Break Easily

Palina walked them across the yard to the annexe, carrying a tray of tea and coffee. She let Zita unlock the front door and turn on the lights. Liam stood back and took a few minutes to look around the room. The brightly lit lounge was decorated with blue walls below the timber dado and above it rag-rolled pale yellow. The settee and armchairs were dark blue crushed velvet and the carpet a deep blue with a black fleck. A log fire burned in the large open fireplace. It was warm and relaxing. The red check curtains were held back with red rope. Potted plants filled every inch of the window cill and a vase of red and white roses had been placed in the centre of the coffee table. Palina led them into the bedroom, decorated in the same colours as the lounge. On the double bed were a pair of dark blue dungarees and a pair of red and white American baseball boots. She placed one of the mugs on each of the bedside tables, picked up the dungarees and turned to Zita. 'Do you remember these?'

'Yes,' replied Zita. She swallowed hard and trembled. 'It's what I wore when I came to you for help.' She swallowed again. 'And to hide,' she said, softly.

Liam looked at her, non-plussed.

Zita waved away his obvious concern and mouthed to him incoherently.

'Yes, I remember it well,' said Palina, brightly. She looked at the clock on the wall and pointed. 'Okay. So, I'll see you both in an hour for dinner.'

They both laid on the bed and looked up at the paintings on the opposite wall. Liam coughed nervously. 'So, what happened?'

Zita exhaled heavily. 'Where do you want me to start?'

'That's up to you.' He paused. 'Okay, how did you two meet?'

'We ... ll, after I left London in 1995, I completed my mission and spent a few days in Amsterdam. I loved the houseboats in London, in Little Venice–'

'Where the rich bastards live, right?'

'I wouldn't know that but David Gilmour – Pink Floyd – lives there.'

Liam chuckled loudly. 'That's what I meant ... the rich bastards ...'

Zita fidgeted. 'Liam, do you want me to tell you or not?'

'Sorry. Yeah. Go on.' He sat up and folded his arms.

'Well, after seeing the houseboats in London I thought that maybe one day I could retire and live on one of dem in Amsterdam.' She chuckled. 'They are much cheaper there.'

'Okay.'

'Well, I was walking through De Wallen and a young girl ran towards me. She was crying and ... and she was bleeding ... her face was a mess.'

'Fuck.'

'It was Palina,' screamed Zita. She paused and thought back to that afternoon. She continued. 'She was on holiday with her friends when she was in the Paradiso.' She turned to Liam. 'You remember dat place?'

He nodded. 'Urchin, yeah?' He paused. 'And … Tommy?'

'That's right. The same place.' She cursed. 'Well, someone spiked her drink and she woke up in a cellar.' She sighed awkwardly and shook her head. 'She was raped and beaten–'

'Don't tell me?'

'Yes, it was … Skipio and De Groot's men–'

'The bastards!'

She shook her head and frowned. 'It wasn't so good for her, Liam.'

'I understand–'

'*Do you*? Do you *really* know what it was like for her?'

Liam blushed, reached blindly for his mug, took a sip, and looked towards the window.

Zita tapped his shoulder and, when he turned, she glared at him. 'Of *course*, you don't!' She brought her fist down hard on the bed. 'How could you?' She shrugged. 'You can *never* … *ever* imagine what it was like for poor … poor Palina.' She covered her mouth with her left hand and rubbed at her face aggressively. 'I had to help her escape from them … *The bastards* …'

'Did you know De Groot then?'

She shook her head angrily. 'No, I didn't! But I knew what he did … and … what he could do.'

'So, how did you meet up with her again when she went to work for Jan?'

'We kept in touch and when I needed her help, she did the same for me.'

Liam was confused. 'Hang on … you *helped her* … and then she *helped you*?'

'Yes. We "helped" each other–'

'But … how did she get to leave Amsterdam?'

'I helped her to leave the city and we stayed in a small hotel, outside of Amsterdam, until she was better and then we drove across Holland.' She paused and smiled. 'And we arrived here–'

'Here?'

'In Domburg. Yes.'

'Fuck.'

'She asked Jan for a job and … she is still here and now they are married.'

'Wow.'

Zita looked at the handmade clock. 'We must get ready now.' She walked off to the bathroom, washed their only other set of underwear and rolled it in towels to dry, before she had a shower.

Liam could see that the room had so much character with a feeling of peace and relaxation. He climbed onto the bed to have a closer look at the paintings that hung on the wall above it.

Zita walked out of the bathroom. 'Palina painted those when she first came here. Aren't they wonderful?'

'If you like that sort of thing,' replied Liam, in a matter-of-fact voice.

'Well … I like them,' said Zita, curtly. 'Your turn for the shower.'

He jumped off the bed and shrugged as he walked off into the bathroom.

They quickly got dressed, stood back and took their time to look each other up and down. 'We look very different now, don't we?' said Zita, as she ruffled her hair. 'I love it. But do *you* feel any different, Liam?'

He smirked at her. 'Yeah, I do.'

Zita tilted her head and looked into his eyes. 'We have come so far and now we can begin our journey.'

He reflected and then smiled at her. 'Yeah, I suppose we can.'

She reached for his hand. 'Come on, we are going for dinner now.'

They walked across the yard and into the huge kitchen. The air was filled with the aroma of freshly baked bread and the mixed smells from several large Tramontina cast iron pots, which bubbled gently on the wood-burning Dutch range. A fire roared in the huge stone fireplace and the light from dozens of candles flickered across the walls and ceiling and appeared to dance magically to the soft jazz that played on the stereo.

Liam sniffed and took in the wonderful aromas emanating from the pots on the range before he turned and glanced at the huge dining table.

'Do you like it?' asked Jan.

'Yeah, I do,' said Liam.

'I made it myself,' said Jan, proudly. 'I love wood, the patterns and colours,' he said, as he traced the grain across the table. 'Nature is so clever and beautiful.'

Liam followed Jan's fingers and ran his hand across the table. He stopped abruptly when he noticed two huge jugs, one of water and the other of fruit juice. *Had Zita told them about his problem?* He didn't see Palina and Zita leave the room.

Jan poured two large glasses of water, handed one to Liam and they both sat in front of the fire in the two huge armchairs and looked into the flames. He pointed at a neat pile of what looked like bricks stacked on the hearth and reached forward. He picked up one of them and passed it

to Liam. 'These are briketten – I think you call them …
briquettes.'

Liam shrugged his shoulders. 'Dunno.'

'We try not to waste very much so we have an
apprentice who makes them from the sawdust.' He smiled.
'And you can imagine we have so much every day.'

Liam offered a congratulatory nod. 'Yeah. Great
idea.'

Jan looked at the clock and knew he had ten more
minutes before dinner. He settled himself into his chair,
before he continued. 'Did you see much of the Euros this
year, Liam.'

'Euros?'

'The football–'

'Ah. No, not much … we were on holiday.'

'Holiday?'

'Yeah, we needed a break after the fire … and …'
Liam turned away and looked into the flames, managed a
painful swallow and coughed. 'We had some bad things
happen before that.' He cursed. 'Some fucking bad things
…'

Jan blew out his cheeks and expelled the air. 'Sorry
to hear that.'

'It's okay,' said Liam, dismissively.

Jan looked concerned. 'No. I really am sorry, Liam.'

Liam smiled and raised his open hands. 'It's okay
now, we're over that. We'll just have to see what shit
London throws at us.'

'But … it will be good to go home, won't it?'

'I've got mixed feelings about going back, what with
my dad having cancer and my mother with dementia.' He
sighed. 'Who knows.'

They both turned in the direction of the giggling.

Palina and Zita stood hugging each other and giggling like young school kids. Palina burst out laughing. 'Today my friend is wearing some of my makeup.' She chuckled. 'Eye shadow, some subtle pink blusher on her cheeks, and mascara on her eyelashes.'

Jan and Liam looked on in stunned silence.

'Is that really you, Zita?' asked Liam.

Palina replied. 'Oh yes. Isn't she beautiful?' she said as she spun her around.

'She really is and with her new hair style … almost … unrecognisable,' said Liam, having to pinch himself.

Liam sat with Zita and Jan at the table and watched Palina as she effortlessly lifted the huge pots from the cooker and bought the kjötsúpa: Icelandic lamb soup, boerenkoolstamppot: a large dish of potatoes, onions and curly kale all mashed together with sliced sausage on top. The third pot contained Dutch hachee stew, a traditional beef and onion stew in a sauce with a wonderfully rich flavour. She laid them all in the centre of the table and Jan proudly served them from the various pots.

For the first time Liam realised how different Dutch life was to anything he had seen in Amsterdam or ever known. It was perfect. He was lost in the euphoric atmosphere: the roaring fire, the warm soft lighting, the aroma of the food, the music and lastly the company.

They all cleared their plates and while Zita washed and dried the dishes, Palina opened the oven and took out what looked like a large pie. She dusted it with sugar and placed it in the centre of the table.

Jan picked up a huge knife, cut the cake into four large pieces and served a slice to everyone.

Palina opened the fridge and took out a bowl of vanilla ice cream and dropped a huge spoonful onto the centre of each slice.

Liam took a bite and drooled. 'What is this? It's fantastic,' he said, with his mouth full.

Zita kicked his leg.

He fired her an embarrassed look, swallowed hard and mouthed his apology.

Palina looked at Jan lovingly.

He smiled back at her and nodded.

Palina flicked her head and faced Liam. 'Liam, it's a cake we have in Iceland. It's called hjónabandssæla.' She blushed as she continued and reached for Jan's hand. 'Marriage cake – and the hope of a long marriage.'

Liam ignored her blushes and, avoiding Zita's stare, he picked up another huge piece of cake on his fork and dipped it in the ice cream that had already melted on his plate.

Palina continued. 'We make it with oatmeal and flour and then add rhubarb. In the long dark Icelandic winter, it reminds us of summer.' She fired each of them a wide grin. 'We all look forward to the summer.'

Jan exhaled as he spoke. 'Yes, we all do that.'

Liam nodded as he cleared his plate. He sat back and turned to Jan. 'How did you meet Palina?'

Jan laughed loudly. 'You may not believe it.'

'Try me.'

'I was working on my stall in the market in Domburg, selling my clogs ... and ... these two.' He paused and grinned broadly at Zita and Palina. 'Stopped and said they liked them.' He sighed. 'It was so busy ... much too busy and I was struggling to sell to everyone.'

'Right.'

'And … they helped me.'

Palina and Zita looked at each other and giggled.

'When I closed the stall, I asked if *one of them* wanted a job.' He reached out his other hand, Palina held it and rested them on the table. 'She, said "yes." So, they came back here and stayed in the annexe.' He paused. 'Zita left.' He grinned. 'And Palina stayed.' Jan laughed loudly. 'As soon as I saw her, I couldn't resist. She was … beautiful,' he said, emphasising every letter.

Palina blushed.

Jan squeezed her hand. 'She didn't tell me she could paint.' He smiled. 'So, at first she worked in the shop.' He squeezed her hand tighter. 'But one day I noticed she was painting some of the clogs and everything changed. She moved into the annexe and six months later we were married.'

Liam grinned. 'Sounds like a fairy tale.'

'Yes, it was,' gushed Palina.

Zita nodded.

Palina blushed again.

Jan continued. 'Do you know she paints all of our clogs now – and they are wonderful. We can't make enough.'

Zita smiled. 'We saw the coaches and busy car park.'

Liam sat back and grinned from ear to ear. 'This has been the best.' He paused. 'The most enjoyable evening … I've ever had.'

It was still dark but Liam and Zita heard the wood working machines whirring in the workshop as Jan made even more clogs. She slid out of bed, stood at the window and looked out at the frost covered fields. 'Come on, sleepy head.' She tapped Liam's foot poking out from the edge of the duvet.

'We need to get going.' She smiled to him. 'After breakfast, Palina said she will drive us to the station in Brussels.'

'Brussels?'

'Yeah. She is happy to do it for us.'

They finished their breakfast and after Palina had cleared the table and washed the dishes, she tapped Liam on the shoulder. 'Would you like to take some clogs back for your children, Liam?'

He silently quizzed her.

'Zita told me ...'

He looked towards Zita who was drying the dishes.

She turned and smiled back at him.

'Ah ...' He forced a smile. 'That would be nice – a great idea.'

'And some cheese for your parents?'

Zita spoke for him. 'Liam, I think they would like that very much.'

Palina grabbed his arm. 'Come on, we can choose something for all of them.'

The car park was already filling with tourist coaches and a group of children were enjoying their time with the calves. Palina led Liam between the vehicles and into the shop. She took her time to walk him along the shelves of clogs.

'So, you painted all of these?'

'Yes. All of them.'

'They're nice. Very nice.'

'Thank you, Liam.'

She helped him to choose three pairs of clogs and, from the other side of the shop, two small wheels of Gouda cheese. As they were leaving, she picked her way through the keyrings and gave him a selection of them. 'One for you

– not an old one, and one for Zita. You can give the others to your children.' She took the woven basket to the counter and placed everything into one of their colourful bags. 'A present from the Netherlands and ... Iceland, for your family, Liam.' She handed him the bag. 'I hope they like them.'

Liam lied. 'I'm sure they will.' *He had no idea if they would appreciate anything coming from him.*

They said their goodbyes to Jan and as Palina pulled out of the car park they both waved back to him.

Two and a half hours later they pulled into the car park at the front of Brussels South Railway Station. Zita opened the holdall and took out all their clothes leaving just their underwear and wash things. She handed them to Palina. 'We won't need these ... we will buy more when we get to London.' She slipped the bag of presents into the holdall and zipped it up.

Zita and Palina hugged until they finally pulled apart.

Palina reached out and hugged and kissed Liam. 'It was such a pleasure to meet you, Liam,' she said. 'Take care.'

CHAPTER EIGHT

Suspicious Minds

They had a two hour wait for the Eurostar to take them from Brussels to the Garde de Nord in Paris before finally taking them through the Euro Tunnel. They sat in one of the many station cafes and ate a second breakfast. Liam finished two croissants before bothering to speak. He looked down at Zita's American baseball boots. 'So, you really helped her,' said Liam.

Zita nodded. 'Knowing that bastard, De Groot … I believe I did.'

'And, probably saved her life.'

'Yes, I did.' She sucked at her bottom lip. 'She was badly affected by De Groot, Skipio and the other bastards … but … meeting Jan …' She sighed. 'Yes, I was able to save her life and …' She lowered her voice. 'She saved mine.' She grabbed Liam's arm. 'Come on you're going home.'

They walked along the platform and sat down.

Liam turned to Zita. 'So, how did she *save you?*'

'Who?'

'Who do you think?'

She shook her head and laughed. 'Ah, Palina. She's a lovely girl.' She reflected. 'Yeah, I was in Amsterdam.'

'Why then?'

'It's a long story.'

He looked at the huge clock hanging above the platform and nodded. 'So, we have more than an hour.'

'Um.' She sighed and then took a huge gulp of air before answering him in one breath. 'Before you ask any more questions – interrogate me. I will tell you how it happened. Okay?'

'Yeah. Carry on.'

'Well, I had a mission in Zurich … It was a banker who had cheated our organisation – stolen some of our money.' She closed her eyes. 'I had to assassinate him as a lesson to any other banker that had thoughts of cheating us.' She smiled proudly. 'I got the money back … and he paid me …' She grinned the broadest of grins. 'He paid me a lot of money to release him – to let him go.' She thought hard before she continued. 'But he died.' She sighed heavily. 'He had to.'

Liam shook his head. 'I can't believe you did that–'

'Liam, I know why you say that … but … with that money … I was able to buy Madonna.'

He sat back stunned, dropped his shoulders and breathed shallowly.

Zita laughed excitedly. 'It wasn't called Madonna then.' She pulled a weird face and laughed dryly. 'It was a stupid French name–'

'Yeah?'

'L'oiseau – the bird.'

'Oh.'

'I spoke to the owner and he said that a robin came every morning … so he called it l'oiseau.'

Liam grinned. 'I prefer Madonna.'

'So do I.' She grinned at him. 'Isn't she cool?'

'Yeah.'

Zita continued. 'I left Zurich and I was returning to Schiphol to take a plane …' She whispered. 'Back to Israel. Okay? But when I stepped onto Madonna for the first time – sorry, l'oiseau … I knew I had to buy it. At that moment I decided that I didn't want to do dat anymore–'

'Do what?'

'The killing.' She paused and her demeanour changed. 'I bought the houseboat,' she said proudly. She shivered and shook her head violently. 'Of course, it was a mistake.' She lowered her head. 'I knew then … it was too late.' She sniffed. 'Because *they* found out.' She trembled. 'From then on it was my death sentence. I had written it for myself.'

'Fuck me.'

He looked on expectantly.

'So, I went back to Domburg and stayed with Jan and Palina … in that lovely place … in the annexe.' She tapped his knee several times. 'And do you know they never asked any questions.' She grinned. 'I even helped Jan to make the Gouda.' She looked around. 'And I stayed there until I felt it was safe to go back to Amsterdam – to hide and live on my new home,' she said, fondly.

'Nice. But where did De Groot come in?'

'Ah. I had Matthijs and his guys do the renovation of Madonna.'

He lowered his head, swallowed hard and gently rubbed his throat. 'Matthijs?'

'Yeah.'

Liam coughed and remembered the smoke and deadly fumes as they seared his lungs and throat before he escaped from the fire at the Love Shack. 'He and his wife–'

'Fenna.' She lowered her head in respect and wiped at her eyes. 'Yeah. It was very sad that they both died in the fire.'

He jumped out of his seat and stamped his feet. 'FUCK.'

The passengers nearest to them lowered their newspapers and all turned in their direction.

Zita pulled him back and coaxed him to sit down.

'Fuck, De Groot!'

Zita pulled him into her. 'We did just dat didn't we?' She paused. 'And don't forget the other bastard in Tallinn.'

Liam grinned at her and nodded wildly. 'Toto. Yeah, and how,' he drawled. He sniggered. 'What a silly fucking name that is?' He pushed himself back into his seat and let out a congratulatory gasp. 'Perfect. That was a result. A great team effort.'

Zita coughed to gain Liams's attention and continued. 'You asked how I met him–'

'Met who?'

'De Groot.'

'Yeah. I did.'

'When the renovation of Madonna was finished, I met Matthijs, to pay him, in the Red Cat, and he introduced me to …' She sucked at her top lip. 'Meener De Groot.' She grinned. 'He knew what I was capable of and so I decided to work for him.'

'Why the hell would you want to do that?!'

She grinned. 'It was only on *my* terms.' She smiled. 'And I got to know the real Amsterdam and how to become invisible.' She paused and smiled at him. 'And guess what?'

'Wha …?'

'You arrived some years later.'

'Right.' He took a moment to think. 'So, it was a coincidence?'

'No. Liam, there is no such thing as "coincidence."'

CHAPTER NINE

Travellin' Light

Their train was announced and they waited until they were seated before they continued their conversation. Liam took his time and picked his words carefully. 'You know, that's all the more reason for doing what we did to him – isn't it?'

Their conversation was interrupted by the Border Control Officer. He checked their passports and tickets and smiled at them before moving on down the carriage.

Zita waited until he was in the next carriage before she spoke. She raised her head and couldn't hide her angry eyes. 'Nothing would *ever* be enough for dose vile sadistic bastards.'

Liam shook his head wildly and took a pained breath. 'Yeah. You are so fucking right.' He paused. 'But the bastards are gone now.' He punched the table and immediately grasped at his throbbing throat.

Zita handed him a bottle of water. He took a sip, swallowed two painkillers, sat back and closed his eyes. She was already making plans and appeared to look blindly out of the window at the never-ending semi-darkness of their thirty-five minute journey through the tunnel. As the train raced out into the daylight, she shook her head and smiled at him. 'Better?'

'Yes, thanks.' He tilted his head. 'So, what *is* the plan?'

Zita was holding the tickets and flicked them while she spoke. 'We are going to London.'

'Waterloo?'

'No, Liam.'

'We go to Ashford–'

'Ashford?!' He flung his head back and laughed loudly in her face. 'That's not London.'

She didn't hide her anger and screamed back at him. 'I know dat!' She paused, took a slow deep breath and smiled. 'Liam, sometimes you are so naïve,' she said, shaking her head. 'Do you forget …?' She licked her lips. 'Dat, they wanted to kill *you* … and me.'

He was embarrassed and shrunk back into his seat.

She lowered her voice. 'If they are following us.' She paused. 'Just maybe … we will have some chance to escape dem–'

'Escape!'

'Sorry, that was the wrong word.' She raised her hands, opened them, wiggled her fingers and waved them in his face. 'Don't be so worried.' She grinned. 'I mean … not to escape … but to lose anyone who *may* be following us.'

Liam nodded his hesitance. 'Okay.'

'When we arrive at Ashford … we will buy a motorcycle.'

She saw him physically relax and he grinned at her. '*Now*, I understand.' He nodded knowingly and his grin widened. 'That makes a lot of sense … *Fucking brilliant*.'

Zita opened two maps. The first was a map of the UK. She pointed at Ashford railway station. Liam looked down and followed her finger. 'When we leave the train, we will buy the motorcycle.' She paused and waited.

He didn't react.

'I know what you are thinking.' She paused again and looked up at him.

He shook his head.

'But we only need one. It is enough.'

'Okay.'

She held up an A to Z of London. 'Can you show me where you lived … and where you mother and father are?'

He took his time to check the East End streets and pointed them out.

She looked up at him and grinned. 'They are very close to each other.'

'Yeah. That often happens in England.' He grinned at her. 'We can walk through the gardens to each house.'

They left the train at Ashford and walked to the nearby café, bought two local newspapers and searched the *For-Sale* sections in both of them. They agreed on their choice, called the seller and arranged to meet in the café in Somerset Road.

An hour later a man in his late twenties arrived on a black 1996 Honda CBR900RR. It was immaculate.

Zita checked it and nodded her approval to Liam. 'Give it a run, eh?' She passed the key to Liam who fired it up and raced away. She guided the man into the café, passed him a coffee and sat down with him at the table overlooking the street. 'Why do you sell it?'

The man smiled. 'We're having a baby and we need a car.'

'Congratulations,' she said with a smile.

'Thanks. I've only had it a few years.' His face broke into a huge grin. 'I love it.'

'Sure. It's a really nice machine.' She coughed. 'You're asking a lot of money for it. Is that your bottom figure?'

He coughed. 'Yes. I need that much to buy a decent motor.'

'Motor?'

He coughed. 'Sorry … the car.'

Zita nodded. She saw Liam pull up outside and he gave her the thumbs up.

The man exhaled with relief.

They shook hands and Zita counted the money, out of sight beneath the table, and paid him. He handed her the log book and was about to tear off the bottom slip.

Zita stopped him. 'We will fill in the details.'

He nodded. 'Alright. Suits me.'

Zita pulled her head back and smiled. 'Can we keep the crash helmets?'

He closed his eyes and wriggled his fingers on the table while he thought.

Zita tapped his arm and handed him three fifty-pound notes.

'Yeah. Sure,' he said, with a grin. 'We won't need them in a car.'

Liam and Zita watched as the man left the café whistling and squeezing the roll of notes in his pocket. Liam bought a mug of coffee, a tea and two sandwiches. While they ate them, they relaxed and looked out onto the street at *their* motorbike. They left the café, pulled on their crash helmets and rode to a motor cycle dealership on the nearby trading estate. They took their time to choose and try on black, second-hand one-piece leathers until they were happy, before choosing outer wax jackets, boots and gloves, and much to Liam's disgust paniers for their scant clothes, the presents, and belongings. Zita picked up a roll of black gaffa tape, tore off several strips and covered the easily identifiable logos on each of the black helmets. She took her time to transfer their passports, debit cards and cash into her different pockets and finally, for backup, placed the other forged passports, cash and cards in the inner pockets of her leathers. She carefully folded the backpack and pushed it into the left-hand panier along with the gifts from Palina for Liam's family, and the holdall containing their meagre belongings into the pannier on the right-hand side.

While Liam rode to the garage and filled the tank, Zita sat in the café and spent her time finalising their route and making a phone call.

Ten minutes later Liam pulled up, she gave him directions and they rode towards London.

CHAPTER TEN

Respect

They left Ashford and took the M20, onto the M25 and the exit signposted London Bexleyheath, and then onto the A2. They passed Dartford and took the A102 through Greenwich and onto the A12. The sixty-one mile journey took less than an hour and a half. They pulled up at the twenty-four room Travelodge in Hollybush Hill, Snaresbrook, just five miles along the A12 from Liam's family and his parents' homes. Zita had already booked their room under the names of Mr and Mrs Reilly using his home address in Gore Road. They checked in and the receptionist handed them the key to room 14. They walked along the corridor and fell onto the bed, exhausted.

Zita was the first to speak. 'What's it like being back home, Liam?'

He shrugged. 'I don't know where "home" is any more.'

The next morning Zita pulled on her beloved baseball boots and walked towards the door.

Liam surfaced from beneath the duvet and yawned. 'Do you have to do that *every* day?'

She held onto the partly open door, stretched the open fingers on one hand and dragged them through her short hair and grinned back at him. 'You know I do.' She paused and grinned. 'Why don't you come with me?'

'Fuck that for a game of soldiers,' was the muffled reply, as Liam slid down the bed and pulled the duvet over his head. He continued from beneath the cover. 'I didn't see you do that in Amsterdam.'

'You were never awake early enough to see me leave.'

He grunted at her and fell back to sleep.

While Liam slept, Zita jogged to the charity shops in the High Street and returned overloaded with several bulging bags of clothes: a suit and tie, several shirts and trousers, jeans, tee-shirts and shoes for Liam. She bought herself a selection of dresses, jeans, tee-shirts, shoes and boots.

The taxi pulled up outside Jimmy and Gwen's post war, brick end terraced house in Morepeth Road. Zita paid the driver and they took their time to walk towards the front door. Liam wore the second-hand grey suit, pale blue shirt and tie that Zita had bought for him. She wore a grey check dress and dark brown jacket, all bought from the same charity shop.

Liam walked towards the front door and trembled as he tapped it softly.

Zita moved him aside and knocked hard and stepped back.

While she waited for the door to open, she took in the front garden. It was not much bigger than a postage stamp and covered in thick weeds, bags of smelly rubbish and sodden cardboard boxes. She knelt down and picked up a dead rat and dropped it into the nearest bag and tied it.

The door slowly opened to reveal a jaundiced, unshaven and balding old man, in saggy tracksuit bottoms and dirty grey tee-shirt.

'Hello, Dad,' said Liam, nervously.

The man took a few seconds to recognise him and then pulled back. 'What the fuck …' He held on to the door for support and swayed back and forth. 'What are *you* doing back 'ere?' He looked over Liam's shoulder. 'Who's that?'

They replied simultaneously. 'It's Zita,' blurted out Liam.

'I'm Sigi–'

'What the fuck is it? Can't you even get your name right!' His body stiffened and sighed heavily as he glared at them. 'More lies … deceit. You'll never learn will yer?'

Zita smiled. 'Both … both of the names are correct.' Her smile widened and she reached out her hand. 'Hello, Mr Reilly … call me Zita – Liam does.' As she grabbed his hand she felt his bones through the loose sagging skin and used the few seconds to check out the faded and indistinguishable tattoos that covered his shrunken forearms, upper arms and scrawny neck.

Jimmy opened the door wider. 'I suppose you'd better come in.' He took a step back to let them pass.

They were met with the smell of overcooked cabbage and urine. It was dreadful.

Jimmy stood in the centre of the sitting room and rocked as he looked Liam up and down. 'Why the fuck are you dressed like that.' He scoffed. 'Have they found out? Caught ya?'

Liam was shocked at his father's comments and was stunned into silence.

Zita gently pushed him to one side and answered in a soft caring voice. 'Liam wanted me to meet his family and

'... he made an effort.' She grabbed Liam's hand and squeezed it. 'I like it. He looks smart.' She pushed Liam forward. 'Don't you think?'

Jimmy grunted. 'He's a great actor - fucking ace at hiding it when he's pissed.'

The kitchen door opened and Liam's mother shuffled into the room. She smelt of sodium powder and piss. Her blank eyes couldn't focus and she dribbled uncontrollably. She didn't recognise them and, after looking the strangers up and down, she began to shake and pulled away. She turned to Jimmy and pointed. 'Who ... who ... who are they?'

'Visitors, Gwen,' said Jimmy nervously, taking care not to put any significance to his words.

While she tried to come to terms with the strangers, Liam took in her shrunken eyes and grey complexion as she shuffled across the room. He sighed heavily and shook his head in disbelief before he moved towards her. 'Hello, Mum.'

She studied his face, shot him a vacant look and grunted.

He forced a smile. 'Mum, it's me ... Liam ...'

She pushed her hands into her dressing gown pockets and replied in a weak and tired voice. 'My Liam's at school,' she said, as she muttered to herself. As she pushed past them, they noticed that the back of her dressing gown was soaked with urine and stained with faeces.

As she struggled up the stairs, they heard her mumbling and moaning to herself with every step she took. 'My feet hurt ... Help me ... My feet hurt.'

Jimmy closed the door behind her. 'That's another thing.' He briefly covered his nose, drew his hand down across his mouth and spoke through his open fingers. 'She doesn't know when she needs to go …' He dropped his hand to his chin and squeezed it. 'It's so fucking sad,' he said, as he shook his head and wiped at his tearful eyes.

Liam tried to hide his shock but his father's faltering speech revealed it. 'She didn't know who the hell I was … did she?'

His father shook his head.

Liam nodded. 'How long's she been like this?'

His father shrugged. 'A year, maybe more.' He thought hard. 'A month or two after you left.'

A beat.

Jimmy continued. 'She left the house last week and I found her in the park feeding the ducks.'

Liam smiled with relief. 'That's nice.'

Jimmy shook his head wildly. 'No, it wasn't! She was feeding them with *our* dinner … *Our sandwiches.*' Jimmy gasped. 'She gets worse every day–'

'Wow,' said Liam. He looked towards Zita and back to his father. 'Can they do anything for her?'

Jimmy shook his head. 'She's got dementia and it will only get worse – much worse.' He briefly broke down. 'It's a fucking nightmare.' He sobbed and tried to hide his embarrassment by turning away from them while he continued. 'Why don't you both sit down, you're making the place look untidy.'

Zita didn't understand that expression.

Liam tugged at her arm and pulled her to join him on the stained threadbare settee. She sat down and took her time to look around. Everything was covered in thick dust, empty beer cans overflowed from the dented metal bins and faded newspapers were piled up on the hearth.

Jimmy sat in *his* armchair and fidgeted until he had made himself comfortable in the deep indentations that over the years had moulded around him. He sighed heavily. 'She don't even know it's me, most of the time. We're strangers to each other … in the same house.' He punched at his head. 'Look at that lot.' He pointed at the notes sellotaped to the light switches and on the walls. 'We got 'em everywhere. They don't do much good.' He swallowed hard and sighed again. 'It's a life sentence for the both of us now.' He looked towards the closed door. 'However much longer … that is.'

Liam stood and read some of the notes before turning to face his father. 'It's really that bad … and … and … and there's nothing they can do about it?'

He looked at Zita. 'Is that right?'

She nodded and cleared her throat. 'It is a serious illness, Liam … and … there is *no* cure.' She tried to give them some comfort with a faint smile. 'They will soon be building special dementia villages in Holland.' She paused. 'And maybe they will do the same here in England?'

Jimmy grinned. 'I doubt it, if Blair and his bastard cronies have anything to do with it.' He paused. 'They'd rather send our money abroad than do anything 'ere.'

Liam stomped around the tiny room and fell back onto the settee. 'Fuck … fuck … fuck …'

Jimmy forced a cough. 'So … what the hell are you doing here, son?' He slammed his hands hard on the arms of the chair and glared at him. 'Have you come back to gloat – to see us die?!'

Zita answered for Liam. 'No. Mr Reilly, of course we haven't.' She forced a soft smile. 'It took a lot for Liam to come back.'

'So why did he? He must have been desperate.'

Zita forced a smile and spoke in a subdued voice. 'Have you ever been *desperate* … Mister Reilly?'

He closed his eyes and scoffed. 'Course I 'ave.' He was losing his temper and patience and tried to think of an answer. 'So, I'll ask you again.' he glared at them. 'Both of ya. Why are ya here?'

Zita sucked at her bottom lip. 'I'm sure Liam will tell you when he's ready.'

'Um.'

Gwen called down the stairs and Jimmy stood. 'Go on. Leave us now. Come back another day.' He tried to force a smile. He failed. 'She does have *some* good days,' he said, apologetically. He let out a pathetic mock snigger. 'We both do. If you can call it that.'

Liam nodded. 'Course.' He closed the front door and immediately grabbed Zita's arm. 'Why the fuck did you do that?'

'Wha–?'

'Use Sigi ... your real name?' You made me look like a fool in there–'

'Liam, please remember.' She looked concerned. 'It is not a name I should be using at the moment.' She exhaled loudly. 'They are looking for me.' She paused and gently loosened his grip on her arm. 'And ... I am sorry ... dey are looking for *you* too.'

Liam sighed.

She spoke softly. 'Please let me decide what name I use.'

CHAPTER ELEVEN

The Way We Were

Liam called his father from the Travelodge, apologised and arranged for him and Zita to visit him again.

Liam and his father sat in the front room and fired each other furtive looks while Zita took in the room. The shelves were overloaded with vinyl rock albums, and one wall covered with framed posters of Deep Purple, Jimi Hendrix, Led Zeppelin and Iron Maiden.

She stood up and walked to the frames and looked closely at them. She turned to Jimmy. 'These are all signed – have you met them?'

Jimmy roared with laughter. 'Course I 'ave.'

Liam interrupted. 'Dad was on the door – pubs and clubs. He was a bouncer and he met them all.' He grinned proudly. 'In fact, Adrian Smith, who was in Urchin, lived with the group around the corner, and in nineteen-eighty he joined Maiden.'

Zita was impressed. 'Wow. I didn't know dat–'

'Why would you?' interrupted Jimmy.

Zita hadn't taken any notice of the huge collection of records the first time. She took her time to flick through the albums and pulled one out. As she read the sleeve notes she jigged in silence, and sang along with the songs in her head.

Jimmy turned to Liam. 'She is quite somefing, ain't she?'

'She's a one-off, alright.'

Zita turned to Jimmy. 'My mother loved music.' She giggled. 'And so do I.' She spun the record between her fingers. 'I love vinyl,' She swooned. 'The covers have so much more information than CDs.'

Jimmy ignored her and turned to Liam. 'Did you hear Reggie ... Reggie Kray died a couple of weeks ago?'

'No.'

'Cancer.' He reflected. 'It's getting all of us these days.'

Zita flicked through the records on the second shelf and pulled out a copy of the Pink Floyd album – *The Wall*, and searched the room for something to play it on. In one corner was a music centre covered in thick dust.

Jimmy noticed that Zita was eager to play it. 'Put it on if you want ... but watch the volume ... because I like it loud.'

As Zita lifted the plastic lid of the turntable and was about to take the record from the sleeve, the kitchen door slowly opened.

They all turned towards it.

Gwen leaned on the door frame, tilted her head to one side and her confused face suddenly changed and gave way to the widest beam.

'Liam ... it is you, innit?'

He couldn't hide his shock. 'Yes ... yeah ...' He stuttered, 'Yes, yes, Mum it's me alright.'

She turned to Jimmy and pointed at him vindictively. 'I told you.' She shook her head wildly. 'I told you he would come and see me.' She grinned mindlessly. 'Didn't I?'

Jimmy nodded. 'Yeah, you did, luv.'

Liam walked towards his mother, took her arm and guided her into the kitchen. 'Come on Mum, let's make a nice cup of tea.'

She grinned. 'Yeah, a nice cup of tea … that will be lovely.' As she turned away, she repeated Liam's name over and over.

Zita and his father watched Liam as he closed the kitchen door slowly behind them.

Zita, still holding the Pink Floyd album, turned to Jimmy and coughed nervously. 'That's nice for her to recognise Liam.'

'It won't last–'

'What?'

He coughed. 'She comes back for a few minutes. Sometimes longer.' He sighed. 'But then …'

She shot him a questioning look.

He sniffed hard and shook his head. 'Then … all hell breaks loose.' He paused. 'Give it time,' he said, slowly shaking his head as he looked towards the closed door.

'Can't they do anything to help?'

He sniggered. 'What do you think? Have you ever seen what dementia does to someone?'

She shook her head. 'No … I'm afraid I haven't.' She sucked her bottom lip. 'So, she has to suffer like that?'

He scoffed. 'She doesn't suffer … it's me … just me and whoever bothers to visit us.' He swallowed hard. 'And that's a rare event now. No one knows how to deal with her moods … her anger … vi …' His voice faded as he slouched in his chair.

Zita slid the record out of the sleeve, read the label and flicked it over to read the other side. She decided not to play it and took her time to slide it back onto the shelf in alphabetical order. She sat down and gazed at the photo on the sideboard of three children: Liam, Tommy and an older girl. 'Mister Reilly, who is that with Liam and Tommy?'

Jimmy pointed at the girl. 'That's Bernadette, their elder sister.'

'Oh. Liam has never mentioned her–'

'Probably because she's a waste of space. She's in Australia.' He shrugged and mumbled under his breath. 'We get a Christmas card some years and that's about it.'

'Ah.' Zita picked up a framed photograph of Liam with his wife, three young children and Jimmy and Gwen. 'Looks like a happy family …'

Jimmy grunted his answer.

She brushed off the dust as she put it back on the sideboard and then picked up a photograph of Liam and Kathleen's wedding. She smiled to herself as she rubbed her finger over his face. 'Very nice,' she said.'

Jimmy reached up and tapped the glass. 'They should never have got married!'

Zita looked at him and tilted her head to one side. 'But … if they didn't get married … you *wouldn't* have your grandchildren.'

He nodded in agreement and struggled to clear his throat. 'Um …' He smiled. 'Suppose you're right. At least *three* good things came out of that mess.'

Jimmy gazed at the wedding photo. 'Kathleen's a good girl. A diamond … and she's got a new guy now.' He reflected. 'Felix.'

'Felix?'

He lowered his head. 'He's French … French Algerian.' He continued speaking quickly. 'He's nice and … he's got a proper job. He's a decent man, not like our Liam … not thievin' to live …'

Zita looked at him.

'Um.' He scowled at her. 'I know what you're finking.'

She forced a smile. 'Do you?'

Jimmy continued with a wild nod. 'I know I lived that way too … and I can tell ya … I'm not proud of it …' He looked around and sniffed. 'I mean what 'ave we got to show for all them years inside?'

He could see she didn't understand.

'Behind bars … in prison.'

She nodded. 'I see.'

They heard the panicked screams coming from the kitchen and both turned towards the closed door. It flew open and a shaken Liam bent his head, and attempted to cover it, as his mother lashed out with her fists and screamed obscenities at him. 'He tried to rape me! The filthy bastard!'

Liam was unable to deal with her sudden change and outburst. He looked at his father confused and disgusted and shook his head in disbelief. 'Fuck … Fuck … Fuck.'

Jimmy sighed heavily. 'You cursed this family, boy!'

Liam sneered back at him. 'Maybe it was already cursed before I was *even* born.'

His father ignored what he'd said. He jumped out of his chair and turned to Zita. 'I'm sorry you had to see that.' He reached out to a stunned Liam. 'Can you go … now?!'

A beat.

'Please … JUST GO!'

Gwen's pained cries continued until they reached fever pitch. While Jimmy tried to calm her down, she continued to scream and hit out at him with her flaying hands.

Liam and Zita left without looking back.

Liam stood, upset and confused, on the pavement outside the house. He took a step back and looked up at what was once his childhood home. 'Can you believe what just happened?' He shook his head. 'How she changed …' He sighed. 'In a split-second.'

'Oh yeah.' Zita shook her head as she continued. 'And, I feel so sorry for your mother.'

'My father's not well either. He's got fucking cancer–'

'Cancer?'

'Yeah, I told you ages ago … on the ship. He's got prostate and pancreatic cancer.' He shook his head. 'We're jinxed … the whole fucking family's jinxed.'

They walked along the road in silence. Zita guided Liam to the nearest bus stop. Liam climbed the stairs in a state of blind shock and sat half way down the empty bus. Zita handed the conductor a five-pound note. She had no idea where they were going and blurted out the first place that came to mind. 'Two to *Piccadilly Circus,* please.'

The conductor looked at her. 'We're not going there but we do stop at the top of Regent Street.'

She smiled at him. 'That will be fine.'

He looked at her. 'Five pounds fifty …'

She reached blindly into her pocket and passed him a handful of change.

'I need another one fifty,' said the conductor impatiently.

She reached into her jacket pocket and took out a ten-pound note and handed it to him. He cursed as he picked his way through his change before he handed her their tickets.

She joined Liam upstairs and they sat in silence as they looked out onto the streets below.

Liam finally spoke. 'This place is a shithole. I can't believe how much it's changed in a couple of years.'

'Nothing stays the same, Liam.' She paused. 'Look at you.' She paused to give him time to think. 'You know you have changed so much since I first saw you at the Love Shack.'

He grinned. 'Yeah. I'll never forget that afternoon. 'How you sorted out the Albanians.' He turned to her and forced a smile. 'Fuck, that was some seeing-to you gave them.'

She pulled a mischievous face. 'It was my job.'

'I know it was.' He shook his head. 'And what a fucking job too … working for that bastard …'

'He's gone. He's history now.'

'Yeah … thank God.'

CHAPTER TWELVE

Streets Of London

Zita sat in the window of the Crusty Cob Café in Lauriston Road and watched Liam swagger up to the counter. He had reverted back to what she imagined he used to be, self-assured, cheeky, loud and brash. It was a bittersweet moment. On one hand, she liked it but she could also see it would not take long for him to revert to his days of robbery, drugs, violence and alcohol, if he stayed too long.

'Hello, George how are ya?' He snorted loudly and looked across at George's wife. 'Hi, Ethel, it's been a while.'

'Bloody hell … Liam Reilly,' said George, with an excited chuckle. He looked across at Zita, nodded and returned to Liam. 'How are ya? Doing alright?' He looked him up and down. 'You've changed.'

Liam blushed. 'Maybe I 'ave, George.' He sniffed and looked across at Zita. 'Maybe I 'ave.'

'So are ya doin', okay?'

'Yeah. I'm existing, George.' He needed to stop the innocent interrogation so he changed tact. 'Listen, can I get two rounds of toast, marmalade and two mugs of tea.'

George handed him a tray, slipped two plates onto it, added the toast, poured the tea from a huge metal pot and handed him a tiny jar of marmalade and butter. 'Enjoy. Good to see ya again.'

'Yeah,' replied Liam, half-heartedly.

While Liam was at the counter Zita noticed the two men that had followed them in. The taller man, in an expensive dark blue suit, white shirt and tie, sat at the far end of the café. As Liam walked towards her, the other man, dressed in dirty jeans and dark blue polo shirt, covered in paint splashes, and sealant which made the white motif on the front illegible, ordered two mugs of tea and spoke quietly to George.

George couldn't keep his voice down. 'Yeah, good old Liam's back.' He chuckled to himself. 'Quite a shock to see 'im in 'ere again.'

The man sat down and slid one mug across the table to the well-dressed man, who loosened his tie and continually stirred his tea while he eyed-up the back of Liam's head.

While Zita buttered the toast, Liam looked out onto the grey street and dreamt that he was back in Amsterdam.

Zita felt nervous. She knew something was not right and she was not in control. 'Come on Liam. We need to go.'

'But I haven't finished me tea.' He looked down at the toast. 'Or the …'

She lowered her voice. 'Liam, we need to go. Now.' She kicked him under the table. '*Come on.*'

Liam was clearly confused but after taking another slug of his tea, he slammed his mug on the table, grabbed a piece of toast. and followed her outside. 'What the hell was that all about?'

'Did you see the two men who came in behind us?'

'Two men?' he said, shaking his head. 'Two men? What? No … I didn't.'

She spoke as they walked. 'They followed us in and were watching you the whole time.'

'You're mad … Fucking paranoid!'

'I heard one of them ask George if you were Liam Reilly.'

He sniggered proudly. 'What you need to remember is that the *Reilly's* are famous 'round 'ere.' He laughed loudly. 'Have been for years.' He grinned at her. 'Don't worry. It's fine.' He huffed. 'I know this place. This is …' He stopped himself and covered his mouth. '*Was* my home. I was born 'ere.' He looked across the street and forced a wide grin. 'This is the *Reilly manor.*'

CHAPTER THIRTEEN

Home

The next morning Liam took a shower and, after breakfast, put on his suit, shirt and tie. 'I'm going to see Kathleen.'

Zita smiled at him. That is a very good idea. And I will do some sightseeing.'

'That's great, I'll see you back her later.'

Liam took the bike and rode to Gore Road and pulled up across the road from what had been his family home. He took a few minutes to sit and look at the house. Although the windows and part of the roof had been replaced, many of the bricks were still blackened from the smoke. He shook his head at what he had done and how he had nearly killed his whole family. He took a huge breath, crossed the road and knocked on the door.

Kathleen partially opened the door and held it with one hand. 'I heard you were back.' She took her hand from the door but kept her foot firmly against it. She crossed her arms and fired him an unyielding look. 'And … wondered when you would spare the time to come and see *us*,' she said, not hiding her resentment.

Liam blushed. 'Sorry, but I needed to be sure before I came' He took a breath. 'It isn't easy.'

'I can understand that, Liam.' She opened the door and ushered him through the sitting room and into the kitchen.

Both rooms had changed beyond recognition, having been replastered, redecorated and refurnished after the fire had destroyed much of the house, all of their belongings and furniture.

Liam ducked to avoid the men's shirts that hung on the door architrave and looked her up and down. 'You look good...' He grinned. 'Very good.'

She stood behind the ironing board, but before either of them could speak, Harry, their teenage son, rushed in and stood at the door. He clenched his fists and his whole body stiffened with anger. 'You! Why did you bother to come back? Why don't you fuck off!' He took a deep breath and continued to vent his anger. 'We're happy now... at fucking last ... and ... And, no thanks to you.'

Kathleen rested the iron on the board with a thump. 'Harry, don't talk like that. He is *your father*.'

'Father?! We hardly saw 'im ... and when we did, he was always pissed!' He took a breath and launched a wry smile. 'Or in prison. How can you call *him* ... *my* father? You know fuck all about me ...' He stuttered and raised one of his fists. 'Any of us.'

Liam looked him up and down. Harry was almost as tall as him and had filled out since he'd left. 'You've grown, son–'

'How would you know?' spurted Harry.

The front door opened and closed and they all turned.

Felix walked in carrying two bags of shopping and a bottle of red wine under his arm. Harry stormed past him and out of the house slamming the front door behind him.

Liam felt jealous as he stared at Kathleen's new partner – his replacement. Felix was tall and slim with Mediterranean good looks; olive skin and dark swept back hair. He was surprised to see Liam but was unphased at finally meeting him. 'Oh. Hello,' he said, in perfect English, with a smooth French accent. He reached out his hand. 'You must be …' He paused. 'Liam … I've heard much about you–'

'I bet you 'ave?' said Liam. He grinned. 'Um.' He nodded and reluctantly reached out and they briefly shook hands.

Felix reached across the ironing board and kissed Kathleen. 'Ca va, mon amour.'

'I'm fine … thanks, Felix,' she said, affectionately.

Liam sniggered.

Kathleen fired him an angry look.

Liam watched as Felix placed the wine on the worktop and took his time to empty the bags and place the contents into the relevant cupboards. He pushed the bags into an even bigger bag and rubbed his hands together. 'Bon,' he said, with a self-congratulatory smile. 'I expect you have much to talk about so I will go and take a shower.' He turned. 'Nice to meet you … Liam.'

Liam was strangely jealous and mumbled his reply.

They waited until they could hear Felix reach the landing.

'I'm impressed,' kidded Liam. 'You've got him well-trained.'

Kathleen picked up the iron and spoke while she pressed yet another shirt. 'He's nice … and steady.' She placed the iron on the board and glared at Liam. 'And … I didn't have to *train* him.' She raised her voice. 'I know you may find it hard to believe but … he *came* like that.'

Liam sniggered. 'Yeah, I suppose so … if you like that sort of thing.'

She suddenly appeared proud and glared at Liam. 'As a matter of fact … I do. He's got a great job … at Harrods.' She paused and then scowled at him. 'A real job. And he hopes to get promoted soon.'

Liam shuffled on the spot. 'It didn't take you long to fuck 'im …' He stuttered. 'Someone else … did it?'

She shook her head and bashed the iron on the board. 'FUCK YOU, Liam.'

He mimicked her.

She moved across to the window and feigned interest in the birds fighting for the seed on the feeder in the garden. She suddenly exhaled her anger and turned and glared at him. 'So *why are* you here?'

Liam sucked in air. 'My bar was burned down on New Year's Eve …'

She forced a grin. 'Maybe the music was too loud–'

'A fucking piano?!'

Kathleen slammed her hand on the draining board. 'Sod you, Liam. Have you forgot how you left us? No contact for months. And … and … and then you expect money to … make that alright?'

He was genuinely shocked at her anger and hurtful words. 'I did what I could,' he said, softly.

'"Did what you could." She glared back at him. 'So, tell me … *what are you* doing back here?'

Before he could answer her, she continued. 'Things will never be the same. I've moved on.' She pulled away. 'I'm happy – *we're* happy … All of us.'

'I know.' He took time to reflect. 'I suppose in a way … I've moved on too.'

'You haven't answered me. Why are *you back*?'

'It's a long story and I doubt if you would want to hear it anyway.'

She sighed heavily. 'No, I don't.' She shook her head. 'So, what now?'

'We won't be here for long–'

'We?'

'Yeah. I have someone.' Liam blushed. 'She's nice too … and …' He paused. 'I believe she likes me …'

Kathleen sniggered. 'Don't *you* know the answer to that?'

He forced a laugh. 'Yeah. Of course, I do … and … yeah.' He paused and nodded slowly. 'She does.' He heard the treads creak as Felix came down the stairs. He grinned to himself. *So, he hasn't fixed that yet.*

The door opened and Felix stood and rubbed his wet hair with a towel.

Liam thought hard for an excuse. 'Listen, I have to go now but I'll pop back and see Sally and Michelle.'

'Okay. We'll see you then,' said Kathleen, half-heartedly.

He turned. 'Maybe I can take them for a pizza?' He thought. 'And, Harry.'

She crossed her arms and laughed. 'Good luck with that, Liam.'

He grunted at her.

'Whatever you want to do. But if you promise them something.' She nodded forcefully and jabbed her finger in his chest. 'Just make sure that you do it!'

He grunted his reply.

As he reached the front door Felix called out. 'Good to meet you, Liam.'

Liam didn't reply. He slammed the door behind him.

CHAPTER FOURTEEN

All By Myself

Gwen had already been taken to the care home in Stepney for her day of respite so Jimmy had a few hours on his own.

Liam knocked on the unlocked front door and let himself in. While Jimmy made a pot of tea in the kitchen, Liam sorted through the pile of old newspapers and post. He opened one envelope and took out the card. Still holding it, he walked into the kitchen. 'Did you know about this?'

'Know about what?'

'There's a session at the community centre explaining about dementia. It says they called you …' He checked the date. 'Weeks ago.' He continued to read. 'Dad, this is today. Are you going?'

'Nah.'

'Come on. It'll take our minds off it all.'

'Fuck, *Liam*. Did you really say that?' He scoffed. 'How can that work?'

Liam nodded. 'Yes, I bloody did.' He paused. 'I'll go with you. Maybe we'll get to see and know more about what's happening to Mum.' He handed the card to his father. While he waited for him to read it, he continued. 'Anyway, it might help – at least I need to take my mind off the shit that's happening to us.' He reached out and tapped his father on the shoulder. 'Come on. Let's go.'

'Yeah,' said Jimmy. He nodded and sucked at his teeth. 'Yeah ... I need that too.'

Liam paused outside the community centre and turned to his father. 'This place brings back some real bad fucking memories, Dad.'

'I can understand that, son ... but ...' He paused and silently questioned Liam before he continued. 'But ... Zita told me you haven't had a drink for a while now.' He forced a smile and tapped Liam on the shoulder. 'It must 'ave done some good, son.'

Liam grunted.

Jimmy grabbed his arm and walked him up the steps and through what were once imposing hardwood doors, now stripped of the varnish by years of neglect, been left to fade peel and eventually rot. He opened the door and pushed Liam inside. 'Come on ... you can do it.'

A young woman walked through reception and recognised Liam from the AA meetings. 'Hello, Liam ... Haven't seen you for a while.' She looked him up and down. 'You look well.' She smiled sympathetically and glanced at Jimmy before she continued. 'How's it going?'

Liam beamed back at her. 'Great ...' He leaned forward and whispered to her. 'Five hundred and seventy-five days now.' He pulled away from her and mouthed the number of days as he counted. 'No. It's seventy six.'

She smiled and nodded.

Liam continued with a brazen grin. '*And* ... I was running a bar in Amsterdam.'

She looked down her nose with a combination of disgust and shock.

He laughed loudly. 'That's right ... in the naughty part of the city. The red light district.'

She was stunned into silence.

His grin grew even wider. 'Didn't touch a drop,' he said proudly.

She patted him on the shoulder. 'Well done, Liam.' She turned to walk away but reconsidered. She edged closer to him and lowered her voice before speaking. 'Liam, remember ... we're always here.' She continued in almost a whisper. 'If you ever *do* need us ... again.'

'Thanks.'

The receptionist, behind a thick Georgian wired glass screen, smiled at them, bent her head and spoke through the narrow gap in front of her. 'Can I help you?'

'We're here for the talk ... Dementia?'

'Ah yes, Room 106, on the first floor - halfway down the corridor. You can't miss it.'

CHAPTER FIFTEEN

As Time Goes By

Imagine a world where your loved ones have no real idea of what's going on around them and how painful that may be. For a brief period, that's exactly what Liam and Jimmy were about to experience. Their journey into another world – the world of someone living with dementia.

They joined eight other people at the large table and eyed each other nervously while they waited.

A middle-aged woman carrying a large cardboard box walked out of a side room and closed the door behind her. She opened a notebook, drew the outline of the table and eight boxes She asked them their christian names, and wrote their names in the spaces. She spoke, without smiling, in a firm monotone voice. 'Good morning.' I will be splitting you up into pairs.' She counted the number around the table and pointed at Liam and Jimmy. 'If you could join me, we can get you ready.' She pushed her chair back, picked up the box and guided them into a small side office. She reached into the box and took out four clear plastic insoles with a raised profile of spikes. 'Could you remove your shoes please and put these inside them.'

They both pulled back.

'Please.'

They sat down and removed their shoes and pushed the plastic insoles inside and put their shoes back on. They both winced in pain but before they could speak, she continued.

'Are you left or right-handed?'

They both replied in unison. 'Right.'

She flicked through the box and passed each of them a thick padded right-hand glove and a much thinner left-hand glove. 'Can you put them on.'

They did as they were told.

She reached inside the box and took out two pairs of headphones and handed one to each of them. 'Put these on too,' she said.

Again, they obliged.

Lastly, she took out two pairs of glasses with lenses that were a combination of tiny pieces of different thicknesses and shapes of glass. She nodded and they slipped them on. They were totally disorientated and found it impossible to focus or see anything clearly. She passed them each a pair of headphones. They pushed them on their heads and she adjusted the glasses. 'If you will follow me, I will explain what we do next.'

They walked into the darkened room, illuminated with a dull light from the black curtained window. She guided Jimmy to a bed and handed him a box of odd socks. 'Can you match these for me please.' She guided Liam to a small table with a tea pot, kettle, tea bags, empty milk jug and two mugs. 'Can you make a cup of tea?' She grabbed his arm. 'Don't worry, the water is cold ... so you won't burn yourself.'

Despite their pitiful efforts They both failed in their simple tasks.

Jimmy was unable to establish any of the colours of the socks through the glasses and Liam fumbled to grip anything through the thick gloves. The pain in their feet shot up into their legs. All the while the cacophony of mixed stereo sounds of sirens, speeding car, fireworks, kids crying and screaming, cars crashing into each other, falling buildings, doors slamming, crowds shouting, barking dogs, screeching tyres, gunfire, car horns and screams of aggression, blasted into their ears, and caused them to rock wildly.

Five minutes later, the woman tapped each of them on the shoulder and sat them down on one side of the room and removed their glasses, headphones and gloves. 'Can you take off your shoes please and let me have the insoles.'

They removed their shoes and Liam handed his to her.

Jimmy handed her one and held the other in his hand and ran his open palm over the sharp spikes and flinched. 'Is it really that bad?'

She took it from him. 'Yes …' Her speech faltered. 'And often much, much worse.'

They both exhaled loudly and tried to stand.

'Can you stay where you are?'

They looked at each other and nodded.

The door opened and they watched the woman guide the next pair in. The tall smartly dressed woman and smaller man in a shirt and tie, who had sat together at the end of the table, and were clearly care home managers, shuffled in.

They were asked to carry out the same tasks given to Jimmy and Liam but were totally unaware of other people in the room. The woman froze and stood in the centre of the small room, and unable to move, shook violently on the spot as the cacophony of sounds blasted into her ears from the headphones and the pain shot through her feet and legs. The man fared much better and was able to sort out one pair of socks but again he constantly struggled to feel his fingers and fight the pain in his feet and rocked erratically as the different sounds pierced his eardrums and caused sheer confusion. What seemed on their own harmless enough, collectively they created a terrifying environment. They were really scared and, needless to say, they failed miserably in achieving little or nothing of what they were asked to do. The obvious sense of relief when they were able to take off the equipment was profound.

They made their way into the small office and handed everything to the trainer who dropped it back into the box. For the first time she spoke with a smile. 'Thank you for doing that.'

They all sighed.

'I appreciate it wasn't easy and I apologise for my tone earlier but that is what people living with dementia are faced with *every day*.' She smiled again. 'Could you please re-join the rest of the group but do not tell them anything … nothing at all about what you experienced.' She paused. 'Okay?'

They nodded.

'Please sit down.'

They dropped into their seats and tried to make sense of what had happened to them.

The last pair followed the same routine and finally joined the others at the table. The trainer served tea, coffee and biscuits and allowed them time to talk to each other. The trainer cleared the table and spoke, 'So how did it feel?'

The female care home manager was the first to speak. 'I was terrified.'

The trainer smiled and nodded slowly. 'That is very common so please don't feel embarrassed. Yes, you did freeze in the room and I wanted to hug you.'

The man spoke. 'We both so wanted *that hug.*'

'That is also very common,' said the trainer. She picked up a pair of the glasses. 'These have been designed to simulate macular degeneration, glaucoma and cataracts. The gloves were made to make you all feel incredibly clumsy and hard for you to move your fingers.'

They all nodded with relief.

She continued. 'And the spiky insoles for your shoes – made it very uncomfortable to walk.' They all looked around at each other and nodded again.

The Care Home Manager spoke. 'Is that why some of our residents don't want to get out of their armchairs?'

'Yes, it is,' said the trainer. 'You felt the pain. Imagine permanently having to suffer like that every time you wanted, or were expected to walk?'

Everyone gasped

The trainer picked up the headphones. 'The most daunting for anyone with dementia is the incessant stream of noise – voices, sirens, traffic, car horns, music, slamming doors, screams and cars braking hard, dogs barking and motorbikes revving past.'

They nodded their agreement.

'You must now appreciate that many living with dementia are unable to stop it or get away from it.'

Stunned silence.

She continued. 'You were able to take them off and shut out the sounds. They can't. And it *never* goes away.'

She turned to Jimmy, checked the names on her table layout and smiled. 'Jimmy, I hope you don't mind me asking … but what colour is the bathroom suite in your house?'

'White,' replied, Jimmy looking confused.

She continued. 'What about the toilet seat?'

Liam answered for him. 'It's white.'

Once more she checked the names on her sheet and looked up. 'Thank you, Liam.' She continued. 'One of the challenges that someone with dementia frequently encounters is trying to make out light colours against backgrounds of the same colour.' She looked at Liam and then Jimmy. 'Black or white … is one of those and they are often not able to see where the seat is.' She forced a caring smile. 'And that's how and when those accidents happen.'

Jimmy blushed.

'Don't worry, Jimmy it is very common.' She tilted her head towards Liam. 'Maybe a red seat would help?' She paused briefly and continued. 'Is it possible for you to do that?'

Jimmy looked confused.

She continued. 'Is that something you could arrange?'

Liam nodded. 'Um. Course it is.'

She coughed and turned her attention to the two care workers. 'Do you find that if the person with dementia hasn't seen someone in their family for a long time, then they weren't sure who they were?'

They all nodded.

She smiled at them with what seemed to be one of her common and well- rehearsed reactions. 'The mood of a person with dementia can often be read from their facial expressions and gestures which can give you a clue and a warning, of not knowing who you are and feeling threatened - fear or anger and very importantly, uncertainty.

Jimmy and Liam immediately recognised those signs.

'What can help is for family members to introduce themselves to that person, and ensuring that they smile. Ask them to bring photographs with them and show them when they arrive. This can often help to stimulate their memory and make them feel more comfortable.' She paused and turned her full attention to the care home managers. 'It may also be worth speaking to the person about their family and who is coming to visit them. It's always a good idea to have family photographs in their room.' Her demeanour changed. 'You will know that a person with dementia may be stuck in a period many years earlier so if they don't recognise you, it is a good idea to talk to them about yourself in the third person.'

Jimmy appeared confused.

She turned to him. 'Jimmy, if it was your wife, you would say, "Jimmy is at work ... but he'll be back later" and show her early photographs of the two of you or ... of you both ... with your family.'

Jimmy pulled a strange face that eventually confirmed he understood.

She now turned her attention back to the care workers. 'Do you use room numbers or the names of your residents on the doors of their rooms?' She paused 'Or their photograph?'

They shook their heads.

'Okay. Here is an idea that works.' She pulled out a handful of photographs and slid them across the table. 'Someone with dementia is often confused by numbers and signage and don't know what they are. Remember some of them may have short term memory loss, so for much of the time they can't remember anything.' She tapped at one of the photographs. 'The best way to use pictures of a resident.' She paused. 'Is to have an image of them now and an image of them when they were younger. If their short-term memory has reduced and long term is good then this will be of great help.'

The care workers understood but were obviously concerned.

The trainer continued with another of her rehearsed smiles. 'Okay. Why not put the room number and resident's name on a small board beside the door frame so their families and visitors, nurses, doctors or new members of staff know who it is?' The trainer realised that everyone was tired. 'Shall we have a fifteen-minute break for a cup of tea or coffee and we'll resume.' She looked up at the large wall clock above the door. 'Three-fifteen?'

They all stood, made their way to the table and poured their drinks.

Jimmy pulled Liam to one side. 'Bloody hell, Liam. This is so fucking bad. Did you realise that this would be coming down the line?'

Liam shook his head and sipped at his tea. 'No. I had no idea. This is an eye-opener but in a bad way. That's for sure.' He paused. 'But it's happening already. It's happening *now*.'

The care workers were as shocked as Liam and Jimmy. One of them left the room and called their director, and told her what they had learned.

Everyone returned to the table and waited in silence to hear what was inevitable.

The trainer stood up and placed a large plastic box on the table. 'You need to be prepared because there will come a time, in *everyone's* dementia journey, that the need to move to adapted equipment will become a *necessity*. This could be plates, cups or even hoists and adaption to their beds. Normally one of the first things that needs to be adapted is a plate or a cup but for people who have never used those products before, they may feel disempowered and maybe embarrassed. It is so important that we approach this carefully and with dignity and respect. You may know or have been advised that at some point anyone with dementia will need adaptations to everything associated with their daily lives. But the person may not understand and probably will not want to do it.' She looked at everyone in turn, took a breath and continued. 'People with dementia can react very negatively to someone giving them adapted equipment and often refusing it or becoming aggressive. Introducing those products and items can be one of the hardest parts of care and they will be sure to tell you in one way or another that they do not want to change.' She took out an adapted cup, similar to that used for young children to stop them spilling their drink. 'If you want them to use this, which they will need to do, then you should drink out of exactly the same cup when you visit them.'

They all gasped.

'I understand your concern but there is a way to help.' She took a second mug from the box. 'When you know they need to use one of these, take two with you but wrap them both up.' She smiled. 'And they will see it as normal and it will preserve their dignity.'

As they left out of the room and walked down the corridor Jimmy was in tears. 'How the fuck can Gwen cope with that shit – live like that?' He closed his eyes and his whole body rocked. 'Nothing but a slow torture!' His head shook uncontrollably 'I can't let her … I just can't.'

Liam shared the same thoughts but held them back. He put his arms around his father and pulled him into him.

'Come on, Dad,' he said, as his lips quivered and his voice faltered with every word. 'Let's go and get something to eat.'

They crossed the road and sat opposite each other in the café. While Jimmy stared into his mug, Liam had half an eye on those who entered and left the community centre and tried to recognise any of his AA group. He finally turned back, sighed heavily and spoke. 'Do you know, Dad. I feel fucking sick after all that in there.'

Jimmy nodded and sighed heavily. 'I know what you mean, son.'

Liam continued. 'The truth is …' He paused and swallowed hard. 'I actually wanted to cry as I walked out of that place.' He paused. 'But do you know what … it wasn't for the fucking drink … but … for what mum and the other poor bastards have to go through … every fucking hour of the day.'

Jimmy nodded his agreement. 'Yeah. You ain't wrong, son. You know I feel wrung out.' He sniffed. 'Fucking numb.'

Liam nodded. 'Yeah. That whole experience had been so sodding bewildering.' He shook his head. 'Think of them and their partners and the pain of being separated.' He swallowed. 'What happened in there, will stay with me for a very … very long time.'

'Liam.' Jimmy's whole body quivered wildly 'You will never forget it. Neither of us will *ever forget* what 'appened today?'

Liam attempted to drink his tea but slammed the mug back onto the table in anger.

Jimmy wiped the tears from his eyes. 'You know … your mother's been gone a long time.' He sighed. 'A very long time.'

'Fuck.' Liam pushed himself away from the table and grabbed at his painful throat.

Jimmy noticed Liam's rasping voice for the first time. He tilted his head and silently questioned what could have happened.

Liam continued. 'Come on, Dad. Let's get out of 'ere.'

They walked in silence, not daring to look back.

CHAPTER SIXTEEN

Hazard

Zita sat at the table nearest the window in the Crusty Cob and blindly pushed her empty mug around the table while she concentrated on watching the busy street. She noticed a teenaged boy riding a bicycle, pull up and stop in an empty shop doorway. He checked his watch, looked furtively around and within seconds he was surrounded by adults and kids of all ages.

A few minutes later they rushed off and he rode away.

Jimmy walked in, bought a mug of tea and joined her. He took his time and sipped at his tea several times before he placed the mug on the table. He wanted to speak and after a huge sigh and still holding the mug he said. 'Can you tell me what the hell happened to Liam's voice?'

Unusually, Zita snarled. 'A nasty bastard had him taught a lesson for getting too friendly with me–'

'Fuck.'

'He was my boss, Meener De Groot?'

Jimmy scratched his chin. 'De Groot, yeah. I remember Freddie mentioning him when poor Laurie died in Spain.'

Zita was intrigued. 'Really?'

'Yeah. Our Liam went over to sort it out. It was his first time on a plane.' He laughed. 'His first time anywhere out of 'ere, 'cept Southend.'

'So ... *he did know* Liam, after all,' said Zita.

'Of course, he did.' He paused and screwed up his face. 'That bastard knew all of us.'

The music stopped and a news flash came on the radio. *"Reports are coming in of an acid attack on a 33-year-old man at Gore Road."*

Jimmy and Zita looked at each other horrified and simultaneously mouthed Liam's name.

Jimmy grabbed the payphone and called home.

Martha, Gwen's carer answered. 'There are police everywhere,' she screamed. 'And a helicopter. It's bedlam, Mister Jimmy.'

'Do you know what happened?'

'Only what I heard on the radio and what's happening now–'

'What happened?'

'Liam was there with Kathleen ... and now .... he's been attacked with acid–'

'Fuck–'

'He's been taken to Mile End Hospital–'

'Fuck–'

'They say he's in a bad way, Mister Jimmy.'

CHAPTER SEVENTEEN

Just One Look

Jimmy and Zita raced to the hospital and stood impatiently tapping on the desk while the receptionist ignored them and continued to talk on the telephone.

As soon as she replaced the receiver, Zita spoke. 'Can you tell us how Liam Reilly is?'

'Are you family?'

'I'm his girlfriend.'

'Ah. I'm sorry I can't divulge that to you.'

Jimmy moved Zita to one side. 'I'm 'is Dad … Jimmy Reilly. So you can tell me how he is?'

She grinned at Zita. 'Certainly, Mr Reilly.' She looked towards the wall and checked the names on the nobo board. 'He is in surgery at the moment. If you can both take a seat, I'll see what I can do.'

They waited for several hours until they saw a bed being wheeled into the ICU ward. They both stood at the door but the nurse held Zita back and nodded at Jimmy. 'You can go in now, sir … but I must warn you that he is heavily sedated and won't be able to speak.' She paused. 'You can stay … but only a couple of minutes.'

Jimmy nodded and walked towards the bed. He looked down at the heavily bandaged Liam, then the wall of machines that flashed and the tubes linked up to his body. He held his breath before quivering and breaking down. 'What the hell have you done this time, Liam? You won't leave it alone will yer?' He looked around the room and then to Zita who remained at the door. His tearful eyes picked out the small area of unbandaged arm and a tousle of dark hair that poked through the bandages. He screamed out and the nurse raced back in.

'I told you, didn't I?' said the nurse, as she took Jimmy's arm.

Jimmy screamed out and wiped at his eyes. 'It's not Liam!'

Zita rushed in and checked the patient's patch of bare skin and tousle of hair. She looked at Jimmy and let out a huge sigh of relief.

The nurse pulled her away and led both of them out into the corridor. 'Mister Reilly, are you sure it's not *your* son?'

Jimmy nodded. 'I'm sorry ... but ...' He paused and exhaled his mixed feelings. '*Yes*, I am.' He coughed hard before he continued and pointed towards the closed door of the ICU ward. 'That is *not* my Liam.'

Zita grabbed at Jimmy's arms and turned to the nurse. 'He's right. It's not Liam.' She closed her eyes and when she opened them, her mood had changed. 'So, who is it?'

Jimmy took a huge breath. 'I'm not sure.' He exhaled with mixed relief. 'But it looks like ...' He trembled. 'Felix.'

The nurse fired him an anxious look. 'You *know* who it is?'

Jimmy nodded.

'Is there someone we can contact?'

'Yeah. There is.' He took her pen and board from her and wrote down Kathleen's telephone number. 'When you call her, take it easy … This will come as a massive shock.'

'Of course, we will.' She took the board and pen from him. 'Thank you very much, Mister Reilly.'

CHAPTER EIGHTEEN

Light Of Hope

Zita took Jimmy home and sat him in his armchair. She poured him a glass of whiskey and a glass of water for herself. *She hated his coffee and tea.*

The phone rang and Jimmy picked it up. 'Hello, Dad. Is Zita with you?'

'Yes, she is.' He looked at the phone. '*Liam* where the hell are yer?!'

Liam grinned into the receiver. 'Visiting some old haunts.' He could hear that his father was upset. 'Just visiting … nothing more. You don't need to worry.'

Jimmy exhaled a long slow breath.

'What's up? What's happened? Is it Mum?'

'You 'ave no idea what's happened do yer?!' screamed Jimmy.

'What the fuck is it – just tell me!'

'It's not yer mother.' He paused and sighed heavily. 'It's Felix–'

'Felix! What happened to him?'

He gave a huge sigh and continued. 'He's been got at … attacked … with acid–'

'Fuck!'

'He's in a real bad way. He's going to need skin grafts.' He shuddered and let out an extended sigh and then a breath. 'The whole nine yards–'

'That bad?'

'Oh yeah.' Jimmy nodded slowly to himself. 'And do you know what?

'What?

'It was meant for *you*–'

'Me? Why? How come?'

'Trouble don't take long to catch up with you, does it, son?'

'Are you sure it was Felix?'

'Oh, yeah.' He lowered his head, closed his eyes and sighed. 'We've seen 'im.' He paused. 'Well … what we could see of him. He's fucked. He's in a real bad way,' he said, as he shook his head in despair.

'Do you know who did it?'

'Not yet … but you left behind a lot of shit … a lot of enemies … and trust me … they *all* know *you're* back–'

'Already?'

He scoffed. 'Course they do.'

Liam shrugged off the insinuation of possible reprisals and instead expressed his shock at the thought of Felix being attacked instead of him. 'Fuck … Fuck … Fuck!'

Jimmy continued in a measured voice. 'But I will find out who did it.' He paused. 'Or more to the point … who paid for the hit.'

'How's Kathleen taking it?'

'She don't know yet.' Jimmy looked at the clock on the mantlepiece and talked to himself. 'She'll 'ave been out. She helps out at the school on a Wednesday afternoon.' He checked the time again. 'Five o'clock. Um … Well, I expect the hospital will have contacted her by now.'

Liam's hands trembled. 'Where is Felix?'

'Mile End–'

'I'm going to the hospital–'

125

The line went dead.

Jimmy fired a futile scream into the phone. 'Fuck you, Liam. Keep the hell away!'

Liam raced to the hospital and made his way to the ICU ward.

Kathleen and her three teenage children were sat around the bed. The twins saw Liam for the first time since he'd come back. 'Dad,' they shouted excitedly.

'Hello, Sally … Michelle.'

'Mum told us you were back,' said Michelle.

Harry moved towards him. 'Wherever you go, shit always follows.'

'What the hell are you doing here?' screamed Kathleen 'This is all your fault!'

As Harry left the ward, he barged past Liam and shoved his shoulder into his father's stomach.

Liam sighed heavily and looked down at Felix bound in bandages and the tubes and wires in various parts of his body linking him to the wall of machines and flashing lights.

He inhaled deeply before he spoke. 'I'm so sorry, Kathleen.' He returned to look down at Felix. 'Is there anything I can do?'

Kathleen's face contorted with absolute hate. 'Don't tempt me, Liam!'

Liam moved towards her and tried to hold her but she forced him off. 'Have you called the police?'

'Course we have. They're just going through the motions – as always.' She scoffed as she flicked her shoulders. 'You should know that.'

Liam nodded. 'Yeah, I do.' He stomped around the room and punched the air. 'Alright. I'll find out who did it–'

'It's too late for that now, Liam. They told us Felix will be scarred for life.' She threw her arms in the air and lowered her voice. 'If he even makes it.' Her whole body shook with anger. 'And do you know what? It was meant for you.' She gasped for breath. 'For YOU ... Liam ... fucking Reilly ...'

The door was flung open and they turned to see a scruffy man in his late fifties with dishevelled thinning hair, wearing a creased overcoat and crumpled trousers – something he could have bought from a charity shop. He stopped and pulled his head back when he saw Liam. 'Well, well, well.' He slowly raised one arm and pointed at him. 'If it isn't ... Liam *Reilly*.' He drawled. 'I didn't expect to clap eyes on you again.' He turned to Kathleen. 'When did *he* get back?'

Liam answered for her. 'A week ago.' He shrugged and glared at the detective. 'I see you've decided to do something after all – detective?'

'It's DCI Fuller ... now,' he said, as he puffed out his chest and pulled out his warrant card and badge. He tapped it proudly. 'So less of the crap, Reilly.' He nodded. 'We always follow up attacks of this sort.' He sniggered as he took his time to look Liam up and down. 'I don't need to ask why you're here.' He paused. 'I can guess. Trouble is your middle name.' He took out his notebook. 'So, where were you this afternoon?'

Liam forced a grin and whispered in his ear. 'We were at the Travelodge in Shooters Hill,' he lied.

'Can anyone corroborate that?'

'Yeah.' He glared back at him. 'Have you gone deaf? I did say … *we* …' He forced a grin. 'Didn't I?'

The detective ignored Liam's arrogance. 'Well … I'll need their details too … sir' he said, as he forced a grin.

'Fine,' said Liam. He slid the Travelodge postcode tag from the room keyring and handed it to him. 'Give us a call, Room 14.'

'I will be keeping a close eye on you … and next time. I'll have you banged up for good.'

Liam shrugged and left.

CHAPTER NINETEEN

Yesterday's Gone

A very drunken Max Player and his cronies were drinking and celebrating at the far end of the pool hall. The large television screen behind the bar flashed with breaking news. *"Acid attack in East London."*

The barman turned up the sound and they all watched. A stern-faced announcer spoke. "We are getting reports of an acid attack at Gore Road in East London."

Player and his cronies whooped with delight.

The announcer continued. "It is believed that the victim may be Liam Reilly." An old photograph of the smoke covered face of Liam filled the screen. "Many of you will remember that almost two years ago Liam Reilly saved his three teenage children and wife from a devastating fire at the family home."

As the screen changed to the weatherman and the sound faded, Player punched the air and led them with another round of celebratory whoops and screams.

They didn't hear Liam as he raced up the stairs. He flung the doors open and burst into the pool hall.

Max Player was shocked and pulled back, speechless. 'Fucking Reilly,' he mouthed. He scrutinised Liam as he walked slowly and deliberately towards their table. Player turned and grabbed the man nearest to him and pushed him onto the table, causing their glasses to fall onto the floor and smash. 'Oleg, you, stupid bastard … you messed up. You hit the wrong fuckin–'

'I didn't–'

'You fucking did!' He punched him in the face and flecks of blood splattered across the table and onto the nearest green baize. 'Reilly is standing in front of you. Look.' He grabbed Oleg's head and directed his eyes towards him. 'He hasn't got as much as a scratch.' He tugged Oleg's shirt and threw him onto the floor. He kicked him in the ribs and face and stamped on his hands. 'You are such a useless bastard. Who knows *what* you've unleashed now?!' Player kicked out at Oleg again. 'Come on. Get up you bastard.' He slowly raised his head and while he glared at Liam with his demonic eyes his face broke into a fiendish grin. 'Hello Reilly. I wondered when we might see you – rear your ugly fucking head.' He raised his empty glass to Liam. 'Come on you prick … have a drink you piss-head.'

'Fuck you–'

Player forced a bibulous grin and sneered at him. 'So, the pissed-up bastard doesn't want to drink with me?' He looked around for support.

A few of his cronies laughed loudly.

'I wonder why? You're always pissed.' He tilted his head and thought. 'In fact, I've never seen you sober–'

Liam retorted. 'You're rotten and so is your fucking money–'

Player sneered and rolled his tongue across his top teeth and poked it out. 'Like you and all the Reilly family.'

Player kicked at Oleg. 'Time to make amends.'

Liam made a move towards Player but he was grabbed by two of the men nearest to him. One of them hit Liam over the head with an empty beer bottle and for a split second he was confused. They grabbed him, dragged him out of the pool hall and down the stairs.

In the car park they tied him up and after knocking him unconscious they bundled him into the boot of Player's black BMW.

They drove to Player's office and workshop off Wallis Road in Tower Hamlets.

When Liam came around, he was stunned and confused. He struggled as he tried to move his arms and legs but they were secured to a chair with cable ties. Player and two of his cronies took it in turns to beat him, first with their fists, then pieces of plastic profile and finally a knotted length of rope.

Oleg grabbed Liam's head and forced it back and Player poured vodka down his painful throat. 'Let's see how the drunken bastard deals with this,' he said, guffawing loudly.

CHAPTER TWENTY

Lean On Me

Zita opened the door and ignoring everyone walked up to the counter. George was frying bacon and eggs on the griddle while his wife dried the plates and cutlery. The radio played to itself while the customers, mothers with kids in pushchairs and the men checking the racing pages before they made their daily trip – a visit to the bookies. 'Hello, George.'

He turned and fired her a wide toothless grin. 'Hello again.' He leaned towards her. 'On your own, Zita?'

'Hello. Oh, yeah.'

'I remember all my customers. I need to ... so much competition out there these days.' He looked over her shoulder. 'Is Liam with you?'

'No. He isn't.'

George stiffened and pulled back. 'It ...' He turned to Ethel while he took his time to choose his words. 'The acid attack ... that wasn't *Liam*, was it?'

Zita sighed and shook he head. 'No, it wasn't ...'

George let out a huge sigh of relief. 'Thank God. That is a relief.' He frowned. 'If it wasn't Liam, then who was it?

She leaned over and whispered to George. 'It was Felix ... Kathleen's boyfriend.'

'Bloody hell.'

Ethel jabbed George in the ribs and looked across at the children. 'Language, George.'

He nodded his apology. 'Sorry, dear.'

Zita fidgeted and flicked her thumb and index finger. 'I've only come for a coffee - milk - no sugar and ...' She looked up at the blackboard and screwed up her face in disgust before she ordered a round of toast and marmalade.

'Righto.' He turned to make her coffee and signalled to his wife, Ethel, to make the toast. When he turned back to place her mug on the counter Zita was leaning across it. She leaned into him. 'You know when we came in last week.'

'Yeah. Oh yeah.' He laughed. 'It was good to see ol' Liam again.'

'Well, two men were watching him.'

He thought for a second and nodded. 'Oh yeah, Max Player and Oleg ... his Russian puppet.'

'That's him. Max,' she smiled, as she lied. She lowered her voice to almost a whisper. 'What did he want?'

George pushed her coffee towards her and flicked the dirty tea cloth from his shoulder and wiped the counter. 'Nothing really. He just asked if it really was Liam.' He chuckled. 'He was probably as shocked as I was to see 'im back 'ere again.'

'Oh.'

George looked towards the radio and pondered. 'Has this got anyfing to do with that acid attack?'

'I have no idea, George but it's not good.' She paused 'Not good at all.' She picked up the coffee and sat in the corner on the only empty table, with her back to the side wall.

Customers sat at every table: very young mums with babies, middle-aged men checking the racing papers for tips, and older men and women who had nowhere else to go or little else to do. She watched them as they voraciously devoured the huge plates of greasy fried food. She shuddered at the thought of her eating it and what it would do to her body. In disgust, she turned her attention to the street. The same football posters she had seen in Lanzarote and Fuerteventura, months earlier, now hung sadly defaced, faded and ripped on the boarded-up shop windows. Multi-cultural people milled up and down the street oblivious to each other. Groups of unemployed West Indian and Jamaican teenage youths, Asian men, women in their traditional clothes and homeless men and woman zig-zagged aimlessly between the people as they pushed their worldly goods in "borrowed" shopping trolleys. She spotted the same teenage boy pull up on his bicycle and stop in the vacant shop doorway. She watched as he blatantly handed out tiny packets of evil, to everyone who approached him and had the money. With one hand he collected payment and passed them their fix with the other before he rode away. She realised that this was part of an organised ring of professional dealers and found it hard to understand the world where Liam had spent most of his life, when not in prison. In disgust, she walked up to the counter and paid. She smiled at George timidly. 'Thanks, George. See you again.' She continued when she reached the door. 'Great food,' she lied.

George followed her with his eyes as he bounced to the music. He continued to watch her as he wiped down the counter until she closed the door and disappeared amongst the crowd.

Ethel gave him a sharp poke in the back. 'Liam Reilly, eh.'

He turned to her. 'What, love?' he said, feigning innocence.

She glared back at him.

He raised his hands in submission. 'She's a nice girl … very noice.'

CHAPTER TWENTY-ONE

Everything Changes

Zita sat in the room of the Travelodge, subconsciously played with her fingers and flicked her nails before she reached for the telephone and dialled.

'Hello, Jimmy. This is Zita.'

'Oh, hello.'

'Do you have any idea where Liam is?'

He hesitated.

'Jimmy, I need to find him. You must know where he is.'

She could hear him taking a lengthy breath which allowed him time to think.

'How do you expect me to know that? He could be anywhere.'

She replaced the handset.

Jimmy decided to get away from the phone and more questions that he didn't want to answer. He called out. 'Martha, I'll be in the garage if you need me ... but unless it's urgent don't disturb me. Alright.'

Martha was putting Gwen to bed and called out to him. 'Yes, Mister Jimmy.'

He walked down the garden and into the garage. He smiled to himself as he fired up his motorbike and knelt down to check the timing.

Zita pulled on her leathers and rode to Jimmy's home in Morepeth Road. She knocked on the door but there was no reply. She climbed back onto the bike and rode down the lane at the back of his house and parked outside. She could hear a powerful motorbike revving in the garage so she opened the side door.

Jimmy had his back to the door when it opened.

Zita crept inside unnoticed, reached over the bike and twisted the throttle.

Jimmy immediately fell back and landed in a heap on the floor. 'What the fu–'

Zita leaned into him. 'Now that I'm here, do you have any idea where Liam is?'

He remained silent as he tried to catch his breath. Still in shock, he spoke as he exhaled. 'Why the hell did you do that?' He took another staggered breath. 'I could have had a heart attack.'

Zita grinned at him and, after flicking the throttle once more, turned off the engine. 'Really. You … a heart attack?' She sucked her teeth and continued. 'Come on, *you know* where he is.'

He slipped his glasses onto his forehead and inhaled sharply as he raised his head to look over the fuel tank. 'I'm not sure–'

'Really?' She kicked out at the rear tyre of his bike.

He was still in shock and struggled to breathe. 'What the hell did you do that for?'

'It was the only way I could get your attention …' She paused and then continued with a sneer. 'Wasn't it?'

Jimmy took his time to get to his feet and when he finally did, he forced a grin. 'You really are sumfink else … ain't yer?

She replied with a shrug of her left shoulder. She knew he wouldn't divulge what she wanted to hear so she changed tack. 'Nice bike.'

His face broke into the proudest of grins. 'Yeah. I bought it when I came out of the nick in ninety-eight … to celebrate–'

'Really.'

He looked down at it and chuckled. 'Yeah, a 1979 classic Kawasaki X400.' He paused and rubbed the handlebars with his dirty rag. 'I know what you're finking.'

She screwed up her face and nodded slowly. 'Go on.'

'How could I afford one of these … New?' He paused and lovingly stroked the fuel tank. 'I bought it second-hand.' He reached across to the work bench and picked up his empty mug. 'Fancy a coffee?'

'Yeah, why not.' She paused and looked at her watch. 'But I am in a hurry.'

He ignored her and dropped the leaf on the pale blue, nineteen-fifties kitchen larder unit to expose his secret stash. He turned and grinned at her as he filled the kettle with water from a plastic bottle and flicked the switch. While he waited for it to boil, he poured two spoons of instant coffee into each mug.

Zita knelt down and, after admiring the black and silver bike, reached down and examined the pristine engine. She stood up and sat astride the classic Japanese bike.

Jimmy turned to her. 'It's a real beast … that one.'

She leaned forward, twisted the throttle and grinned at him. 'Nice … very nice.'

Jimmy removed his glasses from the top of his head and laid them on the bench.

Zita pointed at them. 'I didn't know you wore … glasses.'

'Yeah … but only for working on the bike.' He picked them up and dropped them into a scratched and dented case. 'I don't read the paper … so why would I need them for anything else?' He opened a drawer and threw the case inside.

She nodded. 'Okay.'

The kettle boiled and clicked off and Jimmy poured the steaming water into the stained mugs and added two spoons of dried milk to each of them.

Zita was revolted at the oil and dirt on the mug and pulled her head back as he handed it to her. She took a token sip and forced a smile before she slid a rusty and dented paint tin along the work bench and put the mug beside it. 'Have you any idea where Liam may have gone?' she said as she screwed up her face and wiped the foul-tasting liquid from her lips.

Jimmy crossed his arms and shook his head in a token gesture.

Zita didn't hide her impatience. 'Come on. Where *will* he be now … *tonight*?'

He sighed heavily. 'Well–'

'Come on, Jimmy … Where can I find him?'

He sniggered. 'I knew this wasn't a social visit.' He looked down at his gleaming bike. 'Or … to admire that.' He sipped at his coffee, immediately grimaced and spat it out. 'I never liked dried milk.' He tipped the coffee into an empty gallon paint can and, still holding the mug, shook his head. 'So why now?'

'I have my reasons.'

'Do you?'

'Yeah. I do.'

139

'If you do find' im.' He grinned at her. 'He'll eat you for dinner ... and ... spit you out–'

'Who will?'

Jimmy raised his hands. 'Liam may well have gone to pay a visit to ... Max Player–'

'Player?' Zita looked concerned. 'Do you think he may have done that?'

Jimmy shook his head slowly and took his time to wipe his greasy hands with the filthy cloth. He looked at them and realised they were no cleaner. 'Listen ... Why don't you give the law a chance to deal with it?'

She scowled at him. 'Really? I can't believe you said that.' She took a moment to glare at him and then raised her voice. 'When we both know full well that Liam has already made his decision.'

He replied in a subdued voice. 'Yeah.' He swallowed hard. 'I'm sure he has.'

She took a huge breath and exhaled as she spoke. 'So, tell me then!'

Jimmy sighed his submission. 'Try the pool hall in ... in ... in Manor Road. Player often hangs out there with his cronies.'

Zita turned and rushed towards the door.

Jimmy shook his head and spoke to the invisible Zita. 'I hope you know what you're doing.'

Zita walked out into the lane, fired up her bike and raced to the pool hall.

Ten minutes later she hurried up the stairs. Rock music blasted out in the vast pool hall and bar. It was empty except for two young men playing on one table and the middle-aged shaven headed barman who tapped the bar in time to the music. She rushed up to the table. 'Has Liam Reilly been in here?'

They both shook their heads.

She sprinted across to the bar. 'Have you seen Liam Reilly?'

He immediately stopped tapping and frowned at her. 'Who?'

'Liam Reilly.'

'Maybe.' The barman shrugged his shoulders and turned his back on her and fiddled senselessly with the bottles on the shelf behind the bar.

She was desperate and lost her temper. She grabbed a pool cue from the nearest table and slammed it on the bar.

A beat.

He flinched but continued to ignore her.

She jumped onto the bar, smacked him across the head and pulled the cue up under his chin.

He found it hard to breathe and spluttered.

'Liam Reilly?'

He still refused to answer.

She pulled it up hard against his jaw and forced his teeth to cut into his tongue.

His whole body spasmed in agony.

Using the pool cue, she shook him as she spoke. *'Have you seen ... Liam Reilly?'*

He nodded his head wildly.

'And Max Player?'

He nodded again.

'Where are they?'

She released enough pressure on his throat to enable him to speak.

He blurted out his reply. 'Try 'is workshop ...' He gasped for breath. 'Wa ... wa ... Wallis Road.'

141

She made a fist and pummelled the side of his head. He fell to the floor.

She kicked at his fat body, broke the pool cue in half, looked down at him and systematically used each piece to rake all the spirits from the rear of the bar. 'You should have told me when I asked the first time.' She jumped back onto the bar, ran along it and pulled the phone from the wall, raced down the stairs and onto her bike.

CHAPTER TWENTY-TWO

I Believe in Miracles

When she reached Wallis Road, she stopped twenty yards from the large sign outside Player's office and workshop. She walked through the partially open gates and peered through the window into the empty office. Three computers sat on a row of identical desks and their screens flashed in safe mode and reflected off row upon row of glass samples and chrome door handles. On one wall a large nobo board with the dates of planned fittings was partially illuminated by the blue LED lights around the room. On another large worktop was a display of miniature houses and bungalows with tiny ornate windows and coloured doors.

She walked around the building and, as she approached the rear door, she heard raised voices. She pushed open the workshop door and made her way between the stacked PVC windows, door frames and double-glazed panels. She moved as close to them as she dared without being heard.

She watched and waited.

The vodka they had forced down Liam's throat had already coursed through his veins and he had slipped into a drunken stupor. Player and his men continued to egg him on and poured even more vodka down his throat. He spluttered and struggled to breathe as each gasp triggered unbearable agony through his already damaged throat.

Player slapped him around the head, then turned up the radio and Ricky Martin's, *'Livin' la Vida Loca'* blasted out. While he gyrated to the beat he screamed at Liam. 'Come on, Reilly, why don't you sing for us.'

Liam mumbled his reply before he vomited over Player's suit, lost consciousness and slumped awkwardly in the chair.

'You filthy bastard,' boomed Player, as he made an attempt to brush the vomit from his trousers and jacket.

Zita appeared from nowhere and vented her anger like never before. She picked up a window frame and smashed Player over the head with it and then flayed out at his cronies leaving them all on the floor, moaning and injured. When she was satisfied that Liam's attackers were incapacitated and no immediate threat, she turned her attention to him. She cut him free and immediately put him in the recovery position, raced into the office and called an ambulance. She returned to the workshop and tied everyone's hands behind their backs and then pulled up their legs and trussed them up like chickens. She dragged them outside into the yard and covered them with a tarpaulin.

When the paramedics arrived, they immediately gave Liam oxygen and after making sure he was stable they lifted him into the ambulance. Zita followed them as they raced through the streets, light flashing and siren wailing to Mile End Hospital. She pulled up behind the ambulance, parked the motorbike and followed the stretcher into the Emergency Department and resus. She gave the doctor Liam's details and explained what had happened, that Liam was an alcoholic and had been forced to drink the vodka. It was clear to her that he didn't believe her story. He shrugged and forced his hands into his white coat pockets, tugged it tight and left his thumbs to hang over the side. He slid a tube down Liam's already damaged throat and one of the nurses pushed a cannula into a vein in the back of Liam's hand and connected it to a tube and a clear bag containing a combination of water, sugar and vitamins which dripped slowly into his alcohol swamped blood stream.

A third nurse fitted a catheter and linked it to a plastic bag and hung it from the side of the bed.

Jimmy arrived, threw the door open and screamed at Zita. 'They told me he was drunk – paralytic–'

Zita stood and moved close to him. 'Jimmy, will you listen to me.'

He pushed her away. 'You lied to me.' He gasped. 'What else have you lied about?'

She replied in German. 'Ich habe dich nie angelogen, Jimmy.'

'You lying kraut bastard,' he screamed. He stamped his feet, raised his arms and covered his eyes. 'Fuck. Fuck. Fuck.' He took a deep breath and a grin slowly crept across his face. 'I told yer he would never change–'

Zita pulled back and exhaled her anger. 'Jimmy,' she said, in a soft voice, 'He was forced to drink.'

The consultant followed by two nurses entered the room and heard what Zita had said. He looked directly at Jimmy. 'There was too much damage to his throat for him to have done it himself.' He concentrated his glare on Jimmy. 'I'm afraid … he was forced–'

Jimmy screamed at the consultant. 'Forced?!' He pointed at Liam and jabbed his finger. 'When did *he* ever need to be forced to neck a drink? He had no principles. He'd drink anything – anywhere – any time?' His whole body deflated and he slumped into the chair beside the bed. He shook his head and sniffed hard. 'What are ya talking about?'

The consultant looked down at Jimmy. 'I'm sorry, Mister Reilly. We will do what we can for your son.' He signalled to the nurses, turned, and they followed him out of the room.

Zita reached down and held Jimmy tight. 'He was forced to drink it … by … *Player–*'

'That bastard! How come?'

'They grabbed him in the pool hall and took him to his workshop and forced … I don't know how much vodka down his throat.'

Jimmy pulled away. 'So, you did go after 'im?'

Zita grinned. 'Of course–'

'I'll sort that bastard–'

'Not now, Jimmy. We need to be here for Liam and help him to get better.'

CHAPTER TWENTY-THREE

The Way We Were

The consultant stepped forward, 'Yes, he will need a lot of care.' He coughed. 'He will need to stay with us for at least ten to fourteen days depending on the results of the surgery.' He looked down at Liam. 'He had major throat damage.' He sniffed and shook his head in disbelief. 'I've never seen anything like that before.'

'I know.' Zita looked at Jimmy. 'And ... thank you,' she said.

The consultant nodded. 'I did what I could.' He paused. 'But he needs to be careful. Very careful indeed.' He reached out and patted Jimmy's arm. 'I understand your concern, Mister Reilly, but he is in good hands.' He looked across at the machines and paused while he checked the readings. He turned and smiled at the nurses who reciprocated his positivity. He put his arms on their shoulders and after glancing back at the array of machines, nodded to them. 'We'll leave you both now ... but please.' He paused. 'Don't try to wake him. He needs as much time as possible to heal.'

'Of course,' said Jimmy.

Zita sat down beside him and they looked at Liam, each with their own very different thoughts.

Jimmy wondered how Zita had been able to do it on her own and what had happened to Player?

Zita wondered if Liam would ever recover enough to be able to speak again?

Jimmy still held so much anger from when his parents were killed by the Stuka. He finally coughed and shook his head. 'I'm sorry, Zita.'

'Sorry.'

'For what I called you.'

She flicked her head. 'What *did you* call me?'

Jimmy pulled away, grinned and nodded slowly. 'Thank you.' He paused and his grin grew into a full-blown smile. 'For saving my boy.'

It was thirty-six hours before Liam was conscious. He tried to focus on what was going on around him and he struggled to speak.

He couldn't.

He had oxygen tubes in each of his nostrils and a tube in his stomach to feed him and counteract the damage and effects of the alcohol.

Zita sat beside the bed and held his hand. 'Liam you need to rest and ...' she said, before she turned to look up and smile at the nurse.

The nurse returned her smile, looked down at Liam and adjusted the tubes in his nose. 'Yes, you do need to rest now ... and *we will* get you through this, Mister Reilly.'

The following morning Jimmy joined Zita and sat on the other side of Liam's bed. They both looked towards the door as the consultant entered. He talked directly to Liam who was barely conscious. 'Your throat was very badly damaged, Mister Reilly.' He paused and picked up the board at the end of the bed. 'I noticed there was scar tissue around the oesophagus and larynx and further down your throat.'

Liam raised one hand and grunted.

'It looks like you have been in the wars.' He lowered his voice and leaned into his patient. 'In the past.'

Zita nodded for him. 'Mm.'

The consultant continued with a wry smile. 'We have carried out surgery and it may help you … but …' His faced hardened and he made no attempt to hide his concern. 'You will always have some pain … but we will give you some heavy-duty painkillers.' His voice took on an even more serious tone. 'But please don't abuse them.' He forced a cough. 'As I said … they are very strong.' He looked at Jimmy and Zita and they both nodded. He continued. 'When you leave us, you must take care of your throat, getting too stressed or any attempt to shout will cause irreparable damage.' He smiled. 'But what we have done will allow you to keep your voice.' He leaned over the bed and tapped Liam's arm, smiled at Jimmy and Zita and left.

DCI Fuller had been to interview Felix in the burns unit and suddenly appeared in Liam's ward. He saw Jimmy and Zita at the far end of the ward but when he approached Liam's bed, he took his time to look down at him. He eventually turned his attention to Zita and then Jimmy. He grunted. 'Where have you been hiding yourself?'

Jimmy glared back at him.

D.I Fuller pointed at Liam. 'He hasn't been back long and he didn't waste any time, did he?' He turned to Jimmy. 'So, what the fuck is going on, Jimmy? If he didn't bring trouble back with him, it sure as hell has followed him.'

Jimmy made to stand and thought better of it and sat back down. 'What the fuck do you mean?'

DCI Fuller continued. 'What is it with you Reillys? None of you are ever far away from bother.' He looked at Liam and wanted to spit. 'I spoke to the doctor.' He scowled at him. 'He said you were pissed right up.' He laughed. 'It didn't take you long.' He paused for effect. 'Did it?'

Jimmy made to stand and his chair slid and scraped on the vinyl floor.

Zita pulled him back and kicked at his feet beneath the bed.

DCI Fuller cursed and glared at Jimmy. 'Were you going to say something?' he asked, as he pulled out his notebook.

Jimmy shook his head. 'No. But bad news travels fast.'

Zita looked at the policeman. 'Surely he's allowed a blip ...' She sniffed and swallowed hard. 'Once in a while?'

DCI Fuller grunted. 'Something's not right.' He shook his head wildly. 'What the fuck is going on. We got him here ... and his wife's boyfriend upstairs.' He looked down at the exhausted and barely conscious Liam. 'What do you think about your wife fucking someone else, eh? How many more has she fucked while you've been away?' Fuller's head continued to shake until he stopped suddenly and swallowed hard. 'It's too much of a coincidence.' He paused and exhaled angrily. 'Well. I'll tell you this.' He looked at Jimmy. 'I will be watching you all closely ... *Very closely*. And ... one mistake ...' He looked down at Liam. 'I'll 'ave 'im *and I'll 'ave you* too ... *Reilly*.'

Jimmy and Zita ignored him.

Liam offered a subdued grunt.

Fuller shrugged his shoulders and left.

Zita leaned forward and whispered in Liam's ear. 'They really don't like you, do they?'

Jimmy heard her, sighed heavily and shook his head in agreement. 'You ain't wrong there.'

CHAPTER TWENTY-FOUR

Seven Days

Zita made a number of phone calls with the confidential prefixed numbers used by Mossad operatives until it eventually rang.

'Hello, Zita.'

'Hello, Delfine.'

'We've been expecting your call.'

'Really?'

'Longer than we thought.'

'Oh.'

'You were very lucky last time–'

'Was I?'

'Oh yes, you were. You *both* were.' She cursed. 'They are very upset to have missed their targets.' She exhaled her frustration loudly. 'And … before you say anything … I know *you* would *not* have missed.'

Zita smiled to herself. 'Yeah, we both know that … don't we?' Her voice became more business-like. 'Is there anything that can be done.' She swallowed hard. 'I … I… I can do?' she said, softly.

Delfine sniggered. 'You always want a deal don't you. You're so schlau.'

Zita forced a laugh. 'Of course. Why shouldn't I?' She thought. 'Do I have a choice?'

Delfine laughed loudly. 'Did I really hear you say that?' She paused and took a breath. 'Um. So, why would you ask that question ... when you obviously know the answer yourself.' She paused. 'Don't you?'

Zita nodded at the invisible caller. 'Yeah ... of course I do.'

Delfine coughed as she eyed the chart that covered one wall and the row of large clocks that displayed different times around the world above it. 'Call me this time next week and I'll see what I can do.' She paused briefly. 'And remember *they* won't miss next time.'

CHAPTER TWENTY-FIVE

Every Breath You Take

Zita, wearing her leathers and crash helmet, peered through the side window of the office and saw Max Player shagging a near naked young girl, from behind, on his desk. She moaned with pleasure while he grunted and swore sadistically in between screaming the foulest of obscenities at her.

Zita crept around the building and opened the workshop door and moved in silence until she reached the rear door of the office and slowly opened it. Player was too pre-occupied with the girl and they both continued their animalistic moans and grunts. Zita sneaked up behind them pulled a cattle prodder from her pocket, and jabbed Player between the buttocks. As his body gyrated wildly the girl screeched with pleasure, but that soon turned to agony as his penis drilled and swivelled uncontrollably inside her. Zita dropped the cattle prodder on the desk, and before he could recover, she grabbed Player's hair and simultaneously drove a nine-inch knife up his anus. *Something that had become a common trait with Somalian gangs. It was their way of teaching their rivals a lesson, necessitating their need for a colostomy bag and preventing them from future "plug ins" to hide money or drugs in their anus.*

Zita screamed at the girl as she dragged Player off of her. 'Get the fuck out of here. Now!'

The naked girl shrieked in fear as she gathered up her clothes and raced back through the workshop and out to her car.

Zita continued to scream after her as she picked up her panties and slipped them into her pocket. 'And don't come back!'

Zita dragged the bleeding Player into the workshop and tied the noose that she had already prepared around his neck and threw the rope over a steel beam. She pulled it tight enough to leave Player's toes skimming the ground. She tied it off on the bench, and sliced through his trousers, shirt and underpants and pulled off his shoes until he was totally naked except for his socks. She looked down at his erect penis. 'That's funny,' she said, flippantly. She stared up at him and faked a sensuous grin. 'You like it … don't you?'

He grunted and slowly forced a pained smile. 'How did *you* know that.'

She grinned behind her visor and pushed him away from her. As he swung back she flicked his erect penis with the back of her gloved hand.

'Isn't it obvious?' he murmured.

Her demeanour suddenly changed. She kicked a plastic paint splattered chair towards him and lowered him onto it, then ran yards of gaffa tape around his arms, body and feet until he was unable to move. Player alternated between screams and unintelligible whimpering as his anus bled and the intense pain continued to shoot throughout his naked body.

She looked at him and growled. 'Remember this chair?' She pushed her helmet visor into his face. 'Course you do.'

His eyes looked through her and chuckled dryly. 'The *thirsty drunk* loved every drop.'

'You broke the rules–'

'Rules?'

'Oh, yes. There are always *rules*. Even for someone like you–'

'Who the fuck are you?'

She ignored him and walked across the workshop and picked up a moon knife and pushed it hard into Player's hand. She pressed his palm against it before she wrapped it in a piece of cardboard and slipped it into a side pocket of her leathers. She took a deep breath before she raised her voice. 'Felix was innocent – harmless! He never did you any harm!' She stamped her boot on the concrete floor. 'And what makes it worse.' She slapped him across the face and continued. 'It was Liam you wanted to disfigure … wasn't it?'

Player groaned. 'Yeah.' He yelled. 'The prick did …' He stuttered. 'For what that bastard Reilly did to my stepfather. That drunken bastard left him a gibbering … wreck …' He sniffed. 'A mindless shadow of what he was.' He spat at her. 'He lived a life of hell because of …' He glared at her. '… that bastard … Reilly!'

She grinned at him and, lacking all feeling in her voice, she continued. 'Really.' She stood back and her eyes flitted around the workshop. She noticed the knotted rope on the bench, grabbed it and picked at the dried blood. When she realised it was Liam's blood, she flipped and immediately checked herself. *She had been taught not to get angry – to always maintain control and focus.* She sighed heavily and dropped her shoulders. She walked slowly around the chair ramping up the pressure on Player by repeating the same German nursery rhyme. She lashed out randomly with the knotted rope, before she turned, walked in the opposite direction and lashed out again.

His eyes flitted from side to side in panic as he struggled to try and imagine what she was likely to do next.

Zita took a deep breath and lashed out again and again until Player was almost unconscious. She cut through the noose and left it swinging above him. She grabbed a strap, used to hold the plastic frames in place while they were drilled, threw it over the metal ceiling joist and tied it to the back of the chair. She tugged it hard and Player rose a few feet into the air.

She stopped and tied it off on the bench. She turned to leave but returned and emptied a bottle of water over his face.

The water partially revived him and he slowly recovered. 'You can't leave me up here,' he pleaded.

She ignored him.

She walked back to his office, picked up his mobile phone, dropped the girl's panties beneath his desk and kicked them away.

She returned to the workshop a few minutes later with a plastic supermarket bag and flicked up her smoke grey visor.

Player saw the face of his attacker for the first time and for a split-second, he felt safe and sighed with relief. 'A woman.'

She glared back at him.

He moved his head forward and peered at her. 'It's you again.' His demeanour suddenly changed and he screamed at her. 'Who the fuck are you?!'

Zita could feel his cold evil eyes as they flitted over her; the gaze of a wild predatory animal. She ignored him and pulled two bottles of vodka out of the bag and held them up. 'Is this what you poured down my Liam's throat?'

He looked at the bottles and wriggled and grunted. 'Maybe. How the hell did you get shacked up with that drunken tosser?'

Zita moved towards him and made a fist.

He winced in anticipation.

Instead of punching him she clenched her teeth and hissed at him. 'Did you expect to get away with that?' She cursed. 'Arranging the acid attack on an innocent man and … then doing what you did to Liam?'

'I'm s … s … sorry. I … I … know it got out of hand.' He forced a condescending grin. 'But we're quits … now.'

'"Quits?!"'

Player struggled and made one last attempt to break loose. He soon realised it was futile he remained exhausted and clamped in the chair. He fired her one last desperate and defiant scowl. 'Fuck you.'

Zita pushed the mobile phone into Player's face. 'Who did it?'

'Did what?'

'The acid–'

'Oleg. The fucking idiot.' He cursed. 'Got it wrong again.'

Zita scrolled through the contacts until his name came up and she pushed the phone in his face.

Player nodded.

Zita clicked the number. 'Tell him to come here. Now!' She clicked the phone and pushed it in Player's face.

Still reeling from his beating, Oleg answered. 'Hello, boss, everythin' alright?' he asked, nervously.

'Course. Get over to the workshop … Now!'

'Sure boss.'

Zita grabbed the strap and slowly raised Player's chair a few feet from the floor. She left him suspended while she crawled around the workshop and picked up offcuts of plastic profiles and piled them beneath the chair.

Ten minutes later Oleg opened the door, and walked sheepishly into the workshop. When he saw Player hanging in the air, he tried to run.

Zita was waiting for him behind the door. She slammed it closed and locked it. She smashed an iron bar into each of his arms and when he couldn't retaliate, she pounded both of his legs, breaking them in several places.

The Russian fell to the floor and lay screaming in agony.

She squirted highly flammable solvent over him, stood back and looked across at the terrified Player who thrashed and swung around in mid-air. She maintained her hateful grin as she lowered his chair onto the floor. She grinned at him as she emptied the remainder of the solvent over his waist, legs and feet. She took her time to open both bottles of vodka and drenched Player in the alcohol, stepped back and leaned over him. 'What you did ... was unentscguldbar – kriminell. Inexcusable – criminal!' She sneered at him. 'Ich mag keine feiglinge, die anders menschen benutzen, um ihre drecksarbeit.' She turned and repeatedly kicked Oleg. 'Do you do everything *he* tells you to do?'

He screamed out in agony. 'Het.'

'So, tell me why?'

'On platit mne.'

'Money?' She pointed at Player and grunted. 'So, you do everything he tells you to do ... for money?'

'Da.'

Zita turned back to Player and continued. 'Zu erleidigen – um unschuldige menschen zu verstumeln und zu entstellen.'

Player partially closed his eyes and squinted at her. 'Where did that come from? What the fuck are you saying?'

She snarled at him and continued with an incensed grin etched deep into her face. 'So, you don't understand … German?'

'Fuck no! Why should I?!' He paused and glared at her. 'Why the hell are you speaking in German?'

She shrugged at him. 'Why not?'

He grunted.

She huffed as she turned away, raised her boot and moved towards Oleg.

He tried to protect himself.

But unable to move his broken arms, he failed.

She kicked him again. And again.

Oleg's pained screams and his cries, for the torment to stop, affected Player and he sobbed uncontrollably.

Zita spun him around and spoke. 'Okay. You don't know German so I will make it easy for you.' She clicked her tongue. 'Let me translate.' She wrung her hands as she watched him spin. *'I don't like cowards who use other menschen – people, to do their dirty work – to maim and disfigure innocent people.'*

Player grunted and screamed at her. 'Fuck you! Whoever you are.'

'That's something … you will never know.' She picked up the mobile phone and dialled 999. 'Police, please,' she said. She nudged the semi-conscious Oleg and whispered in his ear. 'Tell them … it was you–'

'Mne — Me?'

Oleg tried to push the phone away with his chin.

She smashed it into his face.

He struggled to speak. 'Kto sovershil kislotnuyu ataku – in Gore Road.'

She grabbed his head and forced a filthy rag into his mouth and stifled his screams as she stood on his broken legs.

'Who is calling?' asked the call-handler.

Oleg couldn't answer her.

Zita punched him repeatedly until he conceded defeat with muted screams. She pulled out the rag and pushed the phone to his mouth. He blurted out his guilt. 'Eto byl ya. Ya, sovershil kislotnuyu ataku–'

'I'm sorry,' said the call handler.

Zita smacked him across the head.

'It was me.' He coughed. 'I did the attack with acid.' He stopped and looked at her.

She twisted his broken arm and he screamed out in agony.

He continued with a stutter. 'V … Gora Rode.'

Zita pulled the phone away from him but left it live so the police could trace it.

She slid it across the warehouse floor and took the Zippo lighter from her pocket. She lit a piece of cloth and waved it menacingly in front of Player.

He screamed out and pissed himself.

She dropped the burning cloth onto the plastic beneath him. The solvent burst into flames and, as they grew, she slowly lowered Player's feet into them and swung him to and fro. Within a few short minutes his screams filled the workshop as the vile smell of burning flesh and the skin on his feet began to melt, and with every breath he took the heat burned the lining of his lungs.

Zita didn't wait for the vodka to ignite, she pulled Oleg away from the flames, stamped on his legs several more times and left by the rear door. She climbed onto her bike, kicked it into life and looked through the window. She waited until she could see the fire taking hold of the building before she twisted the throttle, and took the side roads and lanes as she weaved her way, unnoticed, across Hackney.

CHAPTER TWENTY-SIX

I Heard It Through the Grapevine

Zita visited Liam in his ward and then Max Player on the floor above. His whole body was heavily bandaged and he had tubes everywhere. The expensive machines that kept him alive, bleeped continuously. She bent forward and whispered in his ear – not knowing if he was conscious or not. 'If you do get out of here …' She looked up at the machines, screens and tubes that entered his body. 'It's over. Leave the Reilly family alone.' As she spoke the last word, she smacked what was left of Player's bandaged feet. She walked towards the stairs, but when she saw the lift doors open and DCI Fuller step out, she crouched behind a trolley.

After checking the overhead signs, Fuller walked into Player's HDU ward. He stood beside his bed and spoke to the nurse. 'Will he make it?'

She shook her head. 'Maybe … maybe not.' She swallowed hard. 'The next few days will tell us more.'

He shrugged and cursed as he waited for the lift to take him down to just one floor below. He walked down the corridor, flashed his badge at the nurse on reception, and walked into Liam's ward.

Jimmy and Zita were sat beside Liam's bed when the detective appeared at the door. He looked Zita up and down before he spoke. 'What were you doing up there?'

'This is a big place and I was lost. Do you ever get lost in 'dis place?'

DCI Fuller grunted and glared at Jimmy. 'This is getting out of hand.' He huffed. 'We now know who did the acid attack on the Frenchman.' He took his time to savour every word and looked down at Liam. 'His wife's new squeeze, at *his* old place,' he said, with a broad grin. 'She didn't take long to shack up with someone else, did she?' He sniggered. 'To find someone else to fuck her …' He stabbed his pointed finger towards the unconscious Liam. He huffed and shook his head. 'And now …' He pointed at the ceiling. 'Mad … fucking Max … upstairs.' He shook his head wildly and raised his fists. 'And we've got another bastard upstairs … a Russian … with broken arms and legs.' He took a breath. 'And guess what?' he scoffed and turned to Jimmy. 'He *said* … he threw it.' He shook his head in disbelief and then grimaced. 'But did he?' He exhaled his frustration. 'What the fuck is going on with you lot?! The attack on Player was more than an attack – it was calculated revenge.' He glared at them, stepped back and pushed his hands into his coat pockets. 'None of this is a coincidence.' He took his time to think and after releasing his anger he sneered at Jimmy. 'Where were *you* last night?'

Jimmy grinned back at him. 'With my wife … and my granddaughter … Michelle.'

The detective took out his notebook and turned to the unformed policeman standing at the door.

The policeman shrugged his shoulders.

'Right,' said the detective. He didn't believe Jimmy and confirmed it with a suspicious grunt. 'Can they corroborate that?'

'Maybe.' Jimmy paused and took his time to stare at the detective with a woeful look in his eyes. 'She has dementia–'

'A bit young for that ain't she?'

Jimmy made to stand. 'You fucker!'

Zita reached across and pulled him back into his seat and murmured to him. She glared at DCI Fuller 'Didn't you hear?' She hissed. 'Jimmy's *wife* … has dementia.' She paused. 'And … I was with them too – putting Gwen to bed with Michelle.' She glared at the detective contemptuously. 'Do you know what dementia does to people?'

'Course,' he replied, arrogantly. He sniggered. 'She won't remember much then, will she?'

The uniformed policeman standing at the door shook his head in disgust.

Jimmy made to stand again. 'Fuck you … You bastard.'

The detective ignored him and turned his attention to Liam. He looked down at the sleeping patient and his top lip curled. 'It didn't take *him* long to get back on the piss, did it?'

Jimmy and Zita glared back at him and both spoke at the same time. 'Fuck you!'

DCI Fuller gave his response with the shrug of his shoulders. He took a deep breath before he spoke. 'We've apprehended a young woman who was in Player's office last night.' He looked directly at Zita and grinned vulgarly. 'We found *her knickers* under his desk.' He shook his head and glanced at the uniformed policeman again. 'But I reckon there is no way she could have done something like this.' He sighed. 'She may be able to help us … but whoever did it …' He paused and looked at Jimmy and Zita. 'Gave him a violent beating. It was a professional job – savage … and

165

calculated.' He sniffed. 'Just enough to keep him alive.' He snapped his notebook closed, pushed it into his overcoat pocket and walked towards the door. After a few heavy paces, he paused and turned back, and repeated his mantra. 'Something's not right about all this.' He sucked air. 'And I will be watching you,' he snarled. He looked down at Liam. 'Even that drunken bastard.' He nodded to the uniformed policeman. 'Come on.'

CHAPTER TWENTY-SEVEN

Rainy Days and Mondays Always Get Me Down

Jimmy had a few hours respite while Gwen was at the community centre with Martha, her carer. He agreed to meet Zita in George's café before going back to the hospital with her.

Zita sat at her favourite table in the window and looked out onto the street at the grey November day. She noticed dozens of pigeons swoop in through the windowless top floors of the boarded-up shop opposite and take refuge from the weather. She watched the continuous stream of miserable, downtrodden people of all ages made their way along the pavements. Some ran but the majority walked aimlessly through the cold and heavy rain. *Even at this time of year Amsterdam was so much better.* She shook her head and pitied them and their lives and realised how Liam had had such a lucky escape.

Jimmy was almost unrecognisable when he walked in through the door. 'Hi George, Ethel. How are ya?' he said, cheerily.

They both took a second look before they smiled back at him and waved. Ethel nudged George. 'You could do with doing something about *yourself*.'

George grunted his reply as he ran his hand through his thinning grey hair, turned his back on her, and shrugged away his embarrassment.

Jimmy was a changed man. He'd had a shave and a haircut. Over the past fifteen years his thinning 50s trendy copycat Tony Curtis curled-up front and long-gone ducktail had evolved into shoulder length grey hair. This had now been cut and styled into something more suited to his age. He wore a dark blue suit and waistcoat, a white shirt and blue patterned tie. He looked the business.

Zita was looking out of the window and hadn't noticed Jimmy walk in.

He walked towards the table, pulled out a chair and turned to greet Zita with a combination of pride and an uncomfortable smile.

She couldn't hide her shock and she had to look twice. She whistled at him. 'Wow. A real man about town.'

He was embarrassed and blushed briefly before he spoke. 'Not bad for an old man, eh? I *can* clean up well.'

'No, you look great. Surely you didn't do all this for me?' she said with a giggle.

'Nah, I needed to pull meself together sometime and … and … this is it.'

'Liam will be pleased.'

'Fuck, Liam. I did it for me … not 'im.'

'OK.' She looked him up and down. 'Well, for whatever reason you did it you look like a new man.' She smiled at him. 'I like to see a man in a suit.'

Jimmy sniggered.

Zita was taken aback and frowned at him. 'What is wrong?'

'Nuffin,' he said, as his snigger faded into a sombre look. He shook his head. 'Do you know the last time I wore this?' He flicked the lapels with his thumbs.

'I don't know the answer to dat.'

He chortled as he spoke. 'When I wuz last in court –
I still got three years, so *they* weren't impressed.'

'It still fits you – it looks good.'

Jimmy's blushes were saved by George who waved
at him in anticipation of taking his order.

'Two mugs a tea, George and … two bac …' He had
second thoughts and looked cautiously at Zita.

She sat back, rubbed the side of her neck and
nodded.

He grinned broadly. 'Yeah, two bacon sandwiches
then. Thanks, George.'

George plonked Jimmy's mug in front of him and
carefully placed Zita's mug in front of her, straightened the
handle and returned to the griddle. He sang to himself as
he flipped and pushed the bacon around on the hot plate.

Ethel scolded him. 'Get them sandwiches finished
and over to Jimmy … Stop dreaming. You're too old for
anything these days.'

Zita sipped at her tea and as she placed the mug back
on the table she spoke. 'So, what set Max Player off?'

Jimmy picked at the worn check tablecloth and
shrugged. 'We've been at war for years.' He scoffed. 'They're
our rivals … always have been.'

'Oh?'

He grinned and sipped at his tea. 'It wasn't always
like that.' He paused and took a reflective breath. 'But when
Liam kicked his stepdad into a coma–'

'What?'

He sniffed. 'Yeah. He beat him almost to death.' He
sighed. 'After that, their attacks on us were relentless …
until I had him put away.' He looked at her over the rim of
his mug. 'Your timing – coming back. Couldn't have been
worse–'

'Why?'

'Player's stepfather was attacked by Liam in a fucked-up robbery at the Mount Pleasant Post Office, sorting centre, a while ago now.' He paused and shook his head. 'After that the poor bastard was little more than a vegetable ... until he died.' He exhaled loudly and took his time to finish the sentence. 'A few weeks ago.'

'Oh ...'

He snorted. 'No surprise to know Liam was drunk that day. He was always pissed.' He swallowed hard. 'Such an idiot.' He sighed. 'But he paid for it. He was put away for years but somehow, once again, Liam came up smelling of roses and got early parole–'

'How come?'

Jimmy bit into his sandwich and answered. 'There was a riot, and Liam.' He coughed and took a deep breath. 'Was in the right place at the right time.' He chuckled to himself. 'Saved two wardens ...'

Zita grinned. 'Really.'

'Yeah. And he got out.' Jimmy's mood changed. 'Do you know what that bastard did?'

Zita screwed up her face and shook her head pensively. 'Yeah.' She lowered her voice to a whisper and leaned across the table. 'He told me.'

Jimmy took another huge bite of his sandwich and spoke while he chewed. 'But ...' He paused and looked at her, his eyes open wide. 'Did he tell you everyfing?'

'I don't know.' She tilted her head. 'How would I know dat?'

Jimmy shook his head and forced a grin. 'It didn't last long.' He sighed and closed his eyes as he relived that night. 'He was so fucking drunk he set fire to his own house and ... we nearly lost the kids ...' He swallowed hard. 'And

… Kath …' He took a deep breath and spoke as he exhaled. 'The whole fucking family.'

Zita pulled back from the table.

Jimmy dropped what was left of his sandwich. 'I had no option but to get him out of the way.' He swallowed hard. 'I forced him, yer know.' He exhaled slowly. 'The poor bastard had no choice.'

'So, that's why he ended up in Amsterdam?'

'Yeah. I had no idea where he would go … I didn't care. But I hoped it would make him realise that he had to do something – to sort himself out.'

Zita reached for his hand and closed hers around it. 'Must have been hard to do that … to your own son?' She tightened her grip. 'Well … it worked.' She smiled. 'You did the right thing. You saved *his life*.'

Jimmy sniggered. 'Yeah. I suppose I did.' He looked out of the window and continued speaking without turning back to her. 'Weird, eh?' He sipped at his tea, sat back and relaxed. 'But Player still bore a grudge and I knew he always wanted to settle the score wiv 'im.'

Zita reached for her mug, picked it up, took a sip and placed it back on the table. 'Um.'

Jimmy continued. 'He's only been out a few weeks.' He sniffed. 'He got parole after his stepfather died.' He sniffed hard and looked around and shook his head. 'I guessed when he knew Liam was back.' He screwed up his face. 'It was bound to start again.' He sighed heavily. 'Um.' He wiped the grease from his chin with the back of his hand. 'It was you that sorted out Player – weren't it?'

'What do you think?'

'Dunno. But whoever did it.' He sniffed. 'By all accounts … was the business.' He sniggered to himself. 'Even that bastard Fuller said so much didn't he?'

'He did. But it's over now,' she said softly.

He paused. 'Well, I hope so.'

She grinned back at him and, as she bit into her sandwich, she turned away and looked out onto the street.

CHAPTER TWENTY-EIGHT

Swinging Doors

Zita and Jimmy spent several hours sitting in silence at Liam's bedside before they both decided that he wasn't going to wake, so they walked out of the ward.

Zita stopped and turned to Jimmy. 'I'll meet you in the café upstairs, okay?'

Jimmy ordered and paid for two teas and two cheese and ham toasted sandwiches. Zita picked up the mugs and a ticket with their order number and followed Jimmy to a table near the window. They sat down and he finally began to relax. He fiddled with the grubby chrome top of the retro glass pourer before placing it in the centre of the table with a thump. He watched the sugar settle and straightened it up. 'So, where did you two meet–?'

'In Amsterdam, of course,' she said, flippantly.

Jimmy tried to hide his surprise, instead he forced a grin. 'Really.'

'Yeah, Liam was asked to run a bar–'

'A bar? For fucks sake' He howled with laughter. 'A *bar?* He stopped suddenly. 'How the fuck did he manage that, he's a bloody alkie!?'

Zita closed her eyes and nodded. 'I know.'

He spoke as he laughed. 'He must have been pissed all the time.'

She looked towards the ceiling and gave herself time to think. She slowly lowered her head, looked directly at Jimmy and fired him a proud grin. 'But he *wasn't*.' She paused. 'He's only been drunk … *twice* since I've known him …'

He let out a huge belly laugh. 'Twice? Did you say *twice*? Fuck me.' He shook his head in disbelief. 'How come?'

'Maybe, he's changed,' she said softly. She waited for Jimmy's answer. There wasn't one and she continued. 'Do you think he has?'

He shrugged. 'How would I know that.' He sniggered at her. 'Or … if not …' He adjusted his jacket and crossed his arms. 'He's been a bloody good actor. Well … it *looked like* he was sober before this shit.' He paused and tried to take back what he'd said. 'Sorry. I know it wasn't his doing this time.' He pushed his chair back onto two legs and straightened his jacket. 'Will he slip back after Player's episode … after the Vodka?'

'Who knows but the doctor said he should be alright.'

'Really?'

'Yes,' she replied indignantly. 'He's *sober*. And I want to keep it that way.'

'*You* … want to keep it that way?' He grunted and traced the lines of the table cloth. He stopped suddenly and glared across at her. 'Um.' He reflected before he continued. He looked directly into her eyes. 'So, what do you have to hide?'

'Me?' She grinned back at him and her mood suddenly changed. 'You wouldn't want to know.'

Jimmy chose not to hide his suspicions and as he stroked his stubbly chin, he shot her a knowing grin. 'Erm … I bet.'

She swallowed hard. 'Anyway, it's a long story … A very long story.'

The tannoy called out an order number, Zita checked her ticket, walked to the counter, collected the hot food and two more mugs of tea. She carried them back on a tray and as though she wanted to be noticed she plonked everything heavily on the table. 'Enjoy.'

Jimmy thanked her with a nod and sipped at his tea before speaking. 'Does Liam know *your story?*'

'Yeah.' She nodded calmly. 'Yeah, he knows.' She grinned. 'Why wouldn't he?'

He lowered his head and thought before he continued. 'What about his anger?'

'Oh, he still gets angry.' She looked directly at him, her eyes piercing into him. She clicked her tongue. 'Maybe he got that from you?'

For the first time Zita could see a change in him. 'Course he did.' He wiped at his eyes. 'It started for me when I was six–'

'"Six?"'

'Yeah … When I was *six.*'

Zita stiffened and pulled back.

Jimmy continued. 'My mother and father were both killed by the fucking Germans–'

'What?'

'Right in front of me …' He stared at her through what looked like the innocent eyes of a child. 'Yeah.' He nodded. 'He got it from me alright. I saw me mother … *and father* die … shot in our street … outside our house … by a fucking Stuka.'

'I'm so sorry–'

'Are ya?'

Zita nodded slowly and mouthed her answer 'Yes, I am.' She paused, moved her head towards him and looked into his eyes. 'Do you think that I am … *German* … and I did that to your family …' He whole body stiffened. '*And to you?*'

'Are ya?'

'My grandparents were Polish Jews and were prisoners in Belsen – the concentration camp?'

His face exuded the pain and disgust. He screwed it up before speaking. 'Yeah, I know what that was …'

Zita acknowledged his reply with a slow nod and continued. 'They met in *dat place,* in 1945, a few months before the end of the war and they promised each other if they survived, they would get married.' She smiled. 'They did survive …. and were married in 1946 and then my mother was born.' She hesitated. 'They moved back to Berlin … or what was left of it. I have no idea why they would want to do dat … but they did. When Ursula, my mother, was fifteen, she was given a dull job in the East German government offices. She heard that they were going to build a wall.' She took a huge breath. 'My mother told me that on the morning of 13th August 1961 lines of the huge lorries arrived and came to all the blocks in her strasse … her street. They placed bricks in the doorways and windows on the ground floors and lines of barbed wire across every road to divide them from the American sector. My mother and her friend jumped through the window from the flat above her and escaped into the West.' She gulped at her tea and took a minute to catch her breath. 'She told me others were not so lucky … they ran into the barbed wire, screaming, trapped and bleeding.' She swallowed hard. 'Until they were shot and left to rot ... as a warning to others.'

'Fuck,' said Jimmy, as he exhaled loudly. 'Your mother was *so lucky*–'

'She was.' She swallowed again. 'Yes, she really was.' She leaned further across the table and spoke in little more than a whisper. 'Do you know ... she was one of the *last* to leave?' She sighed heavily. 'After that everyone was starving ...' She gasped. '... eating horses ... and *rats* ... to stay alive.' She could see that Jimmy was getting upset. She leaned back, tilted her head towards the radio playing behind the counter and moved it in time with the music before she forced a huge smile. 'My mother loved music and watched the English groups when they played in *her* part of the city. West Berlin.'

He had no idea what she meant but he agreed. 'Course.'

Zita swallowed hard and as she looked around and her whole body stiffened again. 'My mother was raped by an American soldat – a soldier ...' She exhaled. 'And that's when I was born.' She tilted her head. 'So, you see, I was born in Germany but I am *not* German.' She smiled proudly. 'I am a little bit American, Polish and ... Jewish.'

Jimmy grinned with relief but his mood suddenly changed. He reached out, grasped the mug handle forcefully and it shook, spilling his tea onto the table.

Zita reached out, took it from him, and held it while she wiped it down with a serviette before placing it on the table and sliding it back in front of him.

He thanked her with a grunt and continued. 'After the Stuka killed my mother and father.' He seethed and released his pent-up anger. 'Nobody ... gave .... a ... damn,' he said, splitting up the words with a long pause between each of them. He shrugged and his sad face was slowly transformed into an evil twisted grimace. 'That's when I decided to take what *I* wanted.' His fists tightened and his arms shook. 'And that's exactly what I did.' He tilted his head and smiled at her defiantly. 'It's what I've always done.'

She nodded. 'Why not? We don't get anything unless ... *we* take it.' She paused. 'Or ... fight for it.'

'So, now, you tell me.' He scowled. 'Where did all the fucking money come from?'

'Money?'

Jimmy didn't hold back. 'The bloody plastic cards you keep sending us ... loaded wiv it?'

She let out an outrageously raucous laugh. 'Oh, that.' She reached under the table and gently patted his knee. 'You know how it is,' she said, coyly.

'So, why don't you tell me then ...' He moved his head up and down in a weird, exaggerated and jerky manner. 'So, I can, "*know how it is.*"'

'Well.' She sniggered. 'We both had such generous benefactors ... They were wonderful,' she said, exaggerating the word "wonderful" before she continued. 'I mean ...' She sniggered again but this time into her closed hand. 'Wealthy bastards ... loaded beyond your wildest dreams.'

'And they just gave it to you? Parted with it? Handed *their* money to you and my *boy*?'

She grinned back at him. 'Yeah.' She nodded. 'They did.'

Jimmy finished his tea and swallowed hard. 'Will you level with me now?'

She nodded. 'Of course.' She shivered and shook her shoulders. 'Yes, I'll tell you why we're here.' She sat back and took her time to explain her issue with the Mossad.

178

Jimmy nodded excitedly. 'I knew it. That bastard wouldn't come back without a reason. I know my, boy.'

She tilted her head towards him. 'Now, I need *your* help.'

'ME! Help?' Jimmy pushed himself out of his chair and the legs scraped noisily on the tiled floor. A baby screamed in shock and several of the customers turned to look at them.

Zita touched his right hand and gently eased him back into the chair.

Jimmy raised his hands, stretched his fingers and smiled at them with a submissive apology, then turned to the staff who stood looking at them. 'Sorry,' he mouthed.

Zita waited for the moment and when she sensed the time was right, she continued in a calm voice. 'You helped him before.'

'Yeah, I did. I had no option …' He reflected and shook his head. 'So …' He exhaled loudly. 'What do you need *me* to do?'

'Well, I need to get away from London for a while.'

'Really?'

'Yeah, I promised my mother that one day … I would go to Manchester.'

He stuttered his reply. 'O … o … okay …'

'I'll only be a couple of days … at the most.'

'OK.'

'But I need to you to make sure Liam is kept safe.'

Jimmy shrugged his shoulders proudly. 'Sure. No problem.' He grinned. 'You do what ya gotta do. We'll still be 'ere when you get back.'

CHAPTER TWENTY-NINE

What Becomes of The Broken Hearted?

Zita had photos of the band standing with her mother outside the Liverpool Hoop in Berlin, in 1967 and decided to visit one of the Manchester Playboys. She took the train to Manchester and then a bus to Newton-Le-Willows. She had already checked the name and address on the electoral register and knocked on the door of the terraced house.

A tall man with thinning hair answered. He took a step back when he saw the pretty young woman holding a photograph in her hand.

'Are you, Alan?'

'Yes,' he replied, with trepidation.

She pushed the photograph towards him. 'Do you remember this time, Alan?'

Like so many musicians, from their months, and sometimes years, of – sex, drugs and rock 'n roll in Germany, they had waited for that possible knock on the door, to face someone who said. 'Hello, Dad.'

He stiffened and pulled back. He took the photograph from her and studied it. He shook his head and stuttered. 'I … I … I'm not sure.' He puffed up his cheeks and exhaled slowly. 'It was a long time.'

Zita noticed how her arrival had affected him. She took a step back and gave him time to get over the shock.

He continued. 'A very long time ago,' he said, trembling. He noticed her disappointment and looked down at the photograph again. He smiled. 'Maybe I do.' He opened the door and waved her in.

While he made a pot of tea, she waited patiently and looked excitedly at the sideboard filled with framed photos of the Manchester Playboys in Germany, Sweden and England and silently tried to name each of them.

Alan walked back in and placed the flower-patterned tray on the coffee table. He took his time to pour the tea into the two matching cups before speaking. 'You know, we had such great times in Germany.' He passed her a cup and saucer and turned to look at the photographs.

She smiled and remembered what her mother had told her about her time in Berlin. 'You have some beautiful photographs, and memories too.' She looked across at them. 'Yes, my mother told me about the Manchester Playboys … She loved your group.' Zita took the only copies, taken in Hamburg in the 1970's, and Berlin in 1967, of her mother's photographs, from her bag, and showed Alan.

He took his time to look at them and grinned as he remembered those exhilarating months. He finally looked up and handed them back to her. 'Yes. I do remember her. She came every week … two or three times for the month we were there.' He sipped at his tea. 'She liked, Sandy, the organist–'

'She told me.' She stood and reached for a framed group photo and pointed at the young long-haired musician on the left-hand side. 'That's him, isn't it?'

'Yes, that's, Sandy,' said Alan.

'Would you like to …' He paused. 'Have it?'

'Really?'

'Course you can.'

He sipped at his tea and thought back to what was more than thirty years earlier. 'But do you know what …' He scratched his head. 'She didn't come to see us on our last week.'

Zita shuddered. 'Do you know why?'

He flicked his head. 'No.'

Zita exhaled loudly. 'She was raped by a black G.I.'

'Fuck … The bastard–'

'He was.' She shook her head and exhaled loudly. 'He really was.'

'What happened to him? Surely, he was court marshalled for that.'

Zita shook her head.

'Oh.' Alan was surprised and pulled his head back. 'I thought the Americans were really hot on that sort of thing –'

'"*Thing*?"'

He blushed. 'Sorry, I didn't mean it like that–'

'It's okay. "Thing," just sounds so petty … doesn't it?'

He nodded in agreement. 'Yeah. It does. So, was he?'

She shook her head and chewed her bottom lip. 'He wasn't.'

'Wow. Your mother must have been angry–?'

'She was.' Zita remembered. 'But strangely.' She paused and thought. 'Do you know she really expected him to come back to Germany and take her to America–'

'What?'

'I know. I don't understand that either.'

'And?'

She wiped her eyes. 'She died of a broken heart, Alan.'

'Died? I am so sorry,' he said, shaking his head in disbelief.

'Thank you.'

She reached for her cup and took a huge gulp. 'Nice.'

'Thanks. I thought it might have been too strong for you.'

She smiled and took another gulp. 'I like it like dat.'

Alan waited and looked at her quizzingly.

'I know ...' She grinned. 'You want to hear what happened to him.'

Alan nodded with nervous apprehension.

She spoke softly. 'He *died*.'

Alan stiffened, placed his hand across his mouth, and held his breath.

'Yes. He died last year.'

'Oh.'

She grinned mischievously. 'He drowned while he was cleaning his car–'

'What? How come?'

'He swallowed the hosepipe.'

Alan sighed heavily and tried to think. 'Really ...' He still had no idea what may have happened. 'Oh.' He fired her a blank look and forced a grin. 'He died cleaning his c ...?'

'Yes, he did.' Zita stood and emptied the cup. 'It was so good to meet you, Alan.' She handed it to him. 'If you still are in touch with the rest of the group, please pass on my regards to them. From me ... and ... remind them of my mother.'

He handed her the framed photograph and nodded. 'Course I will.'

'Thank you, Alan.' She looked at it and gently rubbed her index finger across the glass. 'Thank you very much.'

As she walked towards the door Alan called out. 'Do you fancy visiting Liverpool ... and see what it ... the music scene was all about back then?'

'Yeah ... yeah.' Zita was ecstatic. 'That would be *great.*'

They spent the rest of the day visiting Mathew Street, and the new Cavern on the opposite side of the street from the original, then took a bus to Strawberry Fields and Penny Lane.

CHAPTER THIRTY

Rescue Me

Liam was finally discharged from hospital with a month's supply of Tramadol, a painkiller to treat his ongoing severe pain, and the opioid, Fentanyl. Zita pushed his wheelchair to the waiting taxi and they were driven to the Travelodge. Liam took his time and walked unsteadily the few yards to their room. Zita opened the door and helped him onto the bed. 'We need to get your strength back Liam and you will soon be back to normal.'

'Normal? What's normal?' he muttered.

* * * * *

Jimmy felt guilty sending Gwen off for respite as he preferred the twice weekly visit by Martha, the young West Indian carer, he had little option than for her to take his wife to the community centre on some days.

Martha opened the front door and called out. 'Gud merning, Mister Jimmy,' she said, with an infectious tone in her voice. Martha continued to smile. 'And how are yer today, Mister Jimmy?'

He lied. 'I'm fine.'

'And how is Missus Gwen?'

He sighed heavily. 'She's in bed.' He exhaled. 'She's had her breakfast and … looking forward to your visit,

Martha.' He sniffed. 'I don't know how you do it.' He sighed heavily. 'Have the patience …'

She giggled. 'You may dink we carers 'ave special powers, Mister Jimmy …'

'Um.' He nodded. 'You can say that again.'

'It just 'appens.' She grinned. 'Oh, and she loves the foot lady–'

'Foot lady?'

Martha smiled. 'Gina – the foot lady – does 'er feet once a month at de care centre. A massage and foot pamper.' She giggled. 'She really looks ferward to et.'

'Nice.'

'You just need to find the key that unlocks the memory. She walked into the bedroom and smiled at Gwen. 'We'll get yer ready and den we can go to the centre for a few 'ours.'

Jimmy already had his coat on and was sat in his chair staring at the clock when he heard the front door open. He jumped up and smiled. 'Ah, Martha, you're back. How was it?'

She tapped Gwen on the arm and smiled at her while she spoke to Jimmy. 'Do you know she didn't eat her veg on one side of her plate – she left dem … agin.'

'But she likes them.'

'We know dat, Mister Jimmy.'

'OK.'

'Yes, we realised that as 'er 'ead was bent, she couldn't see dem.' She giggled. 'So, we placed small portions on each side of de plate.'

'And?'

She laughed loudly. 'It *worked*.' She turned to Gwen. 'Don't ya have sometheng fer Jimmy?'

Gwen forced a proud smile and her face beamed as she handed him a bunch of fading chrysanthemums.

Jimmy took them from her and kissed her on the forehead. 'Thanks, luv, I'm popping out for an hour, will you be alright Martha?'

'Course, Mister Jimmy. We're goin' to wash Gwen's hair. You won't know 'er when you get back,' she said, with a giggle and a prod of Gwen's shoulder.

Martha washed Gwen's hair and rubbed it with a towel. 'Jimmy well love to see yer shiny her.' She leaned back. 'You luk like a film star.' She giggled in her deep, west Indian Trinidadian voice. 'Very nice… very nice indeed.'

'Where's Liam?' asked Gwen.

Martha replied without having to think about her answer. 'He's at school.'

Gwen smiled. 'Yes, he's at school.'

Martha looked at the clock. 'He be 'ome soon.'

Gwen fretted. 'What about his tea?'

Martha smiled at her. 'We'll do sometheng later. Don't worry. We 'ave time.'

Gwen trembled as she spoke. 'He's always hungry when he gets home.'

'Ain't they all, Gwen?'

Gwen relaxed and laughed. 'I don't think they feed him at school.'

'Come on let's dry yer hair.'

She walked her into the bedroom, sat her down at the dressing table and clicked on the hairdryer.

Gwen looked up at her. 'Can I do it today?'

'Course you can.' She handed her the buzzing hairdryer. 'I go down and mak' us a nice cup of dea.' She paused at the door. 'Don't ferget to turn it off when yer finish.

Gwen ignored her and sang to herself as she waved the warm air blindly over her head.

Martha was pouring two mugs of tea and cutting a fruit cake when Gwen appeared at the kitchen door. 'Dat was quick.' She rubbed at Gwen's still wet hair. 'Looks very nice,' she lied.

'Thanks,' said Gwen with a vacant smile.

They sat at the table and Gwen picked at the cake and dropped crumbs all over it as well as the floor. Martha moved her plate nearer to her but it made no difference. She stopped suddenly and sniffed hard. 'Can yer smell burnin'?'

Gwen tilted her head, smiled back at her and pushed the cake towards her mouth. She missed and dropped large pieces of cake onto the table. She grabbed at the cake and tore another chunk which she squeezed into her hand. She opened her hand and the cake dropped between her fingers. 'It's not burnt. Look.' She attempted to push what was left into her mouth and choked.

Martha jumped up and patted Gwen's back. Relieved, she handed Gwen her tea and she slurped it noisily. She walked towards the living room. 'I can smell burning. You stay 'ere and I go and 'ave a look.' When she opened the door, she was met with a cloud of acrid smoke. She grabbed Gwen and walked her smartly towards the back door. She locked it and returned to the sitting room and grabbed the phone on the sideboard. She dialled 999.

'Operator what is your emergency?'

'We 'ave a fire ... at Morepeth Road. Help!'

She smashed the phone down, returned to the kitchen and slammed the door behind her. She unlocked the door, guided Gwen into the garden and walked her down the path.

Minutes later the wailing sirens of the fire engines could be heard as they raced down the road.

CHAPTER THIRTY-ONE

Too Late Now

Zita and Liam took a taxi to an Italian restaurant in Victoria Park Road for their first real meal on their own since leaving hospital.

Zita opened the door and turned to Liam. 'I expect you feel a little strange being out of dat place?'

He nodded as he looked around. 'Feels like I'm in a mist – everything is blurred.'

'Yeah. I know, but in a day or two it will get better.' She paused. 'As you reduce the drugs.'

Zita ordered and the waiter brought their food. He hovered over the table unsure who had ordered what.

Zita pointed at the pasta and then Liam. 'Thank you,' she said. As the waiter walked away, she called after him. 'Mi scusi. Non dimenticare la nostra brocca d'acqua.'

He turned to look at her, raised his arm and smiled. He returned a few minutes later with two glasses and a huge jug of water.

'Grazie,' she said.

'Prego.'

She looked across the table at Liam and watched him as he nervously forked the pasta. He was unable to eat pizza and thrust his fork into his penne pasta for the second time, taking his time to swallow it. 'Um … very nice.'

She waited until he'd swallowed it. 'This is very nice, Liam,' she said, as she folded a slice of pizza and chomped at it.

The wailing sirens of fire engines approached and raced past the restaurant.

Zita paused when she heard them. She dropped her second slice of pizza. 'Liam, I have a feeling that something is wrong.'

'Wha …?'

She pushed her chair back and stood. As the waiter approached, she handed him a twenty-pound note. 'Scusa, ma dobbiamo partire.' She leaned across the table and grabbed at Liam's arm. 'Come on.'

Liam didn't budge. Instead, he reached for another fork of pasta.

'Liam, we need to leave. Now!'

He rammed the pasta into his mouth and joined her.

It took them a few minutes to reach Morepeth Road and, when they arrived, they saw three police cars and two fire engines blocking the road outside Jimmy's house. They moved as near to the first fire engine as they could but were held back by a policeman. They stood on the pavement and watched as the firemen raced in and out of the house.

Liam walked across the road and Zita followed him. He shouted to the nearest policeman. 'What the hell's happened here?' he asked. He knew Immediately that he shouldn't have raised his voice and he gripped at his throat as the excruciating pain drilled through it.

The policeman replied. 'We don't know too much yet … but … we'll know more very soon.'

Zita could see that Liam was getting anxious and angry and tried desperately to calm him down.

He ignored her and moved nearer to the policeman. 'But?' he asked.

Before the policeman could answer him, a fireman wearing breathing apparatus walked out of the house, removed his mask and took a breath of the fresh, clean air. He spoke to the Incident Commander. 'A hairdryer. The stupid woman turned off the hair dryer but left it on the bed.' He laughed. 'Guess what, Lenny?'

Lenny nodded. 'It caught fire, right?'

'Yep.' The fireman nodded in agreement and grunted. 'The third this week.' He shook his head. 'When will they ever learn?'

Liam's body stiffened and he made fists with both hands. 'You fuckers!' he fumed angrily. '*She's* my mother and … and … *she's* got dementia!' He immediately regretted it as once more the pain shot through his damaged throat.

Zita pulled him away, forced two painkillers down his throat and handed him a bottle of water. 'Liam, you can't be like this. You will undo all the work they have done.'

He took his time to swallow the water and turned to see his shocked and confused mother, and the trembling Martha, being helped out of the house by two more firemen. They walked them to the ambulance. Gwen still wore the full-length once brightly coloured Arabic dress that Zita had bought her, but it was covered with black soot and unrecognisable. The paramedics wrapped them in silver foil blankets and helped them into the ambulance.

Jimmy arrived a few minutes later in a taxi and raced towards the ambulance.

Martha tried to stand and reach out him. 'I am so surry, Mister Jimmy.' She broke down in tears. 'It all me fault.' She stuttered and repeated herself. 'It all me fault, alright.'

Jimmy pushed his way between them and hugged Gwen.

She didn't recognise him. She didn't recognise anyone and she didn't know where she was.

He looked out at Liam and slowly shook his head, his face a combination of shock and what might have been embarrassment.

The Incident Commander approached Jimmy and Liam. 'Okay, it's sorted now.' He paused. 'Luckily, the smoke damage is restricted to the one bedroom and staircase and ... nothing too extensive.' He sucked hard. 'It could have been worse ... much worse.' He looked towards the ambulance and Martha. 'It was lucky that your mother wasn't alone.' He swallowed. 'She wouldn't have got out of that.' He smiled at Martha and waved. He returned to Jimmy and Liam. 'Not all of these ...' He took a deep breath and continued. 'End well.' He tapped his colleagues on their shoulders. 'Come on guys, get packed up. I'm sure we'll soon be needed somewhere else.'

Zita tried to hug Liam. He pushed her off. 'The bastards ... they have *no idea*,' he cursed.

'Liam,' said Zita. Her voice softened. 'They are only doing their job.' She persisted in her attempt to hug him and her persistence finally paid off as he succumbed to her efforts and fell, exhausted, into her arms. 'Liam, listen to me. You heard what they said. "It could have been much worse."'

He sniffed and took a painful breath. 'Yeah. I know.'

The paramedic closed the ambulance doors and it pulled away.

Martha and Gwen were kept in hospital for more than a week. Jimmy stayed with Kathleen, Felix and the teenagers while the bedroom and hall was redecorated by a friend of his. It was finished and everything was back to normal by the time Gwen was allowed home.

Liam and Zita lay on the bed in their hotel room. 'Do you know you are so different here, in London – like another person,' she said.

'Different?' How?'

'More confident and funny – in control'

'I know I've changed. Amsterdam did that.' He paused. 'And meeting you …'

'That's nice.' She smiled at him and kissed him on the cheek. 'It changes most people, Liam.' Her eyes exuded her honesty. 'Even me.'

He chuckled. 'You just need to rise above the shit and corruption, if not you'll get dragged down … and drown in it.'

Zita closed her eyes and thought for a second. 'Do you want to stay here?'

He took a while to think of his answer and finally spoke. 'No, I don't.' He shuddered. 'This place will kill me and I won't be able to fight the temptations–'

'Temptations?' shrieked Zita.

He roared with laughter and stroked her. 'Don't you worry … I meant … drink.'

She smiled. 'I'm so pleased you said that, Liam.

'Yeah. So am I.'

'My life has changed … for the better. I love being with you and … Madonna. I think about it all the time.'

She smiled. 'So do I.'

'Do you think we'll be able to go back?'

'I hope so … But they will want me to do another *thing* for them.

'And.' He sniffed. 'Do you have an option?'

She shrugged and sat on the side of the bed. 'There is one – only one.'

CHAPTER THIRTY-TWO

Handbags and Gladrags

Zita and Liam pulled up outside Jimmy's house in a dark blue 1986, Saab 900. Zita left Liam in the car and knocked on the front door.

Jimmy answered. 'Hi Zita.' He looked over her head. 'Where did you get the motor?'

Zita grinned. 'George lent it to us–'

'You've got him wound around yer tiny finger ain't yer?'

She nodded and grinned coyly.

'Is Liam with you?'

'Yeah,' she said excitedly. 'He's in the car.'

Liam waved regally from the passenger seat.

Zita walked back to the car and opened the rear door nearest to the pavement. 'Come on. We'll take you for a ride. How about Southend?'

'Now?'

'Yeah. Why not.'

'We've got the car ... so, we may as well use it.'

'Shouldn't you be treating Kathleen and the kids?'

'We'll do that another time. Come on.'

A few minutes later Jimmy led Gwen out of the house. She proudly wore her now redundant supervisor's supermarket uniform and climbed into the back seat.

Jimmy joined her.

Zita started the engine, twisted her head and faced Gwen. 'You look nice, Gwen. Very smart,' she said.

Gwen offered a distant grin.

Zita parked the car at the far end of the deserted esplanade and stopped at the first shelter facing out to sea. Gwen was fascinated by the huge waves that crashed noisily onto the pebbly beach and sat mesmerised by the sounds and motion.

Liam sat and watched her. He deliberated before he whispered to his father. 'Can't they do anything for her?' He turned to Zita. 'We have the money. Surely she can see a specialist?'

Jimmy spoke through a twisted mouth and contorted face. 'Do you fink money solves everyfing?'

Liam fired him a vacant look.

'If it did, I would have done it already,' scoffed Jimmy.

Liam looked at his mother and then his father. 'But she's suffering.'

'*We're all* suffering, Liam …'

Jimmy couldn't hide his frustration and as his face reddened, he turned to Zita.

Zita knew what he was going through and spoke softly. 'I do understand.' Her face exuded a caring demeanour. 'I have seen such things before … in Holland and Germany. Sadly, it is getting very common now … everywhere.'

The wind blew in off the North Sea and they all shivered but no one wanted to be the first to submit to the cold.

Liam stood and took Gwen's hand. 'Fancy an ice cream?'

She offered him a childlike smile. 'Yes, please.'

He helped her up and held her arm as they walked slowly along the sea-front. He bought her an ice cream cone with a flake and they sat in another shelter looking out at the sea. He found it hard to control his sadness and frequently looked away. He made small talk but she failed to respond to any of it, instead she concentrated on licking the ice cream which had already melted and dripped onto her coat and scarf.

Jimmy and Zita sat in the deserted beachfront café and watched the waves as they crashed over the promenade and high into the air. He studied her for a few minutes and smiled. 'I 'ave a feeling we're not too different. Are we?' he paused and looked into her eyes. 'I was in Korea … and … I killed …'

Zita acknowledged him with a thoughtful nod.

Jimmy lowered his head and continued. 'War … the killing … and death. It does fings to ya … Especially over there with the Chinese – they are such cruel bastards.' His voice faded, embarrassed at what he had just said and how matter of fact it sounded.

Zita sighed heavily. 'I know it does. It never gets any easier?'

'You sound like you know about it. Maybe done it too?'

She lowered her head and nodded. 'Sometimes I did … sometimes there was no alternative and I did what I needed to do.'

Jimmy suddenly became serious. 'So, tell me straight.' He coughed. 'Give it to me straight … no crap.' He looked up at Zita and stifled a cough.

Zita took a breath before she spoke. 'Liam almost died. If I hadn't gone to see him.' She took an even deeper breath and shuddered. 'He … would have.'

'Again?!' He slammed his fist on the table and shook his head. 'Fuck!'

'He was attacked by De Groot's heavies.' She sniggered. 'One of dem was heavy alright. Skipio, the Greek bastard! He was a weightlifter on serious steroids. He could hardly walk, but he and two others shoved a toothbrush down Liam's throat before they almost beat him to death.'

'Why?'

'For being seen with me–'

'Wha …?' He mouthed. 'That Greek bastard needs a good seeing to.' He coughed hard and the cancerous pains shot throughout his body. 'I would 'ave killed the bastard.' He pulled a face and formed a gun with his fingers and thrust his hand forward, twice flicking his thumb.

Zita nodded and grinned. 'We did …' She paused. 'It was quite a performance …' She bit her bottom lip sensually. 'You could say he went out with a bang.' She paused a long thoughtful pause as she remembered his body exploding into a thousand pieces on New Year's Eve, on the Singel.

Without any warning she shouted. 'BOOM!'

Jimmy laughed loudly and pushed himself into his chair. 'That's the way to do it. Take no prisoners. That's what I say.'

'He took his orders from De Groot – he was a vile boss.'

'The same one?'

'Yeah.'

'He needs to be sorted out too … fucked over.'

Zita grinned. 'He has been.'

'Really?'

'Yeah. He was sunburnt–'

'Sunburnt?'

'*Too* much sun …' She paused and the corner of her lip curled. 'He didn't put on the cream.'

'Cream?'

'Sun cream – so, he burned to death?'

'How come?'

She closed her eyes and remembered that red-hot summer afternoon on Fuerteventura. She opened them and as she spoke, she emphasised every word. 'Yes, he did … He died.' Now it was her turn to laugh. She did. 'He *cooked* … very slowly.' She clicked her tongue. 'Then *he* exploded.'

'Fuck.' He grinned as he compared his pale hands with her olive skin. 'We don't get sun like that 'ere …' He looked at her quizzically. 'So, he was on 'oliday?'

She closed her eyes and smirked. 'No. He lived on the island. After we discovered he arranged the fire at the Love Shack, last December, he was a wanted man and had to leave Amsterdam in a hurry. A great hurry.'

'You are full of surprises.'

'I only "surprise" someone if I have to.'

'Touché.'

CHAPTER THIRTY-THREE

True Colours

They left Southend as the late November sun was setting and drove home in silence. It was already dark when the Saab pulled up outside Jimmy's home in Morepeth Road. A police car was parked outside and waiting for them. As soon as they stopped DCI Fuller left the car, walked purposely along the pavement and tapped the passenger window.

Liam wound down the window and waited.

The detective coughed. 'Did you have anything to do with Max Player's attack?'

'Attack?' Liam feigned ignorance. 'Player?' He grinned. 'When? Where?'

'I see, you want to play that game, do yer?'

Zita spoke in an innocent voice. 'Liam was in hospital, DCI Fuller … surely you remember dat?' She grinned at him. 'I saw you at the hospital … Remember?'

He took his notebook from his pocket and flicked furiously through the pages. He stopped at one page. He reread his notes and closed it but kept his finger between the pages. He hesitated before he made his reply in a defeated and subdued voice. 'Okay,' he said, reluctantly. He coughed. 'Do you know who might have done it?'

Zita spoke again. 'Is that the nasty man who attacked you in the pool hall, Liam?

He grunted. 'Yeah. It is.'

The detective issued a salacious grin at Liam. 'So …' He lowered his head, pushed it inside the car and sneered at Liam. 'You had a motive then?'

Liam could feel his throat tightening up, he rubbed it gently while he answered. 'Maybe I did. But you just said … you saw me in hospital. Check the date and times. I was already in there when the bastard was attacked.'

The DCI pulled away from the car and straightened his body.

Liam continued. 'Listen Fuller, I'm back to see my Mum and Dad.' He turned to look at them. 'They're both sick … So … come on … have some compassion.' He punched the dashboard. 'Why the fuck would I want to get involved in anything at the moment?'

'At the moment?' The detective pushed his head back through the car window and into Liam's face. 'So … does that mean … you … you might have got someone else to do your dirty work?'

Liam shrugged. 'Maybe.' He paused. 'But I'm a changed man. I'm enjoying life. We've all been to Southend and we had a great time.' He turned and smiled at his mother and father.

His father reacted with a slow nod.

Liam continued. 'Haven't we?'

Jimmy grinned brazenly at DCI Fuller and nodded innocently.

The detective pushed his head further into the car and their faces almost touched. 'I've been checking up on you.' He grinned. 'What you've been up to while you've been away.'

'Really?' answered Liam provocatively.

'Oh, yeah.' His face broke into the widest of grins. 'Have you forgotten you were arrested last year for murder in Amsterdam?'

'No. I was never charged ... and ... and I was released.'

Zita interrupted. 'He was innocent!'

Liam exhaled.

Zita sensed he was about to lose his temper and squeezed at his right arm and shoulder.

He sat back. 'You know I didn't kill anybody. Why don't you check your facts?' He fired the detective a crass grin. 'Unless you're incapable of finding the truth.' He hammered on the dashboard. 'Why don't you do what you're paid for ...' Liam twisted his head and pushed into Fuller's face. 'Your fucking job!'

Fuller pulled back and scowled. 'How did you get away with that?'

Liam screamed at him. '*Because* ... you bloody moron – I just said I didn't do it!'

Fuller couldn't hide his humiliation. He stamped his feet and he fired back at them. 'I've said it before ... the Reilly family have always been ...' He stuttered. 'Are ... are ... are drenched in violence.' He took a huge breath and spoke as he exhaled. 'An' I won't rest until I nail ya ...' He looked across at Jimmy. 'Both of ya ... and all yer kids!'

Liam smiled provocatively at him and slowly wound up the window.

CHAPTER THIRTY-FOUR

Every Time We Say Goodbye

Liam and Kathleen were sat in the kitchen drinking tea.

Sally walked in.

Liam noticed her expensive Reebok Preacher trainers. Sally chose to ignore him. 'Hi Mum. What time's tea?'

'When it's ready.'

Sally walked out and slammed the door behind her.

They both shook their heads awkwardly.

Liam turned to Kathleen. 'Have you seen what she's wearing on her fucking feet?'

Kathleen shook her head.

'How could she afford them?'

'I've no idea, maybe your dad gave her the money … or Gwen. She has nothing to spend her money on.'

Liam mumbled to himself. 'I hope she's not been fleecing my mother.' He finished his tea and slammed his mug on the table. 'I'm going to pop round and see them.'

Michelle was reading Gwen a story when Liam walked in. His mother didn't recognise him so he sat in his father's armchair, picked up a magazine and pretended to read it while he waited.

She finished the story and helped her grandmother up the stairs to bed.

Ten minutes later she walked back in. 'Hello Dad. Nan's already asleep,' she said proudly.

'Did she like the story?'

'Yeah. She always does–'

'What?'

Michelle blushed. 'I always read her the same story.' She shook her head. 'And she doesn't remember it.' She sat upright in the chair. 'What are you doing here?'

He forced a cough 'Michelle … is Sally selling drugs?'

She blushed and fidgeted nervously.

'Come on, Michelle, tell me. Because I reckon, she is.' He paused and glared at her. 'Have you seen her trainers?'

'Michelle nodded. 'Yes.'

'So, I am right?'

Michelle broke down. 'Alright, Dad.' She lowered her voice. 'She is.'

Liam jumped up and tried to console her. 'Okay. Then we need to help her–'

'How? She can't get away. She tried and they said they would …' She shook her head and burst into tears. 'Kill her–'

'What? Is it that bad?'

'Yes, Dad. They are vile … disgusting men.' She paused, wiped her eyes and looked hopelessly at him She sobbed. 'That's what she told me … What can *you* do?'

The front door opened and Jimmy walked into the sitting room and slumped into his armchair. 'Alright?'

Liam glared at him. 'No, it's bloody well not …'

Jimmy looked at Michelle and she burst into tears again. 'Will someone tell me what is going on?'

Liam fired him an anxious look. 'Sally's selling drugs.'

Michelle rushed out of the room and raced down the garden to her mother.

Jimmy shrugged his shoulders. 'Is that all. They're all at it these days.'

Liam paced the room. 'What? How can you just say that … dismiss it? 'Have you given up?'

'Didn't you?'

Liam nodded. 'I was lucky … thanks to you …'

'Thanks to me.' He scoffed. 'I fucked you over – forced you to go – to leave everything …'

'I know that.'

Jimmy nodded thoughtfully 'No son, I've run out of energy. I'm fucked.' He covered his face and broke down and sobbed violently. 'Didn't you hate me for that?'

'Course I did. But now, I know it was for the better.' He paused and forced a cough before firing his father a stern look. 'So, what do I do about Sally?'

'Find whoever is supplying the shit and cut 'em up.'

Liam parked his motorbike in the side road, twenty yards from the school entrance, and walked around the corner and waited. He stood on the opposite side of the road outside the school and crouched behind the parked gleaming SUV's and older cars, and mothers with handfuls of young screaming kids. He noticed that Michelle and Sally walked out of school together but as soon as they reached the gates Michelle immediately left her sister and walked off in disgust. He followed Sally and watched as she made her way confidently through the thronging noisy school kids until he saw her openly handing out drugs to some of the older pupils and pocketing the money. He couldn't hide his disgust and shock at what was the reality of what he saw happening to the next generation of his family.

He returned to his motorbike and rode off.

Kathleen was in the kitchen, ironing a man's white cotton shirt and paying particular attention to the Harrod's motive on the pocket. When the door opened, she looked up. 'Hello. To what do I owe the pleasure?'

'Do you know what Sally's been up to?'

'Should I?'

'You should. We both should–'

'We?'

'We are still married you know.'

'I know.'

He looked at her. 'Something is up with Sally.'

'Really?'

'Yeah. She's been selling drug to the other kids–'

'Come on, Liam. What's with the fantasy?'

He shook his head violently and raised his voice. 'I tell you – she's selling fucking drugs to the other kids at her school. Do you realise what could happen if one of them OD's?'

'Calm down, Liam.'

'We'll ask her when she gets home.'

Kathleen made a pot of tea and they both sat at the dining table.

He concentrated as he stirred his tea. He stopped and looked up at her. 'I know it's a bad time ... but should we get divorced?'

She scoffed. 'Just think what you've just told me about Sally, our daughter.' She fumed. 'And now you want to escape your responsibilities?' She paused and forced a chortle. 'That's a bit rich coming from you.'

'Well?'

She forced an ugly grin. 'As far as I'm concerned … we already are,' she said defiantly. ''cept to do it legally.' She picked at the chipped pink nail varnish on her thumb. 'Yes, of course we should.' She jumped up and turned off the iron. 'So, Liam. What are your plans?'

He looked around at the home he hardly recognised and was no longer any part of. 'Okay. Let's do it.'

Kathleen smiled and nodded. 'It won't be so difficult.'

'Okay.'

'So, I'll arrange it then. Alright.'

Liam nodded.

Kathleen lowered her head and then raised it and beamed at him excitedly. 'I'm pregnant.'

Liam didn't know how to react.

A beat.

'Wow.' He bit into the side of his mouth to give himself time to take it in the shock.

'Well … Aren't you going to congratulate us …' She grinned. 'Me and Felix?'

He coughed and spluttered as he spoke. 'Co … co … course. That's great news,' he lied. *She was still his wife and he was strangely jealous of Felix but didn't know why because he had Zita.* He continued to stutter 'Ha … ha … have you told … the twins. And Harry?'

'Not yet … I …' She blushed. *'We will* … When the time is right.'

He took a sip of his tea. 'Yeah. Course.'

Unexpectedly Kathleen's demeanour changed and she reached out to him. 'She loves you … you know–'

'Who does?'

'Come on … Zita. You know she does.'

'Oh. Does she?'

Kathleen lost her patience with him. 'Liam, how the fuck could you even ask me that?'

He grunted.

Kathleen lowered her voice. 'You need to move on, Liam. You have a new life – a lover.'

Liam didn't react.

The door opened and Sally walked in and threw her school bag onto the nearest dining chair. She turned to Liam 'What are you doing here? It's not your home anymore.'

Kathleen raised her head. 'Sally, why are you talking like that? Liam is your father. He came to see you.'

Liam turned to Kathleen and then faced Sally. 'We know what you're doing …' He stood up. 'I saw you, Sally. That is a bloody dangerous game you're into–'

Sally responded immediately. 'Mum, has he been stalking me?' She turned to Liam. *'Have you been stalking me!'*

Kathleen spoke. 'What are you talking about? Why would your own father stalk you?'

'You're selling drugs. I saw you.' He paused 'It's so obvious … and if I can see it … so will the police–'

Sally shrugged and grinned at him

Liam was desperate. 'Sally, you have to stop it – cut it out. Why don't you get a paper round?'

Sally laughed in his face. 'A paper round?' She scoffed. 'Who buys papers these days?' She held up her mobile phone and continued her reply in a shriek. 'Why should I do that when I can earn three hundred a week?'

Kathleen pulled back in horror and turned to Liam. 'Can't the police do anything about it?'

He shook his head. 'I've checked. They can't search kids–'

'What?'

Sally flung herself into the chair and grinned inanely at both of them. 'What's for tea … or shall I order a takeaway?' She laughed loudly and looked directly at Liam. 'I mean I've got the money.'

Liam sighed heavily and left.

Sally called after him. 'Fucking loser.'

CHAPTER THIRTY-FIVE

You Might Need Somebody

Liam and Jimmy had been to the café for breakfast but as they walked through the front door, Martha rushed towards them. 'Kathleen called,' she said, anxiously.

'Yeah?'

'She said Sally didn't cum 'ome last night, Mister Jimmy.'

'Is that unusual?' asked Liam. He looked at Jimmy. 'Has she done that before?'

'Yeah, she has.'

Martha continued. 'Kathleen said "that she has not been home for two days."'

Liam grabbed the phone and dialled.

Kathleen picked up the phone at the first ring. 'Sally?'

'No, it's me, Liam.'

'Thank, God.'

'What's going on?

Kathleen spluttered as she spoke. 'She told me she was staying with Yasmin, her best friend ...' She sobbed uncontrollably.

Liam changed his tone and tried to calm her down. It failed. He continued. 'Sorry, carry on, Kath.'

'I called Yasmin's mother and she told me that Sally wasn't there ... and ... and hadn't been there at all.'

'Wha?'

Liam tried to reassure Kathleen. 'I'm sure she'll turn up. You know what teenagers are like.'

Kathleen spluttered. 'Felix is out looking for her.'

Zita walked through the open front door and pushed her head close to the receiver and listened.

Jimmy grabbed Liam's arm. 'Should we call the police?'

Liam covered the mouthpiece and spoke to him. 'Not yet.' He removed his hand and continued. 'Listen Kathleen, phone here as soon as you have any news.' He sighed. 'Sally will be fine. We'll bring her back.'

Kathleen replaced the phone and dropped down onto the settee, exhausted.

Liam turned to Zita and then Jimmy. 'It's the fucking drug-dealing ... it has to be.'

Zita grabbed their arms. 'Let's go and see Kathleen and find out what has really happened.'

Liam, Zita and Jimmy stood in the kitchen with Kathleen and Michelle.

Zita took control. 'Michelle, tell us what happened?'

Michelle shook as she flicked her mobile phone and silently reread the text she'd received from Sally.

'What does it say?' asked Zita. 'Read exactly what it says.'

Michelle nodded. She shook as she read it out.

'*Mum. My money was short. They will kill me if we don't pay them.*'

She reread the figure before saying it. '*A thousand pounds!*'

'Fuck!' raged Liam.

Jimmy screamed out. 'I'll kill the bastards who've got her! We can hit them now!'

Zita smirked. 'Jimmy, do you know who they are? Where they are?'

Jimmy sniffed and shook his head in embarrassment.

Zita continued. 'OK. We need to find out where they are and we need a plan. Wherever they are, you know they will be waiting for us.'

They both nodded.

Kathleen shook and screamed violently.

Zita raised her hands and attempted to console Kathleen. She waited, took a breath and as she continued she maintained direct eye contact with her. 'And, we don't want them to hurt Sally ... Do we?'

'None of us want that,' screamed an exhausted Kathleen.

Zita stood up and pointed at the mobile. 'Michelle, tell them we don't have the money but *we will* get it tomorrow.'

Liam looked at Zita. 'We've got the money–'

'They don't know dat.' Zita moved in close to Michelle and helped her to finish the text.

We will pay tomorrow - please don't hurt, Sally.

'We need to buy some time,' said Zita.

Jimmy fingered his Nokia, lifted his head and stared vacuously at Liam and then turned to Zita. 'Why the fuck don't you two have one of these?'

Liam grinned. 'You can be tracked ... they know where you are and ... where you've been.' He sniggered. 'Dad, maybe that's how they caught you last time. Did you ever think of that?'

Jimmy grunted. 'Um.'

Zita walked towards the front door. 'I have some things to do.'

Liam's head shook uncontrollably. 'How can you just walk off!' He tried to control his anger and frustration but failed. 'What about Sally?!'

Zita replied in a soft caring voice; one she had used many times when she spoke to him. 'Liam, that is what I am doing. We need a plan and it *must not fail* ... Right?' She forced a smile. 'Everything will be alright and we *will* bring Sally back home.' She could feel their frustration and lack of belief. 'They know we will pay dem ... so why should they hurt Sally?'

They all reluctantly nodded their agreement.

She shrugged and raised her voice. 'Listen, Liam ... standing around and talking about it won't get us anywhere. Go back to the hotel and have a rest. I will call you in a few hours. Okay?' She turned to Jimmy and noticed his jaundiced skin, as the cancer continued to advance around his body. 'Why don't you check your bike. You will need it soon enough.'

He liked the idea of getting out of the confusion and smiled at her. 'Okay.'

Zita looked at the clock and engaged both of them with a loud cough. 'I'll be back in a few hours. OK?' She waited for their agreement.

They all nodded.

'Be ready.' She paused. 'You must be ready when I get back.'

CHAPTER THIRTY-SIX

Sitting In the Park

Zita walked to Victoria Park Road and took the number 303 bus to Camden Market. She walked along Chalk Farm Road until she reached the public toilets. She changed into joggers, black trainers, faded denim jacket, a long black wig and a woollen beanie hat, then jammed her other clothes into a shoulder bag. She knew where she was going and deliberately took her time. To the undiscerning, she appeared to walk aimlessly between the food stalls, and looked blindly in the shop windows until she reached her first destination. She pointed at a 60 litre second-hand black rucksack hanging from a rail above her head and the stall holder hooked it down for her. She paid him and slipped her shoulder bag inside. She carefully picked her way through the market stalls and bought a handful of self-adhesive badges for different countries, walked to the toilet and stuck them all over the rucksack in such a way that they were easily visible. The next stall she stopped at sold army surplus clothes and second-hand workwear. She took her time to choose a dark blue boiler suit and paid in cash. She then made her way inside Stables Market and after taking her time to make her way through the various stalls, she checked the sizes and bought two more boiler suits. From a third stall she bought three balaclavas and a pack of black latex gloves, again paying in cash. When she smelt the sweet cannabis wafting through the open café door, she walked in. She ordered two coffees and while she waited, she spoke to the young girl sitting at the counter. Her answers to Zita's questions were little more than whispers.

Zita paid for the coffees and slid one along the counter, joined the young girl and they moved to a table near the window. They chatted animatedly until a young boy on a blue and white bike with black tape wound around the cross bar and handlebars, left his bike and walked inside and up to them. He passed the young girl a wrap and she paid him. Zita waved him away and watched him ride off.

Zita now had the information she needed, she thanked the girl and left. Her last stop was a second-hand shoe and boot stall where she bought three pairs of lightweight boots. Now, with everything stowed neatly in her rucksack, she made her way back to the public toilets. She removed the wig and changed into her original clothes but this time she put on a short blonde wig and NY logoed baseball cap. Looking every bit the tourist, she mingled amongst the crowd as she made her way slowly through the bustling Camden Market. She passed Camden Lock and crossed the Regent's Canal by the Chalk Farm Bridge Road.

It was a sunny afternoon and although it was late-November the low sun was still warm. After checking her watch, she took her time to begin the two mile walk along the tow path to Little Venice. When she reached the Cumberland Basin, she heard the strange sounds and looked across the canal where it ran through part of the Regent's Park Zoo. She could see the giraffe house and the huge aviary of exotic birds and paused to watch the caged Red River Hogs scavenging around in the mud. She continued her walk but stopped briefly to watch a lone cormorant dive beneath the dark still water and tried to guess where it would reappear. She looked in one direction but it appeared on the opposite end of the canal, and several yards away from where she had anticipated, with a perch which continued to wriggle in his beak. The cormorant swallowed it whole before diving again. When it reappeared without a fish, it balanced its webbed feet on the top of the water, shook its feathers, flapped its wings to remove the excess water and chortled loudly before swimming down the canal and diving again.

* * * *

Before flying to London six years earlier to carry out the assassination, Zita learned as much as she could about Little Venice and the immediate area. It was then that she discovered so much about one particular houseboat, the Astoria. She looked along the canal and, as she eyed a specific houseboat, she remembered the evening of 13th May 1995 and the last time she was there. Her target, a member of Hamas, the Palestinian militant group, had been the instigator of a lethal attack on two Israeli army vehicles, killing eleven young soldiers. He was immediately hailed a hero by the group but, following the euphoria and publicity, his name and photograph was leaked. The Palestinian fled and resurfaced in London under an assumed name and rented a houseboat. It took six days for the Mossad intelligence arm to track him down and Zita, as part of the elite Kidon unit, under the Caesaerea branch of the Mossad, was given the covert mission to assassinate him. She flew into Heathrow on the evening of Friday 12th May 1995 and booked into a dingy B & B, in Paddington. She carried out a reconnaissance trip of the target area at Little

Venice, early the next morning, and later that evening she walked onto the deck of the Palestinian's rented houseboat and tapped gently on the door. She pulled back her hoodie and smiled as the door partially opened. She took a step back and beamed at the frightened eyes that looked back at her. She carefully chose a few Arabic words. 'Hello, Ahmad …' She paused briefly. 'Ahmad Abadi?'

He was clearly in shock and pulled away from the door and thought hard about closing it.

She leaned towards the narrowing gap and smiled at him. She then took a step back and waited until he partially reopened the door. She held up the bulging plastic supermarket bag in her left hand. 'It's alright. I am here to help you … Okay?'

She could see he was confused when he appeared to ignore her question. Zita continued to speak to him in Arabic. 'You are perfectly safe, Ahmad, I live here in London and have been asked to bring you some things.' She continued to hold her smile and paused. 'How are you settling in?'

He nodded and the door slowly opened, a little at a time, until it was wide enough for Zita to reach him.

It was easy.

The Palestinian didn't have a chance.

The chunk of wood in Zita's right hand smashed into the side of his head. It had to be the same as that used to build the boat, to ensure her assassination went to plan and would be considered an accident.

He fell onto the floor.

When he woke up, he was dazed and confused. He reached up and felt the rope around his neck. Zita had control and held the other end. She knew she couldn't tie his hands or feet as that might leave marks and his death would then have been considered to be suspicious.

She tugged the rope and he fell onto the floor. She took a bottle of whiskey from the supermarket bag, opened it and pushed it into his hand. She grabbed his hair, pulled back his head and forced him to drink most of the contents, something he should not have been doing, until he was too drunk to have any idea what was happening. She pulled a plastic sheet from her knapsack flicked it open and laid it on the floor in front of the door. Still holding the rope, she walked him towards an armchair and let him slump into it while she placed a towel on the sheet and a second towel near the door. She took off her hoodie, jeans and shoes, grabbed the bag and quickly emptied it. She carefully laid new underwear, a tee-shirt and socks on the settee.

Assassinations were frequently left to the agent to improvise and Zita, having had detailed intelligence, knew her target couldn't swim. She partially opened the door and checked that there was no one walking along the tow path and bundled him out on deck. She manhandled him along the deck, smashed the timber into his forehead. She looked around and pushed him into the water, between the boat and the bank, and slipped in beside him.

For the first minutes he writhed and spluttered until she used her full weight and held his head beneath the water. Within minutes, his futile attempts at survival came to an abrupt end with a massive release of air as his lungs flooded. She shook her head and mumbled to herself. 'That's for those you killed.'

She climbed back on deck and went inside. Making sure she stood on the towel on the plastic sheet, she stripped and pushed her wet clothes into the plastic bag. She quickly put on her dry clothes, socks and shoes and her hoodie, rolled up the plastic sheet and pushed that inside too. She found his false passport, ID and money and pushed it into her pocket. She laid the empty whiskey bottle balancing on the edge of the table and, after wiping the door handle, she left.

When she reached Praed Street, behind Paddington Station, she deliberately exaggerated her furtive movements as she dropped the bag on top of an already overflowing rubbish bin, knowing that it would be grabbed, by one or other of the many homeless people who rummaged through them every night, and would fight for it as soon as she walked away.

The body of the dead man was found the next morning, by a young woman out walking her dog. Due to his intense black hair and olive complexion, the police called in Interpol, but no one of them were able to identify him. Following a post mortem, he was deemed to have consumed an excessive amount of alcohol, and hit his head before falling into the canal and drowning. The coroner ruled the death of the unknown foreign man to be misadventure and the case was closed.

What had been one of Zita's easiest *assassinations* earned her high praise from Efraim Halevy, the Director of Mossad.

Two days later she took the Eurostar from Waterloo International Station to the Brussels midi-hub and travelled on to Amsterdam where she spent a few days before flying from Schiphol back to Tel Aviv. It was during that visit to Amsterdam, having seen the houseboats in London, she set her heart on one day living on one of the many canals in the beautiful Dutch city.

CHAPTER THIRTY-SEVEN

Another Brick in The Wall

Zita shook away the memory, grabbed the rucksack, pulled it on and walked a few yards further along the tow path. She stopped and stood in awe, as she passed the beautiful and luxurious Regency houses in Maida Vale that backed onto the canal, of the grandeur and elegance of what had been such a decadent period. When she reached the wide-open pool of Little Venice, she saw the first of the many houseboats. She admired the luxurious brightly coloured houseboats and barges with their satellite dishes and decks overflowing with fading dahlias, begonias and fuchsias. She was immediately homesick and yearned for Amsterdam. She checked her watch and stopped again when she saw the empty seat near to the Astoria, the most beautiful and unusual houseboat on the water.

She pulled off her rucksack, sat down, closed her eyes and hummed to herself.

In 1989 she had visited Berlin with her mother and only days later, parts of the notorious dividing wall finally came crashing down. A Pink Floyd song, played by the band at the partially demolished wall, a year later, brought back memories of the jubilation and euphoria. She closed her eyes and began to hum to herself. It became very special to her and rekindled the wonderful celebrations she had had with her mother when Berliners from both sides of the wall were reunited for the first time in almost forty years.

She opened her eyes to see a middle-aged man walking his dog.

He smiled at her, stopped and sat down next to her. After staring across at the houseboats, he spoke to her. 'Hello.'

Zita nodded to him and smiled. 'Hello.'

'Sorry, but I heard you humming that song … *Another Brick in the Wall* … Pink Floyd?'

'Did you.' She blushed. 'Sorry.'

'No, it was nice,' he said. He pointed across at the Astoria houseboat. 'That boat has a wonderful story behind it.'

'Really?'

'Yes, and that song you were humming …' He paused and grinned at her. '… is part of it too.'

'Really, that sounds intriguing.' She smiled back at him. 'Tell me more.'

He took a huge breath. 'Well, the Astoria was built for Fred Carno in 1911. He was born in Exeter, and in 1986 moved to Nottingham before making his fortune from musical hall and his famous circus.'

'Wow.'

The man continued to spew out information. 'Yes, and do you know he discovered Charlie Chaplin and Stan Laurel.'

She frowned as she nodded. 'Sorry, I don't know any of them.'

The man ignored her. 'He …' He smiled. 'Sorry, Fred Carno already owned a hotel … The Karsino.' He pointed into the distance and continued. 'Overlooking the canal … and he wanted the best houseboat he could afford to moor alongside it.'

She faked shock. 'Wow.'

'He had it built with a mahogany frame and it cost 'im.' He paused. 'Let me see.' His fingers flicked out of control as he tried to calculate what may be the current cost. 'Ah. It would have cost what would now be about … half …' He paused, and turned to look at her. 'Half a million pounds.'

'Really.'

He shook his head wildly. 'Yeah. And do you know.' He laughed to himself. 'He wanted enough room to put a 90-piece orchestra on its top deck.' His laugh grew louder. 'And he did it!' He pointed at the elevated top deck roof enclosed with ornate metalwork, balustrades and a huge canopy. 'Fantastic innit?'

'Yeah,' she lied. She had researched it six years earlier and already knew everything he told her. She continued. 'So, what happened to him?'

The man continued his lengthy spiel, something he had done many times before to any stranger who would take the time to sit and listen to him.

Zita didn't hear any of it.

The man finished with a loud laugh, sniffed, leaned over and patted his dog.

Zita reached down and stroked him. 'What's his name?'

The man joined her and rubbed his dog's chest. 'River … he loves the water. Don't you boy?'

The dog licked his hand.

'That is an unusual name,' said Zita.

'It is. I called him that before I knew he loved the water so much.' He sat forward. 'Come on … let me tell you a bit more about this Fred Carno.' He grinned. 'He was a character alright.'

'I can't wait,' she said, as she sat back, stretched out her legs and kicked at the gravel with heal of her boots.

'In 1929 he moved to California for a while and brought the slapstick comedy ... you know ... custard pie fights and all that, to the silent pictures.' He looked at the stars and stripes badge on the rucksack and pointed at it. 'Movies.'

She nodded.

He stiffened. 'They didn't like 'im over there ...' He sniffed hard. 'And ... he didn't like them either. So, he came back 'ome.'

Zita nodded. 'Go on.'

'W ... e ... ll in 1986, David Gilmour bought it.'

She feigned confusion.

He tapped her knee. 'Well. You know ... the song you were humming. That was Pink Floyd – David Gilmour – *Another Brick in the Wall*'.

She threw her head back. 'Ah.'

'Well ... he bought it ... and put in a recording studio.'

'Really.'

'Yeah, he said he hated being inside ... in recording studios, for days ... weeks ... and months on end. So that's why he bought it. He moved here and built the studio.'

'Have you seen him?'

'Oh, yeah,' he said, as he pushed out his chest. 'He knows me, now.' He smiled proudly. 'I 'ad a cup of tea with 'im one afternoon.' He exhaled deeply and looked around. 'Well after all these years. Everybody that lives 'ere ... knows me,' he said, with a snigger. 'And River. Don't they boy?'

Zita nodded and checked her watch. She grabbed the bulging rucksack. 'Thank you … but I have to go now.'

The man stood up. 'Sure. I've held you up long enough.'

'No … no. It's been really interesting,' she lied.

The man reached out and shook her hand before he turned towards Camden. 'Nice to meet you. Safe journey.'

'Thanks,' said Zita. She paused and gave the dog a final stroke. 'Bye, River.'

The man didn't turn, instead he raised his hand and waved back at her.

When Zita reached Paddington, she took the number 205 bus to Kings Cross and a taxi to the deserted car park at the end of Wallis Road. She asked the driver to wait and returned five minutes later, having stowed the rucksack in a closed skip beneath the waste plastic in Player's yard, and made her final arrangements. The taxi took her back to Kings Cross where she took the number 63 bus to join Liam at the Travelodge in Shooters Hill.

Liam was asleep when she arrived. She left him to sleep and, as she had pulled on her leathers, she went through her plan in her mind before she woke him and asked him to call his father.

CHAPTER THIRTY-EIGHT

Leader Of the Pack

Zita and Liam left the Travelodge and arrived at Morepeth Road late in the afternoon. They parked their motorbike in front of the house.

Gwen, wearing the pale green Arabic maxi dress, looking as good as new after the fire, was in the kitchen with Martha who helped her to make a cup of tea.

Liam smiled at her. 'Hello, Mum.'

She fired him a lazy puzzled look.

Liam stammered as he tried to change tack. 'H … h … hello, have you seen, Jimmy …'

Gwen tilted her head and partially closed her eyes as she tried to think. 'I don't know anyone … called …' She couldn't finish the sentence. Her lips quivered in despair and her arms flailed around out of control.

Martha reached out to her and pacified her by passing her a dripping soapy saucepan and a towel to dry it, before she pointed out of the window and the neglected garden.

'Thanks,' said Liam.

Zita nodded and smiled back at her.

They walked down the path and through the overgrown garden.

Liam stopped and turned to Zita. 'I'm pleased we arranged for Martha to stay tonight. Who knows what the fuck is going to happen?'

'Don't worry, Liam. It will be alright.'

Liam mumbled his reply.

They reached the dilapidated garage and the door creaked loudly as Liam pushed it open.

Jimmy was busy checking his motorbike. He looked up at them and grinned broadly. 'Seems like old times, eh?'

Liam nodded. 'Yeah. I suppose it does.'

Jimmy wiped his greasy hands with an equally greasy rag which he threw into an open tool box. 'Give me a few minutes and we can go,' he said as he walked out of the garage.

Zita time to look around. Tools were positioned neatly on the wall inside the black outlines that identified where everything went. Thick cobwebs hung from the timber joists above a workbench and old chests of drawers filled much of the perimeter except for a nineteen fifties, partially glazed, free standing kitchen larder unit with a dropdown shelf. She couldn't resist. She opened each of the doors to reveal neatly stacked pots of paint, spare parts for his motorbike and neatly folded cloths. In the top cupboard was a display of tiny decorated vases, cups and thimbles, all souvenirs of his time fighting in Korea and pinned at the back was a thousand won banknote. She heard Jimmy walking down the path and closed the doors and drawers.

Jimmy's leathers hung on his emaciated body and as he struggled to pull up the zips he laughed loudly and patted his stomach. 'Look, they still fit.'

Zita and Liam looked at each other and forced disingenuous smiles.

Jimmy opened one of the drawers and pulled out a Stanley knife which he flicked open, and grinned to himself. He jabbed the shiny blade menacingly at an invisible assailant. 'I'll 'ave the bastards, alright,' he said, before slipping it into his leathers. He turned to Liam. 'He won't know what's 'it 'em,' he said. He reached into the bottom drawer, moved everything to one side and pulled out a cloth. He unwrapped it, removed a gun and checked it was loaded.

Liam looked at the weapon and shrugged. 'Are you sure you want to do this, Dad?'

Jimmy didn't hide his disgust. 'Fuck you, son. I'm dying anyway so what have *I* got to lose?'

'But … who will look after mum?'

Jimmy snarled back at him. 'Look after her … Do you seriously mean that?'

Liam gasped and pulled back in shock. 'Unbelievable.'

Jimmy scoffed at him. 'So, are you going to look after her then?'

Liam shook his head and turned his attention to a more immediate problem — the gun. 'I don't think you'll need that, Dad.'

'Who says?'

Liam stabbed his finger towards the gun and fired his father a serious but caring look. 'Do you really wanna go back inside for that?'

'Do you know what we'll be walking into, son?'

Zita fired Jimmy an assertive look, reached out her hand and, without a word, he placed it in her tiny palm. She checked it over and looked across at him. 'This is a blue steel 1962, new model Blackhawk.' She spoke as she checked the sights. '"Flattop" model–'

'Is it? All I know is it's a fucking gun and … it does the job for me.'

'Have you used this for anything? Robbery … Murder?' she asked.

He didn't reply, instead he yelled at her. 'It's loaded … be careful!'

Zita flicked the gun and without a second thought skilfully discharged the bullets, dropped them into her open palm and took her time to line them up on the bench. She broke down the gun and examined it. 'It needs to be cleaned … and oiled.'

Jimmy dropped his lower lip and looked at her.

'Well, have you got any?' asked Zita, failing to hide her impatience.

Jimmy pulled his head back and stared blindly at her.

Zita continued. 'Oil.'

He shook himself into action and searched frantically, opening and slamming every drawer and cupboard until he pulled out a dented 1960s Wesco pump action oil can. He handed it to her and watched in amazement as she cleaned and oiled the gun before she replaced the bullets and graciously handed it back to him. 'Be careful …' She clicked her tongue. 'It's loaded …' she said, flippantly.

Liam shook his head in disbelief at what had just played out in front of him. 'Fine. But just be careful, Dad … and leave it to us. We don't want you going back inside again *now*.'

'Fair play, son.' He sniffed hard. 'But I am taking it.' He squeezed the gun into another of his pockets, turned towards Zita and continued. 'And … I *will use it* … if I need to,' he said, defiantly patting the bulging leather.

'Course you will,' jested Liam.

Jimmy didn't hide his disgust. 'Fuck you, son. I've already told you I'm dying–'

'So, all the more reason to make arrangements for someone to look after mum.'

Jimmy snarled back at him. 'Fuck you?'

'You haven't, have you?'

Jimmy shook his head, climbed on the bike, fired it up and dropped it off the stand. 'Come on, son, open the door?'

Zita noticed the mobile phone in one of his top pockets. She pointed at it. 'Can you leave that here … Please?'

'Why?'

'I'm sure Liam will explain …'

'Come on, Dad, I'll tell you later … that's why we don't have one.' Liam squeezed the phone out of his father's pocket and dropped it in the top drawer. He pushed the double doors open and, as Jimmy made his way towards the back lane, he called out. 'I'll see you out front.'

Zita closed the doors, took off her leathers and stowed them in a drawer. She changed into her jeans, shirt and jacket, pulled on a blonde wig and woolly hat and walked to Victoria Park Road where she took a taxi to the deserted car park at the end of Wallis Road.

Jimmy and Liam spent the next hour riding separately in nonsensical routes and in all directions around London, to confuse anyone who might decide to check the CCTV tapes.

Zita had broken into Player's office the previous night and smashed the computer linked to his outdated CCTV and chosen the keys for the vehicle she needed. The van with a side opening door had a dividing rail down the middle, that had been fitted to retain the double-glazed units and pvc window frames and doors when they were delivered to the job.

The yard gate was partially open and wide enough for Liam and Jimmy to ride in. Zita was waiting for them and had already changed into her second-hand overalls, boots and balaclava. She closed the gate behind them and guided them to an area at the rear of the building, hidden from the road. She had emptied the van and after sliding open the side door she walked around and opened the rear doors. She effortlessly picked up a scaffold board and slid it onto the back edge of the van which she followed up with a second. She lined them up side by side, tied them together and pointed. 'Come on, get your bikes up there and … inside.'

Balancing the bikes on the scaffold boards was not easy but one at a time they manhandled them into the van and tied one to each side of the mid rail. Zita checked that they were secure and slid the scaffold boards between them before she closed the rear doors and walked to the front of the van. She opened both doors and pointed at Jimmy's and Liam's boots, dark blue overalls and balaclavas that were laid out neatly on each of the front seats.

She stood beside the van and repeatedly kicked at the ground while she waited impatiently for them to change. *She preferred to work alone, and sometimes with Liam, but to have Jimmy, who was old and sick, did leave her with doubts which seemed to increase as the valuable time ticked on.*

Once Jimmy and Liam had changed and were sat in the front cab, she issued her final instruction. 'Put your balaclavas on but keep them down until we get to the warehouse.'

'Do we have to wear these?' asked Liam.

'Yes. You do … and until we're finished. OK!'

Liam lowered his head in submission.

Zita shrugged as she walked towards the gates and swung them wide open. She waited until the van was out on the road and after closing the gates, she climbed in the side door. She punched out at one of the bulging plastic bags that hung from a metal bar, and watched it swing back and forth before she slid the door closed behind her. She checked that everything was in place and tapped on the bulkhead.

Jimmy pulled away.

He drove the easily identifiable sign written van across the city, and again zig zagging, to confuse anyone who might see them or decide to check any CCTV footage later.

When they reached the dilapidated warehouse on the rundown trading estate in Hackney Wick, they parked fifty yards from the side of the building. Jimmy and Liam climbed out of the van and unusually for Liam he felt a shiver race up his spine in anticipation of what he may find inside.

He shook it away.

Zita motioned to them to pull up their balaclavas.

As they walked slowly towards the large building, keeping in the shadows of the perimeter, they pulled back, shocked at the tangle of pushbikes in all shapes and sizes laid haphazardly against the building. Zita noticed the blue and white bike she had seen several times before and nodded and grinned. She guided them to the side door that she had already identified. When they heard the loud and aggressive foreign voices inside, they stopped. Liam was ready to rush in but Zita held him back. She whispered to him. 'We must wait, Liam–'

'But they may have Sally,' he mouthed. 'We have to do something … Now!'

Zita ignored his outburst and continued in a soft authoritative voice. 'There are latex gloves in your pockets, put them on.' She spoke as she pulled on her own gloves before she checked and adjusted their balaclavas to fully obscure their faces. She patted each of them on the shoulder. 'Stay here and wait for me.'

Liam and Jimmy both fired her confused looks. 'Wha?'

She spoke in a soft reassuring voice. '*You will know when.*' She turned to Jimmy and then back to Liam. 'Okay?'

Reluctantly, they both nodded their adrenaline rushed nervous agreement.

Jimmy's body language exuded excitement and self-confidence as he ritually checked his pockets.

CHAPTER THIRTY-NINE

When The Going Gets Tough

Zita adjusted her balaclava to cover most of her face and disappeared into the darkness of the vast building. She was gone for what seemed like ages. As always, she looked for an exit route and what could also be an escape route for the drug dealers. Her eyes then scanned everything around her as she looked for anything that could be of use. She climbed high into the roof and looked down at what was unfolding below her. The illegal occupants had rigged up a string of temporary festoon lights which they had connected to the incoming electric main. She listened and watched the leader, a Roma with a sculptured beard and nose ring. His long hair raked back tightly from his forehead and tied into a ponytail which exposed the numerous tattoos on his neck, the thick gold chain that framed it and several gold rings in his ears. He wore a tight body-hugging black vest which accentuated his well-honed muscular body. He sat erect and proud behind a raised makeshift desk – a faded sapele office door, with the missing letters **O** and **C**, was laid across a makeshift pile of pallets. He stroked the powerful grey mottled pit-bull terrier, chained to one of the pallets supporting his desk, with one of his boots. He took an extended drag on a joint, while in front of him a long line of young submissive boys and girls, mostly teenagers but some much younger, many still wearing their school uniform, stood to attention waiting for their *interview*. Zita could see that he loved to be in control. He puckered his lips and whistled and when they all turned to him, he grinned and clicked his tongue. His fingers danced across the keys of his Nokia 2110 and he alternated it by tapping the Belgian made, Browning 9mm handgun beside him. It was his way of raising the level of fear, terrorising them and focusing their minds on why they were there. He raised his head and looked towards the door. 'Florin!'

Florin, a giant of a man with long curly hair, who wore a calf length black leather coat reminiscent of the Nazi SS, clicked his ankle boots and feigned standing to attention. 'Da, sefu, Mihai,' he said, with a mock salute.

Mihai shouted back at him. 'Where is Ebanie? Where is my coffee?'

Florin opened the door and looked around. 'She is not here ...' He rechecked the service road and continued. 'Yet.'

Mihai grunted.

Holomek, stood closest to the leader. He wore a filthy denim shirt, cargo trousers and cowboy boots and stroked at his spiky dyed blonde hair with his huge hands, tattooed with swastikas. He chose to answer before he was asked the question. 'Da, Mihai.'

Mihai grunted and took his time to eye up every one of his *agents* in the queue and raised his right arm. He stopped at the young boy, his face a mass of acne. Zita recognised him from Camden Market and his blue and white pushbike. He stepped nervously forward and quoted the number. 'Twenty-one.' He trembled as he stood to attention while Mihai lit another joint and blew the sweet-smelling smoke towards the boy. With the joint still in his mouth he hummed to himself as he flicked through the

235

pages of his notebook until he found page twenty-one. He held his pen poised over the page. He lowered the book and picked up his gun and pointed it menacingly at the boy.

The young boy pissed himself.

Mihai chuckled as the urine splashed onto the dusty concrete floor. He cocked his gun and waved it, purposefully along the line of kids, targeting each of them in turn. As they all pulled back in fear, he grunted and laid it on his desk. He looked down at the urine-soaked concrete, tutted and slowly tilted his head back. He forced an idiotic grin at the boy and exaggerated an intimidating threatening forward jolt of his head. He grinned as he immediately lowered it. 'How much?' he asked, without looking up.

The young boy stuttered his reply. 'Seven … seven … seventy-five pounds.'

Mihai tilted the page towards the light hanging from the cable directly above him and double-checked the figure. 'Eighty pounds. The amount is eighty pounds!' he pushed himself back in the chair. 'Not enough. Where is the other five pounds, eh?'

The boy cowered in front of him and shook uncontrollably as he handed the money to Holomek.

He counted it. 'Seventy-five … Only.' He counted it again and nodded to Mihai before he pushed it through the jagged makeshift slit in the top of a metal box beside the desk.

'So, where is it?' asked Mihai, forcing a phoney voice of concern. Without any warning he grunted and the scared dog, baring its teeth, raced threateningly towards the boy. It was jerked back with a pained yelp as the fully extended chain tightened around his neck. The dog ended up a few inches from the boy's feet. The boy stumbled and fell. He looked at the dog who continued to snarl at him, and then Mihai, his ashen face pale and terrified. Mihai continued to taunt him as the boy scrambled around on the floor and pushed himself to his feet with his urine covered hands. He stood shaking while the dog continued to snarl at him and strain menacingly on the chain.

The boy shrunk in sheer terror as Holomek moved ominously towards him and pulled a knife from his boot. He tried once more to reply but a lengthy nonsensical spluttered response was all he could manage.

Holomek slapped him hard across his head and the boy screamed out in pain.

Mihai slowly raised his arm and after grabbing the boy's attention pointed at the naked young girl, her arms and legs splayed on another door. 'If you do dis again.' To heighten the tension, and fear, he paused and then sighed. 'Dat *will be* you.' He licked his lips and looked around at his henchmen. 'We also … like young boys … *de asememea*,' he said, as he cackled and clicked his tongue.

Florin grunted and repeatedly banged hard on the metal door while Holomek and the fourth man joined him with laughs of depraved madness.

'OK,' said Mihai. He reached into his jacket pocket and took out two ten-pound notes. He made to hand them to the boy but pulled back. 'I pay you nothing this time.' He snorted. 'To teach you a lesson.' He took his time to look along the line of terrified kids. 'All of you must remember this …' He pushed out his chest and beat it with a closed fist. 'Don't cheat, Mihai!' He stood up and after straightening his body his voice reached a crescendo. 'I will kill you all!' He salivated and wiped his mouth. 'Rip out your hearts … and eat them!' He exhaled his anger and sat down. He handed the boy a packet of E's and made a note on his page. 'This time.' He looked up and snarled. 'It is ninety pounds ...' He flicked one of the packets. 'Each of these liddle beaudies is *five pounds*.' He glared at him. 'Okay?'

The boy nodded erratically.

'Remember ... what Mihai says.' He inhaled before he continued. 'Next time. Bring it all!'

The boy rubbed at his throbbing head and shuffled off towards Florin and the closed door. The Roma unbolted it and pushed it open far enough to allow the boy to squeeze through. As the boy crouched beneath one arm Florin grunted and smacked him across his already painful head.

Zita chose that moment and pulled the switch on the electric mains. The lights flickered briefly and Mihai appeared nervous. He stretched out his fingers and they twitched wildly as he looked towards Florin. He screamed out. 'Florin, nu lasati niciunul dintre acesti nemernici sa plece pana cand asa spun!'

'Yes, boss,' shouted Florin, as he nodded and slammed the bolts hard across the door.

Mihai allowed a maniacal self-gratifying grin to escape across his face. 'Next.' He stared hard at a young girl and as she stepped forward, he drew her attention to the other girl, tied to a makeshift table. She trembled with fear. Mihai seemed to relish her panic and licked his lips, salaciously. He beckoned her to come closer and as she approached him, he took a huge drag on his joint and blew the sweet smoke in her face. 'Your nummer?'

Her reply was inaudible to Zita as she moved silently between the piles of empty and crumpled boxes, pallets, crates and redundant machinery. She saw a fourth man who stood over the naked young girl that lay spreadeagled on a table, her arms and legs bound with cable ties. He held a screwdriver in one hand and a hypodermic syringe in the other and alternated them as he made threatening, stabbing actions towards her.

She whimpered and shook in abject terror.

Zita took a second look and realised it was Sally tied to the makeshift table. She watched Mihai grin to himself as he nodded to the fourth man. He was much smaller than the others but also had an intimidating look. His head had been shaved to leave a strip of hair in the centre which formed a Mohican. He wore a dirty Ramone's tee-shirt, advertising their 1977 *Rocket to Russia* album, with the black and white photo and their name in pink on the cover, which hung outside of his ripped jeans, and mud splattered Adidas trainers. He spat and babbled with obscene pleasure as he tormented the naked Sally prodding her pert young breasts and brushing her short vaginal hair with the back of his filthy hand.

Mihai clicked his teeth. 'Yoyo, don't damage her.' He roared loudly. 'Save her for me …'

'Yeah, sure, boss,' replied Yoyo, with a confident shrug of misplaced authority. And as part of a deliberate tactic of reinforcing Mihai's control and ramping up the intimidation of his agents, Yoyo prodded Sally again and grabbed at his groin and thrust his hips back and forth. It had the desired effect and as she whimpered and cried out in frenzied terror those in the queue trembled and mumbled their fear.

Zita quaked with anger and wanted to act on her own. Instead, she took a long deep breath and held it until she had calmed down. She knew she was ready to begin. She held her breath and exhaled slowly.

CHAPTER FORTY

I Don't Believe in Miracles

Zita returned to Jimmy and Liam, pulled them into her and whispered. 'There are four of dem. And …' She paused. 'There are children in there. A lot of dem.' She exhaled. 'We must get them out first.' She paused and lowered her head. 'Well … as soon as we can.' She hesitated. 'There is also a vicious dog, so be careful.'

They froze.

'It looks like he has been used for dog fighting, so, will be very dangerous – if he bites you.' She pointed towards the building and waved her finger erratically. 'The kids must not see what happens to those vile bastards – the dealers.' She glanced at Jimmy and whispered. 'Jimmy, you must take care of the man at the door.' She paused. 'Be careful, he is a big one.'

Jimmy grinned as he felt his bulging pockets and nodded. 'Okay. Just tell me when,' he said glibly.

Zita eyed Liam who was twitching, ready to explode. She moved up close to him and clamped his arms to his side. She lowered her voice and whispered in his ear. 'Sally *is* here.'

'Wha?'

Zita pushed his balaclava hard against his mouth. 'She is safe … I know you will want to go to her but … but first … *first* you must take care of the man beside the table.'

He nodded his dazed reply. 'Table … yeah … yeah … the table …'

Zita continued. 'I will take care of the leader … *behind* the desk.' She paused as she replayed her plan in her head. 'I have released the door at the back.' She smirked. 'It's the broken *blue one*.' She paused again and stressed her next words. 'Take care because it may be noisy …' She pursed her lips, straightened her index finger and pushed it hard over her mouth, also hidden by the balaclava. 'So … open it … slowly. Remember … very slowly.' She paused. 'Okay?'

Their responses were muted grunts as they both punched the air.

Zita continued. 'And … wait until I give the signal.' She looked at each of them in turn. 'Okay?' She took a huge breath and gave herself the time to allow the adrenalin to pump throughout her body. 'This will not be so easy.' She tapped one side of her head with a closed fist, emulating a boxer before a fight, and after raising her hand and tightening the gloves she made a solid fist and disappeared.

Liam and Jimmy took their time to walk around the building, taking care not to tread on anything that would give them away, until they saw the blue door. Jimmy trembled as he slowly pushed it open, wide enough for him to squeeze in.

Liam followed him into the deep dark shadows that were exaggerated by the quickly fading light that managed to find its way through the broken rooflights and corrugated asbestos sheets high above them.

Seconds later, and without any warning, Zita swung out of the darkness on a chain, and screamed like a banshee as she flew through the air making sure to avoid the young girl standing in front of the desk. She kicked out with both feet and one boot crashed into Holomek, who stood beside the desk, and the other into Mihai, whose head lurched forward. Holomek fell and lay spreadeagled on the floor while Mihai's nose was split and oozed blood after it had smashed into the makeshift desk. The impact had spilled the drugs and sent Mihai's handgun clattering along the dusty floor. His chair flew across the warehouse releasing the chained dog.

It raced towards Sally and snarled as it stood guard over her.

On the return swing, as Holomek tried to get up, Zita crashed into him again. He fell awkwardly and lay slumped in a heap on the floor. As Zita released the chain Yoyo, still holding the screwdriver and hypodermic, rushed menacingly towards her.

Liam appeared from nowhere, he grabbed his hand and twisted it violently, until his arm shattered at the elbow with a loud crack. The Roma screamed in agony and dropped the screwdriver from his free-swinging hand. When Liam saw Sally lying naked in front of him, he reached down and grabbed Yoyo's ears, pulled his head towards him and head-butted him, splitting his nose. Then, as he fell forward, Liam punched his daughter's torturer and vented his pent-up anger with an unassailable flurry of violent, well-placed kicks. Liam wasn't finished. He pulled back Yoyo's broken arm and punched him in the throat. While Yoyo lay motionless on the floor, Liam grabbed at his ridiculous line of hair, threw him to the ground and repeatedly stamped on his head and chest. The Roma's mouth was a bloody seeping mess. His lips were split open and several of his front teeth had been knocked out.

Jimmy forgot his cancer and felt alive as he rushed towards Florin who remained, as instructed by Mihai, on guard at the door. In a pathetic token gesture, Jimmy pointed his gun at him and motioned to him to open the door.

Florin ignored him and instead fired an inane grin back at him.

Jimmy cocked the gun and this time it had the desired effect. The giant of a man looked across the warehouse for instructions from Mihai but on seeing what was unfolding, he reluctantly pushed it open. Jimmy raised his free arm and pointed towards the open door and screamed at the terror ridden kids to leave. *He still believed he had it in him to be a successful criminal … but deep down he knew he didn't.* The kids looked across at the tightly restrained Sally and remained frozen in terror.

They couldn't move.

Jimmy screamed at them 'Get the hell out of here … NOW!'

As they all rushed towards him, the open door and their freedom, their horrific screams and shrieks filled the cavernous void.

Jimmy roared after them. 'Don't come back!'

Zita looked furtively around, picked up a shirt, tossed it to Jimmy and motioned to him to cover the naked and quivering Sally. For a split second he forgot he had the gun in his hand and as he reached out to catch the shirt it fired, blowing off the ear and earring of Florin, who for some reason still remained at the now open door. In sheer disbelief, he shook his head and, as the blood poured from what was left of that side of his head, he reached up and tried to cover the damage with his huge fingers.

Jimmy looked down at the smoking gun in disbelief at the fact that he had fired it.

Florin seized the opportunity and disappeared through the door. He raced in the same direction as the kids who were celebrating their unexpected release with whoops of joy. His reappearance rekindled their terror and they screamed as they split up and peddled like hell, racing off in all directions.

Zita rushed towards the makeshift desk and the slumped Mihai who still lay confused and shaken. She jumped on it and spread her legs either side of him. She grabbed his ponytail and yanked it hard. She smelt the stink of him in her nostrils, something that was so common in violent men. She pulled his head back, slapped him across the face with the back of her gloved hand and followed it up with her boot heel to his kidneys. He crumbled in agony, slid between her legs, and landed awkwardly on his knees. She jumped down and followed up with a chop to the throat. He fell back, leaving one leg trapped beneath the other. She now turned her attention to the dazed Holomek that had once stood arrogant and threateningly beside Mihai's desk. After picking him up, Zita twisted his right arm until the breaking bones punctured his skin. His pained screams continued to reverberate around the warehouse as she inflicted even more pain on him until he fell to the floor.

Jimmy watched in disbelief and awe as Zita and Liam continued to mete out their punishing violence. 'Fuck!'

As Holomek and Yoyo lay moaning on the ground Jimmy walked across and looked down at them, not knowing if Zita and Liam had finished their attack or if he should get involved. He silently quizzed Zita and then spoke his thoughts. 'Fuck ... You *are* a killing machine–'

'I know,' said Zita, as she grinned back at him. 'It's my job.' She reached her right hand across her chest and tapped the front of her opposite shoulder. 'What I was trained to do.'

Sally remained terrified and motionless on the makeshift torturers table.

As Liam and Zita, their faces covered, walked towards her with sheer terror in her young eyes, the tears rolled down her face and she screamed out.

When they pulled off their balaclavas, she let out a huge yell followed by quivering sighs of breathless relief. 'Thank God,' she spluttered. She raised her head and looked towards Zita. 'Thank you ... Zita.'

It was the first time Sally had spoken her name.

Sally looked nervously around at the large man still wearing his balaclava and screamed as he walked towards her.

Zita gesticulated and shouted. 'Take it off!'

Jimmy pulled off his balaclava and exhaled his liberation.

She motioned to him to cut Sally free. He pulled out his Stanley knife and relished the moment. With several precise strokes he released her arms and legs, then reached down and pulled the shirt tightly around her.

Zita waited for the terror to drain from Sally's face before she helped the shocked and shaking teenager off the table. 'It's over now, Sally,' she said softly, 'you will be home soon.'

Sally's teeth chattered as she desperately struggled to reply. She looked up at her. 'Th ... th ... thank you.'

Liam reached out, grabbed his quivering teenage daughter and held her tight. He looked over her shoulders at Zita before looking down at Yoyo, Holomek and Mihai.

Her eyes followed his.

He spoke to Zita in a subdued voice from behind his hand. 'We can't let these maggots back out onto our streets,' he said. He turned to Jimmy. 'Can we?'

He didn't react.

Liam turned back to Zita. 'Can we?'

'Fuck,' exclaimed Jimmy. 'Fuck … Fuck …' Although the adrenaline still pumped through his body, he was confused. He raised his gun and the open gloved palm of his other hand, in deference. 'I dunno …'

Liam looked hard at Sally and, seeing how traumatised she was, he made his decision.

Zita beat him to it. 'Jimmy, can you take Sally outside … Please?'

He nodded his relief at the decision that had been made for him.

Zita walked across to the stunned teenager, hugged her and spoke in a soft, reassuring voice. Something she had been trained to do and had done many times before. 'Sally, look at me.' She waited until Sally made eye contact. 'You really are safe now. There are some clean clothes in the bag. It is hanging inside for you in the van.' Sally stiffened. 'Jimmy will take you. Don't worry.' She held her tighter. 'Put them on and we will come and get you.'

The teenage girl stood frozen, her heart racing and her vision blurred with her tears. The dog moved out from beneath the door where Sally had been tied and licked at her bare legs. She looked at Liam and then Zita. 'Can we take him home?'

'What?'

She reached down and the dog licked her shaking hand. 'Please.'

'You need to ask your mother,' said Liam.

Zita removed the chain from the dog's neck, picked up a rope, cut off a length, tied one end around the dog's neck and handed the other end to Sally. 'We can take him with us.' She smiled. 'I'm sure you will be able to keep him.' She turned to Jimmy. 'Don't you think?'

'Course,' said Jimmy, with a restrained smile of reassurance.

Liam finally nodded his approval.

Zita walked across to Jimmy, reached out her hand and asked him for his gun. He handed it to her. She gave it a cursory look, cocked it and told Sally to hold the dog and cover her ears before she fired it repeatedly in the direction of their prisoners, deliberately missing them. When it was empty, she pushed it into Mihai's hand, squeezed it hard against the handle, released it and threw it across the warehouse. She grinned as she picked up Mihai's Browning. 'Have this one,' she said, as she handed it to Jimmy. 'Keep it safe. Keep it very … very safe.' She paused and grinned facetiously at Jimmy. 'Remember …' She clicked her tongue. 'It is loaded.'

While Jimmy admired his new weapon, Zita turned to Sally, hugged her again and gave her a reassuring smile. 'You *must* go now, Sally.' She pointed towards the open door and lowered her voice. 'Please go and get dressed.' She pointed at the dog. 'And don't forget to take your friend.'

Sally looked down at the dog and then smiled back at Zita.

After examining the gun Jimmy slid it cautiously into his overalls. He reached out, put his arms around Sally, scooped her up and carried her out of the warehouse. He slid the side door of the van open and helped her to climb inside.

The dog jumped in behind her.

Jimmy reached for one of the bags of clothes, handed it to her and closed the door. 'Put these on ... and tell me when you're ready. Okay?'

She whimpered her unintelligible reply between sobs and splutters, and licks from the dog.

CHAPTER FORTY-ONE

All Cried Out

Zita motioned to Liam for his help. She grabbed the unconscious Mihai by his ponytail while Liam snatched his feet and they lifted him onto the same door where Sally had been restrained. She tied his wrists and ankles and pointed towards Liam's zip. 'We need to wake him up.'

Liam fired her a confused look.

'Go on.'

At first Liam refused but after she egged him on, he scrambled onto the table and pissed in the Roma's face.

Mihai woke with a splutter. 'Ce dracu.' He shook his head and tried to move. 'What the fuck?'

'Buna ziua,' purred Zita, cheekily in Romanian. 'Good evening. You were sleeping like baby.' She giggled. 'Did you enjoy your sleep?'

'Vei plati pentru rahatul tau.' He scrunched his face and felt the congealed blood in his mouth. He spat some of it out and continued. 'You will pay for this shit of yours–'

'Zigeuner, bastard!' screamed Zita, as she smacked him across his face with an open hand.

'Nu platesc niciodata … I never … *pay*,' sneered Mihai.

'You will this time, mate!' screamed Liam, as he slammed his open hands hard on the door beside Mihai. 'That was *my* daughter!'

Mihai forced a pained grin. 'She was fresh ...' He spat out more of the thick dark blood through his split and swollen mouth. 'Very fresh ... like a ripe piersica – a peach.'

Liam picked up the hammer that Holomek had also used to antagonise the young kids and brought it down on Mihai's hands, crushing all of his fingers. He threw the hammer across the workshop where it landed with an echoed clatter. He raised his right leg and brought the heel of his boot down in the Roma's groin. Mihai's whole body stiffened in agony as once again screams reverberated through the cavernous warehouse.

Zita pulled the moon knife from her pocket and waited until Mihai's eyes were fixed on the blade. It was clear he'd never seen anything like it.

She looked intently at Liam and waited until she had his full attention. 'Liam, turn his head around.' She pointed. 'Away from me, I don't want any of this bastard's blood on me.' She grabbed Mihai's ponytail firmly and made several quick semi-circular cuts on either side of his hairline. She jerked and twisted it until the scalp separated from the skull along the areolar connective tissue. Mihai was left with his exposed skull a mess of red and pink flesh and bleeding capillaries. She pushed her face into his and for the first time noticed his decayed blood-stained teeth. She pulled his mouth open and shoved the intact ponytail into his mouth. 'You won't be needing the haircut any more,' she said, frivolously.

He was unable to answer and her began to choke.

She screwed up her face in disgust and turned to Liam. 'We can do better than that.' She paused. '*Much better,*' she said, with an exaggerated shrug of her shoulders. She tore the gold necklace from the Roma, ripped out his gold earrings and tore the rings from his fingers and nose and slid them all into her pocket. She stroked her chin and paused before she reached down and exaggerated her movements as she theatrically sliced through Mihai's trousers, exposing his tight silk underpants. She looked up at Liam. 'Lift his head – I want him to see this.'

Liam jumped off the table, grabbed at Mihai's bleeding head and jerked it wildly until he held it firmly in his blood covered gloves. He lifted the Roma's neck and jerked it forward.

Zita took a step back and tilted her head and thought. She looked at Liam and drew circles in the air with the index finger of her left hand. She took her time to make a big deal of slowly wiping the blood from one arm of her overalls. She continued. 'Nice … clothes.'

Mihai looked bewildered and trembled. He mumbled his confusion.

She turned to Liam and grinned inanely. 'Do you remember the fat Greek?'

Liam's face exploded with the memory. 'Oh, yeah,' he said, nodding wildly. He stopped abruptly and reached at his throat and recalled the damage and recurring pain caused by the violent action of Skipio, the Greek, as he forced the toothbrush down his throat many months earlier in Amsterdam. He urged and fought to catch his breath before he continued. 'Oh, yeah,' he replied, with a pained raspy voice. 'I sure do.'

Zita held up the moon knife, ran her thumb along the weird razor-sharp edge, and then spat on it. She flicked up Mihai's penis on the wide blade of the knife and held it there. She took her time to taunt him in his own language and with every extended syllable his screams of desperation grew louder.

Liam tightened his grip on their victim's bloody skull and raised it further, ensuring that he could see everything.

It was now Mihai's turn to piss himself.

Zita looked into the Roma's eyes and fired him a tortured grin. She sliced through his scrotum, removed the testicles and placed them on the makeshift table beside him.

Liam smashed him in the face and then pushed the ponytail deeper down his throat.

He waited.

On cue, Zita slit Mihai's throat.

They now turned their attention to the semi-conscious Holomek and both showed their disgust with silent shrugs. She knelt down, leaned over him and sliced deep into his wrists and throat with short, sharp, precise thrusts leaving him to bleed out.

Liam watched as Zita calmly sliced a piece from Mihai's blood-stained shirt and wiped the blade before she pushed his fingers against one side of the knife leaving his prints.

'What the hell is that?' asked a confused Liam.

'Something different.' She grinned. 'Don't you know it – have you seen it before this day?'

Liam shook his head.

She continued. 'It's a mezzaluna – a moon knife – "Don Carlos" and …' She pushed it towards him and grinned as she fearlessly slid her latex glove along the blade. 'Razor sharp.' She pointed her thumb towards him and showed him that she had pierced the latex without cutting into the skin. Her grin widened 'A present from … your old friend Mad Max Player.'

'Wha?'

'They use it for fitting the glass and trims in plastic windows. It will be so easy to be identified by forensics and traced back to him and ...' She pointed at Mihai. 'And him.'

'But Player's in hospital–'

'I know.' She giggled. 'Won't it confuse dem ... all of dem?' She paused. 'And your ... policeman friend ... Fuller?' She slid the knife into the makeshift cardboard case in her pocket.

Liam shook his head in disbelief. 'He's no fucking friend of mine ... right!'

Before Zita could reply, she heard Yoyo behind her.

The Roma groaned in agony as he tried to slide across the floor and make his escape.

Liam turned and took his time to walk towards him. He picked up the hypodermic syringe and stabbed it in Yoyo's right eye. While the Roma screamed out in pain, Liam stood over him and exhaled his extreme anger and bent-up fury with a painful scream as he released a barrage of kicks and stamps until Yoyo was dead and unrecognisable.

Zita had already turned her attention to the metal box. She kicked at it repeatedly with the heel of her boot until it split open. She pulled a carrier bag from her pocket, shook it until it opened and handed it to an exhausted Liam. 'Can you hold this.'

He trembled as he took it from her and held it while she forced all of the money into it.

'Maybe the kids can have a party,' she said, as she took the bulging bag from Liam and held it up. 'Or do something else with this?' She paused. 'Maybe there is a youth club?'

Liam shrugged and looked back at the bloody heap that was once Yoyo. 'I've no idea.'

Zita tugged at what was left of Mihai's bloody ponytail and dropped some of his hairs still attached to his scalp into the bag on top of the money. She picked up his notebook, flicked through the pages and, as she skimmed through them, her anger grew and grew. She cursed as she handed it to Liam. 'Rip out all the pages and burn them. Okay?'

'Yeah. Sure.'

She paused briefly. 'So, do you realise Liam that dese drugs will get much worse over the years ahead of us?'

He shook his head and took a huge breath. 'Yeah, I know.' He took his time to exhale. 'God help us … all.'

Zita looked down at the drugs spread across the warehouse floor. She picked up a handful and dropped them into the bag along with the money. She briefly closed her eyes and, as she opened them, she grinned. 'Liam, we will leave dem where they are. It will confuse the police and maybe they will think it is turf war between dealers.'

Liam replied with a shrug. 'If you say so.'

They left the warehouse without looking back and made their way in silence to the van. Sally was already dressed and squatted against one of the motorbikes, with the dog on one side and cuddled into Jimmy on the other.

Zita smiled at her. 'You are safe now … Sally.'

Sally's heart was racing and her vision still blurred with her tears. She nodded slowly and, as she reached down to stroke the dog, she gave Zita a kiss. 'Thank you … Thank you … so much, Zita,' she said.

Liam still shook with anger as he jumped into the van and reached out to hug Sally. The dog snarled and growled menacingly at him. 'He's protecting me, Dad,' she said, proudly. She stroked the dog and after she murmured to him, he lay down beside her and dropped his head in her lap.

Zita pushed the plastic bag containing the money into her backpack and hung it on a hook above her.

Liam shuddered with relief as he pulled Sally into him. 'You will be alright now. They won't bother you … or any of the other kids.'

'Are you sure?' she asked, through her chattering teeth.

Jimmy moved closer towards her and nodded. 'I'm sure.' He grinned at Zita and Liam. 'That was some show alright.'

Zita remained stony faced as she nodded.

Jimmy shrugged, walked around the van and climbed into the driver's seat and Liam jumped in beside him.

Zita reached through the side door, grabbed the plastic bag and waited to change. She sat beside Sally and spent a few minutes brushing her hair and straightening her clothes. She pulled her head back and looked at her. 'You look lovely, now.'

'Thanks, Zita,' said Sally, appreciatively.

CHAPTER FORTY-TWO

Master Blaster

Zita slammed the side door closed and when she tapped the bulkhead the van pulled away. But after only driving a few yards, Jimmy turned the steering wheel and drove back to the rear of the warehouse and braked hard. It threw Zita, Sally and the dog into the motorbikes.

Zita banged repeatedly on the bulkhead. 'Jimmy, what the hell is happening?' she screamed.

He didn't reply. He left the engine running and leapt out of the van. 'Liam, I won't be a minute.' He rushed towards the warehouse door and kicked it open.

Zita continued to bang on the bulkhead. 'Will someone tell me what is going on!'

'He's gone back!' shouted Liam.

'What?!' Zita slid open the side door, jumped out and pulled Liam's door wide open. 'What the fuck is this all about?'

'I don't know … He just stopped and left …'

Zita looked across at the open driver's door. She punched Liam's door and after telling Sally to stay in the van she slammed the side door closed.

Ebanie, the young diminutive Roma woman appeared from nowhere. She had seen Florin running along the road. The black mud-splattered SUV braked to a halt throwing the coffee she had been asked to get by Mihai, onto the floor. Florin told her what he'd seen but knew nothing of what had happened since he'd left. She gunned the accelerator and threw up a cloud of dust and gravel as she raced towards the warehouse. She continued until she saw the parked van at the rear of the warehouse. She shook her head as she braked to a halt a few inches from the open blue door and rushed inside.

She took Jimmy by complete surprise and as he turned, she smashed her boot hard into his calf and he fell to the ground. She followed up with a kick to his groin.

He screamed out in agony, slumped forward and covered the pain with both hands.

Ebanie pulled a knife from her boot and grinned at him.

When Jimmy saw it, he tried to sit up but his attempt was futile.

She kicked out and dug the heel of her boot into his chest, leaned forward and slashed out at him. Jimmy twisted his body and instead of her stabbing him in the chest she plunged it deep into his upper left arm. He fell back onto the ground in pained exhaustion. Ebanie grabbed at his throat and pushed her knife towards him. He twisted his body to avoid it. He reached into his pocket for Mihai's gun and fired it through his overalls. He shot her twice in the chest. She dropped the knife and slumped onto one knee as blood pumped out of her wounds. She attempted to stop the flow and pressed both hands into her bleeding chest but as the blood continued to gush from between her fingers she fell back.

Jimmy watched traumatised as the life drained from her young body. He stood uneasily and gripped by what he had just done. Taken what may have been an innocent life.

257

He shuddered and cried out. He bent down, picked up her blood covered knife and pushed it into a pocket in his overalls. With his whole body creased in pain he strained to reach into another pocket and took out the hand grenade. He held it lovingly in his open palm before he slowly closed his gloved fingers around it. He briefly remembered the hell that was Korea before he opened his hand again and recalled what this deadly and destructive weapon could do to a person. To anyone. To anything. He took a brief second and respectfully kissed the destructive ordnance, pulled the pin and threw it across the warehouse leaving it to rattle along the floor. He stumbled out of the warehouse and into Zita.

'What are you doing, Jimmy?'

He didn't answer.

BOOM!

The grenade exploded.

Instinctively, they threw themselves onto the gravel and crawled beneath the Roma's SUV. The remaining glass was blown out of the rooflights and the asbestos dust and rusty corrugated sheets flew into the air and covered them in dust. The warehouse burst into flames lighting up the dark winter sky.

Zita got to her feet, helped Jimmy up and walked him back towards the van. She saw a solitary bicycle leaning against the metal cladding. 'Is that Sally's bike?'

Jimmy grunted.

'We can't leave it there. Someone might recognise it.' She walked across, grabbed it with one hand and helped Jimmy into the van with the other. She pushed him into the driver's seat and then noticed she was covered in blood. She checked herself before realising it was Jimmy who was bleeding. She controlled her anger as much as she could. 'Don't you know dat rule?'

Jimmy shook his head. 'Rule? Never heard of it.'

She sighed heavily. 'You should *never* go back!'

He grinned back at her. 'Who taught you that shit?'

She ignored him and walked around the van and dragged Liam out of the passenger seat. 'There is a first aid kit in the back – a large green case with a white cross.' While she waited, she sliced through the blood drenched sleeve of Jimmy's overalls to expose a long deep wound. She tied the sleeve around his upper arm and pulled it tight until the bleeding slowed down. 'Can you still drive?'

Jimmy moved his arm in a token gesture and grimaced at the pain before he replied with a sarcastic grunt. 'Yeah. Course I can.'

'Are you sure?'

'*Yes*. I just *said* I can drive, *didn't I*,' he replied angrily.

Zita shook her head. 'Not like that … you're losing too much blood.'

When Liam opened the side door, the dog snarled at him. Sally spoke in a soothing voice and stroked the dog until he calmed down.

Liam nervously reached inside and took out the first aid kit. 'Is everything alright, Dad?' asked a frightened Sally.

'It's fine,' he lied. 'We'll be off soon and you'll be home before you know it.'

She smiled back at him as he closed the door.

Liam returned with the first aid kit. Zita opened it and her fingers flicked through the contents. She carefully selected sealed packets of gauze and bandages. She tore them open with her teeth, making sure she spat the pieces into the van. She cleaned the wound. 'You will need stitches for dat.'

Jimmy grunted and shook his head. 'No way.'

Zita ignored him.

Liam watched as she skilfully squeezed both edges of the sliced flesh together, laid the gauze on top of the wound and wrapped two of the bandages tightly around it. She unwound several wider bandages, removed the bloody piece of sleeve and made a tourniquet which she tied beneath his shoulder. She turned to Liam and fired him a concerned look as she pointed at the tourniquet. 'We must not leave this on for more than twenty minutes or …' She paused and exhaled. 'Or … your father will lose his arm.'

Liam looked at his father and as their eyes met, they both screamed. 'Fuck!'

Zita tapped Liam's shoulder to regain his attention. 'Remember Liam, you must release it every twenty minutes and then tighten it again.' She jumped out of the passenger seat 'This will be alright until you get back.' She slammed the door. 'Go now!'

Jimmy flicked the key and started the van.

Zita looked cautiously around before she climbed into the van and pushed the bicycle behind the motorbikes and slammed the side door closed behind her. She made sure Sally was safe before she hammered on the bulkhead. 'Let's go. The police will be here any minute.' She bent her head and balanced as she removed her blood drenched overalls, grabbed the second plastic bag and changed into a plain black tee-shirt and jeans and then pulled on a worn denim jacket.

The adrenaline continued to pump through Jimmy's veins and he ignored the pain as he grabbed the steering wheel and squeezed it hard. He gunned the

260

accelerator and as the van raced off Sally and Zita clung desperately to the mid rail.

Liam turned to his father. 'What the hell was that all about?' He pulled his head back when he saw that the blood was already seeping through the bandages. He yelled at him. 'How the fuck did that happen?'

Jimmy growled. 'There was someone else in there–'

'Wha…?'

Jimmy's wounded arm wavered uncontrollably as he took his hand off the steering wheel, pulled the bloody knife from his overall pocket and passed it to Liam. 'She got me wiv that,' he muttered softly, as he tried to hide his embarrassment.

'This is some serious fucking knife,' Liam said. He subconsciously rubbed at his father's drying blood on the blade with his thumb and then contemplated what might have been had his attacker been successful. He exhaled and looked across at his father and realised that he was a very sick man who was holding onto life for as long as he could. He shook his head and grinned to himself. 'What about the explosion.' He forced a cough. 'Did you do that?'

Jimmy turned and grinned back at him mindlessly. 'A souvenir. I've had that grenade since Korea in -53.' He paused. 'Didn't think it would go off.'

'But it did.'

'Yeah.'

Jimmy laughed loudly 'I was finally able to put it to good use.' He clicked his tongue. 'You *see* … I'm not such a useless *git* after all.'

While Jimmy took the planned route, Zita wiped the dust, dirt and the blood from the minor cuts on her face with hand cleaner before she turned to Sally.

261

She was now in shock. Her tears continued to pour uncontrollably from her bloodshot eyes and down her reddened cheeks. 'Come on, Sally, we need to get you cleaned up – we're going on a journey–'

'Where?'

'I'm taking you home but you need to look presentable. If they see you crying people will ask questions and we don't want dat …'

Sally fought hard and forced a smile. 'They?'

'Yes. We can't go so far with your father and granddad. We need to leave soon and travel on our own.'

'Okay.' She reached down at the dog and stroked it. 'Can we take him with us?'

'Yes. Of course. But he needs a name.'

Sally sat back and thought hard.

CHAPTER FORTY-THREE

Sick And Tired

The van pulled up in the pre-planned deserted side street. Zita grabbed the backpack, helped Sally out of the van and walked around to the driver's side, tapped on the window and fired Jimmy an angry glare, which soon changed to a broad smile. 'Nice touch ... That really will confuse the police.' She stopped and looked down at his bleeding arm. 'You're still losing a lot of blood—'

'I told you it's only a scratch.'

She shook her head.

Jimmy pushed out his chin defiantly and grinned back at her. He nudged Liam. 'Just like old times, eh?'

Liam grunted his response.

She grabbed his arm and exhaled through her nose. 'Don't forget, Liam ... every twenty minutes,' she said, emphatically.

He grunted again and turned away.

Zita grabbed Sally's hand, coaxed the dog out of the van and closed the side door. She tapped several times on the side of the van and watched it pull away. They walked around the corner to a telephone box where Zita made one call before walking to the bus stop.

As they walked, Sally ran her fingers along one sleeve of her velvet jacket before she spoke. 'Did you choose these?'

Zita smiled. 'Of course.'

'I like them … You have good taste.'

'Thank you, young lady,' said Zita, with a soft smile.

Sally tilted her head and looked up at Zita. 'You're very different to my mum.'

'Am I?'

'Yes, you are.'

Zita smiled to herself.

'Have you got any kids?'

Zita shook her head as the bus pulled up beside them.

While she paid, Sally raced up the stairs followed by the dog.

Zita joined her on one of the front seats. 'Why did you choose to sit here?'

Sally shrugged. 'Dunno. I just like to look down on everyone.'

Zita put her arm around her and played with Sally's curly blonde hair and whispered. 'So do I.'

Sally answered with a giggle and briefly snuggled into her. She jumped up out of the seat and blurted out. 'Connor!'

The dog jumped up and barked loudly.

Zita whispered as she stroked him and he lay back down. 'Connor? What's that?'

'I'm going to call him … Connor.'

'Why?'

'Well …' She took a deep breath. 'The boy that we saw earlier was called Connor.' She lifted her shoulders and smiled cheekily. 'That's why … and … and *he's nice.*'

Zita and Sally travelled to the Whitechapel tube station and sat on the seat at the bus stop and waited.

'What will happen to my bike?'

'We will buy you a new one … and you can choose the colour.'

'Cool,' said Sally.

CHAPTER FORTY-FOUR

Bits And Pieces

Jimmy drove the van for a little over twenty minutes, stopping at every red traffic light and keeping to the speed limit: along the A12 and through the Blackwall Tunnel until they joined the North Woolwich Road. Liam briefly released the tourniquet and tightened it again. A few minutes later Jimmy turned right into Bradfield Road, in Silvertown, and then immediately right. He drove along the few yards of worn muddy track that led to a large piece of wasteland used for storing skips, scrap and rusty ship containers. The neglected area, flanked by Royal Crest Avenue and Lyle Park, looked strangely out of place between the luxury townhouses and expensive apartment blocks that overlooked the Thames. Jimmy pulled onto an area of compacted gravel where they would leave no tracks or indication that they had the motorbikes. He parked the van with the rear doors facing towards the park that was deserted except for a lone man walking his Yorkshire terrier. Jimmy gave him a fierce growl and the man limped off dragging the dog behind him.

Their feet crunched on the gravel as they carefully guided their bikes out of the van, down the scaffold boards and onto the gravel. They hid them out of sight from anyone in the apartments that overlooked the site and then pushed the scaffold boards inside. Liam climbed through the side door and removed his overalls, gloves and balaclava, tied their boots together and hung them, as they'd been instructed by Zita, alongside hers on the mid-rail, to ensure they would be totally destroyed in the fire. Liam ripped all the pages from the Roma's notebook and pushed some of them loosely into the boots. After crumpling the remaining sheets, he spread them around the van.

Jimmy struggled to remove his blood-soaked overalls and winced as the pain shot down his arm and throughout his body.

Liam reached across to help him, and pulled of his overall and attempted to remove the dripping bandages. As he loosened them the blood pumped out of the deep wound. He shook his head and gasped. 'Dad, you gotta get stitches in that.'

'Fuck off, Liam. I told yer, it's only a scratch.' He pulled his arm away and forced a laugh. 'I got worse than that most Saturdays on the door at the Brecknock.'

Liam shrugged and grabbed more bandages from the first aid box. He bit off the sterile wrapping, spat it into the van and wound them forcefully around Jimmy's bleeding arm.

Jimmy yelled in pain. 'What the f–'

'We need to get on,' said Liam. 'If we stay here much longer …' He pushed his head around the open van door and looked towards the apartments. 'Someone *will* see us.'

While Jimmy stood beside the van and struggled to pull up the zips on his leathers Liam climbed into the back of the van and changed into his leathers. He looked around and systematically covered everything with cleaning solvent. He sliced open the cartridges of window sealant and threw them onto the floor. He poured petrol over their clothes and boots and then the seats in the driver's cab. He tore up a handful of rags and split them. He laid some of them beneath the clothes in the back of the van and the others in the driver's cab, poured the last of the petrol over them and lit it.

His father who had finally managed to pull up his zips now sat astride his bike and waited for Liam.

Liam walked calmly around to his bike. He waited until the van was well alight before he leaned across to his father. 'Are you okay?'

Jimmy flicked up his visor and tilted his head. 'What the fuck is your problem, son? Course I am.'

Liam shook his head. 'Okay. Remember ... we go our different routes now.'

Jimmy nodded.

Liam looked concerned as he noticed the blood seeping down the sleeve of his father's leathers and onto his hand. 'Are you sure you can ride your bike?'

Jimmy took a deep breath and pulled a proud face. 'Course I am.' He swallowed and waved his wounded arm. 'How many more times do I have to tell you? It's only a scratch.'

'Alright,' said Liam. He didn't hide his doubt. 'Well ... if you're sure.'

Jimmy grunted.

'Just ride around until ...?' Liam checked his watch and remembered what Zita had said. He walked across to his father, loosened the tourniquet, waited a few minutes and tightened it again. 'A quarter past eight.' He fired up his bike and revved it hard. 'I'll meet you at home – in the garage.'

It took Jimmy a few seconds to realise what Liam meant before he grinned and slowly nodded in agreement. He flicked down his visor and kicked his bike into life.

As they raced away the van exploded and flames reached high into the dark November night. Jimmy looked back at the burning van, chuckled and talked to himself. 'A bit late for bonfire night innit.'

There were no survivors of the gang.

Florin, the only Roma to escape from the warehouse alive, raced away from the industrial estate. He continued to lose more and more blood and found it harder to focus in the darkness. He staggered blindly across the railway line and as he crossed, he was hit by a train scattering what remained of his body hundreds of yards along the track.

CHAPTER FORTY-FIVE

It's All in the Game

Michelle and Kathleen had been waiting anxiously at home and when they heard the sound of the motorbikes they raced out of the kitchen, down the garden and through the gate that linked both houses. A breathless Kathleen rushed through the rear door into the garage but after looking around and seeing only Jimmy and Liam, she couldn't hide her fear. 'Where's Sally?' she screamed.

'She is alright, isn't she?' screamed Michelle.

Jimmy slowly removed his helmet, reached out, pulled Kathleen and Michelle into him and hugged them. He winced in pain and forced a painful smile. 'They're safe,' he said, He pointed at the wooden front doors. 'Close them will yer.'

Kathleen pulled herself away and slid the doors across.

Liam reached out to her. 'Don't worry,' he said, 'They'll be here soon.' He moved several boxes and tins and pulled out a tea chest, brushed it off and sat his father on it. He loosened the tourniquet and waited until some of the colour began to return to his father's arm and hand and then tightened it again. He stood back and looked down at his pale and exhausted father and sighed. While the blood continued to seep from the bandages, down his sleeve and onto the dusty concrete floor, he unzipped his father's tight leathers, knelt down and removed his boots.

Michelle saw the blood, grabbed at her mother's arm and pointed.

Kathleen looked down and froze before she let out a choked scream. 'What happened? What is this all about?'

Liam saw her reaction and pulled the tourniquet even tighter.

She shook and waved her arms uncontrollably. 'Are you sure Sally's alright?' She grabbed at Liam. 'I mean is she hurt?' She gasped for air. 'Is that why …' She grabbed a breath. 'Why won't you tell me what is going on?' She looked Liam in the eye and, unable to control her fear, she continued with a scream. 'Where is she?!'

Liam grabbed at her arms, pulled her into him and held her tight. 'Shu … Shu … Shush … Sally's fine,' he said softly, as he tried to reassure her.

She didn't believe him and wrung her hands in sheer panic. *What had happened to her daughter?*

Liam turned and looked across at Jimmy for further confirmation.

He nodded back at her. 'She'll be here soon … with Zita.' He nodded erratically to emphasise it. 'She really is … okay.'

'But look at you.' She pointed at the blood pouring from his arm. 'Look what's happened to you – how the hell do you expect me to believe what you've said? Can you honestly tell me my daughter's alright?'

Jimmy clicked his fingers and beckoned Michelle to come to him.

She looked up at her mother who nodded. She shuffled towards Jimmy and he pulled her towards him, squeezed her tight and gently patted her head. He took a difficult breath and forced a smile at Kathleen. 'She is *alright.*' He looked at Liam, exhaled and then back to Kathleen. 'She'll be here soon ... Very soon.'

Liam loosened the tourniquet for a few seconds and tightened it again.

It was an agonising wait until the car drove down the back lane and pulled up outside Jimmy's garage.

Liam held them all back. 'Don't rush outside,' he said. He partially opened one of the doors and looked out. 'You never know who's looking.' They all waited on tenterhooks behind the half open door but when they heard the footsteps Kathleen threw the door wide open.

Sally rushed into her arms and burst into tears. 'Mum ... Mum, I thought I was going to die–'

'You're safe now,' she said softly, as she tried to hold back mixed emotions of relief and sobs of joy.

Zita closed the car door and gave the driver an appreciative kiss on the cheek. 'Thanks, George.'

He grinned his appreciation, turned up the car radio and drove away, singing along with the tune he didn't know.

Zita took her time and walked in with the dog on the makeshift rope, slid the door across and closed it quietly behind her. She passed the rope to Sally. The dog licked her leg and sat down beside her.

Zita dropped the backpack beside the kitchen unit and pushed it into the corner with her foot before she turned her attention to Jimmy. She could see that he had lost a great deal of blood and had deteriorated since she'd left him. She took his attacker's knife from his leathers and tugged at the sleeve. 'Sorry, Jimmy.'

Jimmy looked up at her as he tried hard to hide his disappointment at having his beloved leathers ripped apart.

Instead, he sniffed and wiped blindly at his tearful eyes with his free hand. 'It's alright. I don't see meself ever wearing 'em again.'

Zita nodded and cut through the leather sleeve at the shoulder and sliced it down to Jimmy's wrist. Despite first tightening the tourniquet as she removed the blood-soaked bandages, blood spurted into the air.

Liam pulled his head back in shock. 'You need to get yerself to the hospital with that.'

Zita cursed under her breath.

Jimmy was deathly pale and he struggled to keep his eyes open. He turned and looked at Liam. 'Son, you know, if I go in there ... I won't get out ...' He grinned at him. 'And, ain't that the truth?'

Liam lowered his head in embarrassment at what he'd just said. 'Sorry, Dad.'

Zita turned to Liam. 'Do you have any fishing line?'

'Wha ...?'

'And a hook to catch dem.'

Jimmy motioned by waving his good arm at Liam and pointing towards the top drawer. 'Come on, Liam.' He cursed. *'You know* where it is.'

Liam stood on his toes, reached deep inside the top drawer and pulled out a fishing reel. He held it reverently in his open hand. 'Remember this, Dad?'

'Course I do, son.' He pushed his head back and reflected. 'Good times, eh.' He paused and guffawed loudly. 'Well, the few times we caught anyfing, anyway.'

Liam nodded back at him and forced a grin. 'Yeah.'

The door burst open and they all turned towards it. Each having different thoughts of who it may be.

Harry rushed in. 'What the hell is going on?'

Connor barked at him.

'Where did that mangy thing come from?'

Sally comforted the dog before she spoke. 'It's Connor and he's mine.' She turned to her mother. 'Isn't he, Mum?'

Reluctantly, Kathleen nodded.

Sally grinned back at Harry. 'Told you.'

Liam moved towards Harry and tried to placate him. 'It's alright, son. Your grandad's got a bit of a problem.'

'Doesn't he always?' He glared at Liam. 'What about you? Trouble's never far behind you either … is it?'

Zita was getting impatient and joined Liam and Harry. 'We will explain it later.' She patted Harry gently on his shoulders. 'But now … we do need you to help your grandad. Okay?'

Harry was clearly confused and shook his head as he tried to take in what was unfolding in front of him.

Zita coaxed him to stand back, held out her open hand and sighed until Liam finally handed her the fishing reel and a plastic box of fishing hooks. She flicked through them until she found what she wanted. She took a pair of pliers from their allotted place on the wall and removed the barb. After mentally measuring the line she bit into it, passed the reel back to Liam and threaded the line through the eye of the hook.

Zita had done this many times before, to herself and others and often in much worse conditions, but this time it was special - she had an audience that knew her, and were watching her every move. She couldn't fail.

She fired Jimmy a cautious look. 'Are you sure of this?'

Jimmy glared back at her and nodded. 'No way am I going to hospital.'

'If you're sure ...' She paused and waited for Jimmy's reaction. There wasn't one and she continued. 'I *can* deal with it.'

'Just ... *do* it!' screamed Liam.

She turned and fired him a look of self-assured capability. 'Yes ... of course, Liam ... I *will "do it."*'

Jimmy aimed his wounded arm in her direction. 'Can you just get on wiv it.'

Zita needed no more encouragement and fired her orders at Kathleen. 'I need clean bandages and towels. We mustn't let his arm get infected.' She paused and looked at Liam. 'And alcohol–'

'Alcohol?' asked Kathleen.

'Brandy, whisky ... anything to sterilize these things.' She was losing her patience and raised her voice. 'But ... I need it now ... or ...' She looked towards Jimmy and back to Kathleen. 'He will lose too much blood and ...' She lowered her voice, 'And he *will* have to go to hospital.' She took a breath and waited. 'OK!'

Kathleen nodded and made to move but when Zita continued, she stopped at the door. 'Liam, can you get me some hot water.'

He nodded and followed Kathleen to the kitchen.

Kathleen returned with a tray overflowing with everything Zita had asked her to get and a bottle of brandy.

Liam followed her with a bowl of steaming water and, after sliding the tools and paint cans across the bench with his elbow, he laid the bowl on it.

Zita looked across at the twins who stood open mouthed. She smiled at them and turned to Kathleen. 'Maybe they are hungry and tired ... Yes?'

It took Kathleen a few seconds to take the hint. She placed her arms around the girls. 'Come on girls, let's see what we can find for you, eh?' Despite their fractious wishes to stay, she shepherded them and the dog out and closed the door behind her.

Harry stiffened defiantly, gained height and glared at Zita.

She smiled back at him. 'Not you, Harry. You must stay and help us … Okay?'

He immediately relaxed with a slow nod, pleased at last to be part of what was going on.

Zita smiled back at him. 'Harry, can you help me and hold your grandad steady for me please?'

He stepped forward and stood behind Jimmy and pushed himself into Jimmy's back and held him.

Zita opened the brandy and poured it over the fishing line and modified hook. The alcoholic aroma spread throughout the garage.

Jimmy and Harry looked at each other and waited curiously to see Liam's reaction.

There wasn't one.

Zita tapped Jimmy on the shoulder. 'This will hurt. Do you want some of this?'

He nodded and grunted.

Zita took a metal mug from the shelf, blew off the dust and partly filled it. She passed it to Harry. 'Look after your grandad, will you? It will help with the pain.'

Harry passed the mug to Jimmy and he took a huge gulp.

'Slowly. Take your time … Okay?' said Zita.

Jimmy didn't hear her. He emptied the mug and reached up and passed it to Harry who refilled it. He took another huge slug, shook his head and shuddered. 'Come on, let's get this over with.'

Zita looked at Jimmy's deteriorating condition, his pale-yellow complexion, bloodshot eyes and dilated pupils. She smiled at Harry. 'It will be okay,' she said, softly. She grabbed the bottle from Harry and slid it onto the shelf out of Jimmy's reach.

Jimmy's teeth chattered against the mug and he slurred. 'I'm on morphine anyhow.'

'Wha …?'

'For me cancer,' he replied. Without any warning and affected by the loss of blood his whole body convulsed in shock.

Zita held him gently and whispered softly in his ear.

Within seconds he had recovered.

CHAPTER FORTY-SIX

You Win Again

Half an hour later Zita, Liam and Kathleen sat drinking tea in the sitting room. Jimmy, his arm stitched and bandaged, slumped exhausted in an armchair. He emptied the glass and, although his cheeks had regained some of his colour, he was still shaking. He slowly refilled the glass for the second time from the bottle of brandy, a present from Felix. 'Well …' He exhaled and his cheeks regained some of their colour. 'That was a fucking masterclass.' He shook his head and took another huge slurp of brandy. He smacked his lips and allowed his tongue to taste the last drop. 'I've never seen anything like it,' he slurred.

Michelle and Sally, followed by the dog, walked in from the kitchen still eating toast covered with a thick layer of peanut butter.

Liam stood up and hugged Sally and looked across to Kathleen. 'She needs a bath and a warm bed.'

'Sorry, Dad,' said Sally. She sniffed hard and looked up. 'Thanks, Zita.' She stopped at the door and the dog rubbed against her leg. 'Will they come back?'

Jimmy answered with a drunken laugh. 'I doubt it.' He looked at Zita.

She shook her head.

He continued. 'No. They won't.' He emptied his glass and Zita took it away from him. 'But you have learned a serious lesson today.' He paused. 'Eh, young Sally?'

She murmured her reply. 'Yeah … I have.' She looked around at everyone in turn. 'Zita, dad and grandad rescued me from them vile bastards–'

'Don't talk like that, Sally,' scolded Kathleen.

Jimmy tried to push himself out of his armchair. He failed. 'This time she is right …' He looked across at Sally and grinned mischievously. 'Just this once, eh, Sally, love?'

Liam heard the door open and his mother shuffled in. She looked around and, when she saw Jimmy's blood-stained bandaged arm, she let out a frenzied shriek and soiled herself. 'Did I do that?!'

Martha gasped. 'I'm sorry… Gwen said she heard voices in the gardin and here we are.'

Kathleen walked towards Gwen and held her tight.' No … no … no, Gwen, it wasn't you. Jimmy's had an accident. He fell over and cut his arm … but he's alright now.'

Her kind words seemed to placate the situation and Martha and Kathleen guided her back through the garden and home, up the stairs to the bathroom for a bath and a clean nightdress.

The room was silent.

No one wanted or dared to comment.

Twenty minutes later Kathleen returned. 'She's alright now. Just a bit confused seeing us all here this time of night.' She took a breath and sprayed the room. 'Accidents do happen, don't they?'

They all nodded.

Liam turned to her. 'I would keep Sally off school for the rest of the week.' He forced a cough. 'I suspect there will be a of them lot doing the same after today.'

Jimmy slid back into the armchair, closed his eyes and rubbed blindly at his bandaged arm. Without warning he sat bolt upright and pulled Zita towards him. 'Did you know there was a woman with them?'

'What?'

'The one who attacked me when I went back–'

She glared at him. 'Why did you need to go back?'

His face reddened and he lowered his head. 'I know.' He slurred. 'It was a mistake. A big mistake.' He tilted his head back and reflected. 'I know.' He could taste the brandy on his lips, licked them and grinned like a child. 'But I had an old souvenir I've been wanting to get rid of for years.'

She grinned back at him and nodded. 'Yes, we all heard it.' She paused and chuckled. 'And probably much of London.'

He still wanted an answer. 'So, did you know?'

Zita feigned surprise. '"Know?"' She lowered her head and briefly closed her eyes. 'Yes, I did … but when she didn't show herself, I believed she was either too frightened or relieved to be rid of dose bastards.'

'How could you know that?

'I didn't.' She sighed heavily. 'That was *my mistake*. A "schoolboy error" as you say.' She laughed loudly, stooped down and wrapped her arms around Jimmy. 'This time I had you to rely on.' She squeezed him tight. 'To clear up the mess.'

Jimmy exhaled hard and shook his head. 'I killed her – shot her ya know–'

'I heard that too. I knew that if you missed you wouldn't come out of dere alive.'

Jimmy grunted. 'Fuck.' He sighed. 'You really are somefing.'

Zita nodded profusely, knelt down and squeezed Jimmy tight. 'Promise me ... that was the last time.'

He sniffed hard and, as he winced in pain, he bent forward and clutched at his belly with one hand.

Liam moved towards him. 'We need to get you home now, Dad.'

Zita and Liam took their time to walk Jimmy through the garden and into his house and helped him to drop into his armchair. He immediately reached down the side of the chair and took out a bottle of tramadol, his strong painkillers, flipped off the lid and swallowed several of them. He sighed heavily as he slumped back, closed his eyes, and waited for the pain to subside.

Zita watched him and waited for him to relax. She whispered in his ear. 'Can I suggest you either get rid of the gun or hide it ...' She paused. 'But ... if you keep it ... hide it very well.'

'Course.' He grinned back at her. 'That *was* my plan,' he lied.

Liam sat beside Zita on the settee and hugged her. 'How did you know where to find them?' he asked.

'Who?'

'You know ... them bastards ... and Sally.'

Zita sighed. 'It's my job to know things.' She paused as she thought back to the girl in the café in Camden and the teenage sellers who she had seen as they scurried around London on their bikes. She continued with a troubled look. 'But I didn't know for sure ... that ... Sally would be there.' She turned to Jimmy. 'I need to go to the garage and tidy up the mess. Alright?'

'Sure,' he said, waving his good arm, regally, in her direction.

Liam looked up. 'I'll stay with me dad.'

'I shouldn't be too long,' said Zita.

Zita walked into the garage and looked around at the blood-soaked bandages and Jimmy's leathers. She pulled on a pair of latex gloves and pushed it all into another bag, opened the backpack and took out the plastic bag bulging with the money. She carefully removed the strands of Mihai's bloody hair and scalp and put it on the shelf. She tipped out the money and took her time to select any notes that had blood on them and set them aside. She formed a pile of the newest and cleanest notes. She picked up all the blood covered notes and added clean ones until she had two-thousand pounds. She then split the remaining money into four piles and searched in the drawers for elastic bands. She bound the four piles and rechecked the thicker pile. She recounted and found it was ten pounds short so she reached for the nearest pile and removed a note and used it to make up the two thousand. She picked up a few strands of Mihai's bloody scalp and hair and pushed it carefully between the notes, dropped his gold earrings and necklace into the same blood splattered plastic bag, and folded it tight. She picked up each bundle of money and arranged it carefully, and pushed them into her backpack.

She jumped on the bike and left.

* * *

Michelle slowly opened the bedroom door and lay on the bed next to Sally. She was wide awake and stroked the dog that had snuggled up to her. 'What happened?' She looked across at the dog. 'How did you end up with him?' She took a closer look. 'He's covered in scars–'

'I know ... but he's still lovely.' She stroked his head. 'Zita said he was used in the dog fighting rings. They would fight until one of them killed the other–

'Oh, no. That's disgusting and so cruel.'

'I know. But maybe Connor survived *for me*.' Sally grinned back at her mischievously and pushed herself up on one elbow, gently rearranged her pillow and stroked the dog's head.

'Is that what you've called him?'

'Yeah. 'She took a huge breath and slowly exhaled. 'It was unbelievable. You should have been there–'

'Been there ... Me?' Michelle fired her a look of disbelief. 'What *do you mean?*'

Sally shook her head wildly. 'No ... I don't mean being there.' She took a breath. 'I meant ... to *see it*. Zita and dad. They were amazing.' She paused. 'And even ... grandad.' She laughed loudly. 'Grandad shot him in the ear?'

'Wha?'

'There was four of them.' Her level of excitement rose as she relived what had happened and she sat up. The dog sat up too. 'One of them was at the door. He wouldn't let any of us out. Soooo ... Grandad shot him ...' She shrieked. 'Shot his ear off!'

'Grandad, did that?!'

'Yeah. It was unbelievable. I've never seen anything like it.' She paused and inhaled. 'Well ... I have ... but on TV ...'

Michelle's mood changed. 'Don't you realise how lucky you were? That they came for you.'

'I was.' She reflected on her escape, slid down the bed and pushed herself deep into the pillow. 'I was.' She sniffed hard. 'I know I was.'

Michelle reached out and stroked the dog. 'So, where did he come from?'

Sally didn't hear her. She fell asleep and the dog snuggled into her.

CHAPTER FORTY-SEVEN

I'm Your Puppet

The time dragged while Zita waited to call Delfine, her handler. But, as arranged, at exactly the same time a week after the first call, she walked into the public phone box and dialled.

'Hello?'

'It's Zita.' There was a lengthy silence before she continued. 'Well?'

'We know you're still in London,' said Delfine. There was another extended silence. 'And ... you've been busy ... very busy.'

Zita snorted her contempt. 'Um ... Maybe I have.'

'So, we've held off–'

'Really. That's very kind of you,' said Zita, flippantly.

Delfine screamed down the phone. 'Don't fuck with us! You know you're both already dead!'

A beat.

Zita sighed heavily. 'Alright.' She exhaled shakily. 'So, what am I doing?'

Delfine gave Zita her instructions. 'Go to the WH Smith on Paddington Station, at ten o'clock tomorrow morning and look for an assistant named Denise. She will be expecting you. Tell her you are looking for a book by JK Rowling.'

'What?'

'Listen to me carefully.' Delfine huffed. 'Ask her for *Harry Potter and the Goblet of Fire* by JK Rowling. She will hand you the book and a key to a left luggage locker. When you open the locker, you will find everything you need for your mission.' She paused. 'And, remember to leave the key in the door.'

The line went dead.

CHAPTER FORTY-EIGHT

Who Wants to Live Forever?

Jimmy and Liam appeared at the kitchen door. 'We're going for a ride, alright?'

Zita was sat on the settee reading a book. She looked up at them and nodded. 'Course.'

'Once Martha's put Gwen to bed she'll be finishing. Are you alright on your own?' asked Jimmy.

'Yes. Just go.' As they walked back through the kitchen, she called out to them. 'Enjoy.'

The door was already closed.

She put down her book, flicked the remote control and scanned the channels for something she might want to watch. She stopped at *The Good Life*, yet another rerun on the BBC. She laid a cloth over her lap and settled down with her nail file and varnish, and half-watched the programme.

Michelle joined her and looked on excitedly. 'Will you do mine next?'

'What will Kathleen say?'

'She won't mind. There's no school until Monday … and if she don't like it. I'll take it off.'

'Yeah, go on,' said Zita, as she waved a bottle of nail varnish at her.

Michelle giggled excitedly.

There were a series of what sounded like two-handed urgent repetitive knocks at the front door.

Michelle slid out of the chair. 'Shall I go?'

Zita stood and moved her back. 'You sit down. I'll go.' She passed her the nail file. 'Tidy up your nails.'

'Okay.'

Zita partially opened the front door and stepped back.

'An elderly man, in a worn cardigan, creased trousers and urine-stained slippers, stood trembling at the door, his ashen face etched with deep furrows. 'Is Jimmy in?'

'No. Sorry. He's out with Liam–'

''e attacked me–'

'Who?'

'That bastard son of mine.'

Zita took his arm. 'Come in.' She helped him into the sitting room and let him slump into Jimmy's armchair.

'I wanna call the police …'

Michelle rushed into the kitchen and returned with the cordless phone. She handed it to Zita who dialled 999. She waited until someone answered.

'What service do you want–?'

'Police?'

Zita handed the phone to Sydney.

'What's your name?' asked the call handler.

'Sydney Randall … R– A– N– D –A– L–L.'

'Are you injured?'

'No.'

'What is your address?'

'Thirty-seven Morepeth Road–'

'Are you there now?'

Sydney looked at Zita and trembled.

She shook her head.

He continued. 'No.'

Michelle blurted out the answer. 'He's at thirty-three Morepeth Road.'

'Thank you. We will get someone out to you as soon as we can. Please stay where you are.'

Zita took the phone from him and laid it beside her. 'Would you like a cup of tea, Sydney.'

'Please.'

'Sugar?'

'No fanks.'

Michelle stood and looked at Zita. 'I'll do it. Do you want one too?'

'Please.'

Sydney wriggled and pushed himself deep into Jimmy's well-worn armchair and closed his eyes. He looked very sick and his shallow breathing continued to stop and start. Suddenly he sat forward. 'I want that bastard out of *my* house!' He took a huge painful breath. 'He's fifty-five ... and don't work ... and pays us twenty-five pounds a week.'

Zita lowered her voice. 'I understand that, Sydney. What happened tonight?'

'Me wife ... Lena is really bad. She should be in hospital but she won't go.' He sighed. 'I told her I would call an ambulance and when I said that. The bastard jumped at me and asked me to hit 'im.'

Zita nodded. 'OK. You're safe with us,' she said softly.

'He said "if I hit 'im he would kill me." I'm ninety and I don't need this ... but he and his mother are thick as thieves. I can't even have the remote for the tele ... He controls everyfing I do.'

'Has he done this before, Sydney–?'

'Yeah. He 'it me and gave me two black eyes and broke me nose. I had to go to hospital.' He sniffed and wiped at his nose and eyes with a dirty handkerchief. 'But I told 'em I fell over.' He began to weep. 'I couldn't tell them what really happened or she would have blamed me.'

Michelle walked in with two mugs. 'Are you sure you don't want sugar, Sydney?'

'No fanks.'

Michelle handed him the mug and he sipped at it, totally unaware that it had just been poured.

Zita noticed that his legs were swollen and he continually rubbed them for relief. 'Can you get Sydney a hot water bottle please, Michelle?' Her body stiffened. 'Be careful with the hot water.'

Michelle rolled her eyes. 'It's alright, I always do them for my nan.'

Zita smiled back at her. 'Course. Sorry.'

Sydney slid deeper into the armchair and shook.

Zita gently rubbed his arms and shoulders, and for a few seconds he seemed to relax.

There was a knock at the front door. Zita opened it to a male and female police officer. The policeman spoke. 'We've had a report of an assault?'

'Yes. Come in please.'

They walked into the sitting room.

'Do you want to sit down?' asked Zita

They looked at each other and both answered at the same time. 'No thanks. We've been sitting in the car for quite a while tonight,' they lied. 'We prefer to stand.'

Zita knew they wouldn't sit down until they had heard the details of what had happened from Sydney.

He lay back with his eyes closed.

They took their time to look at him.

He opened them with a start. 'I forgot me stick.'

'That's alright,' said, Zita.

Michelle spoke. 'I know grandad has one somewhere.' She smiled at him. 'We'll sort that. Don't you worry.'

The policeman spoke. 'So, could I ask your name please?'

'Sydney Randall. R –A –N –D –A –L –L.'

'Date of birth?'

'Twenty-fourth of November nineteen-ten. I'm ninety. It was me birthday last week.'

'Thank you.'

'Where do you live?'

'Number thirty-seven – two doors down.'

The policeman turned to Zita. 'Can I ask who you are?'

She answered immediately. 'Eh, Kathleen Reilly.'

Sydney opened his eyes wide and looked at her.

Zita nodded and mouthed to him. 'It's alright.'

He accepted her lie and partially closed them again.

The policeman continued. 'Where do you live?'

Zita replied. 'Gore Road - over the back.'

They turned to Michelle. 'And who are you?'

'I'm Michelle Reilly. I live over the back too.'

The policewoman looked confused. 'So why are you here … in Morepeth Road?'

'My grandad, Jimmy Reilly, lives here with my nan. She's got dementia so we're looking after her.' She smiled at Zita. 'Until he comes back.'

'Ah. Okay.'

The policeman flicked his notebook open and continued. 'So, can you tell us what happened?'

Sydney repeated what he'd told Zita. 'He said "if I hit 'im, he would kill me." Why would I hit 'im? I'm ninety and … and… and I don't need this … He and his mother are thick as thieves. I can't even have the remote for the tele. He controls everyfing I do.'

'Who is this, Sydney?'

'Matt, me fucking lazy-assed, son–'

'Has he done this before, Sydney?'

'Yeah. Jimmy knows, he's the only one I can go to for any help.' He paused. 'Where is he?'

Zita spoke. 'He's out with Liam. They've gone for a ride … on the bike. He'll be back soon.'

Sydney continued. 'Me other two sons won't come near us. He hit me and gave me two black eyes and broke me nose. I had to go to hospital.' He tried to force a grin but failed. Instead, he sobbed.

'Alright Sydney, take your time,' said the policewoman.

'I told them I fell over.' He hammered the arms of the chair. 'I couldn't tell them what happened or she would 'ave blamed me and my life would 'ave bin hell.'

'Any other times?'

'Yeah. Lots. I've been in to ask Jimmy for help loads of times.' He sniffed. 'He offered to sort 'im out.'

The police officers frowned and shook their heads.

'I told 'im not to do anyfing. Maybe I should 'ave let 'im.'

'Do you feel threatened, Sydney?' asked the policewoman.

'Course I do. I can't go back *there*!'

Zita interrupted. 'He can't go back tonight. You do appreciate how serious this is. Sydney *is ninety* and his wife is very ill.'

The police officers coughed.

The policeman spoke. 'We understand. So, if we arrest him …' He hesitated, checked his notebook and looked down at Sydney. 'Matt … Now–'

'Arrest 'im!? You can't do that! She'll 'ate me … and *blame me* …'

Zita walked over, knelt down and stroked Sydney's swollen legs. 'We have to do something. Sydney.' She looked into his sad eyes. 'You do understand that don't you?

He took his time and reluctantly nodded.

The policeman slipped his notebook into his pocket and they walked towards the door. 'We'll go now and talk to your wife and … Matt.' His demeanour changed. 'You do realise, if we arrest him tonight, he will be kept in for forty-eight hours and before he's released, we will need you to fill in a risk assessment.' He took a few seconds to wait for Sydney's reaction.

There wasn't one. He was exhausted.

The policeman continued. 'There are twenty-seven questions and, depending on your answers, he may be held over for twenty-eight days to keep away from your house.'

'Fuck.' Sydney's whole body shuddered as he tried to stand. 'Do you have to do that?'

Zita looked into his sad and veined watery eyes. 'Sydney, something has to be done or … you know what might happen … *next time* …' She gently stroked his arms. 'Don't you?'

He sniffed. 'Yeah.' He made another attempt to stand, his arms gave way and he fell back awkwardly into the chair. 'I don't want 'im in my house.' He sniffed and raised his fists. 'He brainwashed my Lena. He left once before and waited for her to come out of church. He told her he'd been sleeping in his car for three weeks and she asked me to let him come back.' He huffed. 'Like a fool I

293

did … Me other sons said I was mad … but I knew Lena would give me hell if I didn't agree.' He took his time to look at each of them in turn. 'She's not well.'

The police officers moved towards the door. 'We'll go now and we'll come back as soon as we've spoken to them.'

The policewoman stopped at the door and turned. 'Sydney, you stay here with Kathleen and Michelle, alright?'

He nodded and closed his eyes.

CHAPTER FORTY-NINE

Come What May

An hour later there was a knock at the door. The policewoman smiled at Zita. 'Can I come in?'

Zita looked for the policeman.

The policewoman shook her head.

Zita opened the door and followed her into the sitting room.

The policewoman looked down at Sydney and waited for him to look back at her before she spoke. 'My colleague has arrested him.'

Sydney was tired and confused and looked up at her. 'Who?' he asked.

'Your son, Matt–'

'Arrested 'im?!' Sydney burst into tears and threw the hot water bottle across the room.

Unperturbed, the policewoman continued. 'He's in the car with him now.'

Sydney shook his head and sobbed. *'She'll never speak to me again.'*

The policewoman referred to her notebook. 'Listen to me, Sydney.' She waited for him to calm down and then forced a smile. 'At first, Lena said it was *your fault*–'

'What did I tell yer?'

The policewoman continued. 'But then … she told us what really happened.' She paused. 'Sydney, she is very ill and I'm really worried about her legs. She needs to be in hospital.'

Sydney made an attempt to hammer on the arms of the chair but his hands slipped into his lap. 'That's what I've been saying all along.' He gulped for air and sighed heavily. 'That's why this happened …' He looked at Zita. 'She won't go.'

The policewoman gently touched his shoulder. 'Sydney, I am making arrangements for her to go into hospital … tonight.'

For the first time, Sydney looked relieved and exhaled slowly. 'What about 'im?'

'Well, he will be interviewed under caution and held for forty-eight hours. If we deem him to be a risk to you, he will be up in front of the magistrates and *they* will make a decision.'

'I don't want 'im in me house.'

'We understand that, Sydney.'

'How was Lena?'

'She was very angry, but I believe it was the pain. She has anti-biotics and …' She shook her head. 'Paracetamol.' She cursed. 'They will do nothing for her pain. That's why she needs to go into hospital.' She looked at Zita. 'But.' She took a long pause. 'I would like *you* to … *go back* with Sydney … and be there when the ambulance arrives.' She looked directly at Sydney. 'Is that alright?'

Sydney shook violently. 'But … but … but I told yer, she'll blame me.'

Zita stood. 'Sydney, one way or another, this has to stop.'

'I know.' He sniffed. 'When I asked what we wuz having for Christmas dinner they said *they* were havin' duck.' He tried to stand again. He failed. 'But *nothing* for me!' He sniffed harder. 'They just laughed in me face.'

The policewoman spoke softly to him. 'Perhaps Kathleen will go with you?'

Zita nodded.

'Thank you. We will be in touch and keep you informed on your home telephone, Sydney'

Michelle found Jimmy's walking stick and gave it to Sydney. He used it to stand and staggered awkwardly towards the front door.

Zita turned to Michelle. 'Can you wait here until I get back, please?'

'Yes, course I …' She stopped mid-sentence and fired Zita a puzzled look.

'Yes?' asked Zita brusquely.

Michelle took in a gulp of air and hesitated.

'What is it, Michelle?'

Michelle finally blurted out the question she'd been wanting to ask for an hour. 'Why did you say you were my mum?'

Sydney grunted. *He wondered that too.*

Zita forced a disarming smile. 'I will explain later.' She grabbed Sydney's arm. 'Michelle, please stay until I come back.'

She took Sydney's free arm and they stepped outside. She helped him to shuffle along until they reached his house. They stood on the pavement and looked through the frayed net curtains and into the sitting room. 'Do you want me to come in with you, Sydney?'

She could feel his whole body tense in abject fear. 'Ye … es … sss please.'

The front door was unlocked. Zita turned the handle and helped Sydney inside.

He trembled and clung on to her arm.

She looked around an identical sitting room to Jimmy's, except that the legs of the armchairs and settee had been raised onto timber blocks to make it easier for them to get in and out of them. The smell of urine was also identical to Jimmy's house.

They looked around the room but Lena wasn't there.

Zita guided Sydney through the partially open door and into the kitchen.

Lena was sat on a chair in the corner of the room hunched over the table. Her arched back made it difficult for her to raise her head more than a few inches but when she saw Sydney, she ignored the pain, raised it and fired her venom and anger in his direction. 'You fucking bastard! This is all your fault!' Her frenzy grew and she hammered her fists on the table. 'He's been arrested! It should have been you!' She finally noticed Zita, nodded to her, and spoke in her normal voice. 'Sorry, dear. Whoever you are.'

Zita took her time to scrutinise Lena. Her thick swollen legs were partially bandaged and the thick puss had seeped through and stained them a dark yellow. The skin that was visible was red raw with raised blue veins and large open sores that had sealed themselves with the dried puss. She wore surgical shoes with extended Velcro strips holding them in place across her misshapen swollen feet.

Zita knelt down in front of her and spoke in a soft caring voice. 'Lena, I'm Liam's friend. I can see you are in a lot of pain.' She picked up the boxes of antibiotics and paracetamol tablets. 'These will not help you, Lena. You need to be in a hospital–'

'I'm not going to hospital,' she snarled.

Zita reached down. 'Do you mind if I touch your legs?'

Lena grunted.

Zita gently stroked the poisoned inflamed skin which was causing so much of the pain. 'Can I ask you a question, Lena?'

'Yeah.'

'Do you want to get better?'

Before Lena could respond Zita continued. 'Sorry I have another one. 'Do you *want to* die?'

Lena grunted.

'So, do you want to get better?'

'Yes.'

'Do you want to die.'

'No.'

Zita settled herself on the urine covered carpet. 'Well then … you do need to go to hospital.'

A beat.

Zita knew that the policewoman had already called for an ambulance but she wanted to be sure Lena would accept it. 'Do you mind if I arrange it?'

Lena grunted.

Zita sat Sydney down at the table facing away from Lena and pretended to call for an ambulance.

Thirty minutes later Lena was on her way to hospital and Zita put Sydney to bed. 'I will tell Jimmy what's happened and if you need anything call him and he'll come around. OK?'

Sydney was already asleep and breathing heavily.

Zita left the house thinking terrible thoughts and how Sydney and Lena could not look after themselves, let alone each other. She talked to herself. 'Who wants to live long enough to get old.'

CHAPTER FIFTY

The Night Has a Thousand Eyes

There was a chill in the late autumn night air as Liam, with Jimmy riding pillion, rode to a derelict spot overlooking the Thames. They sat on the low brick wall in silence and looked out across the fast-flowing, foreboding Thames and the Millenium Dome, the £758 million vanity project of Tony Blair and his Labour Government, on the other side of the river. The weird structure rose out of the Greenwich skyline and blotted out much of the skyline on the perfect moonlit night.

Jimmy spoke. 'It looks magic at night dunnit son?' He paused and shook his head. 'You can't see the filth and grime.'

'The decay … Erm.' Liam nodded. 'I know … it's everywhere these days, Dad.'

Jimmy studied the Dome. 'I reckon they'll shut it down soon. Do ya know it's costing more than a mill a month to maintain it. And … it's empty' He chuckled. 'One million a month … for what? Fuck all.' He cursed. 'Another white elephant, Liam.' He coughed. 'And a waste of taxpayers' money.' He suddenly broke into raucous laughter. 'You'll never guess.'

Liam shot him a vacant look.

'Last February, Lee, Ray and William and his boys attempted to rob thirty-five mills worth of diamonds from in there.'

'Wha …?'

'Yeah, why would you show off somefing like that in a fucking tent?'

'I dunno.'

'They fucking did … but the old bill got 'em.' He chuckled. 'The flying squad and police had been watching them for weeks. They were so stupid they kept clocking De Beer's diamonds and taking photos.' He paused. 'The old bill knew something was up … so, they swapped the real fings for fakes.' He clicked his tongue. 'Their plan was to do the robbery and get away on a speedboat. Just like fuckin' … James Bond.' He sniggered. 'Guess who they wanted to drive it?'

'I dunno.'

'Terry fucking Millman–'

'Really?'

'The idiots planned to do it at high-tide.' He snorted. 'So they made it easy for the pigs to guess roughly when that would be.' Jimmy stamped his feet. 'Yeah. Lee was never any good at thinking things through, was he?'

'Nah.'

Jimmy shook his head and took a shallow breath. 'Fuckin' losers … idiots' He sat back and sighed, exhausted. 'Terry died – cancer. The others got eighteen years … give or take a few months.'

Liam fiddled with his crash helmet. 'Dad, can I ask you a question?'

'Course, son.'

'How did you know?'

'Know what?'

'You had cancer?'

'I felt tired for months and when I saw the quack, she got me to have a scan and blood test.' He sighed. 'That was it. The oncologist said, "Mister Reilly you have stage four cancer and I'm afraid it's inoperable." I didn't know what to say except to ask him ... how long.' He snorted. 'He just looked at me ... so matter of fact ... and told me it was two to three months–'

'Fuck.'

Jimmy didn't want to repeat himself and changed the subject. He smiled. 'Do you know I used to come here with yer mother ... before we got hitched.' He took his time to look at the dome and the steel arms reaching high up into the sky. 'That filthy monstrosity weren't even thought about back then.' He grinned. 'The good old days, eh?' He looked down at the river and his contented nostalgic memories, now blackened by the dark rushing water, suddenly vanished. He sighed heavily. 'You know, son. I've been a shit dad.'

Liam caught his father's haunted face in the moonlight. 'No, you haven't,' he snapped.

'I 'ave! I wuz ... I wuz never 'ere. I left it to yer mother to bring you all up–'

'Yeah, but ... Dad ... I'm still *here*.' He struggled to breathe. "cept Tommy.' He grabbed at his throat. 'Fuck!' He sniffed. 'That was my fault!'

'No, Liam, 'e lost 'is way.' He swallowed hard. '*Well* before you left ... and he just kept going down that wrong track.' He took a huge breath. 'Listen to me ... No one could help him. Believe me, we all tried.'

Liam sobbed. 'I could 'ave–'

'But you weren't 'ere, son.' He swallowed hard. 'I know he adored ya but it was *my* fault …' He paused and gulped. 'I sent ya away.'

They both paused to watch the fox ignoring them as it rooted around the discarded paper, boxes and rubbish from the overflowing bin.

Jimmy continued. 'What else could you have done?' He paused and looked at Liam. 'Fuck all. That's what.'

Liam wiped his nose with his sleeve.

His father continued. 'It was for the best …' He lowered his voice. 'In the end.' He sniffed and wiped roughly at his dripping nose with a dirty handkerchief. 'But … I didn't want you to leave, Liam.' He placed his arm around Liam's neck and sobbed. 'But what else could I do?'

Liam reached up and held his father's hand. 'It's done now and I'm still here.' He paused and wiped the tears from his eyes. 'There was a Liam before and thanks to you … I am the Liam after.'

Jimmy sat back and let his body slide along the wall. 'Son, you know I haven't got long?'

'Yeah. You told me then–'

'Then?'

'When I … I …' Liam remembered the horrific call he had with his father, when the cruise ship docked briefly in Southampton. He shook his head and continued, stretching every word. 'When … I … last … called.'

Jimmy sucked in air. 'Oh, yeah. I remember that.' He turned to Liam. The despondent and tormented look on his sad face displayed his silent apology. 'I regret that day. I was a bastard for talking to you like that.' He paused and looked hard at Liam. 'If it's any consolation, I'd do different now.'

Liam acknowledged his father's regret with a slow thoughtful nod before he forced a smile.

Jimmy shook his head and continued. 'I thought I'd dodged that bullet, son.' He sighed and continued. 'But I wuz wrong … The fucking cancer has gone from me … me … me pancreas now.' He sniffed his acceptance of what was imminent. 'I'm riddled with it …' he said, as he looked across at Liam.

Liam fired him a vacant look.

'I know what you're thinking.'

'Wha–?'

'How long I've got left.'

'You've already told me that.'

'Yeah, I know. But it's frightening.' He turned and looked directly in Liam's eyes. 'To fink I've got a couple of months left now,' he said, as he slowly nodded. 'Three at best.'

'Fuck.'

Jimmy sniffed hard. 'It's alright.' He forced a smile. 'I'd rather die like that than end up in a fucking home staring at the television all day.'

Liam nodded in agreement. 'Um–'

'Gwen can't look after me …' He continued screaming out his words. 'And … nor would I expect her to … Even *if* she could!'

'I'm so sorry, Dad.' Liam reached towards his father and placed his hand on his knee. 'Can't you have chemo?'

'Oh yeah. Left to rot in bed for months – with no control – shitting and pissing meself … and in fucking agony … and … and what's left of me 'air falling out?' He brushed at his thinning hair and shook his head wildly. 'That's not for me, son.'

'Um.'

Jimmy straightened up. 'Do you remember poor old Laurie?

'Who?'

'Laurie – in Spain. I sent you over to see him for me last year – to get the money he owed me.'

'Oh yeah. He was fucking sick alright. What a state … a vegetable more like.'

'So, you tell me what quality of life did he 'ave?' He shook his head. 'Not knowing where the fuck he was … just waiting to die.'

'Yeah. I can see that, Dad.'

'That's life, son. For me and Laurie and most of us evil bastards.'

'Not everyone that gets sick … is evil, Dad?'

'I know that. But it seems to have got to me and poor old Laurie.' He shrugged his acceptance. 'You go on and enjoy what you have with that Sigi or … Zita.' He sniggered. 'Or, whatever she calls herself … today.' He made to stand and Liam moved to help him. 'I'm not a fucking invalid yet, son.' He grabbed at Liam and looked out across the Thames and smiled to himself. 'Fucking lucky ain't we, eh?'

Liam agreed with a loud snort.

Jimmy reached out to Liam. 'Come on, let's get you back. They'll be wondering where you are.' He laughed loudly. 'Pulling off a job.' He smacked Liam on the back. 'Well … imagine.' He snorted. 'That would be fucking hilarious, wouldn't it?'

As they walked to the bike Liam stopped and spoke. 'It's Mum's birthday next week. How's about a knees-up, Dad?'

Jimmy frowned.

Liam continued. 'It might cheer her up.'

'Um. We can only hope.' He sniffed. 'But, be prepared.'

CHAPTER FIFTY-ONE

London's Calling

The telephone rang on the reception desk of the exclusive Knightsbridge restaurant. The smart woman in her forties stroked her hair and straightened her back before she picked it up. 'Hello, how can I help you?' she said, with a smile.

'I would like to speak to the manager, please.'

'Just one moment.' She clicked on the holding music and called the manager's office.

A smartly dressed middle aged Italian man in a dark morning suit and bow tie picked up the phone. 'Signore Rossi, there is a call for you.'

He smiled as he spoke. 'Thank you.' He settled himself in his seat. 'Good morning, this is Signore Rossi speaking, how may I help you?'

The voice at the other end coughed and then spoke. 'Good morning, Signore Rossi, this is Nick Anstey of the anti-terrorist unit.'

Signore Rossi, inhaled sharply.

The caller smiled to himself. 'I'm sorry. Sorry to alarm you, Signore Rossi.' He softened his tone to reassure the listener. 'There is nothing serious but we do need to follow up on our intel ...' He coughed. 'Intelligence. We understand you have a member of the Saudi Royal family dining with you this evening.' He paused. 'In The Room–'

The manager replied sternly. 'I'm sorry … Mister Anstey.' He coughed. 'But under no circumstances can I divulge who is dining with us.' He coughed again. 'You must understand exclusive clientele regularly dine with us and the press and media are always trying to learn that sort of information.'

'Quite so.' He paused. 'Of course. We understand.'

The manager could be heard to relax with a noisy exhalation of relief.

'We would like to have a member of our security team join you this evening – to assist you. Just in case.' He paused deliberately. 'We can't be too careful now, can we?'

'No, we certainly can't.'

'Thank you, Signore Rossi. That is wonderful. Our agent will be with you at seventeen hundred hours to check everything out. Are you in agreement to that?' Anstey sensed the doubt and he continued. 'I know what you are thinking.'

'Do you?'

'Yes, I do. The member of our team joining you this evening is trained to the highest level.' He laughed loudly. 'They could be an asset to you … and we will have surveillance outside and around the building. We can't have anything happen to your illustrious guest, can we?'

'I understand that. Thank you, Mister Anstey, I will inform our maître d'. Good bye.'

The maître d' was carrying out his meticulous ritual inspection of each and every table, straightening the odd knife, fork or spoon and repositioning the vases of exotic flowers on each table. He turned, and as he passed the table nearest the desk, he took a second to adjust the position of one of the chairs.

Signore Rossi called him into his office. 'Monsieur le Garde, this is a very sensitive matter. We have someone joining us this evening to look after our revered guest, Prince Abdul.'

'But, sir, it is for me to do that …'

The manager smiled as he raised his hands. 'I understand that, Antoine, but I need to follow *their* requests.'

'"Their requests?"'

'Yes. Please understand, it is only for this evening.' He paused. 'And I'm sure whoever it is will appreciate your valuable assistance.' He coughed. 'Tell no one else of this arrangement except to advise them that we have an additional person assisting us this evening.'

CHAPTER FIFTY-TWO

She's The One

Zita rode down Cromwell Road and turned into the side street until she was able to line up the rear of the hotel booked for her. She took a remote control from her pocket and flicked it. The garage door slowly raised in front of her. She rode inside and parked the motorbike. She changed into jeans, a blouse and a tweed jacket. She pulled a blonde wig from one of the paniers and carefully positioned it and checked in one of the rear-view mirrors. She straightened her jacket, took the worn leather travel bag from the other panier and grinned to herself as she walked out. She clicked the remote and watched the garage door close behind her. She took her time to walk around to the front of the hotel. She climbed the steps and walked into the dingy reception. She looked around at the faded and torn wallpaper and crumpled posters that had been on the walls for years. She stepped forward and rang the bell on the desk.

A young oriental woman appeared through a beaded screen. 'Can I help you?'

Zita forced a smile before she spoke. 'Um. I hope so. You have a room booked for Miss Baker?'

The receptionist checked the register and looked up at the clock. It read eleven o'clock. 'Yes, Miss Baker your room is ready for you now.' She smiled. 'They aren't usually ready until one.'

Zita thanked her with a nod.

The receptionist handed her the key and pointed towards the stairs.

Zita's room was on the second floor at the rear of the building with a window that overlooked the side street and opened onto the fire escape. She opened the leather travel bag and took out a toothbrush, toothpaste, hairbrush and face cream. She placed it neatly on the glass shelf in front of the cracked mirror and stained wash hand basin. She returned to the bag and took out a selection of items she had collected from the left luggage locker with the key provided to her by Delfine's contact at WH Smith. She checked the wardrobe, fingered the soft fabric of the formal jacket and skirt, pulled out the white blouse and held it against her face. She closed the wardrobe door and sang to herself as she made herself a coffee, with the complimentary packets and milk sachets. She opened the first of the two packs of sandwiches she had brought with her. She took out the video, which contained the promo video of the restaurant when it first opened, along with a training section of all aspects of restaurant etiquette, from her bag and pushed it into the player. She clicked play, lay back on the bed and watched it repeatedly.

At three o' clock there was a knock at the door. She switched off the video player and rubbed at her tired eyes as she opened the door.

The young woman smiled at her. 'I'm here for your makeup.'

Zita looked down at the makeup case and checked the corridor. 'Yes, come in.'

The next hour of conversation was wasted on Zita as she tried to remember everything she had seen in the video. The woman gave Zita a manicure and painted her nails with a soft pearl varnish. She then sat Zita back and took a syringe and phial from her case.

'What is dat?'

The young woman replied. 'Don't worry. This will wear off in about six hours and you will be back to normal.'

Zita checked the clock on the television and heaved a sigh of relief.

The woman removed a photograph from the makeup case and took a few minutes to examine it before she injected Zita's cheeks and forehead. While she waited for it to take effect, she took a series of accessories from her case, lined them up, and handed Zita the photograph. 'Can you hold this for me, please.'

Zita nodded.

The woman gently pressed Zita's cheeks and forehead and smiled to herself. 'That's fine.' She studied the photograph for a few more seconds and carefully took out a prosthetic nose, pushed it on and moulded it to suit the photograph. What appeared to be a small addition immediately transformed Zita. The woman opened another small container and took out coloured contact lenses. She carefully fitted them and then fixed false eyelashes in place. After adjusting them, she flicked through the rows of cosmetics. She applied a layer of foundation to Zita's face before applying eye-liner, blusher and a tint to her eyebrows. She took a dark brown wig from her case, brushed it out and positioned it carefully on Zita's head. She took another plastic box from the case, walked into the bathroom and washed the contents. She returned and asked Zita to open her mouth and pushed the prosthetic teeth into it. She clipped a tiny pearl earring onto each ear, stood back and compared Zita to the photograph. 'Perfect,' she said, with a huge smile.

She repacked her case and stood at the open door to the room. 'Shalom,' she said, honourably.

'Aleichem shalom,' replied Zita.

The woman closed the door quietly behind her.

Zita flexed her whole body, walked into the bathroom and looked in the mirror.

She didn't recognise herself.

When Zita was a young girl living in Hamburg with her mother, she remembered looking out onto the Reeperbahn, in St Pauli, during the day, and watching the young women walking their dogs and pushing their children along the street. In the evening, when the streets were ablaze with coloured flashing neon lights and loud music, the same women had been transformed beyond recognition into expensive prostitutes.

Zita shook her head and checked the time, took her uniform from the wardrobe and dressed. She tidied the room, opened the window, pulled on a long coat and stuffed a woolly hat in her pocket. She climbed down the fire escape and walked out onto the Cromwell Road and hailed a black cab.

CHAPTER FIFTY-THREE

Hello Goodbye

At five o'clock there was a gentle tap on the front door of the restaurant. The receptionist looked up from behind her desk, tugged at her jacket and walked pretentiously towards the locked doors. She looked through the opaque glazed door, unlocked it and smiled. 'Can I help you?'

The young woman spoke with a soft French accent. 'Hello, I'm Mademoiselle Izzy Dupont, I believe you are expecting me?'

'Yes, Mademoiselle Dupont, we are. Please come in.' She manoeuvred the young woman through the doors and stood her against the reception desk and took her time to look her up and down. 'If you would like to wait here, I will call the maître d.'

Izzy took in the restaurant while she waited? It was not as large as it had appeared in the video and was already tastefully decorated for Christmas with expensive ornaments and baubles, no doubt bought from Harrods on the opposite side of the road, on what were real Christmas trees. The restaurant was horseshoe shaped and was wrapped around the ornate carved oak reception desk. The reception was unusually spacious with a thick glass floor which looked down into the extensive wine cellar and the bottles bathed in soft red lights. The remainder of the restaurant had thick pile, ruby red carpet with a pale grey chevron design. To the right of reception was the bar with shelf upon shelf of bottles of alcohol and liqueurs, of all shapes and sizes with brands that she had never seen or heard of. One side of the bar was the seating area, furnished with soft armchairs, for pre-dinner drinks and liqueurs, and after-dinner brandy and coffee. There were ten tables that could be rearranged to accommodate two or four diners. To the left of reception were nine shoulder high cubicles which could each seat up to eight people, and ten free-standing tables for two, which again could be configured to accommodate four, six or eight diners. The kitchen was accessed at the far end of both sides of the horseshoe.

While she waited, Izzy picked up a menu from the reception desk and skimmed through it. There were no prices for any of the courses, the majority that she had never heard of and certainly not eaten. She had been told by the woman who was responsible for her transformation that those dining at the restaurant for lunch and drinks for two, would have little change from five hundred pounds and for dinner it was closer to a thousand. The private dining area, referred to as The Room, would cost anything from two to five thousand pounds for two people, for the evening. The restaurant was booked weeks and sometimes months ahead and the diners were aristocrats, city dealers, financiers, CEOs of ftse 100 companies, British and American film stars and occasionally members of Parliament who were usually guests of their lobbyists.

It was the restaurant's policy to always keep two tables available for the richest of clientele who may have just arrived in London, and for that they would pay a premium. All diners appreciated the quality of food and service and the special treatment they were given, and the tips were often hundreds of pounds.

The grey-haired, middle-aged maître d' appeared from the manager's office and when he saw Izzy he was taken aback.

She was immaculate. Her dark shoulder length hair edged the collar of her black suit and matching waistcoat, her white blouse with small bow tie, was finished off with the restaurant's logo and name badge on her lapel.

She sensed he was shocked, so she reached out her hand and offered him a smile. 'Mademoiselle Izzy Dupont. I'm here to ...' She paused. 'Help with the arrangements for your special guest this evening.'

As the maître d' felt her soft manicured hands, he immediately relaxed and fired her the broadest of smiles. 'Certainly, mademoiselle.'

Izzy lowered her head and quickly raised it. 'Could you show me where your guest will be dining this evening?'

He paused, pulled back and looked directly at her.

A beat.

Was he suspicious?

Izzy tilted her head and exhaled softly.

He reached out and smiled, 'Les gants.'

She looked down at his hand and the white gloves he was holding. She smiled broadly. 'D'accord,' she said, as she took them from him and put them on.

He performed his well-rehearsed choreographed move and spun around on the spot. 'Follow me.'

As she passed the manager's office she peered through the partially open door and saw what she knew was The Room in the corner of the computer screen.

The maître d' walked between the seating and smoking area and proudly past the eight laid up tables before he turned right. He stood back, exhaled, turned and waited to gauge her reaction. He took his time and slowly opened the pair of ornate, carved teak double doors, as though he was in a theatrical production. 'Eh, voila.'

The Room was magnificent. The pinnacle of decadence. Abstract paintings by famous artists, chosen specifically not to insult or upset the diner or cause issues over their religion, or allegiance to any parliamentary party. One wall was decorated with stunning black art deco Italian wallpaper, designed by Elena Salmistraro, at a cost of more than a thousand pounds a roll. A single stem of the very rare Rothschilds Slipper orchid, costing as much as five thousand pounds a stem, was positioned in the centre of the table.

The maître d' waved her inside.

She took her time to walk around the table making sure that her face was always partially obscured from the security camera. She stopped, leaned forward and straightened a fork.

The maître d' nodded and smiled to himself. He stood upright, clasped his hands and interlocked his fingers. 'Our clients have free rein when they are in here.' He grinned. 'It is very private and discreet.'

Izzy nodded and grinned back at him. Her intense study and repeated viewing of the video had succeeded.

CHAPTER FIFTY-FOUR

Kiss From a Rose

By six-thirty, soft classical music played through the hidden speakers and the restaurant was buzzing with diners at varying stages of their dinner. Many of the tables were occupied while two middle-aged, well-dressed couples sat in the seating area having pre-dinner drinks. Izzy recognised some of them as film stars but didn't know their names.

At seven o'clock Izzy looked out onto the street and saw a white limousine pull up on the double yellow lines immediately outside the restaurant. The front passenger, a tall well-built man with a pockmarked face, buzzed hair, bristled chin and glasses, jumped out of the car and walked briskly towards the restaurant. The receptionist greeted him, clicked the button beneath the desk and the manager appeared. He smiled as he approached the man and briefly lowered his eyes as confirmation to Izzy and the maître d' that it was their special guest.

'Christo Giroud,' said the bodyguard in an Afrikaans accent.

The manager introduced the maître d' and then Izzy. 'Mademoiselle Dupont will be your client's personal server this evening.' He paused. 'And if there is anything specific that your client requires, please ask.' He turned away as he spoke and walked towards his office.

The maître d' stepped forward. 'If you would follow me, sir,' he said as he turned right.

Giroud followed him and Izzy walked closely behind him. It was obvious from the way the bodyguard looked and walked that he wanted to maintain and convey his hard image from his time as a mercenary. Izzy noticed the bulge beneath his jacket and then tilted her head to one side and looked through his lenses from behind. She knew they were clear safety glass, with reactolite lenses, serving a dual purpose as sunglasses and for protection against an acid attack.

They walked past the final couple who were still having drinks and stopped outside The Room.

The maître d' opened the doors and stood back proudly.

Giroud entered and took a mirror from his inside pocket, knelt down on the floor and checked beneath the table and then upturned the ornate chairs and checked each of them.

The maître d' leaned into the room and forced a cough. 'Mister Giroud, we have this room checked every week for …' He paused, bent down and looked directly at him and smiled proudly. 'For *devices*.' He paused. 'And … for our valued guest this evening … it was checked again … *this afternoon*.'

Giroud ignored him and took a small electronic device from another pocket and proceeded to move it along the walls and paintings as he looked for hidden microphones and transmitters. Satisfied with his efforts he slid it back into his pocket and then checked for cameras.

The maître d' turned and whispered to Izzy. 'Privacy is paramount to all of our guests.'

Izzy nodded. She had watched Giroud perform his outdated and inadequate security checks. *He was an amateur.* She scanned the room and when she identified where the *secret* surveillance camera was hidden, she smiled to herself and let out a clipped exhalation of breath to celebrate.

Giroud finally signified his successful sweep of the room with a grunt. He raised his index finger and grinned, at Izzy and the maître d', as he reached for the bottle of the ultra-expensive Dom Pérignon vintage 1998 champagne that was already on ice. He checked the foil that covered the cork and much to the obvious anguish of the maître d', with a sacrosanct move, the bodyguard gently shook the bottle, before dropping it back into the ice bucket. He spoke into the microphone on his wrist and walked back through the restaurant and out to the limousine. He acknowledged his client sitting in the rear seat with a reassuring nod. He leaned forward and tapped on the window of the bodyguard sitting in the second front passenger seat and stood back. At what was a well-rehearsed security procedure the other bodyguard jumped out of the car and opened the rear doors. After looking furtively around and nodding to Giroud they escorted the prince and his guest, a young scantily dressed girl in her late teens, into the restaurant.

As the limo drove away it was immediately replaced by a black BMW, with tinted windows, which again parked on the double yellow lines immediately outside the restaurant.

The maître d' opened the restaurant doors and, after he welcomed the prince and his companion, he introduced Izzy.

The prince, dressed in a handmade, lightweight grey suit, white shirt and dark blue tie, shook her hand. With his intense black hair, sculptured beard and soft skin, Izzy decided that he was in his mid-twenties. His companion for the evening was very young, but old enough for anything he wanted to do to her. Her long blonde hair, short skirt and sleeveless blouse exposed so much pale naked flesh. Her modesty was preserved with a red lambswool shawl which hung sloppily across her bare shoulders and was clearly an afterthought, by her escort agency, to hide her part-time profession.

They followed Izzy to The Room and she took her time to open the doors and waited for them to take in the opulence. It was wasted on the prince, but met with a breathless giggly, 'Wow,' from his young companion.

While Izzy led them into The Room, again making sure that she was not clearly visible to the security camera, Giroud stood outside, spread his feet, clasped his hands and dropped them between his open legs.

Izzy closed one door and deliberately left the other one slightly ajar. She whispered to Giroud through the gap. 'I will be opening the champagne in a few moments and … and there will be a loud "pop".' She controlled her laugh by covering her mouth. 'So don't get too nervous.' She walked towards the table, pulled out the girl's chair and sat her down, then walked around the table, and waited for the prince to sit down. She picked up the champagne and showed him the label.

He nodded.

She removed the foil and the wire cage and let the bottle pop. The cork shot across the room and hit the security camera, in the top corner of the picture frame, and smashed it, before it dropped into yet another huge display of exotic flowers. She waited for Giroud to push his nose through the gap and grinned back at him.

He pulled back in embarrassment.

Izzy spent much of the next two hours outside the door with Giroud listening to the childish giggles and shallow conversation. When instructed by Izzy, a waiter would appear from the kitchen pushing an ornate trolley with each course. He would leave it at the door and Izzy waited while Giroud lifted the shiny and ornate stainless steel plate cloches and visually checked the food, replaced them and nodded to Izzy to enter.

When she delivered the third bottle of champagne, the prince and the girl were very drunk and semi-naked. She dropped it unopened into the ice bucket. They had no need of it as they were now taking it in turns to slurp Louis XlII cognac brandy from the girl's shoes.

The prince turned to Izzy and whispered to her.

She left The Room, and whispered to Giroud. He reached into his pocket and surreptitiously slipped her a gold pill box inlaid with diamonds and a small plastic bag. She returned to the room and handed them to the prince. As Izzy attempted to clear some of the plates, cutlery and glasses, he shooed her away.

When the doors were closed, he smiled at the young girl, opened the pill box and handed her a handful of amphetamines. She giggled as she washed them down with the last of the champagne in her glass and sat back.

He moved the plate on his table mat aside, tipped the cocaine onto it and, with his gold credit card, formed three lines. He cut it with the card and took a hundred-dollar bill from his top shirt pocket, rolled it up and snorted two of the columns. He called her over to join him and stripped her. He beckoned her to sit on his lap and let her snort the final line of cocaine. He wiped the residue from beneath her nose and they giggled mindlessly to each other as the drug fuelled euphoria swept through their bodies.

Izzy looked out of the window and saw the sign written van with the words, FLOWER GIRL - *"Flowers for everyone & every occasion,"* pull up outside. She immediately recognised the driver: the woman who had transformed her a few hours earlier. Izzy turned and walked away and disappeared into the kitchen. *The Flower Girl* wore a pink polo shirt with the logo that matched the one on the van. She opened the rear doors of the van and took a huge bouquet of roses, walked into the restaurant and handed them to the receptionist. She summoned one of the waiters who called Izzy from the kitchen and the woman handed them to her. She spoke in little more than a whisper. 'For our special guest in … The Room.'

Izzy forced a knowing smile and took the bouquet from her. As she made her way past the tables, many of the diners commented on the exquisite bouquet. When she reached The Room, she was stopped in her tracks by Giroud who barred her with his right arm and reached out for the flowers with the other.

Izzy pulled his arm back. 'Be careful monsieur.' She teased. 'They may *prick* you.'

Ignoring any potential nicks from the thorns he checked the bouquet by thrusting his huge hand into the centre. When he was satisfied it was safe, he handed it back to her and waved her to them in. As she opened the doors, she pulled out the tiny needle, loaded with poison, from the bottom of the bouquet, and held it between her finger and thumb and removed the plastic cover. She lowered her eyes to give the impression that she could not see what debauched acts the prince and his guest were performing.

She handed the roses to the prince with one hand and jabbed the needle into his dark hairy wrist with the other.

The Saudi Prince was too stoned to feel it.

She pulled the moon knife from beneath her jacket, dropped it, and while she kicked it beneath the table, she slipped the plastic cover on the needle.

As she walked toward the door the prince called out her name.

Izzy froze.

She took a long slow breath and turned to face him. She tilted her head and allowed a smile to cross her face. 'Oui, monsieur?' she said, evocatively.

The prince pulled a rose from the bouquet and attempted to stand but fell into his chair.

Izzy returned to the table and took the rose from him. 'Merci, monsieur,' she said, softly. She thanked him with yet another smile and left, closing the doors behind her.

She stood outside The Room, and broke off a piece of the rose stem. She reached up, and with a teasing wink pushed the rose into Giroud's button hole and at the same time slid the needle into his top jacket pocket.

She tapped his fat ass, spoke to him in Afrikaans, turned and walked off towards the kitchen.

He stood and watched her – speechless

CHAPTER FIFTY-FIVE

Escape

The kitchen was noisier than it had been the whole evening. Now, at that time of night, it had changed to music from the old cassette player, playing unrecognisable ethnic music. The warm oppressive air was filled with the rattling and clanging of pots and pans as the kitchen porters ploughed their way through expensive cloches, pans and piles of beautifully decorated plates and cutlery before they could deep clean the kitchen and complete their shift. They didn't notice Izzy as she checked her watch, picked up the wall phone and dialled 999. She pushed the telephone close to her mouth and yelled to the call handler, in a frightened high-pitched scream. 'We have a terrorist … attacking us!' She pushed the handset even tighter against her mouth and screamed. 'Help!' She dropped the handset and left it hanging while the emergency call handler pleaded desperately for more information.

There was none.

The phone rang in the restaurant manager's office. He picked it up. 'Si?'

'Good evening, Signore Rossi. This is Mister Anstey. Thank you for your assistance this evening.'

The line went dead.

The Met police had already received a credible, coded message advising them of a planned terrorist incident somewhere in Kensington and had deployed teams to various parts of the wealthy borough to wait for the location.

Izzy knew she had three minutes to get away from the immediate area.

She did it in two.

The naked young girl in The Room screamed hysterically.

Giroud ignored her. He'd made that mistake before when he was guarding the prince in Madrid and he'd almost been fired for incompetence. When Giroud was interviewed for the job, he had been advised that the prince had very special sexual needs and, when he was engaged, he was told never to interfere with whoever or wherever that may be.

The screams grew louder and Giroud gave in to his instincts. He partially opened one of the doors and peered inside. The naked girl looked back at him, her wide swollen eyes a mass of red veins and tears. She shook uncontrollably and was unable to speak coherently. She pointed at the prince who was slumped unconscious on the table, his head amongst the myriad of ornate cut glasses and expensive flowers. His extended discoloured tongue hung to one side of his foaming wide open mouth.

Giroud rushed forward and felt the neck of the unconscious prince for a pulse. He spoke into the microphone on his wrist and raised the alarm with the bodyguards in the BMW.

Before they could respond, four police cars pulled up and surrounded them and the armed response officers jumped out with their guns drawn. They dragged the occupants out of the car and forced them to lay face down on the floor before relieving them of their weapons.

A waitress serving a table nearest to the window looked up. When she saw the armed police, she stood on the spot paralysed in fear until she finally freaked out. She dropped the tray of drinks and ran into the large Christmas tree knocking it over. As the tree fell, the ornate baubles smashed on the nearest table and the fine coloured glass showered the diners. The coloured lights continued to flash until they shorted out and blew the contact breaker.

The restaurant was left in temporary darkness. The waitress screamed as she raced blindly towards the kitchen crashing into tables and stunned diners as she passed. The other waiters and waitresses heard her screams and, shocked by the blackout, joined her. Their frenzied shouts further compounded the fear as they ran in all directions.

All hell broke loose.

Some of the younger diners threw themselves awkwardly onto the carpet and hid beneath the tables while the much older clientele remained, frozen in their seats. The maître d', almost invisible in the darkness, rushed amongst them and made a futile attempt to calm things down.

He was ignored.

A helicopter buzzed above the restaurant and its powerful searchlight scanned the streets below. The surrounding streets were filled with a cacophony of ear-splitting sirens as the security services arrived followed by more police cars and vans, ambulances, fire brigade and anti-terrorist squad. Finally, the armoured truck of the bomb squad trundled down the road and arrived on the scene. The police cordoned off West Kensington High

Street while the building and immediate area was surrounded and secured.

The manager reset the MCB and the lighting flickered back on to reveal the extent of the damage.

The older terrified diners remained at their tables, cringing and shaking uncontrollably, while others crouched on the carpet between the upturned tables, their knees, hands and legs bleeding, punctured and cut by the smashed plates, glasses, cutlery and baubles.

The chaos was about to get worse.

Much worse.

One of the anti-terrorist teams had already pushed their way past the refuse lorry and rushed through the kitchen and into The Room. Two of them grabbed Giroud and knocked him to the ground and thrust the heels of their boots in the centre of his back. The third armed man stood over the prince and the fourth stood at the door, his gun flicking purposefully from left to right.

The second team raised their guns and stormed the front entrance. What they found inside was a restaurant full of diners who were totally confused and shocked, and unaware of what was about to unfold. One of the armed men grabbed the Christmas tree, its lights still plugged into the wall socket, dragged it outside and threw it onto the pavement.

'Get down!' screamed the first armed man.

'On the ground!' ordered the second.

The third screamed just one word. 'NOW!'

For those dining at the restaurant Christmas would never be the same.

In The Room, the naked young girl continued to scream hysterically and her arms flayed around like a windmill. The fourth member of the squad stepped forward and checked the prince's pulse. He immediately shook his head and, while he talked into his mouth piece, a member of the team stepped forward, picked up the girl's clothes and threw them at her. He stood over her and waited while she attempted to get dressed.

She was incapable.

She was marched out of the restaurant, naked, by two of the armed men.

Outside, a policewoman handed her a blanket and, still sobbing uncontrollably, the young girl was bundled into a police car and taken away for questioning.

Two plain clothed middle-aged security men and a younger self-assured woman entered the restaurant, showed the armed men their IDs and were waved in. The woman, clearly of the highest rank, made for the manager's office while the two men walked towards The Room.

The woman stood over Signore Rossi.

He began to sweat, wiped at his forehead and grunted.

'You have security footage – yes?'

He nodded.

'Show me,' she demanded, with a click of her fingers.

Signore Rossi spluttered as he clacked the computer keyboard. 'I can't believe what is happening. We … we … will be ruined.' The screen came to life and he tapped the keyboard several more times until it showed The Room in one corner of the screen.

The woman watched intently as the maître d' and Izzy stood and looked on as Giroud carried out his security sweep. 'Freeze it, there,' she ordered. She moved close to the screen and tried to identify Izzy. She fast forwarded the CCTV and watched with interest as Izzy guided the prince and the young girl into The Room. She watched Izzy open the champagne. 'Who is she?'

Before the manager could reply, the champagne cork popped and the screen went blank.

The woman exhaled angrily 'What the fuck!' She reached down and tapped at the keyboard 'How come?' She dug her fingers into Signore Rossi's shoulders and squeezed. 'Don't you check it!'

'*The Room is private!*' he screamed. He took a deep breath and blushed. 'Our policy is *not* to snoop on our revered clientele,' he said, respectfully. He paused. 'If that ever got out … we would lose them – and our business.'

'Fuck that.' She shrugged. 'So, why do you have the camera in there anyway?'

Signore Rossi coughed. 'We only record it in case there is … an issue.' He looked up at. 'And … there never has been.' He sighed heavily. 'That is why I am the only person to check it.'

The woman shook her head with frustration and grunted. 'What do you do then?' She paused briefly and then pushed her face into his. 'Do you ever look at them?'

'Certainly not,' he said indignantly. 'If there is not a problem …' He turned his head towards her and smiled. 'I delete them–'

'When?'

'Immediately,' said, Signore Rossi, proudly. He appeared to relax and grinned at her as he followed the line of his moustache and sculptured beard with his index finger. 'In fact, we had one of your people … *your agent* … here tonight.'

She snapped at him. 'One of *our* people!' She smashed her hand on the keyboard and kicked out at his desk. 'What the fuck do you mean – one of *our* people?'

'That was her in the video – Mademoiselle Dupont.'

'A fucking French woman?'

Her earpiece buzzed and she turned away. 'OK.'

She turned to Signore Rossi and glared at him before she grunted her anger.

'Yes, she was very nice.' He paused. 'Fantastico,' he said, as he raised his clenched hands and opened his fingers in celebration. 'She must know what happened because she served our guest in The Room all the evening–'

'You said … agent?!' she snapped.

He looked up at her. 'We had a call from your …' He spluttered and checked his note pad. 'Your … your, Mister Anstey.' He paused and regained his composure and followed with a smile. 'In fact, he called a few minutes ago and thanked us–'

'What the fuck? Agent? *Anstey.*' She shook her head in disbelief. 'It had nothing to do with our department … or any other of them.' She sighed. 'We wouldn't do that unless we had strong intel.'

Signore Rossi trembled and grinned mindlessly at her. 'He …' He forced a cough. 'Mister Anstey … he said you had *intel.*'

'Is she here now?' The woman made for the door. She turned. 'Where can I find this … this *agent?*'

Signore Rossi stood and appeared to relax. 'Of course. Come.' He reached out to take the woman's arm and she shrugged him off. 'Mademoiselle Dupont will be in The Room,' he said, confidently. He forced a congratulatory smile. 'As I said … she's been looking after our special guest the whole evening.'

'I see.' She sniggered. 'She did that … so *fucking well.*' She exhaled. 'That *your* guest is … DEAD!'

Signore Rossi was unable to hide the shock. 'How can that be possible?' He shook his head. 'He has his own bodyguard to protect him–'

'That's what I want to know and I'm sure my superiors.' She sniffed hard. 'And the Prime Minister will want to know that too.' She seethed. 'Do you realise …' She spoke as she tapped his grey-haired head. 'In that tiny head of yours … this could cause a major diplomatic incident with the Saudis?' She scoffed. 'If we can't protect their royalty. Urgh … Fuck … fuck …fuck …' She spoke into the radio on her lapel. 'Find the French waitress … Dupont … NOW!'

She left Signore Rossi at the door and rushed out of the office mumbling under her breath.

Izzy had long gone.

CHAPTER FIFTY-SIX

Inside Out

After making the emergency call Izzy walked slowly through the kitchen and out into the rear yard. Something that she had done throughout the evening feigning desperation for cigarette breaks.

Before she walked into the restaurant that evening, she hid a bag behind one of the large waste containers in the rear yard.

She was about to pull it out when the refuse lorry, orange light flashing and safety beeper sounding, reversed into the side street at the rear of the restaurant. Its huge jaws locked onto the first of the large overflowing stinking wheeled bins, lifted it and emptied it into the back of the lorry. Izzy grabbed the bag and crept into the shadows and, now invisible to the driver and his assistant, she took out the long coat and woolly hat, and put them on. She sneaked between the lorry and the wall and took her time to walk out onto a busy West Kensington High Street. Having worn the gloves since arriving at the restaurant she didn't leave any potentially incriminating fingerprints. She finally removed them and slipped them into her pocket and hailed a taxi. She had already picked out a run-down B and B on the opposite side of the road to her hotel and asked the taxi driver to drop her outside. She paid and waited for him to drive away and walked a hundred yards in the opposite direction from her hotel. She took her time to cross the road, doubled back and walked into the side street. She flicked the remote control and the garage door raised in front of her. She walked inside and changed into her leathers, took a plastic box from the bottom of the panier, clicked the remote control and waited for the garage door to close before she climbed the fire escape.

Once in her room, she opened the plastic box and took out three remote fire-starters, already built for her. Something she had only used twice before. She placed one of them in the centre of a neatly arranged nest of sheets and the duvet, on the bed. The second in the centre of a similarly arranged nest of dry towels and her uniform which she laid on the carpet beside the bed. She placed the third fire-starter in the bathroom and surrounded it with towels. She removed the coloured lenses, false eyelashes, earrings, prosthetic nose, teeth and slipped them into her makeup bag. She pulled on a pair of black rubber gloves, refilled the holdall with her remaining clothes and wig, the video tape, toothbrush, makeup bag and anything that could link or identify her. She emptied the bin and pushed the contents into a separate plastic bag and forced it inside the holdall. She wiped down all the surfaces, opened the bedroom window, rechecked the bathroom and left the door and window open. She climbed onto the bed and taped plastic bags over each of the smoke detectors in the ceiling and set the timers on the fire-starters at seven minutes. She raced down the fire escape, pushed everything into the panniers, pulled on her helmet and fired up her motorbike. She closed the garage door and as she gently revved the throttle, she felt something attached to it. She rode a hundred yards down the road, switched off the ignition, and peeled off the note. It contained the postcode

– SW10 0DG. She checked her map, memorised the directions and pushed it into her pocket. She restarted the bike, gently twisted the throttle and pulled silently away into the night. She thought. *Why is it that robbers, murderers and criminals always accelerated away and burned rubber when they have committed a crime – to be witnessed by anyone and everyone around them? This wasn't a film.*

She made her way along the Cromwell Road and, as she turned left onto Palace Gate, her hotel room burst into flames. Four minutes later she rode onto West Kensington High Street and smiled to herself as yet another stream of police cars and anti-terrorist vehicles, followed by more emergency service vehicles with flashing lights and sirens blaring, raced in the opposite direction.

Zita rode along the Embankment until she saw the overflowing builder's skip she had earmarked earlier. She stopped and pulled the bags, coat and hat from the panniers and took her time to empty the makeup bag. She took the white gloves from the coat pocket, and split everything up before she spread it between the rotten timber and pallets and anything that would ignite and burn quickly.

She set the gloves alight and threw them into the skip and set it alight.

She watched and waited as her clothes burned before the rest of the skip burst into a ball of flames. Satisfied, there would be nothing left that could be linked to Izzy, she rode off.

CHAPTER FIFTY-SEVEN

Wild Thing

Zita arrived at SW10 0DG, 106 Cheyne Walk, Chelsea Reach, and pulled into the lay-by immediately outside the Chelsea Yacht and Boat Club. While she waited, she looked down at the luxurious, million pound plus houseboats and motor cruisers that filled much of that area of the river. Seconds later, a black Range Rover, with tinted windows, drew up beside her and the rear passenger door swung open.

'Hello, Zita, come in,' said the deep male voice. She slid off her bike and walked towards the open door. The front passenger's electric window wound down and a hand waved at her to remove her crash helmet. She handed it to him, climbed into the vehicle and slid onto the back seat.

She forced a smile. 'What the fuck are you doing here?' She took her time to look around. 'Where's Delfine?'

'This is *my* decision now – not hers!'

'Didn't you have anyone else?' screamed Zita.

Chayim, the middle-aged dark-haired man, in a navy-blue suit and a dark blue patterned Giordano shirt and handmade shoes, grinned at her and clicked his tongue. '*You know* why we chose *you*.' His grin faded. 'You want to be *liberated*?'

His eyes seared deep into her.

She felt uncomfortable but was determined not to react to his intimidation.

He paused a beat. 'Don't you?'

She leaned into him and aimed her words into his face. 'You *know* I do,' she snarled.

Chayim pulled his head away and grinned. 'Well then … you know.' He opened his mouth to reveal several gold teeth. 'You needed to earn it.' He leaned towards her and scoffed in her face. 'No one can walk away … *Leave us* … Unless *we* say so.'

She took the name badge from her pocket and handed it to him. 'Izzy's gone. She doesn't exist.'

He snorted and squeezed the badge tight in his fist. 'We *trained you* … taught you everything. Moulded and created *Zita* from that innocent … and *angry* young girl.' He tutted, opened his hand and looked down at the badge. 'And fortunately …you haven't changed.' He fired her a crass grin. 'Tell, me. Why would we throw all of that away?' He looked towards the rear-view mirror and sniggered. The driver grinned back at him and he continued. 'Tonight was a master class in assassination.' He nodded. 'You know … you are a natural and … so … so useful to the Kidon.'

Zita grunted and screwed up her face. 'Really?' She looked out at the moored boats. 'So, why did you choose to meet here?' she snarled.

He laughed lewdly. 'Isn't it obvious.' He paused and faked concern before he turned, and looked out of the window. He deliberated and slowly waved his arm at the array of boats. He stopped suddenly and pointed directly at the largest and most expensive houseboat on the Thames.

Her eyes followed his finger but she stifled her anger.

He forced a repugnant grin and relished every word as he emphasised them. 'Well … Aren't you homesick … *yet?*'

She lost control.

She made a fist and punched the seat in front of her.

Chayim ignored her outburst. 'Won't you change your mind?'

She shook her head. 'No. I'm finished.' She swallowed hard. 'I have repaid you … *all of you* … so … so many times.'

'Yes, I agree.' He sniffed. '*We all* agree. But … remember …' He looked directly into her eyes. 'We are tools … *all of us*.' He closed his eyes and paused. 'And you … have done excellent work for us and Kidon–'

'So, will I ever be … *free?*' Zita tilted her head and waited. 'I want a life.'

'Maybe you have. But we own you. We always have.' Chayim mirrored her and tilted his head. He took his time to look her slowly up and down before he replied. 'Perhaps.' He cleared his throat with a cough. 'Maybe … maybe tonight … You have done your most important …' He grinned. 'Or perhaps … your very last mission–'

'*Perhaps?*' seethed Zita.

'I'm sure you know …' His voice tailed off and he paused while he took his time to try and guess what Zita may have been thinking.

She looked past him, took a ragged breath and exhaled slowly.

He realised she had changed and he couldn't work her out. Instead, he shook it off and continued with a huge grin on his face. 'You are very good – the best.' He closed his eyes and rubbed the stubble on his chin with his thumb. He took his time to open his eyes. He looked directly at her.

'You do know we have tracked you … *Everywhere?*' He paused. 'And everything you've done … since … *since* you left *us*.' He covered his mouth and forced a guttural laugh. 'Or … thought you had.'

Zita had always known that but it still incensed her knowing that it was not just her but also Liam's every move they had been monitoring.

'After your assassination here in London in '95, you seemed to be untouchable.' He coughed. 'Our intel knew exactly where you were when you left a few months later after the job in Switzerland but our director gave strict orders to do …' He exhaled and shook his head with frustration. '… Nothing.' He glared at her and shook his head. 'Not a thing …' He exhaled angrily. 'For some reason you were his blue-eyed …' He paused and grinned. '*Girl.*' He fidgeted in his seat and tightened his leather gloves. 'If it had been left to me you would have been dealt with … *killed* – immediately.' He looked directly into her eyes. 'And … I would have been pleased to do it myself.' He gritted his teeth. 'Very pleased.' He paused and forced a grin. 'They were happy to let you go and live in that den of iniquity in Amsterdam and do whatever you wanted. You were no risk to us there.' He screwed up his face and clicked his tongue. 'But all that changed this year when you became a *loose cannon* and a danger to our organisation.' He huffed. 'Our director heard that you were using our communications …' He raised his voice. '*For your own purposes.*'

Zita blushed.

'That was such a stupid thing to do. To risk … in fact to throw away your insane and unacceptable immunity for that drunk.'

Zita raised her voice. 'I did what I had to do! And you would have done the same–'

'Would I?' He briefly closed his eyes and thought about it. He took his time to open them. 'Perhaps I would.' He sniffed. 'But that is something you will never know.' Chayim sniggered and, as if to prepare himself, he shrugged his shoulders and relaxed. 'We loved the roses–'

'Roses?'

'Yes, the *pink* roses–'

'Is that why you sent them ... tonight?' she said, with a smirk.

'What do you think?' He sniggered. 'They worked in Estonia, in Tallinn, didn't they?' He turned away from her and looked into the rear-view mirror and the driver. He laughed loudly. He was joined immediately with raucous laughter from the passenger in the front seat. He continued. 'Why should we let a good idea go to waste,' he boomed. They all nodded in agreement and cheered. He continued and sucked at his bottom lip. 'I'm sure my idea will be used in many future actions–'

'Your idea!' screamed Zita. Her whole body shook angrily. 'Fuck you!'

Chayim licked his lips seductively and leaned into her. 'Do you want to?' he said, as he clicked his tongue salaciously.

Zita's face broke into a vile strained grin and, after taking her time and carefully choosing her words, she spoke slowly. 'You ... are ... *dreaming*, Chayim.'

He tilted his head, grinned at her and spoke softly. 'Zita ... mein schatz.' He reached for her hand.

She pulled away.

Chayim continued. 'Do you not allow me to have my dreams?'

She snarled at him. '*Never*.'

He retaliated with a snide grin. 'So, you'd rather fuck *that low-life … the drunk?*'

She screamed back at him and glared into the rear-view mirror. 'He's worth more than all you vile bastards put together!'

'Only three of us?' he said, as he sniggered loudly.

The other two joined him with celebratory whoops and whistles.

Zita ignored them and stiffened. 'So, what now?'

Chayim folded his arms and pushed himself deep into the soft leather seat. 'That is what I already said to you.' He paused. *'Perhaps.'* His demeanour changed. 'I will speak with Efraim Haleuy, our director since 1998.' He shook his head and forced a cough. 'He and Shabtai Shavit, still talk about your mission here in London, back in '95.'

Zita could hear the jealousy in his voice and grinned back at him.

He smirked at her and flicked his head towards the door. 'Enjoy the rest of your evening.'

Zita remained in her seat and fidgeted nervously.

He glared at her and continued. 'I said … we'll be in contact with you–'

'Where? When?'

He shook his head. 'You already know the answer to that … don't you?'

'Fuck you!'

'That is such a pity.' He tilted his head and humoured her with a smack of his lips. 'A great pity.'

Zita bit into her bottom lip. 'So?'

He exhaled. '"So," yes, you can go.' He reached over the seat and the driver passed him a large brown envelope. He waved it in the air and shook it. 'These are yours.'

She reached out her hand.

He pulled the envelope away, folded it, and pushed it into a deep pocket in his jacket.

'You fucker!'

He grinned back at her mindlessly and tutted. 'I sense there is a storm brewing in that head of yours.' He tutted. 'You know ... *you need* to control *your* emotions.'

She slid along the seat, jumped out of the car and reached for her crash helmet that now hung, once again, from the passenger's hand.

The rear window wound down. 'You know where we are when you need us.' He took his time to light a cheroot. 'Zita, as I said, we know your every move ... We always have.' He issued a snide look. 'I could have had you killed ... *both* of you ... any time I *wished.*'

'You are such a bastard!'

He ignored her anger. 'And we will *always* know where *you are.*' He paused. *'And him.'*

She snapped at him. 'Why do you need to know dat?'

He appeared to ignore her. 'You are too useful ... too good to lose. To waste *your* life ...' He paused and looked directly into her eyes. 'But ... *not ... his,*' he said, emphasising the last words and simultaneously shaking his head.

Zita swung on the car door. 'So?'

He paused, leaned towards her, tilted his head and spoke softly. 'Shalom, Sigrid Obermeyer.'

The driver flicked the ignition key and pressed the accelerator.

Zita left, slamming the door closed behind her.

Chayim waved at her and grinned. 'Auf wiedersehen, liebling.'

CHAPTER FIFTY-EIGHT

Somewhere Between

It was obvious to everyone, except Gwen, that Liam was not enjoying her birthday party. Kathleen guided him into the garden. She leaned on the shed and forced a smile. 'Jimmy and Gwen … and the kids are pleased to see you again.'

'Are they?'

'Course they are.' She laughed. 'And I can say your time here has been a revelation.' She turned away and then took her time to turn back. 'And … you've found someone who cares for you.'

He lowered his head. 'I know.'

'Where is she?'

He had no idea, so he lied. 'She'll be here soon.'

Kathleen looked furtively around and lowered her voice. 'Don't fuck it up like you did with us.'

Liam pulled back and took his anger out on his unfinished cigarette. He pushed it violently in the rain filled ashtray on the garden table and watched it hiss into extinction. He raised his head and like a scolded child looked pitifully at Kathleen. 'Did you know?'

She nodded slowly and her face took on a solemn look. 'Of course, I did.' She took a deep breath and spoke as she exhaled. 'We all knew what you did, Liam.'

'Fuck.'

'You were a lost cause back then ... no use to me ... or the kids.' She paused. 'Something had to be done ... you were killing yourself.' She took a deep breath. 'And you almost killed me ... and the kids with your drunken binges.' She gulped as she relived that night. 'The fire was the last straw.'

Liam swallowed hard. 'I couldn't help myself ...' He hyperventilated and gulped for air. 'Surely you know that?'

Kathleen offered him a sympathetic smile. 'Yes, Liam *we all* knew that.' She shuddered and sighed. 'What else could we do?' She tilted her head and leaned into him. 'Jimmy came up with a plan.' She stepped forward and squeezed him into her. 'We didn't know if it would save you ... or any of *us* ... but we had to try something – anything.'

Liam sniffed and wiped at his tearful eyes. 'Yeah. Course you're right.' He pulled slowly away from her.

She leaned forward and made a token attempt to wipe his tears.

'You ... None of you, deserved any of that. I was so fucked up ... but didn't see it.'

'That's in the past now, Liam. We both have to get on with our lives.'

Liam sniffed. 'Get that divorce sorted and then you can marry your Frenchman ...'

'He's French Algerian!' she retorted. 'And ... maybe you too. Who knows, eh?'

Liam sniggered. 'Yeah, who knows.'

Kathleen took his arm. 'Come on, it's getting cold. Let's go inside and try to enjoy Gwen's birthday.' She sighed heavily and tried to hold back her sadness. 'It might be the last one she remembers,' she said, as she flicked at her tearful eyes.

The tiny sitting room in Morepeth Road was already packed with a few close friends and family members. An elderly man sat on a chair with a piano accordion that looked too big and too heavy for him to lift, and a man of a similar age with a ukulele, were squeezed into one corner of the room.

Kathleen joined the twins on the settee while Felix, his arms and hands still swathed in bandages, had perched himself awkwardly and painfully on one arm. Harry stood at the open door trying his hardest to ignore the occasion.

Zita arrived when they were eating. She handed Gwen a bunch of flowers and gave her a hug and a kiss before she joined Liam in the kitchen where he was refilling his plate from the buffet. 'Sorry I'm late.'

Liam could see she was different. She was relaxed, smiley and couldn't stop touching him. 'What is up with you?'

'I'm happy ... I'll tell you later.'

'Wha?'

Once the paper plates were loaded into the bulging bin bag, the music restarted. The musicians then played *A Picture of You*, a hit for Joe Brown, a chirpy adopted cockney, in 1962. Jimmy looked across at Zita. 'This is *our* song. We danced to it at our wedding.' Jimmy reached out for Gwen's hand. She winced in pain as he pulled her out of the armchair. They managed to stand and moved to their celebratory song by shuffling on the same spot.

Zita whispered to Liam. 'Do we have a song?'

He smirked at her. 'Maybe the summer of 69?'

She grinned back at him. 'Perfect.'

There was a knock at the front door. Harry seized the opportunity to leave the room and opened it.

George, wearing a navy-blue blazer, with a badge on the breast pocket, white shirt and striped tie, was followed by Ethel in a crimplene floral patterned dress.

George, desperate to find Zita, left Ethel with Harry, pushed past both of them, and rushed in carrying the chocolate birthday cake.

Kathleen took the cake from him and walked towards the kitchen. She stopped and turned. 'Did you make this, Ethel?'

George replied for her. 'Course she did … With your own fair hands, didn't yer love?'

Zita appeared at the kitchen door. 'Evening, George,' she said softly. 'Very smart.' She pointed at his badge. 'Oh, I like that.'

He blushed and as he stuttered his reply, 'Korea.' He rubbed it gently with his right hand. 'Thanks, Zita.' He exhaled. 'Yes, I did my bit for the country.' He pointed at Jimmy. 'Didn't we, Jimmy?'

Jimmy ignored him. His mind was elsewhere.

Zita guided George and Ethel to the only empty seats.

As they sat down Ethel dug George hard in the ribs and muttered under her breath. 'Bloody fool, she's young enough to be your granddaughter.' She seethed. 'You're pathetic.'

Kathleen arrived just in time. She had sliced the cake and lit a handful of candles before bringing it into the sitting room. She put it on the table beside the television and began to sing happy birthday.

Everyone joined in and sang loudly.

Gwen froze. She had no idea it was her birthday. 'Where is he? Where's Liam … the birthday boy?'

As the voices faded, Jimmy reached out, turned her away from the clock, held her close and smiled. 'He's still at school. He'll be here soon,' he lied. He sat her down and placed a piece of cake on the paper plate and passed it to her. She tried to pick it up with her trembling hand but dropped most of it onto the carpet. She suddenly flipped and without any warning let out a scream reminiscent of a witch's cackle and slapped Jimmy hard across the face and bit his hand. 'Get away from me you bastard!' She turned and took her time to look everyone in the room up and down. 'Who are you?!'

They all stared blankly at her.

She screamed as she pushed Jimmy away. 'He tried to rape me!'

There was silence.

Everyone was afraid to move and had no idea what they should do.

Jimmy lost control. He pushed past her and raced through the kitchen and out into the garden.

Harry looked at his mother, she nodded and he followed his grandfather.

While Liam and Kathleen guided the stunned and shaken guests and musicians to the door, Michelle calmed Gwen down and with the help of Zita helped her upstairs and put her to bed.

Harry joined his grandfather in the garage.

Jimmy sat on a makeshift chair and sobbed his heart out.

Harry opened the cupboard and took out what was left of the brandy. He blew the dust out of a metal mug before he filled it. 'Will this help, Grandad?'

Jimmy wiped his eyes, reached for the mug and took a huge slug. He fought to catch his breath before he was able to speak. 'I'll need to drink a full bottle of this to do that, Harry.'

Harry blushed.

'No. It will help.' He emptied the mug and passed it to Harry.

Harry refilled it and emptied the bottle.

'You're a young lad, Harry, tell me … what future is there for either of us – me and your nan? We can't go on living like this.'

'I know Grandad. Nan isn't well … but what can you do?' He thought hard before he continued. 'P … p … put her in a home?'

'No way! That will be the final straw. It'll kill her.' He shook. 'And me!'

'So, what then? There has to be a way out?'

Jimmy shook his head. 'But … both are so extreme; I can't even contemplate them.'

Harry gulped. 'Sorry, I couldn't be of more help, Grandad.'

CHAPTER FIFTY-NINE

In The Air Tonight

Liam and Zita tried to leave the anguish and torment at the house behind, but still carried it with them as they walked the short distance in silence to Victoria Park, in the bright moonlit night. They shivered as the sharp frost enveloped everything around them and as they continued to walk the cold hit them. They tugged at their collars and pulled their inadequate coats tight into them as they walked through the deep shadows of the deserted park until they reached the open Chinese pagoda overlooking the boating lake. They looked out at the small tree-lined islands in the centre of the lake until their attention turned briefly to watch a group of rats who foraged around the overflowing rubbish bins for anything left by visitors earlier in the day.

The frost soon covered everything with a layer of fine ice crystals and glittered in the moonlight.

Their silence continued.

Neither of them wanted to be the first to speak.

Liam sighed heavily and finally spoke. '*Everything …* is so fucked up.'

Zita reached across and kissed his cheek. 'It is very sad for anyone when they are older … and for your mother and father it is much … much worse,' she said, softly.

'So, what can they do?'

She shook her head and exhaled. 'Liam ... I really don't know.' She sighed. 'Dare I say ...' She exhaled slowly. 'Sadly, they have run out of options ...'

Silence returned as they both looked out across the lake at the foreboding shadows cast on the water by the huge trees. Zita felt Liam relax into the seat before she spoke. She had learned, when anyone was troubled that they needed time to let their confused mind and the distress in their body work through. She looked into his eyes and silently guided him to look across the lake. 'It's beautiful,' she said. 'It's so peaceful?'

'Yeah. It is most nights until the druggies and fucking alki ...' He stopped himself and shook his head. 'Fuck, I'm one of *them*,' he said.

'Not any more, Liam,' she said emphatically. She bit down hard on her bottom lip and sucked at the warm blood. 'Well ...' She exhaled heavily. '*You are ...* but as long as you control yourself ... you will be fine.' She turned and kissed him softly on the cheek. 'And, you have done *great*.'

'Um.' He turned to her. 'What can I do about me Mum ... and Dad? We both know he's seriously ill and can't look after her for much longer?'

A plane flew over on its way out of Heathrow.

They both looked up.

'Would you like to be on there now, Liam?'

He shrugged and suddenly broke down. 'I don't know what the fuck is happening ... let alone where I'd want to go.' He took a deep breath. 'But ... to be honest, at the moment ... anywhere but here.'

She wiped his tears before they froze on his face. 'I know it's a terrible time for you and your family but things have a way of working out.' She kissed his eyes. 'Try to be a little patient, liebling.'

He sniffed hard. 'Can we go now?'

'Of course.' She tugged his arms and pulled him up from the seat. 'Let's go.'

Jimmy sat in the front room amongst the paper plates of uneaten food and cake, glasses and empty bottles. The phone on the coffee table beside him rang.

'Hello.'

'Is that Jimmy Reilly?'

'Yeah. Who is it?' He half listened to the caller until he finished. He straightened up in his armchair and screamed out. 'Fuck!' He slumped back into his chair with the receiver still in his bony hand and resting on his lap.

The front door opened. Liam walked in and took the phone from his father and replaced it. 'What's happened, Dad?'

Zita stood beside him and held her breath.

Jimmy broke down. He couldn't speak.

Zita and Liam looked at each other and sat on the settee opposite him. They waited in silence.

Jimmy dropped his head into his hands and sobbed uncontrollably.

'What's up, Dad?'

'What's happened, Jimmy?' asked Zita.

Jimmy exhaled a huge shuddering breath before speaking. 'He's killed 'im!'

'Who has?'

Jimmy sniffed noisily. 'I knew that *bastard* would do that. It was only a matter of time.' He rubbed his open hand across his face and spoke through his fingers. 'Matt!' He looked at each of them in turn. 'That fucking bastard has finally killed me old mate … Sydney!' He shook his head and hammered the arms of his chair. 'I knew he would. He should never have been let out. The bastard!' He seethed. 'I should have taken care of him meself.' He quaked and fell back into the armchair, exhausted.

Zita shuddered. 'No, Jimmy.' She paused. 'It wasn't down to you to do dat.' She sighed shakily and lowered her voice. 'The police should have done something.' She looked at each of them in turn. 'We all knew it.' She sniffed hard. 'Instead, they allowed the lives of three people to be wrecked … ruined … tonight.' She broke down and sobbed. 'How unnecessary and …' She shook her head and continued. 'So blutig … so sad.'

Liam held her tight and wept with her.

CHAPTER SIXTY

Catapult

The SOCO team found the moon knife in The Room, during their first sweep of the murder scene, and when the prints were finally checked on the database they were found to match, known criminals, Player and Mihai.

It caused huge confusion.

DCI Fuller was initially asked to comment on the two perpetrator's prints. Unable to come up with any information, he was seen to be totally inept at giving any answers as to how, except for the prints on the moon knife, the murder of the prince would be related to crimes he was dealing with. The case was passed to MI6, the terrorist squad, the Home Office and the office of the Prime Minister.

Giroud was taken to the Metropolitan Police HQ in West Kensington and held overnight pending further enquiries. The investigators were suspicious and sensed something was very wrong. After a forensic search of his clothes, they found the needle, with traces of the poison in his top jacket pocket. He was arrested on suspicion of the murder of his employer.

The Afrikaner sat on one side of the table in the interview room, dressed in a grey tracksuit, and opposite him was the woman who was one of the first to appear at the restaurant, and the second man who arrived with her.

The third and fourth men, obviously special forces, armed with guns, stood at the door, their legs wide apart.

The woman was the first to speak. 'Can you confirm your name?'

'Christo.' He paused. 'Christopher Giroud.'

'Your passport was issued in South Africa. Is that correct?'

'Ja.'

The man tapped the woman on the shoulder. She nodded to him and coughed. 'Mister Giroud, you have waived the right of a solicitor. Is that correct?'

He glared at each of them in turn, nodded and slammed his hands on the table. 'Ja.'

'How long have you been employed by Prince Abdul?'

'Three …' He coughed. 'Three years.'

'Have you ever been approached by, or worked with … a terrorist organisation.'

Giroud let out a loud arrogant laugh. 'Jy kan nie ernstig wees nie.' He stopped laughing and continued. 'Hoekom sale k skuim wil help?'

The man and woman looked at each other.

One of the men standing at the door coughed.

They both turned to him. 'Yes?'

'Do you want me to translate?'

Giroud turned and shook his head in surprise.

The woman nodded and grinned at Giroud. 'Please.'

'He said, "You can't be serious. Why would I want to help scum?"'

Giroud slammed his fists on the table again. He knew it was pointless trying to extend the interview by speaking in his own language when there was someone present who could translate. 'OK,' he said. He was still nodding as he turned and grinned gratifyingly at the uniformed man at the door.

He nodded back at him.

Giroud continued. 'Why would I even consider doing that when I earn more than all of you bastards put together!'

They all wanted to reply but held their mouths firmly closed.

The woman opened a folder and took out a plastic sample bag containing the needle – the murder weapon. 'Where did you get this?'

Giroud shrugged. 'You planted that!'

'But it was in *your* pocket?'

The male interviewer confirmed it with a nod and then spoke. 'Let's put that to one side for the moment.' He pushed it along the table. 'Tell me how you had this.' He turned to his colleague.

She nodded and took another sample bag from the folder containing a faded pink rose. She paused and allowed Giroud to take his time to look at it.

Giroud grinned. 'Fuck.'

The man tapped the plastic bag and continued. 'This was in *your* lapel.' He slammed his hand hard on the table and continued. 'How could you have a pink rose in your lapel when the bouquet was in … The Room?' He paused. 'Can you explain that?'

Giroud nodded. 'I can … but you won't believe me.'

She grinned at him. 'Try us.'

Silence.

The woman straightened up in her chair and looked directly at Giroud. 'Did you *kill* your employer – Prince Abdul?'

Giroud grinned inanely. 'You bastards know this is a farce!' He screamed and spat at each of them in turn. 'A setup!'

The armed men stiffened and made to move forward.

The woman raised her left arm and the armed men stepped back and returned to their adopted position in front of the door. She took a handkerchief from her pocket and wiped her face and offered it to her colleague. He screwed up his face and pulled out his own handkerchief and took his time to wipe the sputum from his face.

Giroud spoke in an almost inaudible voice. 'You just want a scapegoat to blame for *your* incompetence.'

The woman leaned across the table. 'Who ordered the roses?'

He shook his head.

She continued. 'Why would someone do that?'

A beat.

'Did you order them?'

'Why would I order a bunch of fucking flowers for *him*?'

'Would you? Are you having a relationship with him?'

He shook his head in disgust. 'Fuck you!'

'If it wasn't you ...' The woman forced a mock grin. 'Do you have any idea who would have sent them or ... wanted to kill your employer?'

Giroud shook his head. 'Let me just say ...' He grimaced. 'He didn't have many friends.'

There was a knock at the door and one of the guards opened it and took a folder from a young man. While the guard walked across the room, his colleague pointed his gun towards Giroud. The guard handed it to the woman.

She took out a sheet of paper and took her time to read it. She placed the paper on the desk and closed the folder and grinned. 'Mister Giroud, your client was poisoned with ... hydrogen cyanide.'

Giroud pulled back. 'Fuck.'

She glared at him. 'Where did you obtain it?'

'What?'

She opened the folder again and took out the plastic bag containing the needle and placed it on the desk and slid it towards Giroud. 'It was also found in this.' She paused and looked at everyone in the room. 'Let me remind you where we found this, Mister Giroud?'

He shook his head. 'I still have *no idea*.'

She grinned at him and turned to her colleague and then back to Giroud. She dropped her elbows, rested them on the table and glared at him. 'You know it was in the top pocket of *your* suit jacket–'

'Glad nie.'

The armed guard at the door coughed and the woman looked at him. 'He said ... "no way," ma'am.'

'Mister Giroud,' She paused. 'I wonder what the Saudi family will feel about your actions.' She coughed and tuned to the man beside her. 'Or ... should I say your lack of it?'

He slid into his chair and trembled. He muttered to himself.

She reread the document, slid everything into the file and glared at Giroud. 'I am charging you with murder and an act of terrorism.' She shook her head and looked towards the recorder. 'We are terminating this interview at 3:48 am.'

They stood and left the room.

The armed men remained at the door until two heavily armed policemen walked in, handcuffed Giroud and took him to his cell.

An hour later, Giroud was driven away in a heavily armed convoy and taken to a secret location for further questioning by MI6. He knew what Izzy had done but felt embarrassed at how she had so easily been able to dupe him. Although he was innocent, he knew the Saudi family wouldn't believe him. He made the only decision he could, rather than suffer the torturous treatment and painful death that he had often administered himself to victims on their behalf.

He sat on the edge of his bed and removed the soft cover from one arm of his glasses. He tipped it on its end and a microscopic needle slid out. He lay back on his mattress, closed his eyes and inhaled as he pushed the needle into his cheek.

He died instantly – poisoned with potassium cyanide.

CHAPTER SIXTY-ONE

I Feel Free

The cleaner tapped gently on the door of room 14 of the Travelodge. Zita looked through the spyhole and partially opened the door. The plump middle-aged West Indian cleaner in an ill-fitting company tee-shirt, handed her a bunch of pink roses and a thick envelope. 'Someone's a lucky ladee,' she said, with a cheery cackle in her voice.

'Yes,' said Zita.

She left the cleaner holding the large envelope, while she reached between the flowers and took out the card. She unfolded it and read it. Twice. *"You don't exist. Have a safe journey xxx."* She smiled back at the cleaner and continued. 'Yes, I am.' She sighed with great relief, took the envelope from the cleaner and handed her the flowers. She opened the envelope and felt inside. She looked up and finished her sentence. 'Very ... very lucky' She smiled and let out an obvious sigh of relief and pointed at the roses. 'We will be leaving soon ... but can't take them with us.'

'Yu bin 'ere a long time, eh, missus?'

Zita nodded, closed her eyes and thought. 'We have – seven weeks and ... three days.'

'You won't be here for *Christmas*, then missus?' She smiled broadly. 'I luv Christmas 'ere.' She closed her eyes and dreamed. 'It's not like 'ome in the sun ... but I do like it 'ere.'

Zita shook her head. 'I'm sure it's very nice.' She faked a sigh. 'But I'm afraid not.' She pointed at the flowers. 'So, you can have them.'

The cleaner screeched with delight. 'Thank ya, missus. Thank ya zo much.' She took the flowers and placed them neatly on the lower shelf of the trolley between the clean towels and sheets and pushed it down the corridor. She stopped in her tracks and turned to Zita. 'Oh, could you tell de manager you give dem to me.'

'Why?'

'My boss is a bitch and is sure to accuse me of stealing dem.'

Zita grinned. 'Don't worry about that.' She looked at her name badge. 'Amancia. I'll be sure to tell her.'

Zita closed the door, sat on the bed and felt the thick envelope. She pushed herself back onto the bed and, not knowing what else was inside, squeezed it. *Was it another of Chayim's tricks?* She took a few deep breaths and closed her eyes as she delved into the envelope. She shook with trepidation and tears of joy and, as she removed and examined each document, she caressed and kissed each of them before laying them neatly beside her on the bed. She checked the envelope by shaking it and, realising it was empty, she laid back and stretched out on the bed. As well as her original passport, birth certificate, driving licence and ID card the envelope contained other precious documents that had been held by Mossad since she joined them many years earlier. She sighed heavily.

She now had it all.

She exhaled long deep breaths as she celebrated something she didn't believe would ever happen.

She was finally free.

She remembered the plastic bag that Palina had given to Liam, and had lain ignored in the wardrobe since they arrived. She emptied it and laid everything on the bed. She walked to the reception to discover that all the frames on the wall had been draped with silver tinsel and a silver Christmas tree stood in pride of place on the table near the front door. She told the manager that she had given Anancia her roses and then walked down Shooters Hill to the nearby gift shop. She deliberated for ages over the rolls of Christmas wrapping paper until she finally decided on five different designs, five Christmas cards and two flat-pack cardboard boxes.

Back in the room she carefully wrapped the clogs, keyrings and one of the Gouda cheeses. She wrote three of the cards with the same note. *"You can use this for your fare to Amsterdam when you want to visit us. Love Dad and Zita xxx."* She smiled as she counted out three lots of five-hundred-pound notes and placed one of them inside each card, and taped them to the presents. She wrapped one of the cheeses and signed the card for Kathleen and packed the four presents in the larger box, sealed it and wrote Kathleen's address on the label.

The last cheese was a problem. Palina had given it to Liam for his parents but they didn't need it now. She nodded with mischievous excitement as she added the two remaining keyrings and wrapped it, placed a thousand pounds inside and wrote the card. *"To George and Ethel. Thank you for your help, Liam and Zita xx."* She sealed it and after taping it to the parcel she placed it in the smaller box and addressed it.

She walked to reception and called a courier. While she waited, she straightened the frames and reread the posters.

The courier arrived. She paid him and watched him carry the two boxes to his van. She gave herself a series of satisfying shrugs as she walked back to their room and lay on the bed.

CHAPTER SIXTY-TWO

Angels

The crematorium in Grange Road, Plaistow, had opened in 1872 and covered more than thirty acres. It had been chosen by the undertakers because it could only seat thirty people and Jimmy knew that even then there would still be many empty seats. He was right and the sparse congregation was made up of George and Ethel, friends of Gwen who used to work with her at the supermarket who, as a mark of respect, all wore their work uniforms, a few neighbours, a couple of Jimmy's "friends" and Martha, Gwen's carer plus a young girl from the care home where she went for respite. The remainder of the congregation, made up of Liam and his father, Zita, Kathleen, the three teenage children and Felix, his hands still heavily bandaged and the blisters and scars on his face very much in evidence, all sat in the front two rows.

As the coffin was carried in Jimmy turned to Liam and whispered. 'How come we always felt we were indestructible?'

Liam shook his head. 'No one is Dad. You know that.' He coughed. 'If we were honest with ourselves … we've always known that.'

'Fuck,' muttered Jimmy.

The service was over in what seemed like minutes and Jimmy watched as the curtains slowly closed to hide the coffin. 'Bye, love,' He lowered his head and wiped at the tears. 'You will have peace at last.' He sighed heavily and whispered to Liam. 'She left me a long time ago ... without going anywhere.'

Liam shook his head violently.

Jimmy swallowed hard and struggled to get out his words. Instead, he blew a kiss towards the coffin. 'Bye, Gwen. Rest in peace, my darling.'

The meagre congregation soon dispersed leaving Gwen's immediate family standing in the car park. Liam, Zita and Jimmy were huddled together in grief but when they heard the police sirens, they all looked up to see the flashing lights and the three police cars as they raced up the private road towards them. They braked to a halt and blocked the road. They turned off their sirens but left the blue lights flashing, creating eerie reflections on the grey hand-cut limestone building.

Jimmy, Liam and Zita froze, not knowing if the police were coming for any, or all, of them.

The car doors were flung open and DCI Fuller flanked by six police officers strode confidently towards them.

Jimmy, Zita and Liam gripped each other in anticipation and waited.

A beat.

Jimmy reached into his coat pocket and covertly handed Liam the debit cards. 'I'm so ... so ... so ... sorry, Liam.'

Liam squeezed his father's arm. 'Why are you saying that?'

His father didn't reply to the question. Instead, he pulled Liam close and whispered to him. 'Take care of Kathleen and the kids.'

Liam didn't have time to reply.

DCI Fuller strode towards the group and stopped a few feet in front of them. 'James Patrick Reilly, I'm arresting you for the murder of Gwen Reilly on or about the tenth of December 2000.'

The trio froze.

The detective reached into the inside pocket of his overcoat pulled out a folded piece of paper. 'I have the authority to *stop* it ...' He grinned, unfolded the paper, and reached out. He waved it in Jimmy's face. '... the cremation,' he said slowly.

'How the fuck can you do that?' questioned Jimmy, as he attempted to grab the paper. 'It's too late.'

DCI Fuller pulled the paper well out of Jimmy's reach and flashed it again. He sniggered as his face broke out into a wide loathsome grin. 'Urgh ... *I am* stopping it.' He waved the paper again, triumphantly. 'It's signed by a judge.' He paused and snarled at him. 'I told yer ... I have a warrant to ... *stop it!*'

Two police officers stepped forward and they each grabbed one of Jimmy's arms.

DCI Fuller paused and looked at Jimmy with a childlike grin. 'Did you hear me? A warrant from a judge!' he screamed manically. His face reddened as he continued to wave the paper in Jimmy's blank face. He handed it to a policewoman who took it and marched towards the now closed doors of the crematorium.

She pushed her way through the congregation, waiting for the next service, before rushing inside.

Liam dragged himself away from Zita and rushed towards his father's abductors. 'You must be fucking mad!'

Two more police officers stepped forward and restrained him.

'How come?' Liam continued to struggle. 'Surely that can't be right?'

DCI Fuller smirked at him and sucked his teeth. 'We have evidence that suggests otherwise.'

Jimmy strained, leaned forward and whispered to Zita. 'I'm glad he met you, Zita.'

She reached out and stroked his back and arms and felt the suit hanging off his skeletal frame. The suit he had regularly worn in the dock before being sentenced, and he had worn so proudly when she met him weeks earlier in George's café. She shuddered as she tried to hide the shock at the sheer speed of his deterioration from the cancer that was ravaging his whole body. 'You were right, I did give Player a good seeing to.'

He continued and whispered to her. 'I bloody knew it.' He closed his eyes and grinned. He took a weak breath. 'They'll never get me in court, yer know.'

Reluctantly, she mouthed her understanding and watched as his face crumpled in defeated acquiescence. She leaned into him and whispered in his ear.

Jimmy grinned back at her, nodded and grinned at DCI Fuller. He turned back to Zita and mouthed. 'Thanks.' He struggled to take a breath and exhaled raggedly. 'Look after my boy, won't you?'

Zita closed her eyes and nodded slowly. 'I will.' She attempted to kiss him but he was pulled back by the policemen. She tried hard to hide her emotion. She failed. 'Take care, Jimmy.'

Liam screamed out. 'Dad?!'

Jimmy turned to him and pleaded. 'Leave it, Liam ... Leave it, please–'

'But Dad ... they're talking crap!'

Jimmy tried in vain to raise his clamped arms but realising he had no strength, immediately gave in. 'Liam ... I said ... leave it.' He turned and spat at DCI Fuller. 'I'll be dead before you get me to court!' He cursed. 'I'm a dead man walking ...' He struggled to speak and took a breath. 'And, *so are you*, Fuller, you fucker,' he seethed.

DCI Fuller shook his head. 'Your threats are pathetic now. Who gives a damn? I caught you.' He sneered. 'And you didn't get away with it.' He chuckled. 'That's all that matters.' He turned and pointed at Liam. 'An I'll *'ave you as well ...*' he said, mockingly.

Liam smirked, at him. 'In your dreams.' He shrugged. 'You fucking bastard.'

DCI Fuller ignored Liam's remarks, he turned and watched as Jimmy was marched towards one of the police cars and bundled into the back seat before it drove away, siren blaring and blue lights flashing. He now turned his attention back to Liam. He clenched his fists, eyed him up and down and grinned inanely before he motioned to the officers to release their grip on him.

Liam showed his resentment with a symbolic display of strength as he shrugged them off with an exaggerated flexing of his body.

A perverse grin broke out across the face of DCI Fuller and he glared directly at Liam. '*Now ... You ...* Just listen to me–'

'What the fuck have you got to say that I wanna hear?'

'Just listen. Alright?'

Liam grunted.

DCI Fuller spoke slowly amplifying every word. 'Let me tell you about–'

'Yeah?'

He forced a grin. 'The murder victim–'

'Murder?! Victim?!' screamed Liam. 'She was my mother!'

He ignored Liam's outburst and continued in a low celebratory voice. 'As I said ... *the murder victim* ...' He stopped mid-sentence and glared at Liam. 'The *victim* had arthritis and couldn't have taken an overdose.' He stopped to take a breath and then spoke through his clenched teeth. *'She couldn't even open the bloody bottle–'*

Liam exploded. 'Fuck you!'

DCI Fuller antagonised him with a smirk and shook his head. 'We've got your father and ... I *will* get you ... And I will see you banged up ...' He paused and took his time to look at each of the family members in turn before he returned to Liam. 'For a *very* long time.' He tugged at his overcoat, turned and walked slowly back to his car and slammed the door.

His car, followed by the remaining police cars, raced away with their blue lights still flashing.

Liam guessed what his father had done and he bit his bottom lip as hard as he dared. He muttered to himself as the blood seeped around his mouth. 'So, fucking sad ... but a blessing.'

Zita reached out and took his hand and tried to comfort him. 'Liam, do you think your father had any choice?'

Liam shook his head. 'I know,' he murmured. 'Why would anybody want to see someone live like that?'

Felix stepped forward. 'I'm so sorry, Liam. I really am … but I will look after *your* family,' he said, with heartfelt compassion.

Liam was taken aback. 'Um … Okay.' He wiped blindly at his eyes. 'Thanks.'

Felix reached out and winced in pain as he stretched his bandaged hands around Liam's neck. 'You must visit us whenever you wish and …' He turned towards his new family. 'Les enfants.' He repeated it in English. 'The kids, oui?'

Liam pulled away and looked across at his three teenaged children and then Kathleen and allowed himself a discreet look at her yet indiscernible pregnant belly.

There was no reaction from any of them. They were totally shocked at what had just unfolded in front of them.

Liam flung his head back. 'Okay. Thanks, Felix.' He reached down and wedged the debit cards gently between his bandaged hands.

He struggled to grip them but closed them enough to be able to hold onto them.

Liam continued. 'Use them for whatever you want.'

Felix silently questioned what Liam had said.

Liam coughed and continued. 'It's okay, the pin code is Kathleen's birthday.' He looked over his shoulder toward his three teenage kids. 'Look after them for me.' He reached out and patted him on the back. 'And … I'm really sorry about that,' he said, pointing at his bandaged hands and flaking blisters on his face.

Felix smiled. 'Ce n'était pas ta faute.'

Liam frowned and shook his head.

Felix realised that Liam didn't understand so he repeated it in English. 'I am so sorry,' He forced a cough.

'Liam. The attack … and my injuries … It wasn't your fault.' He paused and forced a painful smile. 'D'accord?'

Harry pulled away from Kathleen and Felix and charged towards Liam. He hugged him hard and struggled to speak. 'Dad, I'm sorry it didn't work out.' That was the first time since Liam had returned to London that Harry had acknowledged him, with any affection, as his father. He fought to continue. He wiped his eyes and sniffed hard. 'And for my *shit* attitude.' He coughed and tried to clear his emotion. 'I know I've got a lot of growing up to do …' He continued to wipe blindly at the tears flooding from his eyes and stuttered as he spoke. 'Can I … visit you and …' He turned to Zita. 'And Zita … in Amsterdam and … and … stay with you on the houseboat?'

Liam looked at Zita and silently questioned her.

She smiled and nodded.

Liam pulled Harry into him. 'Course. You know you can, son.' He squeezed him hard. 'You will always be very welcome to come and stay with us.'

Sally and Michelle rushed forward. 'Can we come too?' they shrieked.

Zita replied. 'Sure, you can.' She smiled at Liam reached into her pocket and took out a Nokia 3110. 'We have this mobi now and we will text you the number.'

Liam silently quizzed her.

Zita held up her hands submissively. 'A mobile phone – *just* for Madonna.' She knelt down and whispered in Sally's ear. 'Take good care of Connor, won't you?'

Sally beamed at her. 'Of course, I will. He's my best friend.'

As the family drove away in the funeral car, Liam and Zita held hands and stood in silence, both thinking their own thoughts.

'Come on, Liam.' Zita handed him a second handkerchief and, as he wiped away the tears, she whispered in his ear. 'We can go home now.'

'What?'

'Come on … We're going home'

'Did you say … home?'

'Where do you think?'

He fell silent.

'Amsterdam is also *your* home now.' She paused. 'Or … for as long as you want it.'

He grinned at her through his tearful eyes. 'I know that,' he said, forcing a smile.

They walked in silence to their funeral car. But as they drove through the imposing crematorium gates Liam broke the silence. 'Can't we get my dad a lawyer?' He sniffed 'He's dying … and I can't let him die in that fucking place.' He couldn't hide his anger and frustration. 'It's hell.' He choked. 'And do you realise … I could have died in there too!'

CHAPTER SIXTY-THREE

Reflections of My Life

Liam shuddered as he walked in through the front doors of Wandsworth Prison, the doors he had only walked through once before – when he was released a little over two years earlier for his misconstrued "heroic" actions in saving two warders, when all he was doing was trying to save himself. Some of the warders recognised Liam and while they acknowledged him with a smile, others tormented him with silent grimaces.

He was shown to the hospital wing where Jimmy lay, handcuffed to his bed.

He looked frail and gaunt as he raised his tired head and gawped at Liam through his drowsy eyes. His arms, highlighted by his huge loss of weight, were now little more than folds of pale discoloured skin and bone and the once bright tattoos had now become impossible to distinguish. His whole body was pale and shrunken.

Liam sat in the chair and dragged it as near to the bed as he could.

Jimmy was the first to speak in a weak and almost inaudible voice. 'Son, they think they've won …' He paused to catch his breath and continued with laboured breath. 'But you know I won't be convicted.'

'I know that.'

'So why waste money on lawyers – the leeches – fucking blood suckers!'

'Why not?' Liam's fists tightened and he slowly raised them. 'You know we've got the money–'

Jimmy forced a pained grin. 'It's too late, son. Listen to me.' He sighed heavily and took a shallow breath. 'I said it's too late …' As the grin slowly faded, he continued. 'Who gives a fuck anyway.'

Liam grunted as he looked at the warder who agreed with a slow nod. Liam put his hand on his father's bare shackled forearm.

It was cold.

He pulled the sheet over them, covered his handcuffs and patted it tight around them. He gave his father's bony arm a gentle squeeze through the sheet.

Jimmy sniffed hard and looked up at Liam. His eyes, sad and defeated. 'Listen, son.' He took his time and swallowed. 'You know I couldn't leave her on her own – like that. Don't ya?' He tried to reach his tearful eyes. 'In that hellish world.' He took a laboured breath. 'It wasn't fair.'

Liam leaned towards the bed and wiped his father's eyes with the edge of the sheet. 'I know, Dad.'

Jimmy tried to lift his hands and reach out to Liam but the handcuffs held him back. 'Don't think too bad of me, son.'

'Why would I even think that?' said Liam. He reached beneath the sheet and held his father's hand. 'If it's any consolation.' He paused, looked up at the ceiling and sniffed. 'I would have done the same–'

'Would yer?' Tears reappeared in his father's eyes and he tried to shake them away. He struggled to continue. 'Would yer really?'

'Yeah.' Liam wiped his father's eyes again and looked into them. 'Course, I would.' He paused. 'You *know* I would.'

Jimmy sighed heavily. 'That means a lot. I thought it wuz me being a real selfish bastard.'

Liam shuddered. 'No, you wasn't.' He took his time to look around at the bare painted brick walls and rocked in the chair. 'I hate this fucking place. Urgh ...' He looked at the warder.

The warder nodded in agreement. 'We are prisoners, in here too, Liam,' he said.

Liam continued. 'So many bad memories.' He paused and forced a cough. 'I may well have been in that bed after my ...' He exhaled sharply. 'The riot ...'

'So, is it a coincidence, son?'

Liam grinned, lowered his voice and spoke behind the hand that covered his mouth. 'Zita told me that there is no such thing as a ... coincidence.'

Jimmy grinned. 'Maybe she's right.' He clicked his tongue. 'She's a shrewd one ... that's for sure.' He nodded slowly and gasped for breath. 'You were such a lucky bastard to find her.'

'I know,' said Liam. He sighed. 'Yeah.' He looked down at his father. 'We kind of found each other.'

He had closed his eyes.

Liam sat back and waited for them to flicker and open before he continued. 'Do you want me to contact ... Bernadette in Australia?'

Jimmy appeared to briefly regain his strength and pushed his head up out of the pillow. 'Fuck her.' He struggled for breath. 'If your sister can't be bothered to keep in contact with us.'

Liam felt what was left of his father's skeletal body stiffen.

Jimmy gasped. 'Why?' He exhaled the little breath he had left and continued. 'Should we tell her anyfing?' he said, as he slumped back exhausted and let his head fall into the pillow.

Liam looked blindly ahead and thought so many conflicting reasons; why he should, or shouldn't, tell his sister that their father was dying.

Jimmy found it hard to keep his eyes open. 'Thanks for coming, son.' He briefly opened them but couldn't hold back his tears. He gulped for breath, lifted one arm feebly and tried to reach out to Liam. The handcuffs tightened and held him back. 'After all, we've both been through a lot, eh son?' He let out a raspy laugh and sighed heavily. 'Do you know what, son?'

'What?'

'I've had enough time *with me*,' he wheezed. He attempted to shake his head but failed. 'I just wish I'd had more time …' He wheezed. 'More time with … Gwen.'

Liam reached out and cradled his father's head in his arms. He finally stood, leaned over the bed, closed his eyes and hugged his father. 'I'm so sorry, Dad.' He kissed him on the forehead. 'I really am.'

'I've had me life,' said Jimmy, with a yawn. 'The world is changing and there's no place for me in it.' He licked at his dry lips. 'You go … and enjoy it …' He sniffed away the tears and continued as he gasped desperately for breath between each word. 'And … *don't* … fuck … it … up … this … time.'

Liam wiped at his eyes as he pulled away. 'Bye, Dad.'

'Bye, son,' he whispered. He closed his eyes and fell asleep.

Liam walked out into the corridor and broke down.

The warder nearest to him, one of the two he had saved from certain death during the horrific riots at the prison, tapped Liam gently on the shoulder and offered him a caring smile. 'I'll look after him, Liam. That's the least I can do after what you did for me.'

Liam nodded. 'Yeah. Thanks.'

As he walked out through the front door he stopped and turned. He looked up at what had been his enforced home for many years and clenched his fists. His whole body stiffened as he let out the loudest of screams. He immediately regretted it and held his damaged throat as the excruciating pain shot throughout his body.

Zita raced towards him. She handed him two painkillers and a bottle of water. 'Come on, Liam. Take dese.'

He swallowed them and, after taking a breath, he spoke. 'Before we leave London there is somewhere I want to go.'

'Okay, Liam, we can do dat.'

CHAPTER SIXTY-FOUR

When You're Gone

They bought a large bunch of pale yellow and white chrysanthemums from Kirkham Florists in Grange Road and rode the short distance to the crematorium and cemetery. Liam shuddered as they approached the ornate gates and relived the anguish and anger when his father had been arrested by DCI Fuller.

They parked the motorbike and followed the directions given to them by Kathleen. They walked slowly between row upon row of old graves until they reached an area with mounds of freshly piled earth and behind them a row of the headstones from the earlier burials. Liam's head flicked from side to side as he searched for his brother's name. He left Zita, and walked on ahead of her. He stopped abruptly, knelt and broke down when he saw Tommy's headstone. He struggled to read the inscription through his tears. He shook them away. 'Fucking eighteen ...'

Zita knelt down beside him and stroked his quivering shoulders. 'It wasn't your fault, Li–'

'Yes, it was!' He swallowed hard. 'I will always know it was ...' He choked with emotion. 'It was my fault ... It was *all my fault!*'

'Liam, he chose to do it, didn't he?'

Liam closed his eyes and thought. 'Well ... Urchin were based around the corner from us in Victoria Park

Road.' He forced a smile and nodded. 'Yeah. They got back together last year, and that's how Tommy got to come over to Amsterdam.'

'Liam, have you forgotten what happened when they arrived?'

He sniffed hard.

She tugged at the sleeve of his jacket. 'You have … haven't you?'

He nodded.

'And, what did we have to do?'

He didn't reply.

Zita continued. 'You knew… even then … he was into drugs.' She exhaled. 'Heavy drugs.' She paused and gently turned Liam's head towards her and looked into his eyes. 'It was so hard for him … but it was *his choice* … and … and you know dat.'

Liam sniffed hard.

Zita guided his hand and they placed the flowers on Tommy's grave and both continued to stare blindly at the inscription on the headstone. 'You're right … of course you are,' he said.

'Come on.' She bent over the grave, straightened the flowers, and pulled Liam to his feet.

As they walked in silence past the rows of headstones, they both glanced at the dates and calculated the ages of those that had died. They shook their heads with sadness and in the realisation that they had all lived so many more years longer than Tommy.

Zita took Liam's arm. 'We need to do one more thing and then … we can go.'

They returned to the Travelodge and she forced their clothes into two bags.

Liam climbed into bed. He was still too stunned at seeing Tommy's grave, to question her decision, and pulled the duvet over him.

Zita tucked him in, grabbed the bags, took them to the nearest charity shop and handed them in. She walked down the road and carefully chose one set of replacement clothes for each of them from another charity shop and returned to the Travelodge.

Liam was still in bed when she returned. She dropped the bag on him. 'Put these on and, yes … we can go … now.'

He was totally confused. 'What have you done with the others?'

'I gave them back and …

He scoffed. 'What the fuck.'

She giggled. 'They will be sold again.' She paused. 'We will be impossible to trace if someone else is wearing dem.'

He propped himself up onto one elbow and grinned at her. 'You fucker.'

She pulled back in horror and waggled her index finger at him. 'Liam?'

He forced a cough. 'Sorry, I didn't mean it like that.'

'Okay, Liam. I will forgive you dis time.'

He was still thinking about what she'd done. He turned to her. 'What about my leathers?'

She grinned at coyly. 'They have gone too–'

'Where?'

'They drowned.'

'Okay.' He raised his arms in submission and extended his fingers. 'Let's go then.'

CHAPTER SIXTY-FIVE

Falling In to You

Liam and Zita left the Travelodge and took the bus and tube to Waterloo International Station. There was a huge decorated Christmas tree at the front entrance and inside several smaller festive trees, and glittering garlands that hung from the ceiling. The Salvation Army band played carols creating a welcoming air of expectation for those arriving and departing to and from Europe.

Zita took Liam's hand. 'We will go back on the Eurostar to Brussels this time too,' she said, as she bought the tickets.

Liam fired her a distant smile. His emotions were mixed and he gulped for air.

Zita continued. 'It will give us time to adjust ... Is that, okay?'

He didn't answer. His scrambled mind was elsewhere. *He was still in London. Did he want to leave again?*

She reached across and tapped his arm. 'Look.' She reached into her pocket and took out a wad of notes. 'I sold our bike ...' She laughed. 'And guess what?'

'What?'

She flicked the notes. 'I sold it for what we paid for it ... and my leathers.'

He grinned at her. 'Nice one.'

The departure of their train to Brussels flashed up on the huge electronic board and was called over the tannoy in several languages. Zita tugged at his arm 'Come on, Liam.' She tugged at his arm and smiled at him as they walked along the platform and into their carriage. 'Let's go home.'

* * * *

Christmas came early in Holland and was marked by the arrival of Sinterklaas, allegedly on a ship from Spain. He had arrived in Holland in mid-November, the first Saturday after the 11th November, while they were in London. He was a serious man with white hair and a long white beard. He wore a long red cape and carried a red mitre and a long shepherd's staff with a fancy curled handle. Along with his entourage, which included Zwarte Piet – black Pete – Sinterklaas would parade through the streets on his white horse. While children cheered and sang traditional songs his assistants would throw sweets and gingerbread biscuits into the crowd. A few weeks later on the night of Sinterklaasavond, 5th December, before going to bed, children would put their shoes next to the fireplace or chimney of the coal-fired stove, and in modern homes close to a radiator. The next morning, they would be rewarded with sweets, or a small present in their shoes, with larger gifts beneath the Christmas tree.

* * * *

When their connection from Brussels pulled into a grey Centraal Station, thunder boomed overhead, and it was raining heavily. They ignored the Christmas festivities and the rain and chose to walk. By the time they arrived at the houseboat they were soaked to the skin: they didn't care, they were so pleased to be back in Amsterdam and able to feel the fresh clean rain on their faces.

Liam stood on the deck and tilted his face in the direction of the incessant rain, while Zita checked the houseboat for booby traps, trip wires, microphones and bugs. When she was satisfied it was safe, she motioned to Liam to join her inside.

They giggled childishly to each other as they rushed to remove their wet clothes and strip off before they both fell naked onto the bed. The thunder continued to boom overhead and the heavy rain hammered on the roof. The wind whipped up by the usually still canal water rocked the boat.

Their still wet and naked bodies glided over each other. The sex was wonderful.

The realisation of knowing that they were finally free added to their emotions as they reached a new level of sexual euphoria.

Now exhausted, they lay and listened to the rain until they fell asleep.

Zita had already showered and been to her favourite delicatessen in Laueriergracht. She walked into the bedroom carrying a tray with a mug of tea and two slices of bread and appelstroop – apple syrup. She woke Liam with a kiss on his forehead. 'Good morning, schlafriger kopf.'

He grunted and pulled the duvet over his head.

'Good morning, sleepy head. I have your breakfast.'

He slid out from under the cover. 'Morning ...' He smirked at her. 'Is this for real ... or, ... am I dreaming?'

She giggled. 'What do you think?' She laid the tray beside him and joined him on the bed. '*It is real.* We are home now,' she said, as her face burst into a trusting smile. 'Yes. Liam ... this is *our* home.'

He finished his breakfast and pushed himself deep beneath the covers and pulled her into him.

Zita had been waiting for the question. The awkward question she knew Liam would ask and she would have to answer.

He forced a cough.

This was it.

'You never told me how you ... *did it?*' He pushed himself up and rested his head on the soft headboard.

'"Did it?"'

'What freed you?' He paused and took a deep breath. 'Freed us?'

Zita fell into his arms. 'It is better that you don't know.'

'How come?'

'What I can tell you is that London was my last mission.' She grinned. 'I have Sigrid's passport, birth certificate and ID card.' She grinned inanely. 'Liam, I have *everything.*' She closed her eyes. 'And ... at last ...' She exhaled noisily. 'I have my freedom.'

'For sure?'

'Yes, I have been deleted–'

'"Deleted?" What's that supposed to mean.'

She snuggled into him. 'It means ... I have no more missions. Okay?'

'Yeah.' He closed his eyes. 'At last.'

Two hours later a much-relieved Zita sang along to *Music*, the latest Madonna CD, as she opened all the windows to a blue sky and weak winter sunshine. She washed the dirty mugs and plates that they left when they rushed away many weeks earlier. She filled the washing machine with their bedding, opened a drawer and threw clean sheets and pillow cases at Liam. 'There you are ... you can make the bed while I clean up the rest of dis mess.'

She spent the next few hours cleaning until everything was as it should be. She could see the relief on Liam's tired face so she made him a mug of tea and handed it to him. 'Liam ...' She kissed him on the forehead and fired him a sassy grin. 'Isn't it wonderful to be back?'

He let out a soft warm sigh.

She continued in a soft voice. 'I'm going shopping now.'

His relief was so obvious. 'Fine.' He held up his mug and grinned. 'See you later.'

CHAPTER SIXTY-SIX

It Had to Be You

Their second day home was wonderful with continuing blue skies and the last of the late-December sun. Zita reached under the seat, checked the CD in the player and flicked it on. While she hummed along to the music, she busied herself planting her pots with tulip bulbs, winter flowering pansies and brightly coloured cyclamen. Liam sat on the deck and puffed at his one cigarette of the day and gazed blindly down the canal, mesmerised by the coloured flashing lights and brightly coloured tinsel that now decorated the houseboats and canal-side homes.

Detective Piet Ackerman pulled up and waved to them through the open car window. He turned off the engine and stepped onto the boat. 'Hi. I heard you were back.'

Still kneeling, Zita turned to him. 'Yeah. It's wonderful,' she said, with a broad smile. 'Coffee?'

'I didn't think you were going to ask,' he joked.

She removed her gloves, dropped them into one of the empty pots and disappeared below deck.

'So how are you, Liam?' asked the detective.

Liam sniffed. 'I'm fine.' He wheezed. 'It was a tough time.' He looked into the distance. 'Back there – in London.'

Ackerman lit a cigarette but before he could continue with his interrogation, disguised as small talk, Zita reappeared with a tray. She handed each of them their mug.

Ackerman tapped along with the music.

'Do you like it?'

Ackerman nodded. 'Yeah. I do.'

Zita held up the CD box. 'I bought it for myself in London – I love Britney Spears.'

The CD repeated and, as Britney Spears' *'Oops I Did It Again,'* the first track of the album played. Zita stood and sang along with it.

Ackerman raised his voice to compete with the music. 'What *did you do again*, Zita?' he asked, with a wide mischievous grin.

She shouted her reply. 'Nothing … But I do love this song.' She poked out her tongue. 'Oops, I did it again,' she said, before she turned, looked at Liam, and smirked.

He attempted to show his agreement by nodding in time to the music. He failed. Instead, he rubbed his hand across his mouth and sipped at his tea.

Zita continued to bop along to the music. 'It's fantastic.' She stopped briefly and feigned breathlessness. She spoke as she exhaled. 'In fact, I like the whole CD.'

When the song ended, she sat down and as the thunderous intro of *'Stronger,'* the second track on the CD played, with its soaring synths and distorted guitar, she turned down the volume and let the track play in the background.

Ackerman finished his coffee and hung the cup precariously on his index finger while he lit another cigarette. He turned to face Zita. 'I have one question?'

They all turned as the flock of gulls overwintering in the city squawked noisily and swooped down across the canal, enticed by the parents and their two young daughters who threw chunks of bread into the air.

Zita finally turned back to the detective. 'Sorry. You have a question, Piet?'

'I don't suppose you heard about the murder of the prince …' He faked a cough. 'The Saudi Prince … in London?'

Liam's head spun around to look at Zita and then Ackerman. 'Murdered … in London?' he quizzed.

'Wow. A prince,' exclaimed Zita.

'Yeah. A Saudi Prince,' repeated Ackerman. He grinned at her. 'By all accounts he was a real bastard.' He took one of his usual huge drags on his cigarette and continued to talk through the smoke. 'On his orders … he had three Israeli soldiers … *executed.*'

He waited for Zita to react to what he'd said before he continued.

She didn't.

He continued. 'All women – young women!'

She still didn't react.

Liam did. 'Fuck.'

'The bastard,' screamed Zita, at first feigning total shock, then well-placed anger.

Ackerman nodded. 'Whoever did it … was carrying.' He paused and took another huge drag on his cigarette and watched the smoke rings rise in front of him before he continued. *'Pink roses …'* He suddenly roared with laughter. 'Doesn't that remind you?' He paused and looked down at the ash on the deck and kicked at it with the toe of his shoe. He slowly raised his head and looked directly at Zita as he spoke. 'When that happened …' He winked at her. 'Somewhere else?' He pinched at his cheeks and pretended to think. 'Ah. I know.' He raised his index finger, pointed upwards and held it in mid-air. 'In Tallinn … Estonia. They had pink roses *too*.'

Zita feigned surprise and shook her head innocently. 'No. I don't think I remember dat.' She turned to Liam. 'Do you, Liam?'

'No. I've no idea,' he said, shaking his head. 'Don't ask me. I can't remember what I did yesterday.'

Ackerman flicked the cigarette butt into the canal and lit another one, his third. He grinned to himself and slowly shook his head. He took a drag and as he expelled the huge cloud of smoke he focussed directly on Zita. 'Did Liam show you the sights … Big Ben … Buckingham Palace?'

She fired back at him. 'No.'

Liam spoke at the same time. 'We didn't.' He looked across at Zita and feigned disappointment. 'Maybe next time, eh?'

She grinned. 'But we *did visit* the Tower of London.'

'We didn't have time for much else …' Liam reflected. 'My mother died …'

'I'm sorry to hear that, Liam,' said Ackerman. He slowly shook his head as he exhaled another lungful of smoke. 'I really am.'

Liam continued. 'She had dementia.' He frowned. 'A bloody terrible disease … a life sentence.' He grunted. 'I wouldn't wish that on anybody.'

Zita motioned to Liam with a blink of her eyes, changed the subject, and turned to Ackerman. 'Thanks for taking care of Madonna, Piet,' she said.

'No problem. Happy to oblige.' He tilted his head towards her. 'Just doing my job.'

Zita took a brown paper bag from her pocket and smiled as she handed it to him. 'Thank you. This is for you.'

He opened the bag and was totally shocked. He paused and rubbed the leaded paperweight crystal glass with his thumb. He moved it around to look at the photograph of Big Ben. 'Very nice.'

'I'm glad you like it,' she said.

'Yes, I do.'

'We wanted to get you something for helping us.' She paused. 'You can use it on your desk.'

He lit another cigarette and studied the glowing tip. When he finally looked up his demeanour had changed. 'But ... I do have one question–'

Zita shrugged her shoulders and teased him with a giggle. 'You have already had one,' she said.

He grinned back at her. 'I know.' He raised his hand like a schoolboy. 'Can I have one more ... Please?'

She grinned. 'Of course. How could I refuse after you helped us?'

'We never found out who tried to kill you and Liam–'

She feigned surprise. 'No?'

'No ... Nothing. Whoever it was ... knew what they were doing.'

'Did they?' mocked Liam.

Zita joined Liam with a grin of agreement. 'How could they?'

Ackerman thumbed his bottom lip and shuffled in his seat. 'Do you have any idea who would want to do *that*?'

'Whoever it was ... was a rank amateur,' said Liam, laughing loudly.

Zita cleared her throat and raised her left shoulder. 'One of De Groot's henchmen?' She tilted her head towards

Ackerman. 'Or ... a friend of that filthy ... vile Albanian – Erag?'

The mobile phone rang below deck.

Ackerman fired each of them a surprised look. 'So, you've decided to get one, after all. Eh?'

Zita nodded. 'Yeah. We have.' She grinned at him. 'But we leave it here ... on the boat.'

Liam continued. 'In case my kids want to call us ... That's all,' he said, as rushed below deck.

The detective pursed his lips and nodded animatedly. 'Fair enough.' He lit yet another cigarette. 'Did you know I had a call from the police, in London, asking me about Liam's arrest for the murder when he first arrived here.'

'I'm sure they did ... but he was innocent–'

'That's what I told them.... but they didn't believe me.'

'Why would they?'

'Um.'

They heard Liam's slow and heavy footsteps on the stairs and turned to face him.

When he finally appeared, his face was pale and drawn. He looked at Zita, swallowed hard and gulped for air. 'It's ... dad ... He died an hour ago.' For a few moments he stood frozen on the spot and allowed himself to accept what he'd just been told. 'He was too young to die.' He gently massaged his painful throat. *In his mind's eye were images of him and his father sitting beside the Thames and looking across at the Millenium Dome.* He suddenly snapped and raised his fists triumphantly in the air. 'He beat *'em ...*' He stretched his whole body and punched out. 'The bastards!'

Zita leapt up, reached across and hugged him.

Ackerman offered his hollow sympathy. 'Sorry to hear that, Liam.' He sniffed. 'At least you got to see him when you were in London?'

'Thanks. Yeah, we did,' said Liam, as he exhaled raggedly. 'He had pancreatic cancer.' He sighed and took a slow breath. 'Amongst other things.' He shuddered and exhaled slowly. 'It was everywhere … I'm surprised he lasted this long.' He reflected. 'They only gave him a couple of months.'

Ackerman stood and, as he handed Zita his mug, he forced a cough. 'Liam, can I ask … who did your father …' He paused to choose his last word. '*Beat?*'

Liam didn't take time to think. 'The fucking rozzers, the old bill – the pigs!' He knew immediately what he'd said and in that moment of regret, he lowered his head, and as he slowly raised it, he whispered his childlike apology to the detective. 'Sorry.'

Ackerman shrugged and patted Liam's shoulder. 'I'm sorry, Liam. I shouldn't have asked.'

Liam grunted.

'I know you are upset with the sad news,' said Ackerman, sympathetically. As he walked off the houseboat he turned to Zita. 'See you around, Zita …' He tapped on the side of the boat and when he had Liam's attention, he took a deep breath and traced his nicotine-stained pencil moustache. He continued in a subdued and dejected voice. 'We … are not all the same, Liam,' he said.

Liam frowned.

Ackerman continued. '*The police.*'

'Ah.'

Ackerman shook his head and exhaled. 'Take care, Liam.' He raised his hand. 'And, I really am …, so very sorry.' He opened his car door, looked up at the thick grey clouds building in the distant sky, and pulled up his collar. 'Maybe we will have some snow for Christmas.'

Zita looked up and nodded. 'You may be right. Dat zou geweldig zijn.'

Ackerman closed the car door, and waved to Zita through the open window. 'Elke keer dat je langskomt voor een kop koffie, hè?'

She waved back. 'You are always welcome, Piet.'

Liam slumped into Ackerman's seat and reflected on his news.

Zita joined him, leaned into his shoulders and hugged him tight.

Without warning he sat bolt upright and looked directly into her eyes. He leaned forward. 'That *was you*, wasn't it?'

'Me?' she said, glibly.

Liam continued. 'The pink roses! The prince! The murder!'

She stroked his head and replied in a measured voice. 'Yes, Liam … It was me.' She giggled. 'Well … it was … and it wasn't'

'What the fuck. Was it you, or not?'

'Izzy Dupont did it.'

'Wha…?'

'For a few hours I was French … I was Izzy Dupont. It was on your mother's birthday–'

'That's right … You were late coming–'

'Yes, I was.' She paused and tugged gently at his hair. 'It was the price I had to pay for *our freedom*.'

'Wow.'

She lowered her voice. 'There was no other way for us to ever escape.' She shook her head. 'If I had ignored their orders, we could never live without always looking

393

over our shoulders.' She rubbed her open hand forcefully across her face and neck. 'Until they killed us.' She reached out and grabbed him. 'Would you want to live your life ... *like that?*'

He shook his head. 'No, of course I wouldn't.' He shuddered. 'Look what happened back there.' He pointed into the distance. 'Back there ... In London.'

'Good. I am so pleased you said dat.' She picked up her book, opened it and pulled the blanket tightly around her.

Liam sipped at his tea, slid his other hand into his pocket and repeatedly fiddled with the mobile phone.

Zita half-watched him and finally she put down her book. 'If you want to call to someone, you must do it, Liam.'

He turned to her. 'Are you sure?'

'Liam,' she said, firmly. 'Du hast gezuckt.'

Liam silently quizzed her.

She huffed. 'You have been twitching ... it is up to you.'

'Twitching?'

'Yes, I noticed–'

'Really?'

'Yes, I know you well enough now.' She smiled at him and pointed towards his bulging pocket. 'Go on.'

He hesitated and exhaled raggedly.

'Liam, go on. Do it.'

He pulled out the mobile phone and took his time to pick out the numbers.

'Hello.'

'Hi Kath. It's Liam.'

'Hello, Liam. It's weird to get a call from you–'

'I know.' He nodded, pulled the phone away and looked at it. 'We're back in Amsterdam.' He looked across at Zita and continued. 'On the houseboat.'

She smiled back at him and blew him an invisible kiss.

'Okay,' she said.

He forced a cough. 'I've bin thinking.'

'Yes.'

'I don't reckon we'll be coming back for a while and I wanted to sort things out.'

Zita smiled to herself.

'I can understand that,' said Kathleen, thoughtfully.

'Well. You and the kids can have mum and dad's house.'

'Wow.' She exhaled a lengthy gasp. 'Are you sure?'

'Course, I am.' He looked down the canal. 'And … sell dad's bike.'

He sensed her apprehension. 'That is, if you want to.' He paused and reflected before he continued. 'If not … keep it.' He nodded to the invisible Kathleen. 'His is worth good money. It's a classic – worth a fair bit but who knows … Harry might wanna ride it one day.'

Kathleen took her time to answer. 'Okay, well … I'll have to think about them. But that won't be my priority.'

'It's up to you to decide.' He paused. 'But at least sell the house.' Liam could sense that Kathleen was still in shock.

'There's no rush but … we can't leave it sitting empty.'

'I understand that, Liam.'

'And … share everything out amongst you and the kids. Open building society accounts for them. I'm sure they'll need it.' He forced a nervous laugh. 'Who knows …

they may want to go to university and make something of 'emselves?' He paused. 'Something ... *I* failed to do.'

'*Liam*, don't say that.' She huffed. 'You haven't failed.'

Liam closed his eyes and smiled to himself. 'That's nice.' He sighed. 'Um ... Well anyway ... you do what you want and if you need me to sign anything, let me know.'

He heard Kathleen take a breath.

'Oh. Before you go, guess what Felix told me last night?'

'Felix?

'Yeah. He works with the wife of a policeman.'

Liam sniggered. 'Is that something to brag about–'

'No, Liam. It isn't but she told him that ...'

He suddenly became animated as Kathleen continued with the news. 'Fuck! Bloody hell.' Between breaths, he continued to swear uncontrollably until he was exhausted. He looked across at Zita as he finished the call. 'Bye, Kathleen ... love to the kids ... and ... and happy Christmas,' he said, as his voice faded with an exhaustive sigh of relief.

He couldn't hide his excitement. He continued to hold the mobile for several minutes until he finally slid it back into his pocket. He grinned at Zita. 'You will never guess in a million years what the fuck has happened to that bastard, Fuller.'

'Try me?'

'Well ...' He paused. 'You won't believe it?'

'Believe what, Liam?'

'Felix said they've arrested Fuller for drug dealing.'

'Felix?'

'Yeah.' He laughed loudly. 'His mate's wife told 'im the bastard was involved in drug dealing and the fucking

396

Roma murders. In the warehouse!' He paused for breath. 'Can you believe that?!'

She nodded.' Yes, Liam, I can–'

'The police called them *executions*! And do you know what?

Zita didn't reply.

'And ...' He struggled for breath.

She tapped the seat beside her. 'Sit down Liam.'

He ignored her and froze on the spot. He suddenly became animated and stomped around the deck. 'How?'

'Karma?' said Zita with a grin.

Liam's face suddenly exploded with sheer euphoria and he continued, headlong. 'They had a tip-off. They took his car apart and found ... two grand ... in a bag, covered in blood, the bastard Roma's rings, gold chain and fings ... 'is 'air and scalp ... and ... and ... and the gun used to kill the Roma woman.' He stopped to take a well-needed breath. 'And Forensic evidence proving he was involved in drug dealing and the fucking carnage at the warehouse.' He struggled to continue and leaned back against the side of the boat and took a huge frenetic breath. He spoke as he exhaled and punched the air with his fists. He took his time to catch his breath and then leaned towards her. 'How the fuck?'

Zita screwed up her face and took her time to grin at back at him. 'Yes, I do believe it, Liam.' She sniffed. 'Sometimes, *revenge* can be sweet ... getting even is such a wonderful thing ... Er bekam, was er verdiente.'

He fired her a blank look.

'I'm so pleased for you.'

'For me?'

'Of course. ... For you ... and your father.' She shook her head. 'The detective was not a good man ... and, you are correct.' She paused. 'He was a bastard. And, he got what he deserved.' She grinned at him. 'Don't *you* think so?'

'Oh, yeah. He really has.' He sucked at his bottom lip while he grasped the realisation of everything Kathleen had told him. 'The bastard won't survive … he'll be killed when he goes inside …' His whole body quivered with excitement. '… and they find out he's a bent cop.' He paused and squinted at her. 'Did you do that?'

Zita lowered her eyes and nodded slowly. 'Yes, Liam. I did.' She paused. 'And, do you know what?'

'What?'

She grinned impishly. 'It was so easy.'

'How come?'

'He didn't lock his *car* …'

'That was brilliant. Fucking brilliant!' Liam punched the air. 'I don't know how you pulled that off.' He shook his head. 'But you've done it again!' He took a huge breath and stepped back. He closed his eyes and enjoyed the moment with a deep shuddering breath. Still reeling from the news, he spoke as he exhaled. 'But how? *How* did you manage to–?'

'Liam, you forget it is my job.'

He pulled back. '*Was* your job, alright?'

'Yes Liam, it *was* my job.'

Liam took a huge breath and roared with laughter. 'The funny fucking thing is … he's denied it all–'

'Wouldn't you?'

'Yeah. Course I would. I just wish me dad knew.'

Zita pulled Liam into her. 'Sorry, Liam. I wanted to tell you–'

'Tell me what?'

'Jimmy, *did* know …'

Liam gasped. 'What? How come?'

'I told him after the funeral–'

'What?!'

'Before he was taken away by the police–'

'But … but he never told me when I visited 'im.' He shrugged. 'Kept schtum about it.' He grinned. 'Pffft. The sly old bastard.'

'Liam, he was tired.' She sighed. 'He didn't want to fight any more.' She paused. 'It was better for all of us … better for it to come out when we were back here. If we were still in London, it would have raised so many questions and caused problems …' She paused. 'And who knows if we would ever have been able to leave.'

'But, why the fuck didn't you tell me?'

'I'm so sorry, Liam, but it had to be that way.'

'Okay.' He looked into her eyes. 'I'm tired too.' He lowered his head. 'But … no more secrets, right?'

EPILOGUE

The Love Inside

Although there was an early winter chill in the air, Liam and Zita sat on deck wrapped in blankets and ate their late breakfast. While Liam sipped at his second mug of tea and continued to wave at the ever-reducing stream of tourist boats as they sailed past them. Zita had other plans. She threw back her blanket and jumped up. 'I won't be long,' she said. She leapt off the boat with a wave and made her way to Bloemenmarkt, the floating flower market on the Singel.

When she returned, she handed Liam a warm savoury pancake she'd bought at The Lost Tulip Café. While he ate it, she emptied the bulbs from the brown paper bags and planted out the rest of her pots. Once she had filled all of them, she twisted and repositioned them. When she was satisfied with her arrangement she sat next to Liam and reached out her dirt-covered hand.

He grabbed it and picked at her dirty fingernails.

Zita watched him out of the corner of her eye and smiled to herself.

'You should wear gloves when you're doing that,' he said.

'I know and I do, but I like to feel the plants and bulbs ... and it is easier to plant them.' She looked around, sat back and pushed her head into his shoulder and took a deep breath. 'Isn't it wonderful to be back?' she squealed, with delight.

He answered with a squeeze of her hand. 'Oh yeah. It is.' He smiled to himself as he twisted his neck and looked around at the trees that lined much of the canal, many of which had already lost their leaves. He took a deep breath. 'Yeah. It really is.' He suddenly looked sad, pushed Zita away, and rocked slowly back and forth. 'You know my father knew he would die before that bastard Fuller put him away again.' He sniffed and exhaled a long slow breath. 'Um.' He closed his eyes and sucked in air. 'The poor bastard had nothing else to live for.'

'Does that bastard detective ... Fuller ...have anything to–?'

'No, he is well and truly fucked alright.' He smiled broadly and stood up. 'Fuck you, DCI fucking Fuller!'

Zita drew away from him. 'I'm happy you are pleased, Liam ... but what about us?' she said, softly. She looked into his eyes and smiled sweetly. '*Do you realise* that for the first time ... we really are *free*.' She sighed gently. 'Both of us.' She clicked her tongue. 'So, my liebling, what *are* we going to do now?'

He shook his head. 'I dunno.'

She exuded the widest of smiles and giggled. 'I do,' she said.

He questioned her with a frown.

Dusk was already setting in. She stood and pulled him up. She held him tight and turned him around to look at the coloured flashing lights that now festooned the bridges, trees and houses. 'Liam, have you forgotten today is Christmas Eve?'

He shook his head. 'Is it? Already?'

'How could you forget dat?'

He shrugged and scratched his head. 'Why would I want to know that?'

She grabbed at his arm. 'Maybe not. You have had other things on your mind.'

He nodded. 'You can say that again.'

She tilted her head. 'Sorry, Liam.' She sucked at her bottom lip. 'That was very unfair. I'm sorry.'

'No. It wasn't. You've been part of that too … and … I don't know how I would have got through it without you.'

She hugged him tightly. 'Come on. Let's buy a tree and some decorations for Madonna.'

His solemn face was suddenly replaced with a huge grin. 'Yeah. Why not.'

They left the Madonna and as they walked along the Singel, Liam felt something brush across his face. He tilted his head back and let the first snowflakes fall onto his contented face.

Zita reached out and grabbed his arm. 'Liam, it's snowing.'

He spoke without moving his head. 'I know. I love it.' He stopped suddenly and pulled at her arm. 'Kathleen, thanked me *for the presents*.' He looked confused. 'You didn't tell me about that–'

'Yes, I have given them the presents from Palina and Jan.'

He pulled his head back while he thought. 'Ah. Right.' He reached out for her.

They held each other tight and Zita spoke in a soft voice. 'I didn't want to waste Palina's gifts so I did what I had to do. That's all.'

He nodded. 'Okay. And, do you know what …?' He smiled from ear to ear. 'They'll all love 'em.'

As the snow became heavier, they heard the larger flakes as they fell onto the canopies, plastic bags and boxes strewn around the almost deserted streets. The snow quickly covered the ground and it crunched beneath their feet as they crossed the Kongingssluis bridge. Liam briefly raised his face skywards again to feel the snowflakes cling to his cheeks. He licked the ice from his lips and took his time to rub the melting ice across the whole of his face.

They walked slowly along the canal, through De Wallen, the Red-Light district, and the dirty pavements and piles of broken bottles, fast food containers, wrappings and empty boxes quickly disappeared as they were covered with a thick blanket of virgin snow, beautifying the whole area. The neon lights flashed across the white innocent world as though nothing obscene and dirty had ever existed in this part of the city. It was as though the snow was putting on a show for him and Zita, and them alone, and they didn't want it to end.

He smiled to himself as he recalled the previous Christmas at the Love Shack and the wonderful time he'd had with Zita and the girls. That was how he wanted to remember it, but he shuddered briefly as the memory of the horrific fire came back to haunt him. Just a few days later, on New Year's Eve, the fatal arson attack had shattered his dream and wrecked so many lives and his newfound idyllic life. He grabbed Zita's arm and shook the gruesome memory away.

By the time they reached Bloemenmarkt, the heavy snow had consumed them, along with the rest of the city, and soon everything was transformed into what was now a magical winter wonderland.

Liam watched Zita as she took her time to pick her way between the remaining Christmas trees of all shapes and sizes. He turned away and lowered his head. 'I'm so sorry ... I haven't bought you a Christmas present.'

She tapped him on the shoulder and, without speaking, looked towards the remaining row of bright red poinsettia plants.

He grinned as he remembered that she had bought him one of those for his flat at the Love Shack, the year before. He picked up the largest plant on the stall, paid for it and handed it to her. 'Happy Christmas, Zita.'

He kissed her on the cheek.

She kissed him back. 'That is perfect,' she said. *She knew this Christmas would be very, very special.*